THE KURDISH BIKE

A Novel

By

Alesa Lightbourne

This is a work of fiction. Apart from the well-known actual people, events, and locales that figure in the narrative, all names, characters, places, and incidents are the products of the author's imagination or are used fictitiously. Any resemblance to current events or locales, or to living persons, is entirely coincidental.

Lightbourne, Alesa. The Kurdish Bike: A Novel.

For my parents,
who worried
but still said yes

❊ ❊ ❊

"A work of fiction is an arrangement which
the author makes of his experience
with the idiosyncrasies of his own personality."
~ W. Somerset Maugham

Contents

Prologue

TWO WOMEN laugh exuberantly in a snapshot, their arms around each other, heads close together and aimed toward the camera. This is no pose -- they are caught mid-hysterics. The older-looking Middle Eastern one is wrinkled and mostly toothless, and sports a Gore-Tex traveler's rain hat, something she clearly finds ridiculous. Straggles of gray hair escape from under the hat; she squints, partly because her stomach aches from laughing so much, but also because she can't see the camera clearly. Despite the rapture in her face, she gives the sense that she hasn't laughed like this in a very long time, and this moment is something of a miracle. That's because on this funny, sunny afternoon, right here on her very ordinary concrete porch, she is important to somebody outside of her family. She matters. She is a star.

The Western woman beside her is also of grandmotherly age, but her teeth are white and perfect. Her hair is carefully streaked blonde, and bangs sneak out from under her black scarf, amateurly wrapped and slipping off the back of her head. It's such an American face -- sun-damaged from outdoor fun, not field labor, and nourished by decades of protein and fruit. This is a miracle moment for her, too, but for different reasons. She's re-discovering, after a long, paralyzing dry spell, the radiance of being alive.

Behind them, in front of the rough concrete blocks of a privy, funereal clothes dry on a wire. There's the shadowy opening to a kitchen, a flat corrugated roof weighed down with old tires, and a modest blue bicycle propped up against a water tank. You wouldn't want to place bets on where in the Third World this humble house might be; it could be anywhere, from a village in the Balkans to Africa or Brazil. The only clue would be inside -- a framed portrait of Massoud Barzani, leader of the Iraqi Kurds. Every household has one.

This snapshot is my most prized possession from six months of living in semi-rural Iraq. That was me in the scarf, the day when my village family flipped on a Kurdish radio station, and we kicked up our heels and danced. Widows aren't supposed to kid around like that. But nobody else was there that day except Ara's daughter, Bezma, who took the photo, and she was giddy too, in the early flushes of love. With my camera, which she was good at using by then, she clicked while her mother twirled a scarf the way the men do when they lead the local dances, and the two of us tripped around with our little fingers linked and shoulders shrugging Kurdish-style in time to the music. How daring, how silly! The world was aligned perfectly that day; Allah had indeed been merciful and compassionate, as the prayer goes. For once, all three of us were free of care.

It was a good thing we took that picture. Because before I could even print and frame a copy for Ara, everything had changed. Everything. And without the photo for proof, nobody could have convinced the three of us that that brief shining moment had ever existed. Before hope and safety unraveled. Before the three of us found ourselves utterly bereft, each in her own way, surrounded by danger and scarcity and death — struggling beneath a sense of futility circling like a vulture above her. The utter futility of a world run by men.

One: A Circuitous Route to the Village

IT'S NEW Years Day, 2010.

High on a hill, overlooking the plains of Iraqi Kurdistan, lurks a massive concrete school painted muddy tangerine. A chain-link fence topped with razor wire and interrupted with prison-type guard towers encircles the rocky perimeter. Below, I can make out lights coming on through the chilly dusk in the faraway city. It's all so forbidding. The harshness of bare winter earth, the silence of the empty edifice behind me, the red rear lights of the taxi wending its way back down to the main road, leave me achingly alone.

I'm running on fumes of faith here -- trusting that someone will appear with keys to the promised apartment. Trusting that I'll somehow be able to sleep, and that someone will show me where to get food. Trusting that I will, improbably, learn to survive in this desolate place. The fact that the promised representative failed to meet me at the airport, though, does not bode well.

The school advertised this job as an opportunity to help rebuild a war-torn nation, now that the Kurds are enjoying relative security and autonomy within Iraq, and oil revenues have prompted an economic boom. I'd be happy with something much more modest, like rebuilding my own life, plus educating a few dozen young people at the same time. A long teaching career has made me realistic about how little a person can accomplish in a mere six months. And I know that often it takes more than a clean slate to set your finances and self-esteem aright. Even so, this leap represents boundless optimism, like the Kurds themselves are supposed to be finally feeling. I've left so much behind; they have buried so much.

My hopes ice over as I search that first night for someone, anyone, to welcome me and let me in. How could this place, with its slabs of modernistic symmetry and its machine guns and bomb-detection mirrors at the gate, be something nurturing like a school? It's too male, too impregnable. Too much like a citadel prepared for siege.

Like the thunk of a distant mortar thudding into earth, an image solidifies in my mind, reinforced by the unease of this first windy evening. The sign outside calls this the International Academy of Kurdistan. Before getting here, I'd envisioned it as an intellectual incubator, where young people could be molded with Western values — like democracy — for a more promising future. But now that I'm here, I can see that my new home is more like a military barracks, a bastion of something as yet unclear.

The Fortress.

❊   ❊   ❊

Sleep eludes me. So I bundle up in my wool coat, and shiver on the sandy patio outside my sliding glass door, awaiting the dawn with trepidation. Last night had not been reassuring. A Bangladeshi janitor had eventually appeared to open the apartment, carry in my bags, show me how to turn on the heat, open the mini-fridge to reveal bread and cheese, and deliver a note reminding me to appear in the principal's office first thing in the morning. Typical expat teacher stuff, but not exactly personable. The Fortress expects its employees to be tough, that's clear. And pretty darned self-sufficient from the get-go. That's clear too.

Still, there are homey touches. The apartment is well-appointed, with a comfy sitting room separate from the bedroom, and a galley kitchen with a microwave. The dishes, pots and pans must have been looted by other teachers, but I'm confident that new ones will appear. The Internet works, amazingly enough. They've even put a spotted shag carpet under the glass coffee table, relieving the starkness of the terrazzo floor.

But the odd thing is that everything, from the curtains and comforter to the sofa and carpet, is orange. Not a soft, sunsetty orange, but the jarring color of highway danger cones. A sulfur street lamp, also orangey, stays on all night right outside the apartment, bathing everything in an other-worldly glow. I blame it, and the jet lag, for keeping me awake.

Then there's the morgue-like silence of the hallways. Last night I sat out there on the corridor floor for a long time, hoping a human being would emerge. Names taped to doors told me that people live here. My door says "Rabinowitz." But nobody appeared, and I gave up. Later, I heard the echo of a few doors closing, but no voices — which made me even more lonesome than before. I kept remembering the time I had to put down our German Shepherd, and my son Andy slept in the dog crate all night before it lost the smell of his fur. That kind of lonesome.

Now after a restless night, I'm out on the patio, and it's better; craggy hills beyond the school fence keep me company. They've witnessed so much over the millennia — everything from the birth of human civilization to Saddam Hussein with his land mines. I'm out here because I want to *know* all this, not from books or lectures but in the pores of my skin. Also, there's my (perhaps naive) conviction that simple women in less-developed countries retain a wisdom that we in the busy West have lost. Being a well-meaning and sympathetic person, I will miraculously discover this wisdom, to the wonder of the rest of the world.

People have tried to disabuse me of this idea. One Persian friend was horrified I was coming here. "There's nothing in Kurdistan," he warned. "No beautiful mosques. No great literature. Just a bunch of stubborn people we call mules. You'll be miserable."

But that made it even more appealing. So did the fish-eyed gape the teller at Wells Fargo gave me when I went in to change my address. "Iraq? Really?" she said, and I gloated to be attempting something so outlandish. Had anybody I'd ever known done something like this at my semi-advanced age? No. So, naturally, Iraq qualified as a good idea.

I hadn't expected this heaviness from the hills, though. A sharpness in the air rasps against the lungs, which I take as a warning to be on guard. Against the greying sky, the treeless hills march; at first glance they appear to be rows of bald ogre heads. Fellows like Gilgamesh, the mythic Akkadian hero-king, came from here. Patriarchs like Abraham. This is where Alexander triumphed over Darius. A Who's Who of Ancients chiseled themselves into the gritty embrace of history on this very plain. It's hard to believe it, however, until I try to soak up something from the ambiance, ready for instant reverence, and instead inhale a grittiness of unease. An abrasion, perhaps, from countless centuries of war. An expansiveness that leaves me feeling like the merest dust mote settling inevitably to earth, but in an ominous rather than inclusive kind of way.

I shiver. I'm reading way too much into all this. I'm merely a teacher near the end of her career who grabbed an opportunity to see a new part of the world. And to conveniently leave some inner baggage behind.

I watch the amber rose of dawn creep over the dreary hills, trusting that its light will make The Fortress more bearable.

❄ ❄ ❄

I dress carefully for my meeting with the principal in a floor-length black skirt left over from my years teaching in Saudi Arabia, and a droopy long-sleeved sweater. I've tied a dark scarf around my neck, for whipping over my head in case a male takes offense. The look is meant to be conservative and respective of Muslims sensitivities, but feels downright dowdy. To my surprise, however, my new boss greets me with uncovered graying hair, wearing a snug red pantsuit. She's stubby and stout, probably about sixty, and her clipped British accent has Arabic overtones, throaty in a way I've always found appealing. Her secretary has instructed me to call her "Madame".

"Miss Turner — I trust you found the apartment to your satisfaction?" Madame shakes my hand and steps up to a massive leather chair, elevated on a dais that puts her a head above me. I do my friendly professional smile; this woman wields immense power over my future here, and I need her to both like and respect me. But I also genuinely want to like and respect her in return, so we can be allies. Perhaps even friends. I could use a few of those.

"It's great. Better than I'd expected." Which is the truth, if we're talking about the facilities themselves. I'll leave out the panic at the airport and the despair in the corridor, so as not to seem whiney.

Madame adjusts herself behind the vast mahogany desk. "Excellent!" It comes out more like "egg-cellant". "I spent 20 years in London, and it totally spoiled me. I would never put up with substandard living conditions, or expect my teachers to." The "London" is drawn out, a little haughtily, as if London is somehow superior to the United States. But this is probably my imagination. I've decided to become less hyper-sensitive about things upon moving here.

13

She gets down to business right away. "You'll find that we're organized differently at the Academy than what you're probably used to. We're owned by an Egyptian company, part of a chain of elite schools around the world. We're designed for the children of diplomats, and adhere to a strict schedule that is common across all of our schools. That way a student can move from one country to another without missing a single lesson. A brilliant concept, you'll agree?"

I agree. Jet lag, with its attendant dizziness and mental numbness, is inconveniently sabotaging me. It's getting hard to concentrate, and I'm impatient to meet my students. She must sense this, because she gives me a big-sisterly nod of encouragement.

"You'll be paid in Iraqi dinars at the end of every month. In cash. The Academy representative hands out envelopes in person. Take good care of it, because we've had some problems with theft. Let's see, what else? No open-toe shoes or flip-flops to class. But I shouldn't have to explain to someone like you."

My mind is wandering alarmingly — a pity, because she's just getting started. "Now let me explain some of the Academy's best practices. Please don't get offended. Truthfully, I did at first myself, because naturally I had my own ways of doing things. Any experienced teacher would. Nevertheless. You're expected to follow our regimen to the letter. This means that you will write your objectives and tactics on the board for each lesson, and not deviate one iota. You will not permit the children to interrupt. You will walk the aisles continuously to ensure that they stay on task. You will ask for questions only at the end of each class session."

I blink in an effort to look awake, but am overwhelmed by all the things to remember. I should be writing them down. Suddenly, the polyester of Madame's pantsuit snags my attention; I'll bet the thing came from the London equivalent of K-Mart. It's a deplorable thought, but perks me up with a shot of empathy. I can now see that she's not some pampered society wife who dabbles at teaching in her spare time, but rather is a devoted educator, like me, who puts learning above fashion and other forms of conspicuous consumption. It's like discovering that a stranger comes from your hometown, and can therefore be forgiven the coffee stain on their shirt. I release the stranglehold I've had on the chair's armrests just a bit.

Now she chatters about her popularity with the Academy's owners in Cairo. Her lifelong dedication to students. Her time-tested discipline techniques. She gestures at the wall behind her, covered with gold-framed advanced degrees and diplomas, and awards from being principal at the Light of Christ School for Girls in the U.K.

"Light of Christ?" I wake up in surprise. "Your name sounded Muslim."

"Oh, it is," she assures me, with obvious pride. "I'm Egyptian. But I'm also a modern woman. In fact, I haven't covered since I moved to the U.K. I believe that tolerance is a virtue. Which is why my husband and I have even entertained Christians sometimes. And Jews." She pats her curled and sprayed hair, thinning badly on top, and I sense a breach in the bravado, hinting at the possibility of connection between us.

As if reading my mind, she leans across the desk and reaches for my hand. She is much too short, and the desk is much too wide, to make this happen. "Actually, dear, I've looked forward to you coming ever since they told me about you. We're both, how shall we say, of a certain age? We both have grown children, correct? We both..." She can't think of anything else.

I meet her hand halfway across the desk. Her manicured nails match the pantsuit; on cars, I've heard the color called "traffic cop red". My own hand, bare of either polish or rings, looks naked in comparison. "Of course. We have a great deal in common."

"Egg-cellent. Now, let's get your textbooks and the syllabus your predecessor left behind. Or rather, the rubbish that Rabinowitz called a syllabus. Then I'll take you to meet your class. The children! Ah, such adorable children!" She trills her "r"s. "They will absolutely capture your heart. And don't worry. We won't start observing until you've settled in for at least several days."

Observing? Several days? But she's already parading to the door, pausing so I can gather my purse and sweater. "Do come along, dear. Chop chop. The bell will be ringing any minute now."

I try not to flinch at the "dear", coming so quickly as it did after the mention of being observed. I'm the kind of teacher who gets assigned interns, not the type who is monitored for quality control. Back home I have as many awards and degrees as she does. Doesn't she know that?

But this is no time for testiness. I'm all set for a personal renaissance, a self-induced epiphany, which will no doubt involve some ruffles to my ego. I'd better learn right now to take them in stride.

Then a thunderbolt idea hits me, and I come to an abrupt halt behind Madame.

Up until this very moment, I never once considered that coming here might be a mistake.

What if I have made a very foolish gamble, and the dice have been foreordained to roll against me?

A foolish thought, which I brush aside as cowardly.

❊ ❊ ❊

After piling my arms with texts, workbooks and files, Madame leads me across the quad and into one of the classroom blocks.

She's huffing badly after the first flight of stairs. "I'm afraid that Mr. Rabinowitz left your class in a mess," she says. "You'll have a lot of catching up to do."

"What happened to him?" I'm puffing too, but it could be from 24 hours in the air yesterday and no sleep.

"He was not cut out to teach." I sense an implication that, in contrast, she and I were blessed at birth by a religious calling to education. She ticks off offenses on her fingers. "He wore dreadlocks and a wooly cap, even on the hottest days. He appeared in the same filthy shirt for weeks on end. He never did his bulletin boards. He did not learn the children's names. He failed to show up on time, or sober." Her look says the list could continue.

"Oh dear." Unforgivable, if she's not exaggerating. "He must have really tried your patience. Where did he come from?" Please don't say America.

"He said he graduated from a college in Oregon, but we never saw a diploma." She stops on the landing, turns, and gives me a look pregnant with meaning. For some reason, it gives me the willies.

"You must have fired him then." I start climbing the stairs again, to get her eyes off me.

"Worse than that. One moonless night, he simply disappeared. The guards said that he flagged down a taxi outside the gate and asked for a ride all the way to Turkey. No warning. No explanation. Just poof."

"So his class probably feels like they won the power game." I'm so righteous. I would never abandon an assignment mid-year, or let students triumph over me like that jerk did.

"Such a pity, isn't it? The poor little dears haven't had a homeroom teacher for several months now." She stops to catch her breath again on the third flight of stairs. "They're a wee bit behind on the lesson plans."

I'll bet.

"Another thing. His class — well, now your class — is one of our special groups. Most didn't pass exams at the end of Grade 6. So they're covering two levels this year. We call them 6/7 Accelerated, because they work at a faster pace to catch up with the rest."

"Oh, you mean remedial?" I have no experience with Special Ed, nor have I ever had a desire to teach it. No doubt 6/7 Accelerated is where she has dumped a sorry assortment of kids with developmental, second- or third-language, or behavioral problems, as well as some who are just plain lazy. And it probably has way more boys than girls. Terrific. My stomach lurches with what's likely the start of jet lag diarrhea. I'd better find a bathroom. Too late now. She's pulling open a sturdy metal door, and the unmistakable hormoney stench of middle schoolers rushes out. So does a wallop of noise, raucous and primal, until they see that it's Madame. And me. They jump to attention like a pack of lolling soldiers, and jockey for a better look at me.

"Class, Miss Turner has come all the way from America to be your new teacher." Blah blah blah, be good, show her how smart you are, make me proud of you. They're not hearing a word. They're doing a spot psych work-up on me, searching for the Achilles heel. Every teacher has one. Every class finds it in less than a day.

But I've done this before. Deliberately, I take a full step closer to them than Madame has, and lean into their force field. My lips stay taut; no sign of weakness. Yet. Not for at least a week. I will my forehead to tell them who's boss. At the same time, I'm melting inside with anticipated affection. Every single face will be precious to me soon; this happens without fail with each class, whatever their age or culture. It's what keeps teachers coming back, year after year, a phenomenon akin to bonding your own infant.

The "Missing" starts the minute that Madame leaves and everyone sits back down. "Miss, where do you come from?" "Miss, do you have a husband?" "Miss, will you let us chew gum?" "Miss, have you met Tom Cruise?"

My little cherubs. I gaze out at a sea, no, more like a toxic quagmire of them in white shirts and navy uniforms with hideous orange piping. Nearly fifty of them cram into molded plastic chairs and metal desks, the kind that screech when you drag them across the floor.

A wave of pity swamps me. I've read in *National Geographic* that Kurds love glitz and bright colors – flamingo pink, turquoise, glittery rhinestones on everything from hair clips to flip flops. Even the men are supposed to be crazy about roses. They love being outdoors, too. But here their children wear cadet-type uniforms, and are cooped up all day in a stuffy, overheated classroom. Their parents pay a small fortune in tuition for this?

I drop my books on the teacher's desk, and search for a chair to hang my purse on. No chair. I perch on the front of my desk, and start asking questions.

"Who can tell me where you left off in the English text?"

Nearly fifty sets of eyes turn cold, refusing to let me in.

"Okay, tell me what you did last with Mr. Rabinowitz?"

This gets a rise out of them. "Miss, Mr. Rabinowitz didn't use a book. He liked to talk with us."

"No book?" How absurd. "Then what was he talking with you about? Verbs? Sentence structure?"

"No, Miss. About *jihad*."

This must be a test. They're trying to see how gullible I am, or how little I know about the Muslim world.

"That's ridiculous. Mr. Rabinowitz came from America." And with a name like that, he had to be Jewish.

"No, Miss. He came here from Pakistan."

"He showed us his passport."

"He was in a *madrassa* up in the mountains. With Osama bin Laden's guys."

I assume my authority-figure pose, like an eagle ready to swoop down on prey. "Yeah, right. Look, I was not born yesterday, kids. And I have not been living in the mountains with terrorists. I have been a teacher for a very long time, in America and in Saudi Arabia, and I'm going to make sure that you learn everything you're supposed to in the time we've got left this year. Got that?"

I wait for a chorus of "Yes, Miss."

"Good. I will assume from Mr. Rabinowitz's notes that we should be on page 47 of the blue grammar text. Everyone get out your books, please."

I assign a student to read one of the exercises by pointing a finger, then point to another to provide an answer. It works for about eight and a half minutes. Then chaos begins to dominate — chattering, squirming, giggling, rustling around in backpacks. These kids are wild horses, accustomed to galloping free across grassy meadows. They have no intention of sitting still for yet another foreigner, and a female one at that.

"Hey, let's sing a song." It's worked for me in the past, even with much older kids. We start with 'Head, Shoulders, Knees and Toes,' which gets them out of their seats and motioning in something approximating unison. Then they sit, slightly tamed now, and we move on to 'A, B, C, D.' They're baby songs, but they buy me time.

We're just wrapping up 'Itsy Bitsy Spider', a big hit because of the finger movements, when one of the biggest boys in the back waves at me. With lips pursed, he jabs his finger toward a little window in the classroom door. There a dark head looms, and a hush falls. "Mr. Zaki," the boy hisses. Assuming flagpole posture, the kids maintain a strained silence until the shadow glides away, and the entire room exhales.

After the appearance, they're in no mood to sing. Rats. We still have ten minutes to go until the bell. Already, I feel like I've been run over by a Sherman tank.

"Let me tell you a story." They lean back in their chairs in obvious relief, and await entertainment. I dredge my mind for something funny.

"Okay, once when my son Andy was young, I was giving him and his buddy a bath. They were joking around with their toys, pretending to be scuba divers bringing up sharks from the bottom of the tub." Are they advanced enough to know words like 'scuba'? Who cares. "My son had his naked butt right up in his friend's face, and guess what he did?" I pause for effect, and then make the noisiest, juiciest fart noise that my mouth can do.

Joy! Potty humor never fails. "Another one, Miss! Tell us another story."

I move on to the time I tricked my little sister into kissing the bottom of a snail. They haven't seen snails, but get the general idea and laugh. Yes! It's working. We're bonding. It's great.

Two minutes before the bell, without me saying anything, they magically retrieve backpacks and jostle into a queue by the door. One of the girls hugs me on her way out.

"Miss, we like you so much better than Mr. Rabinowitz."

I can't help but smile now. This emboldens another girl to add, "We're really glad you came here to teach us, Miss."

I beam. I'm a success. Suddenly, the future is bright. Madame is going to love me, and be glad she hired me. I will polish these little Kurds' English skills, so their country will have a better chance of survival in this hostile world of ours. I will be the change I wanted to see in the world. Bravo for me.

My euphoria lasts until I haul my books and purse into the next classroom (no chair again), and start all over with a different group. Same problems, different faces. Then I'll be

21

back with 6/7 Accelerated again before lunch, and will have to come up with something new to keep them busy. Already, a blister is forming on my left heel. Already, the jet lag is making me woozy, and the diarrhea cramps are returning. How am I going to make it to the end of the day, much less the end of a week or school year? And I've signed up for six whole months of this?

Maybe Rabinowitz hadn't been such an idiot after all.

❋ ❋ ❋

I battle my way against the current of adolescents, through crammed, deafening corridors, searching for the faculty room. Everywhere I've taught, it's been a haven of blessed relief and easy adult camaraderie, the one place where teachers can chuck their bulletproof armor and be something approximating their normal selves. In The Fortress faculty room, however, something funny is going on, which smacks me along with the sour coffee smell. On one side of the room, the Westerners, or rather the teachers wearing Western-looking clothes, sprawl on sagging sofas, their heels propped on a coffee table heaped with text books. On the other side, women in Arab-looking outfits sit at straight chairs around two work tables, hunched over stacks of copybooks. They're a very serious lot who barely glance up as I come in. I sense an invisible Green Line, like the one that divided East and West Beirut during the civil war.

The Westerners make room for me on a sofa and introduce themselves. There's Jake, a lanky blond kid from Los Angeles with spiked hair and a flashy ruby stud in his ear. Pat from Vermont, via a Peace Corps in Burkina Faso, is the only person about my age. Louanna from Texas is the sole veteran of previous years here. Jennifer, a fresh-faced teacher from England, recently married a Kurdish Academy employee, so she lives off campus — getting to know the "real Kurdistan," she hastens to add — which I take as a form of culture-junky one-upmanship. Plus a handful of Europeans, and a few Arabs like Khalil and Layla, who claim they're British yet look and sound Arab. Eagerly, the expats launch into survival advice.

"Take the bus tonight into town for groceries. We'll show you where to go," says Layla. She looks at Khalil in a protective way that makes me think they're related, maybe mother and son. "My apartment's right next to yours, by the way. Come over if you need anything."

Khalil, incongruously attired in a starched designer shirt and cashmere jacket, goes next, as if we're in an AA circle. "Turn in your lesson plans for the next week by Wednesday afternoon, or they'll threaten to ding your bonus."

"Write your tactics on the left side of the board at the start of each period, or they'll ding you for that too," adds Jennifer.

"Watch your back with Madame. She's a foul one," says Jake. "And watch your back with the Arab teachers over there, too. They're Madame's spies." It strikes me as scripted, like they've done this with many newcomers before.

"Hey, shut up all of you. Can't you see she's still got jet lag?" It's Pat, a stocky woman with permed reddish hair. In sturdy laced shoes and a no-nonsense blazer, she looks like someone who can steer a steam roller backwards with one hand. I feel like I've known her forever.

"Now, let's get you a nice cup of tea and let you settle in," she says. "You're lucky nobody has swiped the tea bags yet. Sugar? I wouldn't trust the powdered creamer myself. Your goal is to merely make it through today in one piece, and then get a decent night's sleep. I'm in apartment six. After classes are over, we'll take a walk. It'll help you feel better. Okay? Good. Everything is going to be just fine."

I stare at her in amazement. Is it that obvious, how overwhelmed I am — how I can barely keep my head from wobbling? I hope she doesn't have a best friend here yet. I want to nominate her for sainthood.

* * *

Pat knocks on my apartment door that afternoon, and announces that we're walking to the village for vegetables. "They look ratty, but they're fresh. Sort of like the organic bin at Safeway before organic got trendy. Now put on some walking shoes and grab a coat. It's freezing out there." She fails to notice that I can barely stand up after almost eight grueling hours of teaching.

We set off through the back gate toward the hills, past a pack of snoring wild dogs the size of small lions. "Rumor has it that they're toothless," she says, but we give them a wide berth anyway, picking a path through deep dried mud. Once we get to the paved road, all we have to contend with is the wind, whipping up ash from a smoldering mountain of trash on our left.

"What's in the village?" I ask.

"You're going to anthropologize?" She makes it sound inane. But yes, that's what I've been hoping, once I learned there was a settlement between The Fortress and the sprawl of the city.

"Forget it. One, you'll be way too exhausted from teaching. Two, Madame would probably fire you for fraternizing with the natives. And three, there's nothing here to see. Zip. Nada."

"That's impossible," I protest. "If you look hard enough, there's something interesting everywhere."

She flares her nose and snorts. "Oh, you're one of those diamond-in-the-rough believers?"

She must not have meant it to cut so much, because her tone softens. "Well, I haven't been past the grocery store, myself. But if you want, we can take a look-see, since there are two of us. I certainly wouldn't do it alone."

It's about a mile to the outskirts of the village, past bare hillsides, litter-strewn verges, and a few copses of leafless trees. Pat keeps up a brisk pace as we pass rough goat or sheep sheds pounded together from tree branches. She has to point out the grocery once we get there, a gray square of concrete blocks with some crates stacked outside. If not for a faded Pepsi sign tacked to a pole, it could have been just another sheep stall.

"We'll hit the store on the way back," she says. We zip up our jackets in a vain effort to look less conspicuous and enter one of the lanes with faux nonchalance. Too late, I realize it might have been a good idea to cover my hair.

The village is a rambly scattering of concrete houses crammed alongside a soggy ravine. The six streets in either direction must have been paved once. High cinderblock walls, some topped with broken glass, line the lanes, interrupted by rusted metal gates. Over the top, all that can be seen are corrugated iron roofs weighted down with stones and tires.

An old patriarch totters toward us scowling, his staff like something out of a Sunday school coloring book. He ignores us as we pass. A rooster glares from a heap of rubble, threatening to peck us to death if we come closer. "This is freaking me out," says Pat.

"Just a little farther," I beg. The lane ends with a drab little mosque on one side and a four-room school on the other.

"That's it. Now you've seen it."

We hustle even faster on the way back. It's the kind of place where my son Andy used to hunt snipers in video games, where commandos crouched beside piles of wreckage.

"Don't you wonder what's going on behind all of these walls?" To ward off the sniper idea, I'm imagining women doing intricate embroidery, children memorizing homework, men philosophizing over hookahs.

"Nope," she says. "I spent two years teaching in an African village. I know what goes on in places like this. Cooking. Eating. Sweeping. Scrubbing. Arguing. Pissing, crapping, periods, screwing, birthing, dying. All the boring stuff of life, except that the details are a little different in each country. A spice here. A prayer mat there. Same same."

"Yeah, you're probably right." But I don't mean it. The village fascinates me as much as it intimidates. The place surely has a name, and so do each of the people behind these faceless, crumbling walls. After learning a person's name, there's a story. After hearing the story, there's a relationship. "I want to come back."

"Be my guest. You might want to learn some Kurdish first, though. I doubt if anybody speaks English."

"I can remember some Arabic, from the years in Saudi. Not a lot. But some." Arabic is the official language in Iraq, of course, but I've read that most Kurds don't speak it.

"Try it out here in the grocery," she dares me.

So I clumsily negotiate the cost of potatoes and a can of juice with a toothless old woman at the counter; even after blowing the dust off the can and standing over by the light bulb, there's no price to make out. I wrangle a small discount for Pat on some bananas, balanced out on an antique metal scale. This will make a great first entry for the blog I'm going to do.

"Very impressive," she says as we march back toward The Fortress. "And brave. I walked down here twice before I had the guts to buy anything."

"You did not." I can't imagine her being scared of anything.

"Okay, you're right. But I still didn't like having to ask how much everything costs, and then count on my fingers. That's why everybody else takes the school shuttle into town to the supermarkets."

"None of the teachers ever come down here?"

26

"Not unless they run out of cigarettes."

"Well, I'm going to. Maybe if I come often enough, I'll get to know somebody. Or get invited to tea some day."

She laughs. "You go, girl. Just make sure you've got my number loaded in your phone, so you can text me if you get into trouble."

"I won't be needing a phone. I've got to save every penny." I hadn't needed one back in Saudi. Actually, cell phones hadn't even existed back then.

"Uh, wrong. We may be in Kurdistan, but we're also in Iraq. I'll take you to the city and you can get one like mine for fifteen bucks. We'll go on the bus later this week."

I stare in wonder at this force of nature. Resistance will be futile.

I wish she'd been around when I was extracting myself from a certain unnamed person I'd had the misfortune to be married to recently.

❋ ❋ ❋

In the middle of the night, I bolt up with a start. What a stupendous idea! I can't wait to announce it in the faculty room the next morning.

"We'll buy bicycles! We can toodle all over the hillsides when the weather warms up. We can go buy stuff in the village whenever we want, and get to know people there. We can even ride to that Crusader's castle up the road you guys were telling me about. Or go all the way into the city, once we've been training a while."

I wait for their inevitable enthusiasm. Can't they envision us with our hair streaming out in the breeze, flying over hill and dale with that freedom only cyclists know?

Pat finally breaks the silence. "I've never seen a woman riding a bicycle in Kurdistan," she notes dryly.

"I've never seen anybody riding a bicycle, period," says Jake. "Anybody alive, that is." He could easily have a career in soap operas. "Haven't you seen the traffic out there, Twinkle Toes? Ragheads don't have driver's licenses. Fricking lunatics."

"Hey…" Pat points with her lips toward the Arab/Kurd work table. "Talk nice."

"Yeah, yeah, yeah," he whispers. "Sorry, Mommy."

"Seriously, I want to travel around on my own, without the school shuttle. And get out into the hills. It looks like there are roads out there." Mostly, I want a way to get outside and away from all this concrete.

"Roads with land mines." Jake sounds a lot like Eeyore.

"You don't know that's true," says Pat. "I've seen shepherds wandering around out there."

"Ragheads. They know what they're doing. But old Theresa here, with that gorgeous blonde hair…. Tell me, darling, is it true blondes have more fun? Or is it only true blondes who have the fun?" He mimics twirling a lock around his finger and bats his eyelashes. Beneath his platinum spikes, dark roots are growing out. I hope it will be a long time before mine do the same.

Pat grins at me. "Thank God for Jake. Despite his naughtiness, this would be one dull place without him."

But I'm not giving up so easily. "So where do you think I could buy a bike? Do they even sell them here?"

Nobody knows. They suggest the Kurdish bus drivers down in the school's garage, who, it turns out, speak neither English nor Arabic. So I try the shuttle driver. No, too dangerous, he says.

Next, I try Mohammed, the Academy's government liaison officer. He's a rakish young Kurd in a glossy Western suit whose office lies just down the hall from Madame's. He's rumored to come from a "big" family; no one is clear about his exact duties. Obtaining bicycles for teachers, he informs me

28

while stroking his wispy moustache, is certainly not one of them. He would be violating the trust Madame and the government placed in him by putting a British teacher at risk on the roads around here. Plus, he is much too busy. He motions at the single manila folder decorating his desk and the impressively full ash tray.

"Just for the record, I'm not British," I interrupt. "I'm American."

"American?" He glances at the door, which is securely shut. "Really? American?"

"Yes. Does it matter?"

Another look at the door. Maybe Madame keeps tabs on him? "Certainly it matters. Americans are best friends of the Kurds. You freed us from Saddam." He opens the file, frowns at the piece of paper in it, and shuts it with great fanfare. "Okay. You promise not to tell anybody that I'm helping you? You'll never tell Madame or Zaki? Okay?"

"Sure."

"Tomorrow afternoon at three o'clock, we shall meet at the bus garage. I shall arrange a ride to the city. You shall bring money. Together, we shall buy a bicycle."

I wonder where he learned his English. Does anybody really say "shall" anymore? It strikes me as kind of quaint and endearing.

The ride turns out to be in Madame's company car, a late-model Camry, driven by her personal chauffeur, through pounding rain to a muddy alley near the bazaar. The bicycle proves to be a bright blue Chinese marvel akin to those on clearance at Target, with little spangly gew-gaws to make clicking noises in the spokes, plastic streamers erupting from the handlebars, a tinny bell, and a skinny black seat designed for castration. I pay extra for a girl's seat and wire basket, and gaze in wonder at my new wheels. The bike feels like a new friend, as adorable as a puppy still in a shoe box with newspapers.

Mohammed ties down the bike with twine in Madame's trunk. The front wheel dangles precariously out the back, so he makes a feeble effort at lashing the whole thing shut. "You are very good at bargaining, for a white lady," he says, struggling to make complicated knots. I had, in fact, gotten the price down by more than a third, probably because no other cycle purchasers seem to be venturing out in the rain today. So why is he buttering me up? As we splash our way back to The Fortress, my prize possession bashing around with each pothole and speed bump, I discover why.

"I would like it very much if you could get me a U.S. visa," he says, as if the thought just occurred to him.

I sigh. This is out of my league. "I don't know anything about visas."

"Perhaps you have met President Obama?"

"Not even once."

"I'm sure you have a special friend at the embassy."

"I don't know a soul there."

"Then maybe you are related to a lawyer."

"Sorry. If I'd been related to a lawyer, I wouldn't be here now."

This plunges him deep into thought. He smacks his forehead with great force. A fresh idea has surprised even Mohammed himself with its brilliance.

"By George, I've got it. We should get married!"

I guffaw. "What, you and me? I'm older than your parents."

But he hadn't been kidding; the pout on his mouth proves it.

"I like old ladies," he assures me. "Really. They make much better wives than young and beautiful girls. Old ladies are smarter. They take care of you like mothers. And they're good cooks." We experience a long break in the monologue as I let him assess his damage, which any fool can see is considerable. "But you are both. Young. And very beautiful." It's the best he can come up with.

I cough. Mercilessly, the minutes tick by. When at last we reach The Fortress, I slip him a large tip, and he pretends to be offended, but pockets it nevertheless. It probably isn't enough to offset the favor he's done me getting the bicycle, but it's all I've got left after tipping the driver. He presses his business card into my palm.

"Whatever you need here in Kurdistan, I am at your service. Keep my number. I can make things happen."

This guy just won't give up. "You're a nice kid," I assure him. "And you're smart. I'm sure you'll make it to America one of these days. Even without my help."

He shakes my hand with wounded dignity, and I wonder how many times he's tried his spiel on an American before. I also wonder how long I will remain in his debt — and what it will take, short of marriage, to pay him off.

         ❉ ❉ ❉

The minute classes are over the next day, I take a test ride down to the village, bundled up in a jacket and black balaclava designed to make me look male. Bracing cold whips my eyes, but I do a "yippee" anyway. The bicycle has to be one of the greatest inventions of all time. Cheap. Simple. A ticket to freedom. I can't believe my good fortune in owning one; it's more like a pair of wings than wheels, letting me soar away from the dismal Fortress and off through the countryside. I keep it parked next to my bed, and name it the Blue Angel.

It's easy flying downhill, but once at the village itself I have to get off and walk around the ruts and dried mud ridges.

Today the sour-faced elder with the staff is nowhere in sight. A handful of kids kicking a ball around the street stop mid-play when they spot me.

"Hallo?" one of the braver boys ventures. It sounds like a taunt, so I ignore him.

"Hallo? Hallo?" His buddies join in; it's becoming a joke. In cheap acrylic sweaters and tattered no-brand sneakers, they don't look too dangerous.

I stop and smile. "Hello." Now they're swarming all around me.

"Teacher?" I nod. "School?" They point up the hill. I nod again. "Ingleezi?"

"No, American."

"Amreeka! Amreeka!" Jumping up and down with excitement, the brave boy pantomimes a bomber hovering above us. Now he's jackknifing as the bomb wobbles its way down, his arms tight for the dive, his cheeks ballooned to make a deafening explosion. Somebody else mimics pulling down the great statue of Saddam in Baghdad, shaking the earth as it crumbles into pieces. I'm not entirely pleased at the associations. But at least I'm clearly a friend. One of the Great Liberators. The boys come close enough to touch my bike.

We try to talk, but don't know many words in common. They can do a few lines from Hollywood movies, mostly involving guns. "Make my day." "Hasta la vista, baby." "My name is Bond." I've got goosebumps now from the cold and swing my leg back over the bike to take off again.

"Wait! Ingleezi!"

A smaller boy bangs frantically on one of the closed metal gates. The others hold my bike so I can't move; it's got to be a set up. Nobody at The Fortress knows where I am. I should never have come out here alone without getting a phone. I take a deep breath and tighten my grip on the handlebars, ready to plow my way through the boys if they won't let go —

And then the gate creaks open. Out peeks an ample-figured young woman, hastily adjusting a headscarf and floor-length black cloak. She wipes her hands on her thighs, as if coming from some wet or messy task. Her hearty peasant face scowls; she's irritated with the boys wasting her precious time, and starts shaking a finger at them. Then her mouth drops as she sees me there astride the bicycle, in my absurd balaclava, ready to push off.

"You speak English?" She's imperious, like a warlord demanding to know why I'm on her turf.

"Of course."

"You are woman!"

Is that a crime? Is she going to call the police?

Instead, she drags the gate open, motions for me to get off the bike, and wheels it awkwardly inside the yard. There's no invitation, or even a question about whether I'll obey. I follow as she shoos away the boys like an experienced auntie, shuts the gate in their faces, and slides a heavy iron bolt in place.

"So." She turns to me with hands on beamy hips. I am her captive, and she's got more heft to her than I do; if she sits on me, I'll never get out from under her.

She's obviously calculating how much I'll pay to get the bike back. Will she believe that I only brought enough money to buy a couple of oranges? I can pour out my wallet and show her it's true. The only other thing of value I have on me is my key chain from home, but I need the keys on it to get back into my apartment.

And then, just when it dawns on me that she wants to take my beloved Blue Angel, not a cash ransom, she breaks into a smile, an incandescent burst of pure graciousness. It's as sweet as a curtain call, when the villainess drops her facade, revealing the lovely person she is in real life. I'm floored.

"My name Bezma. I study English, learn be teacher. You drink tea with me and mother?"

"Wow! Sure!" I can't believe my luck.

We sit in molded plastic chairs on her little patio and try to relax. Her mother, an ancient thing completely enshrouded in black, shuffles in with a tray of dainty little glasses and a metal pot of tea, then disappears back into the shadows. Bezma spoons at least a teaspoon of sugar into each glass, and we experiment to see how well we can communicate.

"Treeza." She repeats my name several times. "Do you speak Kurdish?"

"No. I'm sorry. Do you speak Arabic?"

"No." She bristles inexplicably. I thought Arabic was the second language here. "Old Houda, friend of my mother, speak Arabic. You, me, speak English. Good for me practice English."

"Your English is really good," The praise mollifies her and earns me a grin. "You must be taking your studies very seriously. How old are you?"

"I am 21." Oh my. I would have guessed at least 30, because of the hardship chiseled into her face. "How old are *you*?"

"Fifty-seven."

She holds up five fingers and then seven. "Really? Five seven? Not possible. I think 40. My mother Ara is 47."

I'd pegged Ara at mid-sixties, given her cataract squint and the criss-cross of wrinkles on her forehead. Time to change the subject. "Are you married?"

"No. I care for mother. She is widow." Bezma gives a furtive glance. "But I have secret love. Soon he ask for me, *in sh'allah*. Please you do not tell mother. You have husband?"

Divorce is probably a taboo topic here, so I just shake my head and talk about my son Andy. My mind keeps flitting around, though, terrified of making some unforgivable cultural blunder. I sense the eyes of the entire village on me, lying in wait for a trespass against Muslim values, or an offense against the government that would land me in jail.

Bezma is nervous too. She has never spoken with a Westerner before, she admits, and has only used English under duress in class. No stranger has ever come inside their home. She apologizes for not having prepared herself, or the house, or taken down the laundry pinned to a wire across the porch. Still, she carries it off with amazing aplomb, as if foreign cyclists drop by on a regular basis, and invites me to stay for dinner.

"I'd love to. But it's getting dark, and it's uphill all the way back to the school. I was just testing out my new bicycle…"

She seems both relieved and disappointed; I suspect the cupboard was bare. "Then you come back Friday after prayers." Friday is the Muslim holy day, and the first day of the weekend at the Fortress, so I can make it.

"My mother makes dolmas. Or kitchen?" I'm puzzled, and she realizes her mistake. "Chicken! Not kitchen. You like eat chicken?"

"Sure. I like to eat anything."

"Then you promise. We will wait."

I give my word. I will be waiting too. In truth, I'll be hoping the rest of the week that this chance encounter will launch me miraculously into the heart and soul of the village. Or, even better, into a new understanding of my place in the world in some yet-to-be-determined way.

I can't wait to write it up on my blog.

❖ ❖ ❖

At lunch time the next day, Jake grabs us some suspicious-looking pizza from the student canteen, and he, Pat and I stretch out on the sofas again. We've got the faculty room to ourselves now. Since they'll surely make fun of my bike escapade, I ask Jake how he got here.

"You mean, how did a graphic designer slash surfer dude end up so far from a zipper club?" He grins and leans back, pleased for a chance to talk about himself. "Well, girlfriends, after I got my diploma, nobody came knocking on my door with a job in a corner office. I was shocked, literally shocked." He slaps the side of his face; I can't tell whether he's making fun of us, or of himself. "So I waited tables. And waited. Jeez. I was bored out of my mind. Then my partner — and a very lovely little milk-and-cookies fellow he was — had this brilliant idea. We'd go to Taiwan and teach English. Just like that. And we went."

He's eyeing me, to see how I'm taking all this. Maybe he's run into some of the fundamentalist missionary types who turn up frequently in expat staff lounges. He needn't have worried.

"And after that?"

"China. Then Turkey. Then this patch of paradise. Hah!"

"Which was best?" I could easily have ended up in one of those places instead of here, given my lack of due diligence in the job search department.

"There's no best. There's only different kinds of crap. The pay was lousy in Taiwan, but then I was a newbie and didn't deserve any better. It was my first time living abroad, too, so I had some shockers to get over. Like learning that not everybody on the planet loves Americans. Or that the NBC Nightly News might not be telling the whole story all the time. Hah! Then there was China. They had great massages, but ghastly pollution. In Turkey, the food was out of this world, but, oh man, those kids were lazy little bastards..."

"Everybody says Indonesia is the best," says Pat, interrupting. "But I haven't been there myself. They say it's good if you like beaches, and bad if you like money."

Listening to them is a relief. My stomach starts to unknot. I want to keep them talking. "Which is the worst?"

"It's got to be Saudi, from what everybody says," Jake says. "Hands down, the armpit of the universe. Expat teacher's hell. Human being's hell."

"I taught in Saudi." They both stop mid-chomp, riveted. "It was a really long time ago. But still, been there, done that."

"Whoa. I'm stunned! Little Miss Twinkie, under an abaya." Jake shakes his head. He leans forward and gives my knee a quirky little tap. "So, what's your story? Prurient minds want to know."

My poor brain, still partly on West Coast time, can hardly string words together, so I get up to make another cup of tea. "You mean, how I washed up here four days ago?" They both nod. "Well, one day my son Andy and I were out walking. And he asked me, 'Mom, if you could do anything in the world, what would it be?' I didn't have to think for even a second. It just popped out of my mouth. Teach overseas again."

"Mmm hmm," says Pat. "That's more or less how I ended up in the Peace Corps in Burkina Faso, a country nobody has even heard of."

"The Peace Corps offered me something in Libya, because I used to speak Arabic," I continue. "But I thought, oh yeah, sure, go to some Muslim country all alone. Might as well hang a big sign around my neck that says 'come rape me.' Even in my late fifties. So I took this instead."

"Older women are invisible." Pat does a floozy shimmy. "Which is a handy thing, after you get over the bruised ego. It means we can get away with murder. Except in the Middle East, where your blonde hair and my red hair make us like movie stars."

"Even if it's dyed."

"Yep. Even if we're almost over the hill and twice as dusty."

Jake isn't letting me off so easily though. "It had to be more than just adventure that brought you here," he mumbles through a mouthful of pizza. "I mean, sure, we were all drawn toward something unique about Kurdistan. But we were also running away from something. Right?"

Oh, so true. I'm not sure I'm ready to talk about it yet. But expat teachers tend to become like family overnight. So what the heck...

※ ※ ※

We had been walking around the neighborhood after dinner, Andy and I, in misty dusk that encouraged speculation. "If you could do anything in the world, what would it be?"

I flashed back to a time when life had been purer, freer, more vivid than this rut I was in. Back when I sprang out of bed each morning eager to discover new synchronicities, dazzled with hope instead of cynical and victimized.

"That's easy. I'd teach overseas again."

"Like where?"

"Practically anywhere." My years in the Middle East had been the most memorable of my life. They had become, in retrospect, what defined me. And I missed them – including the discomforts, heartaches, terror and, often, abject misery. I missed that daily undercurrent of the unknown.

"So what's stopping you?"

I rolled my eyes. "Uh, a life. A career. You."

"No, I mean it, Mom. What's stopping you? You've gotten rid of The Leech. It's been way too long since you've laughed. Plus, I can take care of myself now. You don't have to worry about me." Said with the utter confidence of an 18-year-old college student who plays video games in his single mom's basement. With the bravado of someone who has never faced tragedy, except when his orc got killed off too early on the screen. Or who isn't in a position to take humongous leaps himself.

I shrugged, and asked what he would do. Practice hard enough to win the Computer Athletic League World Championship. Or live at a Krishnamurti ashram to study philosophy. Or hitchhike to Nicaragua. Cool kid.

But his question haunted me, like a smell that teleports one to childhood, and makes the eyes tear up with lost innocence.

A few months later, I was on a plane flying into the unknown.

❖ ❖ ❖

When Andy asked his Big Question, let's just say that it had not been a good year. The person I'd been married to (it now seems crazy to have ever called that person a husband, or rather second husband) invested everything we (I) had owned in a grandiose real estate scheme. His timing was perfect. He bought when the market was at its peak. Then real estate went to hell.

So did he. As his business imploded, he spent more time every day in his Lazy Boy watching Fox News. Pretty soon, he wasn't even going into the office. He stopped taking phone calls or making decisions. He just sat, drinking, taking pain pills, shouting along with Bill O'Reilly, and staring at the bookshelves. When he wasn't yelling at Andy, that is.

"Pull up your trousers, boy. You look like a goddamn faggot."

Sullen teenage silence in reply.

"Pull up those trousers I said, or you're grounded for a week."

Slam went the bedroom door, followed by the chiming of a PC boot-up. Then the inevitable roar of video-war Armageddon. Every wall of the house reverberated with rage.

"You come out of that bedroom for anything but school and meals and you'll wish you hadn't."

Oh joy. Bills went unpaid. Decisions went unmade. With nobody at the helm, our family frigate dashed against the rocks. My health insurance was the first thing to go. Then Andy's. When Mr. Financial Genius eventually declared bankruptcy, as he had in his previous marriage, and — worse — wouldn't go for therapy, we split. He got any liquid assets, so he could start over. I got any assets that had mortgages attached.

Then my father died. On the road trip to the funeral — oh Jesus — the nightmare freeway skid, scream of locked brakes, slow-motion crunch, smash, g-force wham, whiplash, wham-again, concrete-barrier bash, rusty-blood taste, splintered glass everywhere, rain-soaked gurney, how come my brain stopped working, not sure I can even move my elbow, Andy I don't want to be alive if you're not, open your eyes, pleasepleasepleaseopenyour eyes, no don't take him in a separate ambulance, nonononono that's my son ...

✼ ✼ ✼

After something like that, priorities change. Andy and I make it out of a seven-car pile up doing 65 on a dark rainy interstate, and risk takes on a new meaning. Maybe two heartbeats of warning, that's all we had before the wreck materialized out of the torrent before us. Two windshield wiper swooshes. What could possibly happen next? What else — good or bad — might life hurtle at us in a matter of seconds?

Maybe I'd been setting the bar of life too low.

I started staying up late at night, following admittedly bizarre ideas on the Internet. A couple of clicks, and a whole new realm of possibility opened up. The Peace Corps wasn't the only game in town. Plenty of other places were looking for teachers. Most of them paid enough to live on (barely). They didn't mind if applicants were getting a bit long in the tooth, as long as they weren't 60 yet.

I got an online ESL certificate. I window-shopped for jobs. And then late one Friday night, I emailed my resume to five schools in places like Tajikistan, Surabaya and Fujian. I couldn't have found most of them on the map.

Half an hour later, the phone rang. Someone with an enigmatic accent asked for me, mangling my name. The connection made her sound as faraway as Outer Mongolia.

"Would you like to help the Kurdish people build a new nation?"

What an odd way to start a long-distance conversation. "Well, sure." I'd read a book about the Kurds several decades ago, and thought they were heroic. I'd even watched an obscure Iranian film about Kurds once on Netflix.

"Can we do an interview right now?" At 10:30 on a Friday night with no preparation? Why not?

She sounds skittish, bringing to mind the image of grenades going off in the background. She didn't want to talk about herself, though. She wanted to go down a long list of canned questions.

"Are you respectful of other cultures?" After teaching in Saudi, tolerance was one of my theme songs.

"Can you manage a classroom with 60 students?" Oh yes, I lied.

"Are you a firm disciplinarian?" I hedged a bit on that one. Discipline has never been my strongest suit.

"What do you think about teachers who drink too much and don't show up for work?" What a silly question.

"Can you teach from a strictly defined syllabus?" That depended on how you defined "strictly"; I usually prepared detailed syllabi, and followed them fairly closely.

And then the clincher. "Can you be here in six weeks?"

41

I should have asked why the rush. And it might have been wise to tell her how hard it would be to get my affairs in order. Instead, I gulped and said, "No problem."

Six weeks to rent my house. To help Andy find a place to live. To sell my business. Find a home for my little dog. Give notice for my college teaching jobs. Put my belongings into storage. Buy some long skirts and long-sleeved blouses. Write a will.

The contract arrived by email in less than 24 hours.

❁ ❁ ❁

When I'm done telling my story, Pat glances at the clock. "The bell rings in a minute. But I've gotta hear more about The Leech. Let me take a guess. You were a single mom before, and he spent the money you'd saved up while raising your son on your own?"

I nod, and Jake whistles in disbelief.

"No child support, either. I'd earned every penny by myself."

"Mmm hmm." You can tell Pat has seen this movie before. "So what do you mean, he got all the money and you got everything with a mortgage? How did your lawyer let that happen?"

"We didn't use lawyers. We did it ourselves." It's something I've been proud of.

She stands up abruptly. "Then I'm not going to feel sorry for you, sweetie. You should have screwed that sucker and taken every penny. Too bad you didn't hire a shark attorney like my first-and-only ex. He would have taken care of that loser for you in a New York minute. Like he did with me, by the way. Okay, back to the salt mine, everybody."

Two: Forms of Obedience

I FRET the rest of the school week about Friday's lunch. What should I wear? How will I communicate with the widow? I borrow a phrase book from the school library, but it's too confusing, with jumbles of consonants in what looks like the Turkish alphabet.

Fortunately, I spend my days surrounded by little Kurdish language experts. Using an exercise book, I start my own dictionary. The kids love the diversion. We're still getting to know each other, and switching roles from teacher to learner is a great way to break the ice.

"How do you say 'thank you' in Kurdish?"

"*Spas*, Miss."

I write *spas* on the board. "And 'how are you?'"

"*Choni*, Miss." Nearly fifty preteens swing their arms around like cheerleaders, practically exploding out of their chairs. "Then you answer *bashi*."

"Sit down!" Their bottoms are supposed to remain attached to the chairs at all times. Madame has been emphatic about this.

"*Danisheh*, Miss." Oh, very funny. But surely, this will be a useful word to learn.

"*Danisheh, danisheh!*" They obey. I proceed to write other teacherly phrases on the board like "be quiet" and "very bad" -- more appropriate for a classroom than a village meal. They insist on *wiss ba* — "shut up". I especially like 'very bad'. *Zor krappa*. Like crappy — easy to remember.

We agree that the kids will teach me one new word a day, which they can quiz me on. Whoever has been especially helpful gets to write my word on the board. Helin, one of my favorites, prances up and writes '*zor krappa*' as our first example. She curtsies to a hearty round of applause. I'm buoyed by their enthusiasm, and they by mine, and by my fascination with their world. We're mutual learners, and the atmosphere is electrifying.

I'm bragging about my success in the faculty room when a summons comes via student courier from Mr. Zaki.

"Who or what is Mr. Zaki?"

Pat and Jake roll their eyes at each other. "He's basically God around here — the so-called Academy rep, from headquarters in Cairo," says Jake. "We're not sure who's higher on the pecking order, Zaki or Madame. In general, he's a royal pain in the patooty, enforcing all his stupid rules. I'll bet he's discovered you didn't check off your tactics properly." He makes it sound like a mortal sin.

"Tactics?"

"Didn't Madame tell you? You've got to write your learning objectives and teaching tactics, including the textbook pages you'll cover, for each period on the board, and put a tick mark as you do each one. In order." Jake puts his hands on his cheeks, as if to say "oh my!"

"And they've got to match what you wrote on your lesson plan, word for word," Pat adds in a more no-nonsense manner. "They come around and check."

"Madame told me, but I didn't think she could be serious." I had, in truth, assumed it was just administrative micromanagement, designed for first-year teachers, and forgotten all about it.

"Better believe it. And too many days without tick marks mean bye bye bonus." Jake waves a limp ta-ta.

"But that's stupid."

They agree. Louanna, the Texan who's been here the longest, looks up from her crime novel. "You get used to it. Just forget you've taught any other way and it's not so bad."

I grab my lesson plans as ammunition against Zaki. I've been following them pretty closely, just not writing them on the board.

"Stiff upper lip," Jake advises. "Remember that you're at least a foot taller than he is. And white."

"And you know what you're doing in a classroom," says Pat. "You don't have to listen to his ridiculous corporate crap."

An enormous brass plate mounted on Zaki's door announces "Mr. Nazir Zaki, B.Science (Honors), Representative to the President, International Academies Worldwide." Behind the door, a trim young Arab sits decked out in a commando outfit. Mirrored aviator glasses hide his eyes. A black trench coat covers him down to the ankles, and a black KGB-type briefcase rests next to his desk. All that he needs is a sash of bullets slung across his chest and he could be a guerrilla, banging his machine gun against the door in the middle of the night. Although the look must be designed to terrorize little children, it doesn't do much for my comfort level, either.

He stays seated when I come in. "Miss Turner." It's an indictment, not a welcome. "I received reports of unauthorized content in 6/7 Accelerated this morning. May I ask what was going on?" His murky Egyptian accent comes across as both officious and weasely. At first I suspect that he's putting on an act, like an extra in a forgettable low-budget movie.

"Oh, that." Whew. I relax my stranglehold on the lesson plans. "The kids are teaching me Kurdish. I've got this system to reward good behavior by letting them write a word each day for me on the board." I wait for praise.

He blows his nose into a handkerchief, then extracts papers from the briefcase, held together with a common tailoring pin. Can't the school afford a stapler?

"Kurdish vocabulary is not mentioned in the 6/7 English syllabus. You should have been on page 64, past perfect verbs."

"May I see that?" It's a copy of Rabinowitz's old syllabus. "We're way behind all this. The children haven't had a teacher for several months. So there's no way…"

"All the more reason to avoid straying from the syllabus." Cough cough.

"Mr. Zaki, do you have a cold?" I'm attempting to humanize the situation, although he's obviously got a smoker's hack.

He ignores me and drills the desk impatiently with his fingers.

"Your contract clearly stipulates that teachers shall not deviate from the approved syllabus or texts. They shall not introduce unauthorized concepts or pedagogical methods."

This is getting way too heavy. "So I can't ask them to teach me one Kurdish word a day?" It comes out more flippantly than I'd intended.

"That isn't what I meant." The brusqueness surprises me. "You may do whatever you like within the confines of the syllabus. I'll repeat. Within the confines of the syllabus."

I can hear my heart going faster. Damn. This guy is getting my goat.

"Mr. Zaki, I won Teacher of the Year in my district several years ago. I know how to achieve learning objectives in a classroom." I regret this the minute it pops out of my mouth — too defensive.

"I'm certain that is true. Please realize, though, that the parent company of the Academy has been in existence for 61 years. We have dozens of schools throughout the world. Each one is on the same chapter of the text every week. It's a formula, yes. And it works."

I guess it sort of makes sense, if teachers and their students aren't acknowledged to be human beings.

I must have waited too long to agree; his eyebrows knit into a solid brush across his forehead. "Let me remind you that you signed a contract to teach in the manner this school requires."

True. But I hadn't spent much time reading the fine print.

"As we say at the Academy, no one is irreplaceable. Your contract clearly stipulates…."

I hate words like stipulate. They feel like bullying. I try to zone out.

But I'm still too new here to fight him. I cave. "Perhaps we could have talked about the Kurdish language if it had been within the context of past perfect verbs?" I try brightly. "For instance, 'I have spoken Kurdish, she has spoken Kurdish,' and so on?"

The brows separate. "Precisely." Maybe he wasn't picking a fight after all.

"Kurdish, within the context of page 64 of the Grade 6 English book, in other words?"

"Ah." He leans back, inhales and blinks, as if thanking me. "Now you're following."

"Okay. I understand." I gather my lesson plans and stand up. "I will do my best to teach within the confines of the syllabus in the future."

He does another noisy inhale and laces his fingers together into a tent. "Yes, I'm sure you will."

I'm heading out the door when he calls me back. "Miss Turner? Let me add just one thing." Uh oh. He must have heard about the fart in the bathtub story, or one of its cousins. He coughs again, this time as if embarrassed. "We are extremely grateful that you joined us."

I listen for irony, but it's not there. "You are?" Even though I've already been such an abject failure?

"We were actually relieved when your CV came through from Cairo. It's quite noble of you to sacrifice your pleasant life in America to give us assistance here."

To my amazement, he sounds sincere. I take a closer look at the paramilitary get-up and feel a spasm of compassion. What a job, having to shape up a crop of new teachers every year — coercing people from all over the world, trained in different methods, to get them to obey.

I give him a wan smile, feeling a little like myself again. "Thank you for saying that, Mr. Zaki. I'm glad to be here too."

❊   ❊   ❊

I'm not so glad in the middle of the night, though, when I can't stop crying about all the great teaching ideas that now get flushed down the drain — or about a much more sinister issue.

"Say, Pat, how did Zaki know the kids were teaching me Kurdish? We only did it for a couple of minutes at the beginning of the period. And we weren't that noisy, for once."

We're hauling bulging book bags upstairs from the teacher apartments to report for work the next morning. She pauses to see who is within ear shot.

"He's got informants," she whispers. "He picks a few kids to be his quote special helpers. They're usually the sons of big politicos, who know how loyalty works. They report to him every time something unusual happens."

I wince. One of my little angels, a secret agent? Unbelievable.

"But I've got a solution. You know that window in the door? I appoint a kid to watch it and warn me when Zaki skulks around. He hasn't summoned me since I started doing it. Jake does the same thing."

I can't even imagine Pat wrangling with Zaki; she'd take up way too much of the psychic space in that wretched office of his.

"What if I mess up and pick one of his spies as *my* spy? Then he'd find out…"

Pat laughs sarcastically. "Jake says they've got video cameras and microphones hidden in the ceiling lights anyway, taping everything we do. But I don't believe it. The Academy's so cheap that we have to get Madame's permission to photocopy every blessed worksheet. They'd never pay for a video system. Remember, this whole thing is a business, not a charity."

"Oh yeah." The idea of schools being profit centers is still an anathema to me.

"We Westerners are what make the place so-called international, so they can charge the big bucks. As long as you keep looking American and don't rile up Zaki too much, you'll last just fine." She shifts the book bag to the other shoulder with a groan.

"Last? Is that the goal?"

"Yep. It's all about that end-of-year bonus. Assuming you can make it through each torturous day from now until the end of June."

"I've been collapsing on the couch every afternoon when I get home. I don't wake up for about an hour." I've been too embarrassed to admit this until now, viewing it as a sign of age.

"Layla, next door to you, crawls right under the covers and cries most afternoons. If she's gotten Zaki'ed that particular day, she doesn't come out for hours. And she's actually friends with Madame, so go figure. For me, it's a shot of rum after work. To each his or her own."

"I could hold out better if only they'd let me have a chair to sit on. It's cruel, making us stand up all day."

49

"Against the rules. Standing keeps us on our toes — ha, ha. Just wait. Pretty soon Madame will quote invite you to go on chummy little walks with her after school. As if she has no idea how our feet ache by that time of day."

"Maybe it's easier for the younger teachers."

"Like Louanna? She doesn't count. She turned into Teflon after her first year here, so we all call her Roboteacher. Now she's beyond redemption. Note that she's the only teacher — got that, the *only* one? — who returned after last year, poor desperate thing. The Academy boasts a practically zero percent retention rate. The data speaks for itself, wouldn't you agree?"

We've reached the classroom blocks, four-story towers of orange that loom above. "Happy tick marks on your chalk board," she says with forced cheeriness. "Seven hours to go, for today. One hundred thirty two days. Nine hundred twenty four teaching hours until departure day. Chin up. We can do it."

❖ ❖ ❖

Early Friday morning, I take the faculty shuttle into the city to find a hostess gift for Bezma and Ara. It's just the driver and me; none of my colleagues feel like rising this early and braving the howling wind.

As we descend from The Fortress, I scout out possible bicycle rides. Saddam demolished almost all of Iraq's Kurdish villages, including the orchards they'd been famous for, and the place still looks like a vast battlefield, bare and bleak, with ragged palms here and there, and winter stubble poking out from fallow earth.

Maybe biking to town isn't such a great plan after all; as we approach the city, the roadway becomes utter chaos. Lanes don't exist. When traffic bunches up, trucks merely bounce off onto the shoulder — where a cyclist could easily have been trying to ride. And who would want to breathe all this exhaust?

My search for camera-worthy exotica out the window isn't too fruitful either. The sprawl of the city is like every CNN shot from a nameless Arab town. Squat cinder-block buildings march to the horizon, surrounded by tangles of utility wire. Muffler shops, one-room minimarts, and unmarked storefronts hide behind rolled-up metal doors. We pass a dusty little mosque or two. I almost doze off.

Suddenly, the walls of the ancient part of the city rise to fill the entire bus window. It's supposed to be one of the oldest continuously inhabited places on earth, here for at least 6,000 years. I can't even see to the top from inside the bus. An old bazaar spills maze-like around it on all sides. The driver lets me out, pointing to his watch that he'll leave if I'm not back at eleven thirty sharp. How will I ever find him again in this mess?

I blithely hop off the shuttle, hear the doors suck shut behind me, and start to take in the jumble. Men crouch on the sidewalk behind stacks of pirated videos and music CD, priced at a dollar. Table after table offers "designer" watches and wallets mixed in with cigarette lighters, key chains and combs. From dim stalls, strings of prayer beads beckon, many with the blue-and-white *hamsa* "Eye of Fatima" to protect against the evil eye. White crocheted skullcaps pile like overturned bowls beside checked turban cloths in red, green or black. It's a wonderland for the senses, this cacophony of colored plastic, traffic honks, donkey brays, dust swirls and smells of chicken fat dripping from spits — even before entering the bazaar itself. And best of all, the vendors don't call out, or otherwise pester me. Mercifully, I don't exist.

Then I feel a scream of panic rising, and barely manage to choke it back. I've just noticed an appalling fact. I am the only woman in this entire throng of humanity.

Tense scenes from suspense movies and TV news footage accost me. Which are the more treacherous — the scowling older guys in baggy khaki bloomers, with safari vests and checkered turbans? Or the sly younger ones in tight jeans and fake Adidas? They all leer when I raise my eyes from the sidewalk; any of them could have guns or knives tucked away. The guy with a black backpack is definitely a suicide bomber, waiting for me to get closer so he can detonate himself (and me) into blood and guts all over the place. He's biding his time to verify that I'm an infidel, maybe even an American under my Amish-length skirt and black scarf, the perfect target to get him into heaven and earn those 80 or however-many adoring virgins.

I stumble on a pile of cables; a ragged end rips my hem. Blood trickles down my ankle, but there's nowhere to stop and wipe it — nowhere to hide. I hurry toward a coffee shop at the end of the block, but it turns out to be narrow, deep and dark inside, jammed with men staring out from wobbly metal tables. My lungs hurt; I've been breathing too fast. Isn't there a Starbucks, or a department store where a woman can wander safely by herself?

A teenaged juice vendor two doors down seems trustworthy. He squeezes fresh oranges and hands me a glass still wet from the last customer. I shrink into the back corner of his shop, sipping slowly to make the juice last as long as possible, all the way down to the last bubble of foam. The sweet chill seems out of place in this biting cold. As I calm down, I notice how fast my heart had been racing.

Framed on the wall is a poster I'm seeing everywhere, like the Pope in Italy or the Virgin of Guadeloupe in Mexico. It's Massoud Barzani, the president, in red-checked head wrap and traditional Kurdish trousers. He exudes both confidence and competence, as if promising to protect me in his country. This is oddly reassuring. Maybe I can make it through the throng of men outside after all.

I wedge back onto the sidewalk, and let myself be swept along by the current. We're all swimming, like salmon, toward a mosque with chipped green plaster and rows of tattered sandals piled inside the gate. Curious, I start to slip off my shoes to join them — the loudspeakers' call to prayer is so close overhead that my ribs rattle — but in the nick of time note, with a start, the lack of women's shoes. I shove aside and let the men eddy around me.

At long last, the crowds of men thin out. But I'm not invisible after all, as I'd hoped. Someone taps my shoulder from behind. My stomach seizes, ready for the worst. I'm paralyzed, my inner trigger cocked for something practiced and speedy — the inevitable rag stuffed in my mouth, or rude rope around my wrists, or knife tip in my ribs, warning me to obey. But I turn, and it's college-aged kid in jeans and a leather-like jacket. That first horrific moment passes, and there's no pain, no ambush, no accomplices. My hands are still free, grabbing my purse like a life preserver. My elbows are unpinned. My lungs start to work again. Why did he let me live?

"America, yes?" He reaches inside his jacket for what must be a gun. It's a smart phone.

I nod, still unconvinced.

He grins and does a double thumbs up. "Okay, okay. America, big okay."

Now he puts his arm around my shoulder and pulls my head close, so we're cheek to cheek. His hair reeks of cigarettes and pomade. With the other hand, he stretches out the phone to take a selfie. Click. "Again! You smile this time, okay?" Tentatively, not sure this will be allowed, he tugs down on my scarf so my hair shows, and takes several more photos. "Now wait a minute. See?" He fiddles with the screen. And there we are together on his wallpaper, posing like long-lost friends, the Kurdish youth and the aging blonde teacher.

"Coffee?" He's pointing to one of the all-male dens of seeming iniquity I'd passed earlier. "I pay. You friend. Nice coffee."

I shake my head, still not quite recovered from my foolish fears.

"Tea then, yes? We practice English?"

I burst helplessly into a smile as he transforms before my eyes. Or maybe it's me, the viewer, that transforms. I can see him now as one of the undergrads I'd been teaching back home, avid to learn once they remembered how much fun it could be, and hungry for a nurturing adult connection. "Sure. Tea."

Being the only woman in the coffee shop isn't scary now with my young guide, who swaggers as he shows me to a table. The tea glasses are spotted and tea way too sweet, but I find myself dropping into a familiar ease as we practice phrases from his text book.

"My name is Hamid. Please tell me yours." "I am a university student. What is your profession?" "I am interested in football and music. What are your interests?" His words come out choppy and rehearsed, and he keeps glancing over his shoulders, both directions, at the guys at the tables around us. 'Look, Ma, no hands!' That's what this feels like, an act put on for the benefit of the old codgers hunched above torn cardboard checkerboards. They can't be bothered to look up from their deliberations over the bottle-cap markers, prongs up for red, and down for black.

I want to thank them all — Hamid as well as the sleepy waiter and all the checker players — for letting me be here, for this soaring sense of strangeness and liberation from everything in my past, for letting me smell the rasp of extra-strong coffee wafting between the tables, hear the guttural babble of a language still incomprehensible, taste the woodiness of cheap tea-bag tea. It's gratitude for being right here, right now, at this improbable intersection of time and space.

When we run out of English phrases, I point to my watch and mimic running. "My bus is coming. I have to go. Thanks for the tea."

He slaps his heart and turns dramatically to the ceiling; I've ruined his life by leaving, ha ha. With a gallant bow he opens up the phone to show me the wallpaper again. "Beautiful," he says, implying that the tea was a small price to pay.

But now I've got to rush. There's barely time to buy a box of Turkish delight from a turbaned guy pushing a handcart. The fact that he's shaved within the past week reassures me, irrationally, that he's not Al Qaeda, and probably has no ulterior motives. After the tea with Hamid, though, I'm less worried about Al Qaeda. A scum of flies swarms over the open piles of candies on display, but the prepackaged ones look sanitary enough. I can't remember how many dinars to the dollar; it's over a thousand. I'm nervous about making a multiplication mistake and looking foolish. I fish a small wad of dinars from my wallet and hope it's enough. It is. The vendor thanks me in Arabic, *shukran*, and grins when I answer *afwan*. He says *shukran* again when I refuse a plastic bag, and nods approval at my canvas shopping bag. Then he goes back to gazing over the heads in the crowd and flipping his prayer beads, as if this is an utterly unremarkable transaction, putting my nerves to shame.

Safely back on the shuttle, I fold my black scarf, which certainly hasn't worked as much of a disguise, and ruffle through the shopping bag. Lo and behold, no one has stolen the Turkish delight. My wallet is still there too, with all my money in it.

On the ride back to The Fortress, I wish Pat were here to discuss the existential reality of ugly Muslim terrorists and ugly

Americans. I want to articulate my chagrin with somebody. When I was so certain of being a terrorist target, I was instead a photo-worthy woman. When I thought I was a rich American ripe for purse-snatching, somebody sold me candy and forgot about me. What a provincial rube I am.

But no longer, I realize with a start, am I a provincial rube mired in boring old sameness. I have just survived an entire morning in an ocean of cultural, religious and gender strangeness — all on my own. And it has been a record 48 hours since I have wasted a single thought on my humiliating marital mistake. If only he could see me now, I think with a smirk.

With another start, a brightness shafts through my inner cloud cover, so habitual I hadn't even realized it was there. I've rediscovered an amazing new word on this brief but stressful outing. It's one I'd assumed was lost to me forever. Fun.

※　※　※

That afternoon, the guard at the back gate is napping, and so are the wild dogs. It's even silent in the Bangladeshi janitors' little slum behind the school, where rags droop on clotheslines and plastic buckets lie strewn here and there. Friday is the janitors' only day off, and they're getting some rest.

In a long skirt hitched with clothespins so as not to tangle in the gears, and a windbreaker as an all-purpose cover up, I glide on the Blue Angel toward the village intoxicated with freedom. I am alone outside The Fortress! I am alive! I am really here in this amazing place!

Beyond the first rise, billowing black smoke chokes me. A bomb? No, it's just the trash heap, about an acre in size now, and almost as tall as the young eucalyptus nearby. The smoke follows me to the village and down the lanes, which all look confusingly similar. I bang on one of the metal gates, hoping it's the right one, and there to my immense relief is Bezma. Her face radiates anticipation and intelligence, like someone who has just won a spelling bee and awaits her prize. I marvel at my good fortune; out of all the young women in this village, I meet up with one as clever as this.

"Come, come!" She grabs my handlebars, props the bike against the water tank, and leads me up to the porch. I unclip the clothespins to lower my skirt and kick off my jogging shoes outside the door jamb. Next to the rubber slippers heaped there, the shiny swishes on my Nikes remind me of a phase when my son Andy refused to wear Nikes once they were scuffed. I can't believe I'm the same person who allowed something like that.

"*B'kher hati. Ser tchow, ser tchow.*" Ara, Bezma's mother, covers one eye with a wrinkled hand, choking back sobs.

"She say, 'Welcome. You are my eyes,'" Bezma explains. Something must have gotten lost in the translation.

"Why is she crying?"

"She cry many times this week," Bezma says dismissively. "She afraid you not come. Now you here, she very happy. You see my house?"

There's not much to see. Unpainted concrete blocks form two all-purpose rooms plus a kitchen. One room has a pressboard wardrobe across the back. The other has an old unplugged TV. Besides a pile of sleeping mats, cushions and a carpet, that's the entire extent of their furniture. The only wall decorations are a cracked mirror, a framed photo of Massoud Barzani, a small sepia photo from decades earlier, and a nail holding several black headscarves.

I search in vain for a kitchen sink to wash my hands. There are no counters or cabinets in the kitchen, either, only a stove and a free-standing cupboard. I wonder where they cut vegetables or put mixing bowls when they cook.

Bezma leads me to a spigot down low in the outhouse, a windowless block that's half wash room and half pit toilet. There's a bucket to fill with water to flush. I squat to rinse my hands, and watch the run-off flow through a hole to an open gutter.

Ara lays out lunch on a plastic tablecloth spread over the carpet: flatbread, cucumber and tomato salad, watery bean soup, and dolmas, her *piece de resistance*. The dolmas are stuffed grape and cabbage leaves, as well as stuffed peppers, onions, and little eggplants, filled with rice and tiny pieces of meat. We sit cross-legged near a portable kerosene heater that holds a tea kettle, and eat with tablespoons and hunks of bread.

I try to imagine how life could have made a woman in her forties look like this — the straggly gray hair, the lumpy figure, the black gaps where teeth had been, the creases in her face. "Bezma, please tell me about your mother."

Bezma leans back on her arms. This could take a while.

"My mother life not like other woman. She marry for love. She was village girl. Not this village. From mountains. She love boy and he love her. But families say no. My mother and love wait many years. Never able talk. Only look sometimes. After years, families say yes."

"Wow. Good for you, Ara." Since we're speaking in English, she hasn't been able to follow any of this, and gives a confused smile.

"My father was driver for Big Man," Bezma continues, tearing off more bread. "One day, bomb go off for Big Man's car and my father die. My mother have four children. Only two alive now. I am youngest."

"What happened to the others?" I hope this won't cause offense.

"My brother and wife live next door. You will meet. My oldest sister die two years ago. She had three children. Other sister die. Burn when heater explode." I shrink warily from the kerosene device beside me. "Yes, like that one. I almost die too." Bezma rolls up her sleeves; angry purple scars torture the insides of her arms.

My heart skips a beat. "I'm so sorry." Flustered now, she hurries to re-cover herself, while I search for a diversion. I unfold my aching knees and get up to admire the sepia photo on the wall. An angular, mustachioed man in a traditional khaki outfit glares from under a checked turban; he totes an archaic rifle across his chest. The grimace is both jagged and proud. It's hard to imagine anyone holding out for a love match with him.

"Tell Ara I think she must miss him."

Bezma translates, but Ara looks away. I've made a mistake.

"My father not good husband. He take second wife. Ara no talk to him. Ever."

"A second wife? I didn't know Kurds did that."

"We must. Saddam kill too many mans. We not have enough for all womans."

It's an interesting, if heartbreaking, justification for polygamy, one I'd never considered before. "Still, Ara must have been really jealous."

"Yes. Father make more children with other wife. He give money to other wife, not my mother. We poor. We have little food. No new clothes. Quran say no, not do like this. All wife should be same. But now father is dead, better. One time in month, my mother get money from government."

"Oh, like a widow's pension." It couldn't be much -- probably less than a fifth of my expat teacher's salary. "No wonder she wants you to become a teacher."

"Hmmph." She forces a laugh. "Maybe mother want. But *I* do not want."

"You wouldn't like being independent? Having an income of your own?" Not to mention the gratification of wearing a holy mantle, nurturing little minds...

"For teachers, six days every week with children, but not my children. I want husband. *My* house. *My* children. Not always live with mother." She pushes her lips into a pout. "But mother say no. She say mans no good."

"Please tell your mother that I agree with her, based on personal experience." We'll leave it at that. This probably isn't the best time for a feminist polemic about money and power.

Ara nods and sniffs, fishing a cotton handkerchief from inside her bodice. Without a bra, her breasts hang down to a string belt that pouches her dress at the waist. I wonder if she'd let me sew pockets in the dress sometime.

"Ara say, why you have no husband here?"

I pantomime tugging off a wedding ring and hurling it out the window. "My husband was bad. It was for different reasons than Ara had, but still bad. He is gone. Finished." The ring toss wins me big points with Ara. Bringing out the photo of Andy from my wallet wins me even more.

"My mother say God is good, God give you boy. You bring him, my mother she cook dolmas."

"Oh, that's not possible. My son is back in America," I say bravely. "Far, far away. Eighteen hours on three different airplanes. I won't see him until the summer, when the school term is out."

This sets Ara to crying again on my behalf.

I want to reassure her. "It's okay. I'm getting used to being alone."

But really, I'm not. Sometimes my whole body aches with missing Andy. On days when school is particularly awful, which is more frequently so far than I care to admit, I stare at a photo of him beside me on the sofa back home. That was about a hundred years ago. Summer is at least six hundred years away.

Ara must sense this, for she takes my hand in hers, and looks seriously into my eyes. Through the creamy blur of cataracts, it's like she recognizes me as a sister in some international mother's club, where the only membership requirement is having given birth and loved. Her look is one between equals; any intimidation she felt by my "otherness" earlier has vanished. Without dropping her gaze, she speaks and Bezma translates. "My mother say, we family for you. You never alone. You come here always. All Fridays."

I swallow hard, trying to collect myself. "Thank you." I hunt for a way to say more, to acknowledge how touched I am to be included. But suddenly my stomach is stabbed by doubt. Maybe she's just being polite, and Kurds do this all the time. I'd probably be making a big mistake to read too much meaning into this.

Perhaps it's time for a joke. "In that case, I'd better learn a lot more Kurdish." Drawing back from Ara and her intensity, I rustle around in my backpack and pull out the dictionary I've started making, and pass it to Ara. "Please write the word for delicious?"

The spell is broken; Ara leans against the wall and makes a big show of adjusting her skirt, avoiding my outstretched book. Something's wrong. Oh damn. How did I offend them?

Bezma grabs the book. "I write. My mother cannot. She did not school."

The shame on Ara's face tells me this is true.

"But I saw a school at the edge of the village."

With great tact, she deflects me. "Yes, but this not village of my mother. Her village in mountains. Her family have sheep and trees with fruit. Her village very beautiful. Saddam want it, make palace. He make everybody move. Push down houses. Push down trees. Put concrete where water come from earth. Many peoples go Iran. After, many peoples go here."

"All of your neighbors? Everybody in these houses around us?"

She nods. "We know all peoples here in village, always, from mountains. My uncles here." She motions around the block. "Mother and father of my father here." She motions across the street. "Everyone, family. Some peoples not come here. They go back to mountains. Family of my love go back to mountains. We take you there, when warm days come."

"That's a good word to learn today — warm."

We struggle to write phrases, Bezma in her childish English letters and me in my childish Arabic script, while Ara clatters around in the kitchen and brings out tea. My mind is stuck picturing Ara's dark world of illiteracy. How does she make a grocery list? How does she navigate without reading road signs?

"Ara, I'll teach you to read!" I blurt when she rejoins us. "We'll get a book. Every time I come here, Bezma will practice English, I'll learn Kurdish, and you'll learn to read." The teacher in me is getting excited.

But Ara shrinks back with her tea tray. "No." She taps her forehead, frowning as if to say that she's too stupid, or maybe it's too old. What I really think she means, though is too scary.

She's adamant, so I give up. Instead, she teaches me to do the *der tchow* thing, where the right hand covers the eye. I've read that it means something like, "You're as precious as my eyes to me." We move on to *min dulum khosh*, my heart is glad, hand-over-heart like the pledge of allegiance. To her great delight, I remember how to do both successfully when leaving that afternoon.

My pride is short-lived, though, because a frowning Bezma heads me off at the gate. "Treeza, you no talk again to children in street."

Another cross-cultural blunder? "Why not?"

She glances around for an answer, as if one might be hiding behind the water tank. "They bother you."

"No they won't. I'm a teacher. I like kids." There's some polite dissembling going on here, but it's over my head.

She pauses, as if weighing the comparative value of tact versus bluntness. "Now you my family. Look not nice when talk in the street. You come only here. Okay?"

She plants her hands on her hips, exactly the way she did on my first visit. There's no question she could command a village classroom, and a crowded one at that. "I guess," I say, but with great reluctance, and start to hike up my skirt again with the clothespins.

"Stop please. You not put arm over bicycle." She pats her calf. Oh, she means that I shouldn't swing my leg up. "Rude," she continues. "Please you walk bicycle to store."

"Okay." Maybe I'll try leggings underneath the skirt next time.

I obey her about baring any skin, and walk the Blue Angel slowly out of town, weaving through a flock of sheep. The dour old man herding them won't meet my eye, but the warmth inside insulates me from caring. He can't make me feel alien. Two women in this village now know my name, and I know theirs; one iron gate is special to me. In some small way, I belong.

* * *

"Miss, I saw you on a bicycle yesterday!" Seema, one of the 6/7 Accelerateds, announces this like it's up there with extraterrestrials landing on the roof.

We're in that honeymoon period of the school week, namely the first twenty minutes of the first day, before we're beaten down by boredom and fatigue. A girlish hand has written "We love you Miss Turner" on the board, surrounded by daisies. And I love them too, these eager little faces filled with trust and guilelessness. I hate having to erase the daisies to make space for tactics and agenda items. I want to prolong this brief interlude when we're still genuine, excited by the light sifting of snow out the windows and feeling fresh from the weekend. I plunk the dreaded text onto my desk and try for an American-style class discussion instead.

"Who has a bicycle?" Only a few students raise their hands. But they've all perked up, now that I'm no longer holding a book.

"What about you, Helin?" The few kids whose names I know get called on more frequently than the others.

"Miss, I had one when we lived in Sweden." Her skirt is much shorter than regulation length; by some fashion miracle she has made the uniform look chic. "I loved it. It had 21 speeds, and my dad taught me, and he used to take me around the park with him on Sundays." Who would have expected such flawless English? Or such a dazzling smile?

My father had taught me to ride too, jogging beside me around the high school track, holding the seat of a second-hand clunker with balloon tires. And after a while, he wasn't answering me, and — a miracle — I was gliding along alone, and he was laughing in triumph behind me, sharing that exact instant of bliss. And then it didn't matter that the bike was red, a boy's color, instead of blue like the girls down the street, but only how it gave me wings; my father understood, and we were buddies in a fraternity of bicycle fanatics. A pang of anguish swells up in me at the memory of him, the funeral I never reached, the ache of not having been able to phone him from here and tell him about this adventure, which he would have cheered, or even just getting an email from him. But I've got to stuff it all down quickly, because my students have become infected by the euphoria of their own memories, and clamor to jump in.

"Miss, I lived in Sweden too."

"Miss, I lived in California. I had a skateboard."

Ah, this is what language lessons should be like. We are engaging as a class, even if it's getting a bit chaotic. The mere mention of words like bike and skateboard and California lightens up the room.

"So, Helin, where do you ride here in Kurdistan?"

A roar of laughter erupts from the back. "Miss, she's a girl! Good joke, Miss." Helin presses her lips, glaring at the floor.

To rescue her, I whip out the roll sheet to call on a boy. The problem is that gender is not readily apparent. Some of the names ending in "a" are boys, and some are girls. Aside from the raft of girls named Sara, Sana, Lara, Vana, Hana and Tara, I have to just guess.

"Barav, how about you? Do you know how to ride a bicycle?"

A gloomy character in the back hauls himself to his feet, as if he's doing me an enormous favor. "Miss, no Miss." He collapses back into his seat.

I don't want to encourage one-word answers. "Well, why not? Don't you want one? Won't your parents get you one?"

He studies his lap, morose as an abandoned watch dog. I smile encouragingly. More silence.

A helpful-looking girl in front whispers to me. Thank God for little girls.

"What? I can't hear…"

"Miss, he doesn't have any parents. He's a Child of Martyrs."

Martyrs? It has an ominous ring to it – like something we probably shouldn't be using for English practice. I decide it's time to switch gears.

"Okay, never mind. Everybody open your books to page 47. We left off when Alexander was getting his favorite horse. Who remembers the name of the horse?"

"No, Miss. Tell us another story about your son Andy."

"Tell us again about when he threw toilet paper all over the neighbor's yard and it rained. That's our favorite."

"We don't have time for that." That's not the real reason. Although we Skype once a week, the thought of Andy crushes my chest right now; I miss him that much. So I get stern. "The name of Alexander's horse?"

Rows of little faces sag in disappointment. It's going to be a dreary old English day, like any other. No longer am I a Fun New Bicycle Miss. Suddenly, I have morphed into Just Another Old Boring Miss. It's heartbreaking. But Zaki will be pleased, if he happens to be snooping outside at the peep hole.

When class is over and the other children have left, Seema sidles up to me. She's one of the shyer kids who doesn't seem to have many friends; I've been trying to draw her out in class, with only limited success. "Miss, did you see me Friday?"

"See you? Where?"

"My grandmother wouldn't let me come out, but I was peeking behind the gate. My grandmother is Old Houda, Ara's friend. You can't miss her. She's the one who always wears a white scarf."

"Really? You live in the village?" She morphs before my eyes from any ordinary student to a long-lost relative. "I'll look for your grandmother next time. Maybe your mother too?"

She shakes her head, flustered, and ducks into her shoulders. "No, Miss. I don't have a mother. Or a father." Before I can ask more, she's out the door, leaving an odd scent of sweat and orange peel behind. And I'm left with the guilt of having blundered twice today in front of the children, which bugs me the rest of the day.

❊ ❊ ❊

That evening on the shopping bus, Pat fills me in about Children of Martyrs.

"Most of the families who send their kids to the Academy are millionaires. They pay more for a year of high school than I did for my daughters' college. They basically run the country. That's why security is so tight." She keeps her voice low and her eyes on the scarved teachers in the front of the bus.

"I'd been wondering about the guys with machine guns at the front gate. And those sticks with mirrors on them that they poke under all the cars. And the way they open everybody's hood and trunk. It's like teaching at a Russian embassy."

"Yeah, well there's a reason for it. The rich kids come in Land Rovers every morning, escorted by their personal body guards. But then you've also got some kids in rattier uniforms, whose parents were killed in the fight for Kurdish independence. The Academy has to give free tuition to a certain number of them, in return for getting so much free land to build on. A few Children of Martyrs probably come from your village."

I beam. After just two visits, it's already become "my" village.

"How did they get to be millionaires? I thought most of the Kurds were refugees when Saddam was in power."

"They were. About a million of them walked across the mountains to Iran or Turkey with only what they could carry on their backs. The whole place emptied out. Then Saddam brought in bulldozers."

Jake pokes his head between us from the back seat. "Good old Uncle Saddam. Doing his best to look after his people. And moving in Sunni Arabs wherever he could, to de-Kurdisize the north." Is that perfume he's wearing? To go out shopping?

"And it's why so many of our students spent time overseas," says Pat. "Sweden took in a lot of Kurdish refugees during Sadaam's time. So did Germany. A few went to the U.S. and Australia. Now it's safe again and business is booming, so they're coming back in droves. With money.

We've reached the shopping area, and the bus jolts to a halt. The Egyptian teachers cram their way to the door. Pat holds me back. "Let them get out first," she advises. "They'll stampede us if we get in their way."

Jake nods at the chemistry teacher, who is retying a dark head scarf. "Miss Junk in the Trunk up there stepped on my foot and bruised two of my toes the first week we were here. Wish I'd been wearing steel combat boots to kick her back."

Pat whacks him on the shoulder. "Would you just shut up? It's no wonder some of them don't like us, the way you talk about them." But despite the fierce tone, Pat's sounds as if she's gotten stomped once or twice too.

I hope none of the teachers up front understand English.

When we finally get off, Pat takes charge of me like a seasoned tour guide. She shepherds me around sinkholes in the sidewalk, piles of construction debris, and knots of abandoned rebar on our way to her favorite vendors. Dark is falling fast, and an icy wind knots our skirts around our shins.

"This is a Christian part of the city. Its Assyrian families came here in the first century, and never converted when Islam swept through. You don't need to worry about a head scarf, or about counting change, by the way. People in Kurdistan — both Christians and Muslims — are so honest, I just hand them five thousand dinars and see what they give me back."

We buy misshapen, dusty tomatoes and tiny finger-like cucumbers, then a whole roasted chicken for each of us, fresh off the spit. Nothing looks very good. But it all *smells* delicious — the tomatoes pungent and viney, the flatbread yeasty and warm. This food is alive, like a garden is alive, each potato or onion unique because you've hand-picked it from a bin, rather than prepackaged in plastic net. The little minimart they call a supermarket is the opposite; its aging tins and boxes look like they've been hauled over from Turkey by pack mule.

"You'll learn to cook with what you've got," says Pat when we fail to find ketchup, oregano or tonic water. "Still, whatever you see here beats Burkina Faso any day of the week. We're not in the first world, but it's not the third either. Maybe something like second and a half."

We barely make it back to the bus on time, only to find that it's not going anywhere. Somebody's missing. We sit in the dark getting colder by the minute. Jake, reeking of beer, is not amused.

"Let's place bets on who's holding us up *this* time. I have a sneaking suspicion…"

By the time the chemistry teacher heaves herself onto the bus, Jake calculates he could have had two more drinks plus a much-needed piss. The driver helps her with bulging sacks of cookies, chips and Coke. "Our cherished Lard Ass," murmurs Jake, a bit too loud.

"He means Mrs. Zaki," Pat says once the bus starts moving.

"Really?"

She nods. "Big mucky-muck Egyptians from headquarter, like the Zakis, live free on campus like us gringos. And really, they're not half bad, once you get to know them. *If* you can get to know them, that is."

"Except that they hog the washing machines on the weekends. So do your laundry on school nights."

"Thanks, Jake." But he's almost passed out on the seat behind us.

❊ ❊ ❊

"Treeza, you need Kurdish dress," Bezma announces. It's Friday again — they assume I'll appear every week now — and we're stretched out on mats on the floor, waiting for Ara to finish fixing lunch. "We make one?" It seems that this is a matter of some urgency.

"Well, sure." I've been secretly hankering for a local outfit, so I could theoretically blend in better.

"Good. We buy cloth after eat."

"Wouldn't it be easier to get something ready made in the bazaar?" I've seen sack-like house dresses like Bezma wears, fake velvet studded with rhinestones, probably mass made in China. They look nice and warm for chilly days like we've been having.

"No, better dress. Then look good with guests. Or maybe for wedding." Her eyes glint with barely concealed implication.

She means the spangly Cinderella-type outfits that I see in the village on Fridays. They probably cost a fortune. "But I only brought 60,000 dinars." It's about $50.

"Enough." She brushes her palms decisively. It's settled then, though I haven't seen a fabric shop or tailor in the village.

Ara rolls out her plastic tablecloth and serves chicken – one scrawny but delicious fowl stewed up for eight adults and several children. Out of nowhere, Ara's son, his extremely pregnant wife, their two-year-old son, and several older men introduced as uncles materialize for the meal. Every few minutes, Bezma leaps up, surprisingly quickly for a girl her size, to text on an old-school cell phone. Each time she returns, she tucks the phone back into her dress and suppresses a grin.

"What's going on?" I whisper.

"My love," she sings cryptically. "You see today."

Bezma explains the plan in English, which no one else speaks. Her "love" is driving down from the mountains to visit her. She and I will walk to the outskirts of town, where a fabric vendor parks his truck on Fridays, and I will buy cloth for a proper Kurdish outfit. Meanwhile, Mr. Love will be nearby, watching. It's all very cloak-and-dagger.

"You won't even get to speak with him?"

"No. Too dangerous. Somebody tell my mother."

It seems like an awful lot of maneuvering for a couple of glances.

After the food scraps from lunch are carried out and tea goes around and the uncles finally leave, Bezma wraps herself in her head-to-toe abaya and we trip off to find the fabric vendor. She hides around a corner to put on lipstick, then teeters in high-heeled sandals I've never seen before through the mud ruts. We find the vendor's pickup parked beside the trash-clogged stream that runs through the village. An old man in traditional garb smokes behind the wheel, waiting for nonexistent customers, while tall bolts of cloth propped up in the bed sway in the wind.

"Where is he? Mr. Love?"

"Coming." Actually, he's been phoning every few minutes. Between calls, we check out the fabric options.

"Black good for you," she assures me.

"Won't I look like a widow?" But she's not brooking any discussion. The pickup has several dozen black bolts to choose from, so making a selection is a complicated endeavor. We finally agree on a fusty georgette with yellow flowers for the outer dress, a black stretch knit for the bloomers and under-tunic, and a black knit for a cropped vest that will tie in front. The vendor knows exactly how much to cut.

What would otherwise probably be a five-minute transaction ends up taking about twenty because the phone keeps ringing, and we spend so much time scanning the empty road across the stream.

"I see Seema a lot at school now," I say to kill time. "She doesn't seem to be a very happy girl." Now that I know who she is, I can't stop noticing things about her. She's scrawny, like the runt of the litter. Sometimes her hair isn't plaited freshly, like she's slept in the braids. She often has a funny squint, too, as if she's peering through smoke. The overall

71

image is of a little gypsy who's traipsed in from the forest. I've moved her to the front row, to keep my eye on her; as soon as class is over, she hops up to grab my book bag and lug the thing down to the faculty room. Jake has started calling her my puppy.

"Difficult for young girl in old lady house," Bezma answers, reluctant to leave her own thoughts. "Kurds say, girl with no father like mountain with no rider."

"Rider? Like a man on a horse?"

"No, like water." She runs her fingers through the air.

"Oh, you mean river?"

"Yes, of course river. I am sorry. Like mountain with no river." She makes a quick recovery, continuing, "And Seema no brothers, no sisters. No friends."

"The girls at the school stay away from her." If I didn't know better, I'd suspect that she smelled bad.

"Of course. She not clean. Never get husband." She shrugs; Bezma clearly considers herself in a different category entirely.

The "unclean" part bugs me. "Maybe it's hard for her to bathe." Come to think of it, I haven't noticed tubs or shower stalls in the village.

This earns me a look of amused disdain — whether for Seema, or something else that I'm missing, I can't be certain.

Maybe I can sneak Seema into my apartment sometime for a nice hot shower — and wash her clothes at the same time. Her uniform blouses could use a good soaking in bleach. Wait. Maybe I could just buy her a couple of new blouses instead. Would she accept them? Would the other kids tease her even more if they found out? Worse, what would Madame say?

The fabric vendor has long since driven away when a dented white truck pulls up across the ravine, and out jumps a tall Kurd, dressed exactly like the uncles at lunch and the fabric vendor. In one hand he offers a pinkish rose, not a long-stemmed florist variety, but one plucked from a garden somewhere. But wait — no flowers are blooming yet; it must be plastic. With the other hand, he waves to us. We wave back. He tucks the rose into his cummerbund, lights a cigarette with great ceremony, and puffs a string of smoke rings. Bezma titters with admiration. She points to me with great melodrama. He nods vigorously. Her cellphone rings.

"Treeza, say hello to Hevar." This is weird. He's standing right there across the gully.

"*Salaam aleikum.*"

"*Wa aleikum assallam.*" There's not much more we can say, given the language barrier, so he and I gesture vaguely at each other.

She grabs the phone back and there's lots of fast talking, coy posing, crazy smiling, frantic waving, more smiling, and a woeful wind-down full of regret. Then he gets back into his truck and drives away in a cloud of dust. We head back to the house.

She sighs contentedly. "Hevar handsome, yes? Perfect, yes?"

Handsome? Yes, in a swaggering sort of manner. Perfect? I'm the wrong person to have opinions about male perfection. "He was too far away for me to see. Even with my glasses," I try. Wrong answer; she was hoping for more gush. "And he smokes. That would be a deal breaker for me."

She shrugs again. "All mans smoke."

What had struck me most, albeit from afar, was his posture — regal and imperious. American men don't usually stand like that unless they're in a uniform for the first time.

She's powerless to stop talking about him, though. "You hear him speak in telephone. Very beautiful, yes?" I nod evasively. "Hevar say he love me. He want me."

"Well, that settles it then." She doesn't catch the sarcasm. "Bezma, you don't even know him, do you?"

"His family my family, same village in mountains for long time. We know too much about family."

"I think you mean *so* much…"

If only I could protect her from infatuation; it's hard to do, when she has no interest in being protected. "Okay, what does he do? For work?"

She has to think; this must not have been an important consideration. "I think sell cars. He have money. You saw. He have truck."

Oh wow; major qualification for life partner. "Does he know you're going to college? That you'll be a teacher?"

"Oh yes. He want smart girl. He say I finish college after married. Okay if I want work too."

It's starting to sound a little better; I've probably been projecting my own disillusionment onto the poor couple. Time to lighten up. "How are you going to convince Ara?"

Ah, I've finally asked the right question, because the corners of her mouth twist. "I think *you* talk with my mother." This must have been her plan all along.

"No way. The last thing I want to do is meddle." Still, it seems like Ara is being unreasonable. Who wouldn't wish a happy marriage for their child?

When we get back, we join Ara on the floor, where she fingers the fabric for my dress. She praises the fact that I'm becoming more Kurdish by the week and will look more presentable when guests come over. But she scowls the minute I ask her about Bezma getting married.

"My mother say I must take care for her," Bezma translates. "She say I know this. I know this all my life. She say I am rude, ask you talk for me."

Now Bezma is crying. "This not fair," she continues. "Mother marry. She have children. Me, I am very old. This last chance."

Over the hill at 21? It's ludicrous. And yet... her hips would be a tight squeeze in some airline seats. And when she does that dazzling smile, a dark gap shows on the side where a tooth is already missing. Yes, her personality is so ebullient that I don't pay much attention to her body, but potential suitors surely would. For a village girl, it's probably now or never.

"Ask Ara how she felt when she was your age. See if she can remember pining away for her love match. Maybe that would work."

In wordless reply, Ara purses her lips. She won't meet my eyes. I have gone too far.

I scoot over to my backpack in the corner and slip it over my shoulders. "I'm sorry. I'd better be getting back to school."

Bezma is still crying, and now Ara is too. "She say you still best friend," Bezma translates. "She angry with me, not you. Now afraid you not come back. You promise come next week."

"Of course." To change the subject, I add, "And I could teach you to ride my bike next week. It's great exercise. Good for the figure."

"No, not possible." She seems tempted, though. I figure I'll ask her again another time, until she adds, "Hevar not like. Someone say to him Bezma on bicycle, he not want me." End of discussion.

As I pedal the Blue Angel back up toward The Fortress, I keep imagining how much freedom Bezma would have on a bike of her own. It gripes me, the way she gave up so easily. She's not even engaged, and already she's letting a man control her? Muslim men! I'll step in and say something to Hevar, if I ever get to meet him in person, and convince him how good the workout would be for her. I'll tell him how girls ride bikes in America, and even compete in races. I'll help be the architect for a new Western style of marriage here in Kurdistan, starting with Bezma and Hevar ...

Then I remember hats. Mr. Financial Genius, bless his controlling little heart, hadn't liked me in hats. All it took was a single comment, and my favorite straw sunhat went to Goodwill. Same thing with short skirts. He didn't like other men being able to check out the goods. Same thing with grilled lamb, which I love to cook and he hated. I hadn't been willing to risk even a frown from him to keep doing things that had previously made me *me*. One by one, I thought "no big deal", and let go of a habit here and a preference there, all in the spirit of marital compromise. Until after a while, I started making decisions based on what I imagined he would think, instead of what I thought myself — like an awful lot of other women I know.

In other words, who am I to talk? Maybe America isn't really that different than a Muslim country beneath the surface.

Three: Going Local

AFTER a month at The Fortress, it seems like I've been here forever. It's no longer odd to start the work week on Sunday. My students have learned to respect me, or at least pretend I'm not a total pushover. The day progresses from one transfusion of sweet black tea to the next.

Today Mohammed has left me a note on crisp Kurdish Government letterhead in the faculty room, asking me to come see him at 2:00, my free period. I haven't spoken with him since the bicycle expedition. In his smoky office, angular in a shiny brown suit and the pointy-toe dress shoes that young city Kurds sport, he's all smiles.

"Please sit, Miss Treeza. I am so happy that you are here." This is odd, overly familiar; locals at The Fortress usually call me Miss Turner. He leans back in the leather chair with hands laced behind his neck.

"Hey, Mohammed," I say as evasively as possible.

"Are you happy with the bicycle?"

"Happy? I love it! I use it almost every day. Thank you so much." Hadn't I been appreciative enough?

"Ah, you like the bicycle. But you never come to see me." Like a wounded infantryman, he slaps a hand over his heart.

"Well, we're both pretty busy." Uh, duh -- why would I want to visit in his office anyway?

"So true. Never enough time at a place like this. In a country progressing as quickly as Kurdistan." He gestures abstractedly at his empty desk, almost bare book shelves, and the telephone. Oh yes. The telephone can keep one extremely busy here.

"I have a proposal you will like very much." I pinch my lips with barely concealed impatience as he drags out a pause for suspense. "Come with me to my cousin's wedding Tuesday night. You'll get to see a real Kurdish celebration."

My eyebrows shoot up. I've been hankering to go to something like this. But there's surely a catch.

"Lots of music," he tempts. "Food. Dancing all through the night." I feel like a big juicy fish on a hook, being reeled in word by word. Still, I can't afford further social debt with this guy.

"I don't know, Mohammed. Tuesday is a school night. I have to teach the next day..."

"No problem," he adds, eyes wider now that it's going well. "You'll stay at my family's house. Then I'll drive you back here in the morning." He lifts both palms; it's all settled. "Easy."

I take in his tie, crumpled where he has tried to rub out a stain, and the cheap cotton of his shirt. The effort to appear Westernized is obvious. But so is the dilemma of being a young single man in a Muslim country, with no chances to speak with the opposite sex. Lust practically oozes from his pores like teenage acne -- it's almost a smell, thick like sweat, uncontrollable, embarrassing. Heartbreaking, really.

"I'm sorry, Mohammed. Maybe some other time."

The 'other time' is a mistake. "Then we'll go out for dinner. Any place you want. I have money."

A date with somebody two or three decades younger than me? "You're cute. I'm flattered. But honestly..."

He flinches. "You don't like me?"

"No, I do like you." I'd better not protest too hard, though. "You're a very pleasant young man..."

His sharp shoulders drop, as if jacked down a notch. "You think I only want sex. Is that it?"

I laugh. "Of course not." What a preposterous idea. But the droop of his face tells me that that is indeed the issue. Given our ages, the thought is mind-boggling. "I'm not having sex with anybody."

"Why not?" he fires back without an instant's reflection. I get the impression he's been rehearsing this for weeks.

I draw a quick breath, struggling for composure. "Well, because I'm not married, for one thing." How strange this conversation would sound back home.

"So what?"

"What do you mean, so what? This is a Muslim country." Let's see him get around that one.

He leans forward, drawing his face closer to mine. "You are not Muslim. You don't count."

My jaw drops. "Are you kidding?"

"No." And he isn't. "I watch movies," he continues. "American women have sex on the first date all the time."

He's sounding like a student protesting an unfair grade — a tactical error on his part, because my Righteous Teacher kicks in. "Surely you don't think that all Westerners behave like in the movies."

"Don't they?" He's not arguing now. He really wants to know.

"No!" Well, maybe some do. "Not me, anyway."

"You are beautiful like an actress." He's doing some Hollywood-type thing with his eyes beneath bushy brows, like a Rudy Valentino caricature except that he's not joking. I can't help but smile. It's midway between adorable and pathetic.

"We have a saying that flattery will get you everywhere. But not in this case." Will he take it as a joke?

He holds the Valentino look, not sure what to do with his face. "I do not understand this word 'flattery'. But I know you are wrong about certain things. Maybe you don't think I am as handsome as Mr. Khalil. Is that is?"

"What in the world are you talking about?" How dare he insinuate… Indignant, I stand up and turn for the door.

"Not you, Miss Treeza. But I am not stupid. Or blind." Then, more softly, "And I did not mean to offend you. I really do want to take you to the wedding. You could meet a lot of important people. And have a good time, too."

Probably just wants to show me off. To have a Western woman on his arm, no matter what her age.

"It was a nice idea, Mohammed. Very thoughtful of you. But not this time."

He sighs and holds his palms up in defeat. He has tried his best.

I leave him to ruminate behind the empty desk.

"You still have my card though, don't you?" he calls as I reach for the door.

"Of course." In truth, I tossed it after the bicycle escapade.

"Good. You may need a Kurdish friend sometime."

"Quite possibly." I can't imagine when that might be.

"And Miss Treeza, you know I was only joking about the sex. No offense meant. Right?"

"And none taken. We were merely having a casual conversation about cultural differences."

He gives me a little grimace of relief. "Good. See you around."

I wonder where he learned a phrase like that — and whether he'd had better luck with any of my predecessors in previous years.

❊ ❊ ❊

When nobody answers my pounding on Ara's gate later in the week, I'm ready to cry. It has been a terrible day. Zaki gave me a black check mark for not having had suitable bulletin boards up yet. Black marks accumulate in a database, and are used to calculate my bonus, he warned me from behind the aviator shades. But where am I supposed to get construction paper to decorate said boards? Pat wasn't home when I looked for someone to commiserate with. So even though it isn't Friday yet, and Bezma and Ara aren't expecting me, I flee to the village.

With empty streets and the afternoon thickening into dusk, the place doesn't look so friendly any more. A rooster strutting on the sidewalk tries to peck my legs, and a mangy dog snarls. I've been stupid to think of this as "my" village after just two visits. In truth, I am an intruder, a cultural spy. I shiver, cinch up the hood on my jacket, and turn back toward The Fortress.

"Treeza! *B'kher hati!* Welcome." Bezma appears from a gate across the street. Surprised but clearly delighted, she kisses me on both cheeks. "Come eat with us. Yesterday my father's father die. Everyone here." She doesn't ask why I've come; I needn't have bothered preparing an excuse.

I slip into the long housedress I've brought to keep in their cupboard, a baggy velour thing studded with rhinestones that I found in the bazaar. Bezma claps in delight at the sight of it, making me wish I'd picked up one in a different color for her. I help her carry heavy pots of rice from Ara's kitchen to the grandparents' house, where several dozen women are crammed cross-legged on the floor and mumble *"B'kher hati"*. They look even more downtrodden than I feel, each one draped in a black head scarf and abaya; a smell of sour milk only intensifies the dreariness of the stark little room. Bezma introduces me to her grandmother, the widow. Blind, partially deaf and utterly bereft, the widow barely notices me.

"When someone die, we eat together three days," Bezma explains. "All women bring food. Mans go pray at mosque with body."

Ara is already inside; she says *"ser tchow"* with her hand over her eye, and makes me sit right beside her. The women wince when they shift to make space for me on the floor; they must have been sitting here for hours. They flood me with quiet questions through Bezma. What am I doing here? Where is my husband? How many children do I have? Am I a Muslim? I'm less a curiosity than a welcome diversion.

As we run out of polite topics, they make fun of my head scarf falling off, and I ask a woman to teach me how to tie it properly. This is hilarious. How could a grown woman not know something as basic as tying a scarf? Once they show me the secret, namely starting under the chin, going around twice and tucking in the end, they watch me do it myself and cluck in approval.

Just when it's time to eat, the power goes out, which causes a murmur amongst the women but not much more. They scurry to light candles. Girls join us, including my student Seema, who beams adoringly at me. We cluster on disposable plastic tablecloths that they've torn from a big roll, around circular trays on the floor, dipping soup spoons into communal bowls. Rice pilau with green peas. Green beans in a wan tomato sauce. Rice and yogurt pudding. Dolmas. Squash with nuts and raisins. Fried potato with egg. Pickled beets, cauliflower and cucumbers. Raw bell peppers. These must be special dishes. Maybe the men are having meat, because there's none here. The women toss pieces of flat bread and leaves of lettuce to one another as they eat, but there's no talking.

After tea, we get down to business praying. Off come the prayer beads they've been wearing around their necks; someone passes me an extra plastic set, which makes me feel wonderfully included. One wizened woman in a white scarf leads the chanting, droning on and on in Arabic. Her fingers are so bent with arthritis that it's a miracle she can manage the beads. When she glances at me, the clarity of her greenish eyes pierces straight through me, and I shiver, as if she's a clairvoyant reading my thoughts.

"That is Old Houda," Bezma whispers. "She best friend my mother, and also midwife. She know all the prayers. She wash dead peoples. She very close with God."

"I can believe that." The quiet dignity of her chanting peals like a monastery bell through the din in the room, commanding respect.

"Why isn't anybody crying?" I ask.

"Grandfather old and sick. Time for die. Only grandmother sad."

"But what about you? You don't seem very sad." Bezma hasn't joined the chanting yet, and it doesn't look like she's going to. "You must have loved him."

She tosses her head. "Father's father very bad to my mother." I wait for more. "He have money, but not give to us. He like second wife my father, not my mother. He see us hungry, just look, no food."

"But he lived right across the street." I can't imagine such heartlessness. She just shrugs. Such is life.

As the chants continue, the women start rocking back and forth, lost in inner worlds, made mysterious by the flickering candlelight. "They pray not about grandfather now," Bezma says. "They say to God about life. They ask God many things, many things sad."

I can certainly commiserate. Zaki's upbraiding today has left me cold and deflated. "I want to pray too. What can I say? Without looking stupid."

She tilts her head prettily. "Prayer not stupid. You say 'Allah, Allah.' Or 'ayatal kursi.' From Quran."

Allah Allah is pretty easy to do, and it doesn't interfere with the other one-way conversations going on around me. Now we're all swaying in time, like we're all sitting on the same porch glider, and the private chants harmonize into a peculiar shared rhythm. *Allah Allah*. We've become a church choir. Old voices. Teenaged voices. Mothers. Grandmothers. Widows.

Virgins. All spontaneous, each woman doing her own private litany.

It's hypnotic and irresistible, this chanting and pulsing in the shadows, congealing into a shared sorrow. The mystery of phrases not understood forms a heady drug. Words themselves don't matter; we're singing a universal female song – the inevitability of loss and tragedy. And there's a certain comfort in the mutual emotion. "We are here together, and together we can bear anything" — that's what all those Allah's translate to inside me.

Then a quickening happens. My shoulders relax; my worry about being conspicuous vanishes. I am a nameless female surrounded by sisters, all awash in an unutterable sorrow that goes far beyond the dead grandfather. The grief is huge; like a heavy black gas it saturates the air and fills our lungs. Babies lost before they had a chance to grow. Sons blown up in war. Husbands who betrayed or disappeared or beat us. Daughters who married and moved far away.

Oh damn. Tears are streaming down into my lap, and I can't sniff them back.

What's going on? I never even met Bezma's mean old grandfather. Then it hits me. This is mourning, the real thing. Because of the car crash, I missed my father's funeral. Even if I had made it, it wouldn't have been like this; we Turners think it's ill bred to grieve. The only emotions we're allowed to show are cheery.

Now I am shuddering uncontrollably with sobs. I miss my father so much. Gone is the firm shoulder in a tweed jacket, scented with his special pipe tobacco mixture. The sideways squint when he cracked a joke. The way he loved to quote Ouspensky, even when we knew he was making it up.

Ara scoots closer and kisses my head. "*Khosh, khosh,*" she says; good, good. Several other women come close too, patting my leg and shoulder, their leathery hands rough but kindly.

Their droning fades to a stop. The women search my face to try to understand.

"Bezma, tell them that my father died right before I came to Iraq." I wait for her to translate. "I couldn't reach the funeral. I never got to cry for him."

They murmur amongst themselves; this is something they understand. A stone slips aside within me, making a poignant thud. We sit in knowing silence. Not smiling or speaking. Just sitting. And in doing so, they are offering me something, which they automatically share with one another as a matter of course and now extend to me. I don't know what it is, but don't really need to know either.

Never in my life have I sat silently in a group with eyes open for more than an awkward second or two. Never have I just *been* with other people. There's always been a purpose to fill up the space between us, talking, moving, fixing, accomplishing, doing. Not like now, where some invisible seam binds us beyond awkwardness.

As quickly as the seam coalesces, it vanishes, and I'm doubting myself again. Maybe they expect something from me and I'm letting them down. Maybe I'm supposed to entertain them, to take their minds off the dead man. I should give them a token, to thank them for accepting me. I have nothing. But then, I have an idea…

"In America, we have a song for funerals," I offer. "Want to hear it?"

They do.

Hesitantly, I stumble through the first verse of Amazing Grace, above the evening muezzin whining in the background. My voice wavers, with little strength left after weeping. I sound feeble and pitiful like a child whimpering in the night. "I once was lost but now I'm found, was blind, but now I see." Hah. I ought to quit; nobody should be subjected to such lousy singing. A guitar would help. But when I stop after the first verse, they motion me to keep going. By the second verse, the song takes shape as a recognizable tune. "How precious did that grace appear the hour I first believed." I am surrounded by women who believe a whole lot more than I do, and who do a better job practicing their faith. I hope they won't see me as a fraud. I launch less apologetically into the third verse. "Tis grace that brought me safe thus far and grace will lead me home."

The words echo in my mind as silence creeps back amongst us. I don't have a home anymore; the divorce messed up all that. I still feel blinded, or maybe blind-sided, by the car wreck / train wreck of my life back in the States, and rudderless without a father. I want an hour here when I first believe in myself again, when I understand who I am beyond now-irrelevant roles of wife, mother, daughter, professor, or business woman. I want the song to work a miracle in me, and deliver a tiny touch of grace here in a very bleak part of the world.

And then, meeting the gaze of first Ara, then Bezma, then Old Houda, then the women whose names I will probably never learn, my first-world needs become dwarfed by the reality of Iraq. By the immensity of sorrow each of these women has lived through. And by the boundless forbearance these women seem to possess.

Their poise settles like a gentle powder of snow around me, and I take a deep breath. The candlelit gloom is different now, peaceful, inclusive. I am certain, suddenly, that each woman here is exactly where she is meant to be, doing exactly what she is supposed to be doing, by her simple presence helping the widow to shoulder her grief. And me to acknowledge mine.

I wonder whether recognizing that you're in the right place, at the right time, can itself comprise a form of grace.

✣ ✣ ✣

Madame likes company on her walk around the sports track in the late afternoons, after all the students have gone home and before dinner. She asks me to join her, but won't venture past the school gate. "Much too risky," she says. "I only leave the school to shop on Saturdays with my driver. Sometimes Layla and Khalil come. Maybe you could join us."

"That would be great." Although I hate to commit any time on weekends, when I could be down in the village, a car sure would be easier than hauling groceries to the school's van. "How about Pat and Jake? Do they come too?"

I assume she hasn't heard me. Then she says, "If I were you, I'd keep my distance from that Jake. I don't like his attitude."

And I don't like *her* attitude, trying to control my friendships. "Really? He keeps us laughing. And the kids love him."

She continues, overlooking my defensiveness. "Layla would be a more suitable friend for you. She's much closer to our age."

I like Layla, but don't know her very well yet, as she teaches the elementary grades. Being Egyptians who lived in the U.K., she and Khalil are the only teachers who straddle the Green Line, mixing with both groups in the faculty room. Petite and perky, she dresses like a Vogue model, and I've been amused by the little coquettish toss she does with her hair, especially when Khalil is around.

"You're kidding. If she's our age, Khalil could practically be her son."

"In truth, he *is* like a son to both Layla and me," she confides. I wish she would walk faster. My heart rate will never get up the way we're ambling along. "Layla was my best friend in London, and I got her the job here. Then we brought

Khalil over this August. We promised his mother we'd take care of him."

"That's nice." My mind is wandering. "Tell me, how can I get invited to some of my students' houses? I want to learn more about Kurdish…"

"Oh, you mustn't even think of it. It's strictly forbidden."

"What's forbidden?"

"Visiting families. Having a relationship with students outside of school. Didn't you read your contract?" Her tone resembles the one behind her big mahogany desk; my teeth start to grit.

"Well, yes, but I just assumed…"

"You must assume that every word in your contract is sacrosanct. Including no contact with students. You would be terminated immediately."

"Just for making friends with them?"

"Egg-sactly. No personal conversations. No home visits. No rides to town. Nothing. And especially no tutoring."

"Huh?" It takes maximum willpower to keep ambling beside her and not stomp off in irritation.

"Tutoring English is big business. You could triple your income with private lessons to the wealthier families. But don't try it."

"The thought hadn't crossed my mind," I reply, probably too huffily. Who would have the energy to teach extra hours after the grueling school day and all of the paper marking on the weekends? Still, I hate agreeing with her, even on something small. I stuff clenched fists into my pockets and try to change the subject.

"So what's with the guys bringing food to the cafeteria every day?" Serious-looking men in *khak* Peshmerga outfits carry elaborate baskets to the lunch room, spread white tablecloths, dish steaming meat and rice onto china plates, and then pack the whole thing back when their child has eaten.

"Admittedly, the food's pretty bad. But a private picnic every single day? And delivered by fathers?"

She sniffs. "Those aren't fathers. They're body guards. The school cafeteria is run by Turks, and Kurdish politicos don't trust them. They might poison the heirs. These are very high-ranking children, the crown jewels of the country, so to speak."

"Funny. So that's why some of them act so ... not haughty, exactly, but with such dignity."

"Egg-sactly." My jaw clenches tight at hearing the phrase again. "And it's why you must keep your distance. You don't know which family is which, and could do something that gets us all in trouble."

"I can see your point." What a passive/aggressive coward I am, lying to her like that. Because I have no intention of stopping my trips to the village. They're what keep me alive.

❋ ❋ ❋

Pat is making biscuits for dinner when I knock the next evening. She's actually wearing an apron; I haven't seen one in about forty years. It gives her the appearance of a frumpier version of Donna Reed, which is as welcome as home-cooked comfort food right now. "So how do I get out of walking with Madame every night?" I blurt.

She wipes floury hands on the apron and lets me in. "Hah! She asked you too? I spent all of September tramping around that blessed track with her until I finally just said no."

"I guess it's a form of exercise. If you are totally out of shape."

"And if you don't mind being a double agent. Pretty soon she'll start asking you about the rest of us." She rolls the dough flat with a wine bottle, then punches out biscuit rounds with one of our Academy-issue water glasses. "But it's a one-way street. You'll get nothing out of it, except maybe a better bonus at the end of the year. If you give her what she wants, that is."

Pat sounds almost cavalier; for some reason I want to give Madame the benefit of the doubt. "I don't know. She seems genuinely lonely. Like she needs a friend."

"Maybe because there's something amiss with her little campus 'family'." She tilts her head down as she waits for me to catch her meaning. "Layla and Khalil have been riding the faculty shuttle with us lately instead of going with her chauffeur. Noticed that?" She zaps a cup of water in the microwave and dangles a tea bag in it for me.

Yes, I had noticed. On my last trip to town, Layla and Khalil shared a seat in the back of the shuttle, and whispered with their faces close together. Odd, if they could have gone in Madame's car instead.

I'd also noticed that Khalil was unusually jolly, beaming at the young Arabic teachers, chatting them up around the wooden work table. "I think he's got a crush on one of the little Lebanese babes. I just haven't figured out which one."

"Maybe, maybe not." She slides the biscuits into her toaster oven and twists the timer.

"Oh come on. Any of those girls would want him for his British passport. Not to mention his looks." Thin and sultry, he reminds me of a younger version of Omar Sharif. Maybe it's because of the boarding-school accent he affects (shame on me – maybe the accent is real), and the cashmere jacket he wears to work almost every day.

"Here's my secret for expat happiness," Pat says, brushing hair out of her face with a floury wrist. "See no evil. Hear no evil. Speak no evil. Because things are not always what they seem."

"Yeah, you're probably right." I should have thought of that myself. "I think I've got a migraine scheduled for the next time Madame wants to walk."

❀ ❀ ❀

"Com3 tomrw. We ho taylr."

Bezma and I have figured out how to text. However, we both have the world's most basic phones, requiring four pushes on the '7' key to get an "s". Messages often get messed up.

I stuff the black dress fabric into my backpack and glide on the Blue Angel down to the village. The mud leading up to the road is starting to harden, and green shoots are popping up between rocks beside the road. After the closeness of a classroom, breathing great gulps of almost-spring makes me giddy.

At the house, Old Houda the midwife is hobbling down the steps to leave, and greets me like a favorite cousin. "Ah, Treeza the singer. Welcome," she says in Arabic, thanking me with a nod and a friendly flash of the jade-colored eyes. It's like the sun has come out from behind a cloud; Houda's presence lights up every corner of Ara's humble courtyard. I wish she'd stay longer, so I could get to know her better.

Ara sits cross-legged on the porch, chopping vegetables on a wooden board. She looks up and beams. She struggles to her feet and kisses both sides of my head. *"B'kher hati. Ser tchow!"* Her eyes tear up when she covers the right one with an oniony hand, while Bezma brings my housedress from the cupboard.

After a day trying to tame adolescents, this hero's welcome is just what I need.

We settle on the floor, and I search for topics to stretch Bezma's vocabulary. "Houda looks so happy, so peaceful," I say. "She must have had a better life than the other women."

Bezma pours us tea. "No, Houda have hard life. Saddam soldiers shoot husband in field, like other mans in village. Then two sons die. Daughter tooken. Now Houda have sad work, wash dead peoples, bring babies, do other private lady things."

Despite my curiosity, I'm not bold enough to ask what these private lady things might be. "Then what makes her so different?"

"Houda not different. She like other widows."

But she isn't. At the wake, the other women had deferred to her, and treated her like their leader. She has an unmistakable inner light, projecting an aura of calm.

"Where did she learn Arabic?" None of the other women seem to speak it, to my dismay.

"I think Saddam prison. Many Kurds learn Arabic at prison. Kurds hate speak Arabic, but Houda say language of God, language of Holy Quran. She can say Quran with no book."

Memorized the entire Quran? A remarkable feat. I wonder if it's true. "I like Houda a lot," I say.

"Me too. She and my mother best friends, many many years." She rests her fingers on my hand. "But now you best friend. When Mother say Treeza, she smile. No other time smile."

Embarrassed, I want to downplay it, but am deeply touched. I've done nothing to earn their friendship except to barge in and eat their food. We're not eating today, though, because Bezma says we have to rush to the tailor's to get her started sewing my dress. We barely have time to finish the third cup of tea.

Once outside the gate, she pulls me into a rock-strewn gutter between two house walls. "We need talk." This sounds like life or death.

"About your love?" I guess. His name has slipped my mind.

"Yes, Hevar. Store lady say bad thing about me." She jerks her head toward the little grocery at the edge of the village. "Store lady daughter love Hevar long time. Now Hevar love *me*." Just saying the words is clearly a delight. "So store lady say to Hevar mother I am bad." Clearly an outrage.

"What could she say about you? You're smart. You're going to college. You're a good daughter…"

"She say I am fat." She spits the words like food gone rancid. "She say college girl talk to mans and get dirty."

"That's silly. Of course you see men at college. Everybody does. It's part of a modern education." And fat would be an overstatement. Bezma's pudge is more like "pleasantly plump," which seems to be the "in" look around here. The grocery woman isn't exactly svelte herself.

She wipes her nose on a corner of her abaya. "Hevar know I am good. But Hevar mother and my mother say too much talk. Talk give family black name."

"Sounds like Ara's grabbing any excuse to keep you from getting married."

"Yes." We start walking again. There's really no need to talk secretly; nobody can understand our English.

"Her life would be so empty without you." I want her to see both sides.

"But now Hevar say we live here. Not in mountains, not with mother father Hevar. With *my* mother."

"So you'd be just down the street from your mom…" A puff of optimism lifts me, and I stand up straighter.

"In house of my mother. Yes."

I smile and Bezma nods back. It's an ideal solution. "And she still won't agree? That's just plain crazy. Here's my advice. You keep trying. That's what my son did with me whenever I said no. It usually worked."

And it had worked when my nameless former spouse, the Financial Genius, did it, too. I'd still be the proud owner of a sizeable savings account if he hadn't been able to wheedle it out of me in the divorce proceedings. But surely this is different. Surely Ara is just being a stick-in-the-mud.

We pound on a gate that's indistinguishable from any others, and a cut-out metal door creaks open. Maia the tailor turns out to be a young second wife who sits yoga-style on the floor behind an ancient hand-powered Singer. Scraps of spangly fabric and bits of thread litter her sitting room. She acts like the Queen of Sheba has come to call, and can't believe that someone as important as me — a foreigner, an American! — wants to hire her.

We've barely started negotiating when Bezma's phone buzzes and she disappears. Maia chatters to me in Kurdish, oblivious to the language problem. Stand up, she motions. Here, hold the fabric to your shoulder. With black iron scissors like my grandmother used to have, she nicks the fabric where it hits the floor. Now hold it there. Another nick records my bust size. Now here. A third nick marks the length of my arms. Without tape or chalk, my measurements are all clipped on the selvage edge of the cloth.

Bezma returns, glowing; all must be well in Hevar Land. Now she can help design my dress. She pantomimes medieval-styled sleeves with triangular hems that drape to the floor.

"I'll trip over them!"

"No, we tie in back, like this," she says. "Pants to ankle. Tunic to knee. Vest tie here in front." Ah, the vest knots to cover the boobs. The tailor seems to know exactly what she means. It will be ready by the weekend.

"Is there some rush?"

"Nowruz coming. You need good dress then."

The kids at school have been telling me about Nowruz, something like Christmas (feasting without the presents), Easter (a spring celebration without the religion) and the Fourth of July (patriotism and picnics, with bonfires instead of fireworks) all rolled into one on the equinox. Although these are mostly urban, plugged-in children, up on the latest trends, they rave about getting new traditional outfits, and wearing them out on hillsides with bonfires.

"Nothing before Nowruz?" I mean it mischievously, hinting at an engagement, but she takes it in earnest.

"Maybe. Who can say? Maybe Hevar change my mother mind. Hevar very good, get what he want. *In sh'allah.*" The sorrowful tone she uses, however, makes the prospect sound unlikely.

We're just settling down to tea back at Ara's when there's thudding at the gate. A child runs in, out of breath. I don't recognize her at first. "Seema!" In a long house dress and gauzy blue scarf, my shy homeroom student appears to be out of a different century; it's impossible that she ever stepped foot in a place like The Fortress.

"Grandmother says the baby's almost here," she pants. "Come."

"Wife of my brother," explains Bezma, throwing her abaya back on. "Mother and I, we hurry."

When no one invites me to come along, I wheel the Blue Angel home sullenly, unreasonably disappointed. All night I wait for a text from Bezma, announcing a new niece or nephew. Nothing comes. I get up the next morning heavy with dread. What's gone wrong? Second babies usually come quickly; surely it has been born by now. I text Bezma, but get no reply.

All day I'm snappy with the students — partly out of worry, but partly, I'm embarrassed to admit, out of wounded pride. I thought I was an honorary member of Bezma's family, enough to be notified if there was some emergency. But as it turns out, in reality I am merely a guest.

I chalk it up to American hubris.

Four: Nonessential Body Parts

"WHO MESSED up the frickin sugar jar again?"

Jake stomps right across the Green Line and shoves the jar into the center of the locals' work table. "Look at this mess. When you stir your tea and put a wet spoon into the sugar, it turns into nasty clumps. Like this!"

Nobody raises their eyes. The Arabs and Kurds are a polite bunch, more into avoidance than confrontation. Jake heaves a dramatic sigh and throws himself onto one of the expat sofas.

"Yesterday somebody used up the last of my Constant Comment too. But I won't even TRY with that one." I'll bet he did theater in high school.

Only Pat has the sassiness to reply. "Is this about tea and sugar, or all the noise down by the gate last night?"

He takes the bait. "Those guards know me. How dare they ask for my ID?"

"They've got to obey the rules…"

"Rules, schmules." His chin juts up.

"I thought I heard glass breaking," Pat says testily.

"Hey, I missed. The bottle was almost empty anyway."

"Don't tell me you threw a bottle at the guards." She sounds like she already knows his answer.

"Yeah. And they caught everything on video. Or said they did. They got Old Baldie out of bed to yell at me."

"No. You didn't call her that…" Pat shoots me a worried look. Then her mouth twists wryly.

"Maybe. I don't exactly remember." His sheepish slump says otherwise. "But look – I'm here today, aren't I? I didn't take a sick day. Although I sure felt like it."

"I'm grateful for that," I say. His class is next to mine, and The Fortress doesn't hire subs. The last time Jake took a hangover day, his kids were supposed to teach themselves. I was hoarse by noon, trying to teach over the din.

Mrs. Zaki glowers at us from across the Green Line. I wonder how much she understands, and how much of this will get back to her husband.

"Never mind," says Jennifer, the roly-poly Brit married to Shahaz, one of the Academy's Kurdish employees. She's so fair that even her eye lashes are blonde. Floating about her is an air of tender goodness and ingenuousness that I always find refreshing. "Here – you can use this word puzzle I made about Alexander. I made extra copies. It'll keep the kids busy while you calm down."

"Frickin Alexander. But thanks."

"You mean we're all teaching Alexander this term?" I thought it was just my "accelerated" group.

"Yep," Jake adds. "Just like we all taught Hannibal last term. Academy textbooks are about long-dead war heroes, as Binny loved to point out."

"Speaking of Rabinowitz," says Pat, "somebody with an Arab-sounding name posted on Facebook about him. He's in Baghdad. In prison."

"What? Our Binny?" The entire room perks up. Even the locals are all ears.

"It turns out he didn't go to Turkey after all. He went to Mosul," Pat adds.

"But we all have to stay inside Kurdish Iraq," I protest. "It says so in our visas."

"Binny spoke Arabic pretty well." The smooth voice of Khalil pipes up from over by the tea kettle, where Layla is stirring creamer into two cups of coffee. "I'll bet he talked his way through the check points."

I try to imagine someone from our expat group in the squalor of an Iraqi prison. Blurry TV stills from Abu Ghraib well up. Suddenly, I don't resent Rabinowitz so much for leaving me a class in shambles.

"So maybe he wasn't joking that night when he told those stories." Jake whistles. "I thought it was the vodka talking. How would somebody with a Jew name, and a Jew nose, end up training with Al Qaeda ..."

The words "Al Qaeda" act like a gigantic stun gun. Everyone freezes, even the teachers who supposedly don't speak English. "Jake, I'm sure he was just kidding." Pat does her mother-hen cluck. "He was always showing off. You can't believe everything you hear."

But it's clear that she does, in fact, believe the Facebook post, and is worried about Rabinowitz. We all are. We might be a motley lot, but when push comes to shove, it's us against Madame and Zaki. Us against The Fortress. And, if it comes down to it, probably us against the world.

❈ ❈ ❈

The next day Jake has brought his own sugar and a new box of Constant Comment. He offers a bag to Jennifer, but she declines.

"How's life in the Real Kurdistan? Prying minds want to know."

How does Jake pull this off, being catty yet at the same time ridiculing his own cattiness to make it less offensive? He's better than any woman. Still, I'm glad he does it, because Jennifer has become a great source of information — and often entertainment — for us.

"Oh, okay I guess." She sighs. "Mother gets so tired doing all the cooking. But when I offer to help…" She sighs again.

We wait. Sometimes she needs a little nudge to confide in us. "But what?" Pat finally asks.

"She says I'm unclean." She holds up lily white hands and shrugs.

"But you said you became a Muslim. What else could she want?" Pat still hasn't gotten over Jennifer switching religions. Neither have I, for that matter. Jennifer is carrying this Kurdish thing too far; Pat and I can get downright snarky about it sometimes.

"Conversion is one thing. But getting *khatana* is another. I'm much too old to get cut."

Pat and I share a look of disbelief. "Cut? You mean, like female circumcision? They do that to girls here?"

Jennifer nods. "It's about 90 percent in this part of Kurdistan, and almost 100 percent out in the villages. The outside world doesn't really know about it. And Shahaz sort of forgot to tell me before I got here."

"I'll bet." Pat has never held a high opinion of Shahaz, even before we learned he was married to Jennifer. "They still do female genital mutilation, FGM, in Burkina Faso, even after the government outlawed it."

"It's not such a big procedure here as in Africa." Trust Jennifer to get defensive about 'her' people. "Here they only do a little snip. Just the clit itself. They don't sew the whole labia shut so you can hardly pee, like a lot of Africans do."

"Well, praise the Lord for that. I mean, praise Allah." Jake is getting into his element. "*Just* the clit, Jennifer? The word *just* cannot be logically applied to the removal of any body part, much less something like a woman's clitoris!" His voice rises.

"They do a little snip back home in Egypt too," Layla adds. "But of course, it's only backwards people who do it." Not somebody who exudes sex appeal, like she does. Nobody's paying any attention.

"Technically, it's not a necessary body part," Jennifer continues, still prickly. "And the government keeps saying they're going to prohibit it. But I agree with you, Jake. It's too horrible to contemplate. That's why I'm refusing."

"Wait," I interrupt. "If you're not cut, they say you're unclean?" A light is starting to dawn.

"Yes. Nobody wants a wife who will be lusty and unfaithful." Jennifer makes it sound so clinical. "And if a man is strict, he can't eat food that you've prepared. My husband says he doesn't care about that old-fashioned stuff. He'll eat anything I cook. Of course, it helped that I was a virgin."

"Bully for him," says Jake, at the same time Pat is saying, "Of course."

"Hey, I just thought of something," I muse. "That means that most of the girls in our classes are cut."

"Not the rich ones. Or the ones who lived abroad and then came back. Which is a good portion of our students." Jennifer knows it all.

"How about the Children of Martyrs? The village girls?" One in particular comes to mind…

"Oh, definitely," Jennifer answers solemnly. "It usually happens when they're younger, though. Not in the higher grades like you teach."

I shudder. My stomach is churning. I make a mug of tea with the communal sugar, ignoring the vile brown crusts in it.

The heater kicks in with a rumble, a sound that goes unnoticed unless the room is very, very quiet. "That means my first graders," Layla says finally. "When one of my sweet little girls suddenly turns into a brat, maybe there's a reason for it. It never occurred to me before." Her eyes, big pools of loveliness, tear up. When she wipes them, black trails of mascara streak her cheeks.

"Maybe they do the procedure in hospitals here. So it's more sanitary." Good old Pat, trying to cheer us up.

"When I lived in Saudi, they sometimes amputated thieves' hands in hospitals, instead of chopping them off in the public square on Fridays." It sounds irrelevant after I say it.

"Oh thanks, Twinkle Toes. So much less barbaric that way." Jake yanks his head hard to the side to make it crack. Layla winces.

Across the invisible Green Line that segregates East and West, three young Kurdish teachers are straining to listen.

"What do you ladies think?" I ask them, in an effort to be inclusive. "Is it true, about our students being cut? You're the experts here, after all."

Three scarved heads duck back down over copy books, as if avoiding tear gas. Oh damn. Another cultural faux pas.

Jennifer says something to them in Kurdish and they unhunch a bit. Then she moves her book bag over to their table to chat, presumably doing damage control. Jake rolls his eyes. Pat shrugs. Khalil drifts in, closing the door gently behind him, and Layla springs up to make him coffee. We're back to normal.

I set off for class in a haze. I can imagine particles of dried blood in the air soiling my lungs, or some rusty residue of pain leaching out of the walls. The crazy thing, I realize, is that this horror applies to only half of the people who will ever walk this corridor. The female half. I will study the girls in my class carefully now, and see if I can tell which of them have a clitoris, and which have a ragged scar instead. To put it that way, in words, is crass. In reality, it's one of the most disgusting things I've ever contemplated.

❈ ❈ ❈

A toothache is one of those things people try to avoid in the Third World. But when it can't be ignored any longer, taking care of it becomes an obsession. On one of our evening strolls, I ask Madame to recommend a dentist.

"I can tell you one *not* to go to," she says. The testiness we've both felt on previously walks has temporarily vanished, and we're friends again. "First, the dentist told me that because of my age and gender, my gums were inferior to those of a man. He therefore refused to do the crown that I wanted. And then the filling that he eventually put in fell out in a week. Oh -- and he didn't believe in novocaine."

"Yikes." My chest shudders. "What did you do when it fell out?"

"Waited until the summer when I returned to the U.K." Oh great.

But Jennifer knows a dentist that her Kurdish family likes, and gives me his number. To my surprise, it is not a secretary who answers, but Dr. Zewar himself on his cell phone. He makes all his own appointments, and sets me up for that very evening. His office is in the Christian neighborhood, near the old church. How will I find it when the streets have no names? No problem, he assures me -- just ask anyone. They'll show you.

A helpful old fellow outside the church points me to a dentist, but it's the wrong one. After wandering through six blocks of construction debris, past parched bushes in rusted metal cages and skeletal stray dogs, I finally locate Dr. Zewar's office. It's unmistakable, thanks to the gigantic drawing of a tooth outside.

To one side of Dr. Zewar's stairwell, a barber crouches over a heated game of dominoes with a child, his towels drying on racks on the sidewalk. He gives me a distracted *salaam*. To the other side, dozens of parakeets and little gold-colored birds chitter from cages in a shop window. I can hear them all the way up the narrow staircase, past an uncovered electrical box, to the dentist's office, which is marked with a piece of printer paper masking-taped to the door.

It is probably unfair to judge a dentist by his entry way. However, the steps going off at odd angles, the cracked plaster walls, and the bare light bulb dangling from the ceiling give a very disconcerting air. So does the toilet, which I make the mistake of visiting before going in. It has a Western-style commode, complete with a seat, but no water intake. Instead, there's a plastic bucket to fill from a tap near the floor, and then dump in all at once to flush. The same tap has a gnarly greyish bar of soap for washing hands.

"Miss Treeza? Please wait a moment." A bored receptionist sits at a rickety metal table beside a TV blaring an Arabic soap opera. My fellow patients, six of them ranging in age from about eight to utter decrepitude, look like they'd been there since the dawn of time, along with the faded dental hygiene posters curling on the wall. Nobody protests when, to my embarrassment, the receptionist rushes me in ahead of them all.

Dr. Zewar is in his 30's; towering and slim, he bears himself with the confidence of a man aware of how attractive he is to women. He is proud of having trained in Denmark and Italy, and is up on all the latest techniques. Or so he claims. He escorts me across snarls of electrical cords to the single brown dental chair, with the kind of spitting sink and overhead light I remember from childhood. The motor for his drill rests on a concrete block beside the chair.

He chats pleasantly, wanting to know what brings me to Iraq, whether I am married, and what I think of Obama. He loves Obama, although he admired George Bush too. "Liberator of the Kurdish people, and victor over Saddam," he explains. "Okay, we'll start the examination. Where is it hurting?"

104

The fact that he wears rubber gloves is some comfort. But has he changed them since the last patient? He taps on my tooth with a metal instrument handle, this direction and then that. "Does that give pain?" My ankles twist in agony. He pokes at my gums with a wiry-ended tool, much too aggressively. Then he is done.

"Okay," he announces, snapping off the gloves. "We'll do a root canal. It will cost $150 cash."

What? No X-ray? No explanation of different treatment options?

"No, we won't require an X-ray. I know what's wrong by the feeling in my hands. It saves you the cost of an X-ray. But I can't do the procedure today; you saw all those people waiting out there. You'll have to come back in a few days. Can you tolerate the pain that long?"

The sudden realization that there is no running water in the treatment room is giving me pause. Did Dr. Zewar wash his hands and instruments in the bathroom I'd used?

"Or if you prefer, we could remove the tooth entirely and do an implant for $600. That's the best price in all Iraq, guaranteed. And the best long-term solution."

Wow. I'd had an implant once back home and it had cost about $5,000.

"Uh, let me think about it. I'll give you a call in a day or two." I scramble out of the chair to escape.

His limpid eyes squint. That isn't what he'd wanted to hear. "We can squeeze you in whenever you like."

I thank him and the receptionist — no charge for the initial consultation — and make my way back down the crooked staircase, heart pounding. It has grown dark, and the caged birds have stopped chirping. The school's shopping shuttle won't arrive for at least an hour, so I find a place three doors down for dinner. The shwarma looks good; a huge upside-down cone with slices of lamb, grilling and dripping herb-scented grease before an electric heater. They use an electric hair trimmer to shave off the meat. I choose the local pizza instead, a pita the size of a dessert plate topped with a tomatoey lamb sauce and an egg baked on top. While I wait for it to come out of the oven, the cook poses for a photo, flattered by the attention.

Eating inside with a bunch of men staring at me seems intimidating, so I eat standing on the sidewalk instead, contemplating the state of dentistry in Kurdistan. Am I being a snob, judging a book by its cover?

In the U.S., a person never even thinks about whether dentists' doors hang squarely in the jamb. We take it for granted that offices will be marked with gold engraved signs and have lots of parking spaces outside. Invisible wiring brings power through the walls, not in cables across the floor, and invisible plumbing brings water to sinks in treatment rooms. In the waiting room, patients catch up on trendy magazines they'd never pay to subscribe to. The whole place exudes a practical type of luxury; it's okay that the dentist drives a new Mercedes, because his office treats patients in a Mercedes way.

But nothing I've seen in Kurdistan so far has that kind of luxury -- not government or professional offices, or even the brand-new shopping mall downtown. Construction is shoddy; second-rate materials are thrown together by Bangladeshi laborers in such a way that buildings never look new, or even entirely finished. So is it Dr. Zewar's fault if he had to practice in semi-squalor? Maybe I should learn to be more tolerant.

Back in the faculty room the next day, my story provokes not-so-hilarious anecdotes about dentists in Burkina Faso, rural China, Cambodia, and other places where my colleagues have taught. The unanimous consensus is that returning to Dr. Zewar for the root canal would be madness, especially since I'd forgotten to verify that he used novocaine. Which leaves me back at square one — without a reliable dentist, with a mouth

106

that still hurts — but at least with a dramatic blog post to show for my troubles.

❀ ❀ ❀

The next day, I find myself in Mohammed's office, in response to another summons. Various certificates stamped by the Kurdish government now adorn his walls, red and gold seals and burnished frames gleaming with fresh importance.

"So, maybe you find you need a Kurdish friend after all?" He has the air of a waiter leading me to a choice table in a crammed restaurant, and snapping away the "reserved" sign.

"Excuse me?"

"A dentist. Here. She's my cousin-in-law. Very reputable." Out of his suit pocket comes a tattered wad of paper, folded over about five times, which he places in my palm. I cringe; the fact that the paper resided for a while in his jacket makes it somehow contaminated.

And yet I am desperate. So I go to see the cousin-in-law, a charming young woman in a starched lab coat and high heels, trained in Vienna. She doesn't speak much English, but has a spotless establishment. She takes an X-ray, repairs a cracked filling, charges me $30, and about ten minutes later my toothache has disappeared. No root canal, no implant, no trauma. Her toilet even flushed.

Mohammed deserves a peace offering for coming through, and for my skeptical attitude. So I bake him a batch of cookies, and decide to stop being so wary of him. I also update my blog post, in case the photos of Dr. Zewar's staircase give anybody the impression that all Iraqi dentists are the same.

❀ ❀ ❀

That weekend, the plan with Bezma is to pick up my dress at the tailor's right after the Friday midday meal. But when I reach Ara's, the gate gapes wide open, and a familiar-looking pickup takes up most of the yard. On the porch, several older couples and two younger women sit stiffly on the plastic chairs, all decked out in their Friday finery -- the men in starched tan *khak* outfits with bulky red-checked turbans, the older women beamy and buxom in black drapery to the floor, and the younger women in rainbow-sequined splendor. *"B'kher hati,"* they welcome me in a chorus. The men smoke and fiddle with prayer beads. Ara wears a scary-looking grimace above folded arms, like she is trapped in the middle of a siege. Obviously, I am interrupting something serious.

"Treeza!" Darn. Bezma has seen me, and it's too late to escape. "Come. Here is family Hevar." She has a lot in common with Oprah, introducing a movie star to her celebrity guests, opening her arms wide, embracing the yard with her magnificence. I can almost hear applause for her grand performance.

Ara gets up to hug me, and *der tchows* me with her hand over her eye. She is as stiff as a rifle. I gesture that I'll gladly go home, but no, she begs me with her foggy eyes to stay. She clings to my hand, searching for an extra chair for me beside her. There are none. So we all move into the formal sitting room, the one I've never been into before because it's for important guests (meaning men), and select cushions on the floor. This involves careful positioning, as first the three older men take places of honor at the far end, then their women bunch together on one side, and Ara and I take the other. Bezma shuffles to the kitchen, serves glasses of water to everybody in order of importance, and then hovers outside the door. She isn't missing a word.

Hevar and his family speak no English. But when the pleasantries are over, any fool could follow the drift. We suffer through lots of "Bezma"s and "Hevar"s. Lots of nods toward the pickup outside. Gestures in the direction of their home in the mountains. Then the trump card. Hevar draws a a blood-red velvet box from inside his jacket, and pops it open to reveal six solid gold bangles and a layered gold necklace something like a breastplate. It must have cost more than the truck. He lays the box reverently in Ara's lap. She refuses to even glance down.

Bezma's there in a flash, screaming with delight. The gold is like a super-magnet; she has to touch it. Ara slaps her hand, hard. She threatens to slap her face, too, if she comes any closer; she's furious, treating the box like a live grenade, and she's protecting an innocent child.

"No!" I've never seen Ara speak to a man before, much less shout like this. "No. No wedding. Bezma will not leave here, ever, ever, ever." Her meaning would be clear in any language.

"But…" The men have plenty of reasons. They are unruffled in a united front before this deranged old woman, patronizing in their assurance. Their prayer beads click like metronomes. They've got plenty of time and nowhere to go. It doesn't matter what words they are saying. Their posture, their poise while lighting more cigarettes, their smugness, says it all. The matter is already settled. Now foolish Ara should just shut up and accept it.

A young woman in red spangles meets my eye; her beauty electrifies the space around her, and she stands out like a single sunflower in a sea of weeds. There's a flash of intelligence, or perhaps autonomy, as she follows the proceedings with amusement. I wish I could have been her teacher when she was younger. She has the kind of presence that says, "I'm going to be a somebody. Just wait and see!"

Hevar puffs away, letting his elders do the talking, sneaking a glance my way with a presumption that gives me goosebumps. Oh, he's a handsome bastard all right, the creases on his khaki shirt all stiff and perfect, hair poofed up and sprayed, like a Middle Eastern Elvis, and shoulders thrown back like a drill sergeant. His bulging arms can probably hoist a rocket launcher with ease. And all of this is undeniably sexy -- the power, the raw maleness of him. No wonder Bezma has fallen so hard for him, and so quickly -- why she is so proud that he wants her. I get the feeling that wherever Hevar goes, he's in charge and gets what he wants.

Not with Ara, though. The longer that the men assume her assent, the more furious her breathing becomes. Can't they see that each word lays another stick of dynamite on her pyre? Finally, the fuse of her patience burns up.

"Go!" She leaps to her feet, and the gold falls out onto the carpet. "Go home. Leave. Get in your lousy truck and drive back to the mountains and never come back. Out! Out! Out!" Or some Kurdish equivalent.

Hevar gathers the jewelry and struts out calmly, as if this is only a small blip in his plans. Perplexed — how could anyone possibly refuse a suitor like Hevar? — his family piles into the truck, the four men in the front seat, the three women in back. From behind the wheel, Hevar leans out the window to wave, and the young woman in red steals a mischievous look at me from the rear window. I can almost hear a movie orchestra swelling in the background, promising the audience that the entourage will be back, no doubt triumphant next time.

I try to leave too. Sobbing, Bezma clings to me. "I love him! I love him too much. You must speak my mother. You make mother say yes." She must be nuts; no sane person would try to reason with the glowering Ara now.

At some unknown signal, they switch; Bezma gets mad, and Ara sobs. They're akin to two squirrels chasing around a tree, trading places at intervals between rage and heartbreak. I can't understand any of it except the emotion, so acute that my lips ache from pursing. When I sense another shift coming in their roles, I make my break.

At the gate, though, I stop and turn back to the porch. "Bezma. Listen. Something has been bugging me for days. You never told me about the baby. What happened?"

She frowns at me in pained annoyance.

"Your brother's wife. She was having a baby. Right?"

"Oh, she have," Bezma says, wiping her nose; she can't be bothered with such an irrelevance.

That's it? "Was it a long labor? How big was the baby? What was the birth like?"

Another Kleenex, another blow. Bezma glowers. "She have girl."

"Nice!" From their faces, however, it's clear that neither Bezma nor Ara agree with me, nor do they want to be diverted from their argument.

"What's her name?" I continue, undaunted. "What kind of present should I get for her? When can I see her?"

Bezma shuts her eyes for a long minute, as if praying for patience. Finally, doing me a huge favor, she states, "I — said — she — have — girl."

At first, I want to duck out before her annoyance can register. Then I feel the corners of my mouth twitching. Hah -- I'm a close enough friend now that Bezma can be irritated with me.

I take it as a compliment, give them a bright farewell salute, and leave the two of them to their catfight.

❊ ❊ ❊

"This has got to be a mistake…"

I shake my head in mild amusement at my bank statement online. I've maintained an account to cover stateside bills while overseas. Reconciling the statements once a month is a two-minute routine, barely enough time to finish a cup of tea.

But this time when I log in, the friendly five-figure balance that always greeted me has gone AWOL. In its place, a platoon of ghost-eyed zeroes taunts me up and down the screen. In the checking. In the savings. In everything.

Obviously, a computer off in the Civilized World someplace is malfunctioning.

I have always been fiscally conservative. Okay, the term miser has been applied at times over the years, rather uncharitably but not completely unjustifiably. I have been known to recycle manila folders and toothpicks and leftover pieces of cheese. I'm not a person to squander – or ever "mislay" – money.

Add to this the fact that Wells Fargo isn't exactly a fly-by-night institution. They will rectify their error with typical American efficiency. I calmly punch their phone number into Skype and connect with "Linda".

"There's no mistake," her chirpy voice assures me. I imagine her adjusting a sari over her head and trying for an audible smile. "The funds were transferred yesterday to cover a credit card debt."

"That's impossible. I pay off my card the day the bill comes in." I take a sip of tea and muse at the funny world we live in. Here I am in Iraq, discussing a computer glitch that occurred in the U.S., with someone located in Bangalore or Delhi.

"It wasn't your card, ma'am. It was one you opened with a Mr…" and she mentions the name of a certain Financial Genius that Andy and I had once shared a home and life with. "Many years ago."

Oh, that. No biggie.

"The gentleman in question" – I can't bring myself to pronounce his despicable name – "is no longer my husband. In our divorce, he assumed responsibility for all of his outstanding

112

debt." Which had been considerable, given his pending bankruptcy.

There's a long pause as Linda scrolls to find the right script. "Madame, obligations to financial institutions are not affected by divorce decrees."

"I beg your pardon?"

"It does not matter what your divorce decree said. You are still legally responsible for payments on this card if your former husband chooses not to make them."

Ha ha. I've got Linda there. "He was party to a legally binding agreement." The words 'party' and 'legally binding' taste terrific. "He knew what it all meant. The judge signed it, and it's filed with the court."

"That may be the case. But he did not pay. And now the debt has accrued to..." She names an obscenely large figure, at least double what it had been when we divorced. "The bank was authorized to deduct the entire sum from your accounts. Including fines and interest." I wonder if her script instructs her to sound more forceful at this point.

"You can't do that! You can't take every last penny I own!" I jump up in rage, yanking out the ear buds connecting me to the computer. Damn. Now where is that pesky little hole in the laptop?

But Linda, when I can hear her again, is certain that they can take every last penny – and, to be more specific, they already have. The deed is done. And the bank is definitely not going to consider a refund. She promises to email me a copy of the fine print proving my responsibility, and justifying the theft. "Did I answer all of your questions during this call? Is there anything else I can help you with?"

HELP? Oh yes. She could set off a bomb at Wells Fargo headquarters for me. She could hire a hit man to dispense the Financial Genius to the bottom of some polluted river wearing concrete shoes. She could put her supervisor on the line. It takes her a few minutes to find him, while I steam.

But "Brendan" is even less helpful than "Linda" had been, and proves to be a great deal more articulate about the bank's rights. He listens to my pitiable plight, and "understands" my "concerns". He patiently listens to how unfair all of this is, and "appreciates" my situation. It's like shouting from a little rubber dinghy bobbing around beside the steely side of a battleship; the metal wall echoes back at me, but doesn't budge. He has clearly heard many desperate pleas from sinking lifeboats in the past, and knows how to rev up the ship's engines to move on.

I click Skype's hang-up symbol, wishing there was a way to slam it. I stomp around and around the little rattan coffee table, pounding fists against my thighs.

No! The universe could never be this unfair! That scumbag got every liquid asset that remained after his squandering frenzy. We cashed out my personal account to buy him a car. We even cashed out my IRA, losing a big portion of it to penalties, so he could have an RV to live in.

I barely make it to the bathroom to throw up, but nothing comes out. The dry heaves burn as badly as real vomit.

"Pat!"

Thankfully, she's home. Thankfully, she learned quite a bit about contracts from her shark attorney ex. Not so thankfully, she frowns.

"There's not a damned thing you can do."

"There has to be." I'm a confirmed optimist. There's always a way out. Always.

"I could tell them I'm teaching in Iraq, and have nothing left in the U.S. to pay any of my bills." I imagine the nice driver on the Wells Fargo stagecoach gazing down at poor little old me in benevolent pity, having compassion for my plight, and giving me one of his money bags.

"Don't tell them that. They already know you're out of the country and helpless. Why do you think they waited until now to do this?"

"Oh." Of course. "Well, I could call the manager at my Wells Fargo branch." His son played high school tennis with Andy. We'd shared countless hours on the bleachers together, shivering in Pacific Northwest springtimes.

"It's not his decision. And don't think corporate gives a flying rat's ass either. You're screwed, honey."

I'm sure she's wrong. I pore over the contract "Linda" emails, sure to find some loophole or statute of limitations. I check site after site on the Internet to prove that banks really have no right to take everything I own. To my shock, I learn that they do. Unbelievable.

The next morning, the other teachers can't believe it either. When living overseas, things back home seem better than they really are (or ever were). The Good Old U S of A takes on heroic proportions. Uncle Sam will come to your rescue if terrorists strike. The nice folks at the embassy will provide a new passport, loan money for a ticket home, and generally do whatever it takes to resolve Americans' artless bungles. After all, America is that great paternalistic world power, where everything is done Right. Full stop.

Pat disabuses my colleagues of all this. I choke with tears. I can't hold it back any longer, especially after the entire faculty room converges to give me a group hug. Even the locals, who probably don't understand what's going on, join in.

Later that day, Jake slips a note under my apartment door. Layla 30K dinars. Jennifer 45K dinars. Mrs. Zaki, 10K dinars. Every single teacher on both sides of the Green Line has pledged to chip in if I need money until payday. My eyes tear up all over again.

I have about $200 worth of Iraqi dinars to my name. It's enough for the rest of the month, but just barely. I'm pissed, with a capital P — at the bank and The Financial Genius, but mostly at myself. Once again, I've failed to suspect the worst, and to protect myself accordingly.

❋ ❋ ❋

As might be expected, classes do not go well the rest of the week. I lose my temper with even the fair Helin when I catch her with a comic book in her lap. The appropriately named Jaber doesn't have a chance. I give him so many demerits that he has to spend every afternoon in Zaki's gruesome detention hall.

After the last class of the week, Jaber swaggers up to me. I've been expecting this. They all try to get out of punishments on Thursdays.

"Miss, I want to make a deal with you."

Jaber is proud of being one of the rare Arabs at The Fortress. Like the few Christian kids, he points out that he's not Kurdish whenever I try to discuss Kurdish language or culture. In the U.S., he would have been a star – smart, athletic, handsome, and with a quirky quickness to his mind. But he's bored to death at The Fortress, and a royal pain in the neck.

I'm in no mood for his jokes. "Yeah? In exchange for detention? Forget it." When he doesn't leave, curiosity gets the better of me. "Okay, tell me. What kind of a deal?"

"The kind you can't refuse." Where did he learn such a good Mafia imitation? Despite my crankiness, he's irresistible.

"Like maybe you'll stop talking all day long in my classes?"

"Something like that…" His expression reminds me of a carnival hustler. "I promise to become the very best student you have ever had. Number one on every test. No games. No tricks. No leaning back in my seat, even."

"Oh wow, wouldn't that be too hard for you to pull off? That's not a deal. It's more like a miracle."

He's close enough that I can give him a playful little swat on the butt, and my defenses dissolve. We've been hassling each other all week long, but now I can finally appreciate that innocent bravado of his posture, that affectionate boldness in his eyes. "So what's the catch?"

"Simple. You become a Muslim."

I start a guffaw, and immediately stifle it. He's serious! Dead serious.

"Jaber, I'm a Christian." Not technically the truth, according to Fundamentalists, but close enough. "All of my people are Christians. Most of my country is Christian."

"So?" He grabs an eraser and starts smearing chalk dust around the board. "Mohammad Ali changed to be a Muslim. So did that English singer."

"Cat Stevens."

"Yeah, him. And once you're Muslim, you can go see Mecca." Had I mentioned in class how much I want to go?

"But I'd also have to wear long skirts. And cover my hair all the time." My lips twist to josh him a bit.

He doesn't catch the humor, though. "Covering's not so bad. All women do it. Scarves are cheap. I'd buy you a couple."

"Thanks. But I'd also have to learn a bunch of prayers." The repartee is becoming kind of fun.

"No problem. You're smart!" A juvenile prince of flattery. He clearly thinks he's winning.

"Really, Jaber. I respect Islam. It's a great religion. But I'm quite happy with my own beliefs."

He folds his arms over his chest. I sense the clincher coming. "But look, Miss, if you change then you could go to Heaven. You could be my teacher in Heaven."

If there is one reason NOT to convert it's the prospect of a whole classroom of little Jabers for eternity. Yet there's such sweetness in his face when he turns to see my reaction, a childlike compassion, that I scramble for something nice to say.

"Hhmmm. Interesting idea…"

"Miss, I've been thinking a lot about this." What, Jaber serious about something? His face tells me that he is. "If you're not a Muslim, then you probably won't get into Heaven at all. Even though you came all the way to Iraq to teach us."

I gulp. "That frightens you." Astonishing.

Some invisible gear in the room shifts downwards, and we are no longer skating along on trivialities. We have done a quantum leap. We are no longer authority figure and kid. Nor female and male. Nor Christian and Muslim. Nor even old and young. The air is dense with caring, and words move slowly through an emotional soup, with extra significance.

"Yes, Miss." He's felt the shift too.

"You're trying to take care of me after I die," I murmur, the muscles in my cheeks softening.

"Yes, Miss." He stares at the eraser in his hand. "I can't let you to go to hell."

I consider the hell he puts me through on a daily basis, the revenge hell I've consigned him to in the detention hall, and how little I deserve his concern. I consider the way "Linda" and "Brendan" spoke with me yesterday (how dare they!), and how alone I am here in Kurdistan, and my awful vulnerability to Madame and that goon Zaki, and how somebody who supposedly loved me enough to marry me sneakily plundered my very last penny, and it's all too much to process in front of this little Arab boy with the goofy proposition.

"You know, Jaber, that's about the nicest thing anybody has said to me in a really long time."

I write him a hasty pardon from detention, as a reciprocal gesture of sorts. If he hurries to turn it in at the office, he can still catch the early bus home for the weekend.

When the door slams behind him, I squeeze into one of the desks in the back, put my head down on my arms, and try to hide from the tides of fate. It doesn't work. My elbows get sticky from something spilled on the desk, but I can't leave; my chest is too shaky to contain this wellspring of emotion. I stay there a long time, until the last janitor comes through to sweep.

✵ ✵ ✵

"My mother say, why you sad, Treeza?" We're finishing a simple meal on the floor, salad and flat bread, plus an egg Ara scrambled just for me. I've been trying to put up a good front about the bank thing and pretend it never happened — not very effectively, apparently.

"I'm not sad." More like steaming, fuming, furious, like a raging bull pawing dust in an old cartoon.

Bezma, on the contrary, is at her most manic, fussing endlessly with the tea paraphernalia and checking her phone screen. She's put on lipstick, too; it's the first I've ever seen her with makeup. It seems a bit much for going to the tailor's to pick up my dress.

"Yes, Treeza, you sad. We see."

Ara says something in a big rush of emotion, and waits for Bezma to translate. "Mother say we family. We talk. We help." There had been a lot more to it than that, but that's all she's translating for me.

They both wait patiently. I fiddle with the end of my headscarf, which keeps slipping off. My knees hurt from sitting cross-legged so long. My heart hurts, from holding it all in. So when Ara reaches her gnarled old hand to hold mine, it all comes spewing out.

"Someone stole all my money in America."

They gasp. "Not possible! How? From house?"

119

"No, from the bank. My ex-husband did it." I pantomime taking off a wedding ring and hurling it out the window. "He did not pay his debts, so the bank took my money away from me. Just like that. All of it. Without even telling me."

They stare, dumbfounded. Things like this aren't supposed to happen in America. Only in places like Iraq.

"How much?" Bezma blurts.

I can't give them a number; it would be a life's savings here. "Everything I had in America, down to the last dinar."

Ara starts moaning and rocking back and forth. *"Allah akbar."* God is great. Even when really bad things happen, God is great. *"Allah kareem."* God is compassionate, even when people totally screw you. She fishes for the black prayer beads inside her dress. *"Allah kareem,"* she repeats. She keeps hold of me with her other hand, so pretty soon I'm rocking too. She embarks on a long monologue.

"My mother say mans are bad. Very bad. Not good for trust. Kurdish people say, better for one day to be man instead for ten days to be woman. But my mother say, everything good in life, it is from woman and child."

I nod. Wells Fargo is definitely a male institution. And the person who didn't pay the debts was undeniably male as well. "I trusted too much. I was stupid."

"No, Treeza, you not stupid. You good. Mans bad, not you." Then Bezma hastens to add, "This what my mother say to you. Kurds say, 'In your face the man is mirror, but behind back he is shoe.' But I do not think this. I think some mans can be very good."

I pass up the idea of a detour about women's liberation, or the potential virtues of Hevar, or even a request for explaining the shoe metaphor. "I was positive my husband would honor his promises. And I thought I was finally safe here in Kurdistan, and could start over again." I'm probably talking too fast for translation, but it doesn't matter. "And it wasn't just money. There were a lot of other bad things, and I was trying to forgive him, and not be so angry, and move on..."

"My mother say, did husband hurt you?" Bezma interrupts me and mimics whacking with a stick, wincing with each blow. This is not play-acting. They both know what it's like.

I nod reluctantly. The shame of it burns, even now, even so far away. I thought I'd gotten over it months ago, but here it is, burbling out again, the fear mixed in a poisonous way with indignation. Yes, my husband had hurt me, not with a stick or a belt, but with shaking, shouting, threats, pinning me to a wall. No, that hadn't been the worst. The worst was him battering my son.

Ara shows no surprise. She merely nods, as if it's all inevitable.

"We know this about mans," Bezma says, so slowly and deliberately that nothing more needs to be put in words. It's an "amen" to a well-worn prayer; it's how I imagine concentration camp survivors might share the tattooed number on their wrists, meet eyes, and just know.

They scoot closer on the carpet until our knees touch. We're three women draped in black on a faded red carpet, arms wrapped around one another, swaying gently back and forth. No tears this time. Just a sweet togetherness. It's what I imagine peace might feel like, if I were ever lucky enough to experience such a thing again.

The moment crescendos like an ocean wave; the closeness becomes moist and viscous and fertile. Together, we are one pulse of female feeling, of exquisite nurturing, like the combined pain and rapture in the first suck of breastfeeding.

When the feeling starts to ebb, Ara nudges Bezma to ask, "Treeza, how much you need?"

"Nothing. I have enough until the next payday." I hope they didn't think I was asking them for money.

"How much? We have." She mimics shoveling a deep hole.

"No, I could never take your money. I will be fine. Honestly."

Ara speaks carefully, so Bezma will translate correctly. "My mother say, maybe no money. But Treeza, you never poor. This your home, always." She motions to the bare concrete walls, to the bed cushions stacked in the corner, and the little metal tea tray. "You live with us like sister. You eat here. You sleep here. You never alone or hungry when Ara and Bezma live."

She means it. Every word. The truth of it resonates like a tuning fork through my being, and realigns me deep within with gratitude.

I sigh from the pit of my belly. With the exhale, my shoulders drop and a weight falls from them. I've been hauling a backpack filled with rocks up a slope, and now gentle hands have lifted the burden so I can breathe. I feel naked. But it's okay now.

"Thank you." If I say it a bunch of times, will they understand how much I appreciate them?

I'm overwhelmed and can't stay much longer. When hoisting my backpack to leave, I discover that Ara has stuffed it with little bags of raisins, walnuts, raw rice, a couple of onions, and hard candies – most likely a good portion of what she has in her pantry. She spanks my hand when I try to give it back, and shoves the pack over my shoulder. The widow's mite. I'm raw with love/guilt.

In faint moonlight I push the Blue Angel back toward The Fortress, prolonging the trip so my feelings can percolate. Walking helps. A breeze chills through my jacket, but I'm thankful for the shiver; being present in this vastness slows down the poor-me poison that's been torturing me all week.

I ponder the pocked asphalt. The Kurds from the village must have walked on this same road when they fled Saddam's bombs and bulldozers. I've seen photos of Kurds snaking up a mountain path toward exile in Iran, tens of thousands of them on foot. A few had suitcases. Even fewer had donkeys. Most of them carried bundles in their arms, or exhausted, terrified children. In one photo, a mother tried to nurse her infant while stumbling along.

I stop pushing the bike, stunned with new comprehension. Ara and Old Houda had been hungry, thirsty and desperate — maybe even pregnant — when they trudged for weeks on this road to Iran. They couldn't carry enough food and water for themselves, much less their children. How did they bring blankets or pans to cook with, or even spare clothes?

In contrast, I've been *afraid* of being hungry, thirsty and desperate; humiliated because of being cheated; angry because of being victimized. I thought it was the end of the world. But it's not even the same category of misery.

Standing still there in the middle of the road, my moon shadow long and wan, I take stock.

I am a well-educated woman.

I possess the most sought-after passport in the world.

I own a house in America (albeit mortgaged to the hilt), and an older but reliable car.

I have a secure job (albeit stressful and exhausting), and am well paid compared with the majority of people on the planet.

I live in a very comfortable (albeit orange) apartment with central heat, air conditioning, a flush toilet, no cockroaches and only the rare rodent.

I am in excellent health, and have decent insurance should I fall ill.

I have a mouthful of teeth, and none of them hurt any more.

The one child I've borne is still alive.

And I've been whining because somebody took my *extra* money — my surplus, socked away over the years after all my needs (and, truthfully, an awful lot of desires too) have been met?

In other words — and this is what devastates me — I'd had *extra* money all that time, and didn't even recognize what a luxury that was.

I shake my head at my shadow, my only companion out here in the night, and wonder if the "extra" idea had been obvious to Ara and Bezma the whole time. Had they empathized with my sense of loss, while also knowing that I am still rich beyond their wildest dreams — and yet they offered me part of their meager savings?

If yes, as seems likely, I have a long, long way to go before I'm as evolved as these simple village women.

* * *

By early March it's no longer dark in the afternoons when Madame and I make the rounds of the track. A verdant smell from green wheat, now nearly knee high in nearby fields, tickles my nose; the wind puffs friendlier on my cheeks, carrying hope.

"I heard about your financial misfortune," she says. "I'm very sorry."

I wonder who told her. Probably Layla or Khalil. "Yes, the shock of it was really something. But I'll survive. I've survived worse in the past."

"Still, I'm sure it makes you feel more precarious."

"To put it mildly." I laugh, hoping it doesn't sound too bitter.

"Let me confide in you a moment, if I may." Odd that she's demurring, when she's my boss after all. "I have had my eye on you ever since you arrived. And I think you have great potential here at the Academy."

"Potential? Even with all my demerits in Zaki's database?" The guy is still driving me nuts with his meddling.

She brushes the comment aside. "You're still adjusting to the system. It takes everybody a while. Even myself, when I was new."

The revelation gives me courage to be a little more candid than usual. "Well, the more I adjust, the more doubts I have about the Academy's philosophy. There are so many restrictions. The surveillance. The emphasis on final exams instead of ongoing work. I was trained as a Montessori teacher, which is just about as opposite as you can get."

She is not fazed. "The Academy has been around for decades. It has schools all over the world. It is the favored choice of diplomats…"

"So I've heard." How tiresome to have to listen to it again. "That doesn't mean that its style of education is best. Take, for instance, the way that we expect all the children to learn at the same pace. I have at least thirty kids who would be labeled special ed back home…"

"The Academy does not believe in special needs. No ADHD. No dyslexia. Its methods are effective for all children."

The company line is an insult to intelligence. "Oh come on. You can't really believe that. We've both taught for most of our lives. We know from experience…"

"What I know for certain is that the Academy rewards loyalty over everything else," she replies dryly, slowing our pace for emphasis. "And they reward very generously, I might add."

I bristle at being in a category of people who get "rewarded", rather than paid fairly for services rendered. "Then why is turnover so high?" Who cares if it sounds rude? "I've never seen a place like this with only one repeat teacher. One!" And that one, Roboteacher, acts like she's got PTSD, I fail to add.

"We lose teachers because the expat labor pool is so flighty." Was that a touch of defensiveness? "English language teachers are mostly young, barely out of college, and they care more about seeing the world than about devoting their lives to children."

She has a point there, if our faculty room is any example. But I'm not ready to admit it.

"They come to the Academy because we pay so well," she continues, "and then they leave as soon as some little thing displeases them. They move on to Bali, or Japan, or wherever, and pick up another assignment easily enough. But those aren't the educators we really want. We want ones like you and Pat, who are committed to students. The professionals."

Losing all sense of proportion, I let my ego puff up. My Zaki problems seem a bit smaller, for the first time in weeks.

"So, as I said, think about the economic benefits to making this a long-term appointment. After the second year, the bonuses become even more substantial. Also, there will be opportunities for promotion. We have openings next year for a head of department, and head of the senior school, for example. They pay better than teaching. You'd have more responsibility, and make more of an impact on the children."

"Are you asking Pat too? She's been here longer than I have, and probably deserves it more."

"Of course. She's a fine woman. I know you're friends. You'd enjoy the years ahead more if you were together. Think about it."

I promise I will. And this gives me the nerve to ask something that's been puzzling since my arrival. "So what about you? What keeps you here?" I can't bring myself to call her Madame when we're walking. "It can't just be money. Isn't it tough to have your family so far away?" Professionalism and responsibility are great, but they only go so far.

She does a funny little bark of a laugh. "My marriage thrives on distance. Also, we're saving for retirement. You can live on practically nothing here, so we're saving much more than we could if I worked in the U.K." She waits for me to agree. "It's all about attitude, really. Once you set your mind to it, you can get accustomed to anything. Now I practically think of this place as home."

I shudder. The thought of calling The Fortress home is nauseating. Home means soft foggy breezes through Douglas fir trees, damp green and cedar colors, privacy and safety. Not concrete walls and hard terrazzo floors, spy holes through doors and machine guns at the gate.

And then I glance down at her, this stunted, brittle woman who barely comes to my shoulder. Not for the first time, I try to imagine what life is like for her here. What type of stress makes your hair fall out like that? What kind of marriage thrives on distance? Not one that I would want.

"Yes, I suppose you can." It's more than just throwing her a bone. I want to show her a little affection, maybe even call her by her first name. No, that's too much. "I really appreciate you thinking about me for next year, by the way."

"I hadn't planned to mention it so soon. But when I got wind of your, uh, difficulties back home..." She coughs discreetly, making an attempt at delicacy. "I can't get you more money for this year. But next year is a different matter."

"It's very thoughtful of you. A relief, in fact — knowing that I might have some options." It's also a relief that Zaki's database might not be as important as he makes it out to be. "I feel better now."

"Yes, these little walks are good for both of us. Let's do them more often."

She pulls her hands out of her coat pockets and swings her stubby little arms as we saunter through the twilight. We circle the track a few more times. A stranger might take us for a couple of nuns, promenading affably with a common — and noble — purpose. Two selfless women, out to educate the world. Here on a barren hillside in northern Iraq. At a school that prizes loyalty over common sense.

Sometimes this place beggars belief.

❊   ❊   ❊

Pat and I have taken to rum and Cokes after work. Her patio is covered in fine sand, so we brush off the chairs with our hands. "How old do you think this dust is?" I ask, looking at my fingertips.

"Older than the Flood," she jokes.

And that starts me thinking. I've been reading on the Internet. The lands surrounding The Fortress have been occupied since proto-humans first migrated out of Africa. In nearby Shanidar Cave, human remains date from 65,000 BCE, and the earliest forms of domesticated wheat have been found in the region. The first evidence of writing comes from a little to the south.

This part of the Fertile Crescent was the breadbasket for ancient Assyria starting around the 25th century BCE, and was ruled at various times by the Sumerians, Akkadians, Babylonians, Persians, Greeks, Parthians, Romans, Islamic Arabs (Abbasids, Ayyubids, Seljuks), Mongols, Ottomans, and Islamic Arabs again. Some Kurdish scholars believe Kurdish culture originated with the Medes, of Old Testament fame. Dreaded Saladin, sultan of a vast empire and conqueror of the Crusaders, was a Kurd.

"It's quite possible that one of these specks of dust contains a tiny fragment of Abraham's camels," I venture.

She clinks plastic cups with me. "Not probable, but possible."

"Same with Hammurabi or Genghis Khan. The genius who thought up cuneiform. Or irrigation." I rub my fingers together. "These very specks of dust could come from the bones of some shepherd just like David, roaming around writing beautiful psalms. But he lived at the wrong place, at the wrong time, and never became immortalized in a Bible."

"You could probably say that about any speck of dust anywhere on the planet, the way stuff gets mixed around."

"True. But what if there's something special about this place, which made people think up agriculture and writing and religion as we know it? Maybe there are spirits in the caves and boulders. Giants. Gods. And people in the olden days knew how to communicate with them, but we don't."

Pat gives me that dubious look over the top of her glasses. "I'll admit that there's a grandiose vibe to the place. You can't exactly put it into words. It creeps me out sometimes. But not as much as the idea of land mines still buried out there."

I decide she's being melodramatic about the mines. "It'd be fun to try to see if we could pick up some of the vibes. Go out and soak up whatever is there."

"We?" she says. "You go right ahead, baby. All you'll soak up is a whole lot of hay fever, turds on your shoes, and a sore butt from sitting on boulders."

But I don't really mean giants and gods. I mean God. 'I will lift up mine eyes unto the hills' was written about country just like this. I want to find Him here. I want to be transformed, awestruck like Moses with the burning bush, and zapped without too much effort on my part into a finer person. Well, it's possible, isn't it? And a person would never know for sure unless they tried.

❊ ❊ ❊

She's probably right, I decide upon reflection. Pat's always right.

Nevertheless, I take the Blue Angel early one Saturday morning to see how far a particularly promising dirt road will take me. It starts at the smoldering trash heap on the way to the village, and meanders out beyond the last wire fence and plowed field. At first I pass the remains of picnics — plastic bags, juice bottles, candy wrappers and a glittery aqua scrap of fabric from the dress-up outfits Kurdish women wear on Fridays. Then even the garbage peters out, and it's just rolling hills with stickery tufts of weeds, endless blue sky and me.

I find a suitably lonely knoll. Not a single sign of human existence is visible, most importantly The Fortress. From afar, the hillside was brown; up close, tiny white and yellow are pushing up in random clumps. Spring is coming. I prop up the bike on its kickstand, spread out a towel, and wait.

How is a person supposed to go about something like this? I'll make it up as I go along. I pretend that my legs are made of sponge, and there is a colored Gaia/Jehovah/Ishtar substance in the earth that can seep up, like dye, through my being. I *want* to experience something so badly; I put great deliberation into the wanting. My consciousness *should* be able to make it happen. David and Isaiah were humans just like me. I summon the mystery without knowing its name or its secret password, vaguely counting more on intent than on skill.

It doesn't work. All that I notice is how my hair keeps whipping in my face, because I've sat in the wrong direction. I move to a better knoll that faces into the wind.

Back onto the towel. Back to the sponge image. Instead of a nice ancient effusion wafting its way up from the earth, though, I start smelling animal droppings. Oh damn. I've put the towel right on top of a dung heap, not smooshy and moist, but still stinky and stainy.

One more try. Rolling up the soiled towel, I find a relatively stone-free, poop-free, bramble-free patch facing windward, and sit directly on the earth this time. Eagerly, I await inspiration and contact with The Universe.

❋   ❋   ❋

My back hurts. My Nikes are too bulky to tuck easily under crossed legs. Flies have found me, and keep trying to climb into the corners of my eyes.

Lying down will expose even more of my body to the ancient wisdom, and maybe less to the flies. I stretch out on my back and admire the sky. Cloudless days like this are so rare in the Pacific Northwest. Now there's a wisp of white forming above me, like a horse's tail. I watch as, slowly, it grows, and re-forms into a tablet. A tablet like Moses used? The shapes might be trying to tell me something profound, if I could just pay better attention, and decode the nuances of the clouds. Maybe there's a message for me on the tablet. My eyes start to burn at the sky's brightness. I let them close for just a second.

❋   ❋   ❋

Something brays in my ear. I wake up surrounded by a sea of wool, smelly and matted with burrs and twigs, and a boy about the age of my students astride a donkey. His flock is as curious as he is, but they keep a distance, which is great because I'm afraid of being bitten.

"Good morning." His nonchalance says that he comes across teachers sleeping out here every day.

Peeking out from his unbuttoned *khak* Peshmerga jacket is a soiled Superman shirt, torn at the neck. He has wrapped his checked turban exactly like the old men with canes in the village.

He shoos away the sheep and sits beside me, accepting half the jam sandwich I've brought in my pack. We try talking, but have a serious vocabulary problem. He motions to the Blue Angel. Can he take her for a spin?

I'm sorely tempted to say no. I don't want a single scratch on my prize possession. But politeness gives me no leeway. Sure.

Although he's cocky about knowing how to ride, he crashes on the first two attempts. I wince, but he grins to me that everything is fine. How could anybody learn to ride on this hillside, dodging stones and clods of earth? But he does, and pretty soon he's figured out the hand brakes too, and is cruising along the ridges of this little dale, whooping and hollering.

He's probably assuming that I'm minding the donkey and the sheep while he rides, but the creatures have minds of their own. They're straggling all over the hillsides, some even beyond where I can see. The shepherd boy circles around them on the bike, restoring a semblance of a flock, and then disappears again.

When he finally comes back, he wants to trade the donkey for the Blue Angel. Fat chance! But I'll take his picture. He's amazed when he sees the image captured on the digital camera. Can he try it? He takes some great shots of sheep, mostly rear ends and udders. Then he motions me onto the back of the donkey, which is covered by a coarse blanket. My feet nearly touch the ground. Click. Sure enough, there I am on the little screen, hair flying every which way from under my scarf, hanging on for dear life to a scruffy blanket. I can't remember looking so elated or present, in a Zen sort of way, for nearly a decade. Wait till Andy sees it.

Later in the week, I make prints and ask Bezma how to find the boy. She has no idea. Too bad, because he could have gotten a lot of laughs from the other boys at school with the sheep butt shots.

But wait. Maybe he doesn't go to school. This makes me more obsessed with finding him, as if there's some connection between the simple wisdom of an untutored pastoral existence like his and my own potential encounter with God. Less can be more; limited intellectual sophistication can lead to heightened spirituality. Was it any coincidence that David was a shepherd? Or that Jesus wandered into the wilderness for inspiration?

No, I am trying to read too much into a chance encounter.

❖ ❖ ❖

"Did you find any trolls up in them thar hills? Goliaths? Maybe a centaur or two?" Pat waits to ask until practically everybody is there in the faculty room, for maximum humiliation.

"Oh, shut up." I love Pat. I show her the photos, both the shepherd's and mine, and she passes them around.

"Whoa. Great tits and ass," Jake says. "Almost makes me want to turn raghead."

Pat stares at him in mock shock. "Grow up, would you?" We all know she's saying this for the benefit of the local teachers across the Green Line, so they don't think we're a bunch of perverts. Which they probably do anyway.

But maybe not, because Mrs. Zaki yanks her scarf over her mouth and turns away toward the windows. Her back shudders, and it looks like she's dabbing at her eyes with the scarf. When she finally turns around, she winks at me.

Offensive as we probably are, we must certainly make The Fortress more entertaining sometimes.

❖ ❖ ❖

Thinking about Ara's entire village being bulldozed makes me wonder about my students and Saddam Hussein. He was toppled only six years before; they would all know about his brutality. Telling stories about a villain might be a great way to get them engaged in English conversation.

I've held off asking, though, worried that the name "Saddam" might be offensive here, like evoking the Evil Eye. The syllables themselves sound eerily similar to other repugnant words. Sadistic. Satanic. Sodomy. Serial killer. Google tells me that Saddam means "one who confronts" or "powerful collider." How appropriate. Too bad his mother hadn't named him something like Khalil, "friend", or Habib, "beloved".

I keep the Saddam discussion in reserve for a time of pedagogical crisis, when monotony lurches perilously close to pandemonium. At times like these, I usually pull a song or game out of my teacher's bag of tricks. This time, I close my text book and say brightly, "Okay, let's change the subject. Who wants to tell me something about Saddam Hussein?"

Almost fifty little faces stare at me in bewilderment. "Like what, Miss?" someone finally asks.

"Well, I'm from America, and I want to learn what it was like when he was in power. Who can tell me about it?"

Not one student raises their hand. Instead, all eyes are glued to desktops.

I'll try a different tactic. "Who lost someone in their family due to Saddam?"

"Lost? You mean disappeared?" Helin asks.

"Yes, vanished. Or died."

Tentatively, with surreptitious glances at one another as if seeking group permission, every student raises a hand except one -- Jaber, the lone Arab. I'm stunned.

"Every single one of you?" I ignore Jaber, who is doing his best to look invisible.

"Yes, Miss."

Barav, one of the sullen lumps in the back row, stands up. It's the first time he has volunteered anything in class; I take this as something of a triumph — until he speaks.

"Miss, my people all came from a village that was gassed during Al Alfal. My parents were out shopping the day the planes came. That's the only reason they lived. It was just like Halabja. You know about Al Anfal and Halabja, Miss?"

The room has never been so quiet. It's a silence much deeper than emptiness -- hinting at years of screams stifled, sleepless nights, tears unshed, secrets untold, hearts overflowing with dread.

I nod. I've read about Al Alfal, Saddam's genocide against the Kurds. From 1986 to 1989, 4,000 villages were systematically razed -- out of 4,655 total. About one third of Iraq's Kurdish population was displaced, and about 100,000 civilians were massacred. Firing squads. Mass graves. Routine torture. Nighttime raids on towns; every male who looked like he was between 15 and 50 taken away, usually to be shot. Dumping the women and children in so-called camps without food, water, sanitation or shelter. And worst of all, air attacks on 250 towns and villages like Halabja, dropping napalm and chemical gas that killed every living thing, from song birds flying in the sky to infants in their cradles.

Reading about it in my apartment was one thing. I'd think, "Oh, how terrible." My mind would stop for a moment, stupefied, trying to fathom the vastness of the numbers. A million and a half people driven out of their homes; that's half the population of metro Seattle; each person walking with a lumpy bundle of belongings and food, or carrying a child, or supporting an elderly parent. A million and a half people with nowhere to go except away.

Seeing the impact of atrocities on the faces of twelve-year-olds is another thing entirely. The kids who watch silly cartoons after school had relatives who died in prisons, or froze to death walking across mountain passes in winter. The knowingness in their eyes doesn't match the youthfulness of their little faces.

"Miss, we don't talk about some things at home. Some names we don't say." This is from the beautiful Helin with the pink nail polish today, whose goal is to become Hannah Montana when she grows up.

"Neither do we. And we're Christian." Louai comes from one of the old Assyrian families in the Christian area. The kids call him Orange Fizz, partly because of his carrot-colored hair, and partly due to his temper. "Not too many people ever think about what happened to the Christians," he adds defensively.

Jaber's head is buried in his arms. It strikes me how untenable his position is here, a hated Arab in a school of Kurds. No wonder he's such a pain.

"Maybe this discussion was a mistake," I say. "Let's move on to something different. We'll sing 'If You're Happy and You Know It Clap Your Hands.'"

They dutifully chime in, but without their usual revelry. I'll get in trouble for singing, that's for sure. But it won't be as bad as if Zaki and Madame find out about me floundering into politics.

I am so naive. Well-intentioned, yes. But when you come right down to it, a babe in the wilderness of global politics.

※　※　※

On Friday afternoon, the grocery woman motions to me as I pass her shop, pantomiming that she wants a photo with her little grandson. My popularity in the village has risen exponentially since I started carrying around a camera.

Disregarding Bezma's ultimatum to ignore the local kids, I take pictures of anyone who seems photogenic (or who asks), get them developed in the city, and hand out prints on my next visit. Now adults have started asking for pictures too, saying they've never had one before.

But the grocer's request takes me by surprise. Since the advent of Hevar, she has been chilly toward me, and her prices have gone up, too. Still, I say yes. She poses with the grandson in front of some blackening bananas, refusing to smile — maybe to hide bad teeth — and pesters me to bring the prints as soon as possible. Sure. Maybe the photos will just mysteriously disappear from the camera, I think, as revenge for her slandering Bezma. And then I laugh at my own pettiness.

I find Bezma, Ara and her daughter-in-law over at Old Houda's house, along with the two-year-old son and newborn baby. The women lean against the wall with legs straight out in front of them. How do Ara and Houda sit that way at their age, when they otherwise move so arthritically? They've apparently achieved a sort of truce; a glassy tranquility overlays the spitting of the kerosene heater.   I join them under the inevitable photo of Massoud Barzani, as they sip the inevitable tea through sugar cubes between their teeth, and take turns cracking walnut shells with a hammer. The little boy is being a nuisance, running all over the place, threatening to spill the delicate tea glasses, and mocking his mother when she yells at him. They ignore him, and ask me to practice my *ser tchow*, with my hand over my eye, and *min dulum khosh*, with my hand over my heart. They're trying to teach me the basic Muslim prayer, the *Surah Al Fatibah*, too. It's a pleasant diversion from marriage battles, but I'm not making much progress.

I crawl over next to the new mother and ask to hold her tiny bundle. She passes it over with a gentle smile.

The infant is swaddled, wrapped tight as an ace bandage. I can't cuddle or nestle her in my arms; it's like trying to embrace a bread board.

"Why is she all tied up like this?"

"It's good for the legs," Houda replies in Arabic, and begins a discussion with Ara. The names Bezma and Hevar keep cropping up in perturbed Kurdish, and Ara starts to cry -- angry tears this time -- and chops at the air like a ninja. It's a little unnerving.

"What's her name?" I ask the new mother, nodding at the baby.

"Shirin." She holds up a cube of sugar. Sweetness. How lovely. The little boy tries to swipe the sugar, and she shoos him away. He sneaks around to touch the turquoise evil-eye protector pinned to the baby's cap. His mother swats at him again.

I give up trying to make out what the women are saying, and creep to a quieter corner with baby Shirin. I prop her up on my knees for a closer look. I don't want to see her as a generic newborn; I want that wonder of looking into my own child's eyes — if nothing else, to get my mind off the squabbling on the other side of the room.

Tiny grey eyes stare blindly up at me; shallow little breaths barely raise the swaddling. No hands nor feet peek out of the milky cotton, only a face still bruised red from the birth. Her eyes are like bottomless wells leading straight to infinity.

"Shirin," I whisper. "Sweet little Shirin." I will myself to keep meeting her gaze and not flee from the bald intimacy. I float downward into her, close to the place she has just come from. Where is that? I have no idea, but can sense it, like a remembered dream. A spark quickens in my empty womb, reminding me of times like this when Andy was an infant; the rest of the world dropped away and we held the entire universe suspended between us. Shirin is Everybaby, and I'm

Everymother; there's a holiness to it. Or rather, there is a holiness to this innocent baby, which I am privileged to bear witness to.

A deep peace settles in, and baby Shirin and I drift off together to an island somewhere, far from the contention in the room, from Iraq, from the world itself. Her breath and mine, swelling in and out, one quick and one slow, create a single pulse with two beats to it. All of this beauty in the wake of war. In a village without flush toilets, kitchen sinks or central heat. Little Shirin, born into such uncertainty, yet the very essence of trust.

We sit this way until my poor feet grow numb and my knees stiffen. Old Houda brings me a fresh glass of tea. "Very beautiful," she whispers in Arabic; she's also sensing the spell. I nod. "It's from God," she adds, resting her fingertips on my arm. She understands.

"We are sisters," I say, hoping it doesn't sound lame. "The baby girl, Ara, you, me..."

"Yes, sisters." By virtue of being female, by having gone through childbirth, by knowing how everything of value in the universe can be found in a newborn's gaze.

It's getting too intense, so I try to make conversation. "How many babies have you delivered, Houda?"

"Too many to count. Praise be to Allah."

And how many are still alive? I'm not brave enough to ask.

Things are finally calming down on the other side of the room. Ara sits up straight again, more composed now but with a resigned bitterness to her squint. "Is everything solved now?" I ask.

Yes, no, Ara nods and shakes in both directions. Putting it into words will make the decision more real, but she does it anyway. "Houda says that Bezma is right. The marriage must take place." She waits for Houda to translate for me. "If I say yes, I am sad. If I say no, I am sad. No matter what happens in

139

life, being a woman is sad." She sounds like a judge, issuing a tragic decree against her will.

I nod. "I hope it will be better for Baby Shirin. She's lucky. She has a mother and a father, plus a grandmother next door. She's surrounded by love." And she was born into a tight community that will help sustain her. Her country is no longer at war, at least for now, and her people are not being bombed, gassed, tortured or taken away in the middle of the night by the government. She will no doubt go to school. And if she is like Bezma, hopefully she will one day get to choose her own husband. Compared with Ara and Houda, her life will be heaven.

After a long pause, Houda draws out her beads and begins murmuring a prayer. With a single glance, the sea depth of her green eyes seals the emotional tenor for us, blessing what has been agreed. *Allah akbar, Allah kareem...* The rhythm of the prayer soothes us, and even Ara is breathing freer now. The prayers are doing their work. Allah is surely listening. Allah has a plan for us all. In His wisdom, he will ensure justice, and heal even the saddest of hearts.

I want to bottle the air in the room, and remember how Old Houda did this — reconciling the irreconcilable. I want to become a peacemaker like she is, not denying pain but weaving it into a larger fabric of meaning and acceptance.

Five: Faces of Longing

IT'S THE morning of Nowruz, the spring equinox, the Kurds' biggest holiday. With the general discord at Ara's house, an invitation to celebrate never materialized. So I take the Blue Angel for a ride toward the city to check out the red poppies, tiny white star-shaped flowers that hug the earth, and swaying yellow hollyhocks that, miraculously, have carpeted the countryside almost overnight.

The highway is one humongous parking lot. As far as the eye can see, cars and trucks roll at a snail's pace out of the city, bedecked in Kurdish flags, honking their horns, and piled high with folding chairs, rolled rugs and ice chests. If not for the music blaring and the holiday atmosphere, this could be an endless convoy of refugees.

Crossing the mess of a highway would be suicidal. I pedal along the dirt shoulder against traffic -- where a shoulder exists, that is. In most places the verge is filled with cheater traffic, ramming over dried ruts and weather-matted trash, and crushing the newly sprouted wildflowers. I laugh, buoyed by the sheer ecstasy of humanity surging around me. Kurds of all ages give me thumbs ups, and laugh back at me. One little boy sticks his flag in my hand; it fits perfectly in the grip of my handlebar. Now I'm officially part of the parade.

"Excuse me, Miss." An oversized SUV with an intimidating mess of antennas pulls up alongside me, rolled-down windows leaking chilled air. "We'd like to speak with you."

"Who, me?" They could be with the police or the military; I can't make out the writing on the car. I'm in my hopefully-male-looking bicycle disguise -- a *khak* vest with about two dozen pockets all over it, a red Peshmerga-style kerchief wrapped around my head in a semblance of a turban, and jeans. It's not exactly what Madame wants school representatives being seen in, that's for sure. I clinch my handlebars for a quick getaway.

"You are a foreigner, yes?" An absurdly handsome young man in a Western suit and Ray Bans jumps out, followed by a technician lugging a video camera and microphones.

"How did you guess? Yes, I'm American," I say warily.

"American! Oh, wonderful! We're putting you on TV." He motions for the tech guy to set up the camera, and passes me a mike.

"I don't have anything to say. My employer wouldn't like it…" But nobody is listening. Children appear out of nowhere, gathering around the fellow in the suit, trying to get him to film them making faces.

"Take off the scarf so we can see your hair please? Oh nice. Very pretty. Here, tuck this poppy into your hair. Now, name please?" The cameras are already rolling. "Where are you from? And what brings you to Kurdistan?"

I answer carefully. There's probably a clause in my contract forbidding this.

"Wonderful! A teacher, coming to help educate the Kurdish people. We are very thankful to you, Miss. Now, please tell us what you think of Nowruz and Kurdistan."

Why has my brain frozen? Why can't I be clever at times like these?

"I love Kurdistan!" I say to buy time. "Uh, my Kurdish students are absolutely the best -- smart, polite and hard-working." What nonsense. Then a stroke of brilliance. "It is a privilege to be here, helping the Kurdish people build a new nation. I want to tell everybody in America what a terrific place this is -- and how Kurdistan should be an independent country."

The kids all clap. They probably have no idea what I'm saying.

"And what do you think of Nowruz?"

I gesture at the jubilant traffic jam around me. "I am so lucky to experience Nowruz first-hand. Look at how happy everybody is. Your country is such a success. *Kurdistan, min dulum khosh*!" Oh, thank God that "my heart is glad" popped to mind instead of "shut up" and "sit down", my most frequently used Kurdish phrases. I grab the flag from my bicycle and flutter it gleefully for the camera.

The anchorman's translation takes at least three times longer than my little speech had. What on earth did I supposedly say? Then mercifully he switches back to English. "Thank you so much. Soon you will see yourself on Zagros TV. Very beautiful."

Like heck. I barely even know how to turn on my television at The Fortress, much less find the right station.

I've pedaled another couple of miles when a second SUV with similar contraptions pulls over to do another interview. "But I already did one," I protest. "With your buddies down the road."

"No problem. Do it again." So I spout the same PR foolishness to a different city slicker, this one in a tie sporting the Kurdish flag. My spiel comes out a little smoother this time. The *Kurdistan, min dulum khosh* is right there on the tip of my tongue.

By now, the hillsides are awash with picnic groups; cars and trucks park haphazardly any old place, and families squeeze through wire fences to spread out sheets, blankets and rugs on the fields. The shoulder is so crowded that I have to walk the bike. It's a battle of the bands with boom boxes and car radios -- whiny bouzoukis, drums, men singing.

143

About every third party beckons for me to come join them, but I'm too timid, until a mob of kids surrounds the Blue Angel and won't take no for an answer. One of the older boys lifts the bike over the fence for me, then, to my horror, mounts it, crashes, gets back on, and takes off cross country into the hills. This is worse than a hold-up, more like a kidnapping, watching my treasured steed vanish beyond a rise. I'm helpless with rage.

Meanwhile, the younger kids drag me by the hand to deliver me, their prize, to their parents. "Sit, sit!" About twenty adults speak at once. I can't figure out which is more polite -- sitting on a webbed chair with the men, who most likely speak some English and Arabic, or down on the ground with the women, who probably speak only Kurdish. I opt for a spot on the blanket where I can scour the horizon for my bike.

Then there's another dilemma. Should I use my checkered scarf to cover my hair, like the other women, or over my lap to cover my crotch, which is shamefully exposed by the jeans? I go for the lap, and somebody passes me an extra black veil; it smells smoky and musty, like cheap rose oil and spice, when I wrap it around my face.

Who am I? Where am I from? What am I doing here? They've never met a foreigner before, and haven't heard about expat teachers. But I don't want to talk; I want to learn about them and be sure of getting the bike back. Who is the patriarch? Whose children are these? Who is married to whom? They patiently explain, and I immediately forget most of it because the names are so strange.

The plate they pass me has enough to feed three normal-sized people. Stuffed cabbage dolmas. Stuffed onion dolmas. Stuffed eggplant dolmas. Stuffed grape leaf dolmas. Rice pilaf. Pita bread. Homemade yogurt. Rank-smelling off-white sheep cheese. Roast chicken. Then more platters go around -- tomatoes, cucumbers, cut-up apples and oranges. And little tulip-shaped glasses with sweet tea filled and then refilled from a battered old thermos.

"Someone cooked for days, making all this!"

The matriarch grins. She's draped from neck to waist in gold — probably most of it fake, but still very impressive. Sets of gold bangles march all the way from wrist to elbow. She even has a gold headband with dingle-dangles across her forehead.

"How old are you?" she asks.

"Guess."

The women bicker and eventually agree that I'm 35. They're astonished (or pretend to be) when I admit to being 57 — and don't even have grandchildren yet.

Then it's my turn to guess their ages. This is risky. I gauge the wrinkles, dental condition, size of waistline, and amount of black in their outfit, arrive at a number and subtract 20. I'm still sometimes off by a decade. It's a great crowd pleaser.

"Let's dance!" What, out here in a rocky field beside the highway? Why not? One of the men cranks up a cassette in the car, and we women join baby fingers in a line. Hems snag on low pricker bushes; evening slippers stub into clods of dirt, and we bob up and down in time to the music, shoulders shrugging, prancing in dainty little female steps. Every now and then someone starts a high-pitched ululating, and they all laugh. The men stay smoking in their chairs, paying us no mind, which is fine, as the music goes on interminably.

Dancing with Kurds — at first, I'm mortified, my jeans so unisex compared with the other women's gaudy femininity, as I stumble to learn the intricate steps. Then the odd tempo gets into my blood and breath, and my feet start prancing of their own volition. I'm carried along on a stream of Kurdishness, two beats to the right, then one beat dipping toward the center, in an irresistible current. Step by step on this primeval piece of earth; for just an instant it's pure sky above, earth below, and a

145

line of dancing women channeling some universal joy in between, happily keening to the music and stirring it all together in a mystical soup — until the music stops and we hug each other around the waist and swing this way and that, not knowing what else to do with ourselves. It's too much goodness to bear for very long; it's too exquisite an essence to hold in humble human bodies.

The golden cobweb stretches, snaps, and we're ordinary people again. The grandmother to my left pulls my ear to her head. Her skin smells sandy, and her cuticles are weed-stained. She asks something that I don't understand. Furtively, she rubs her fingers together. Money. It's Nowruz; she is poor. I shake my head; I have come by bicycle, without a purse. But she doesn't believe me, and asks several times more before I leave, each time a little more insistently. And worse — the teenager who rode off with the Blue Angel pleads for me to give it to him. This is the first time that Kurds have asked me for anything, and I recoil. How offensive. If I had really been part of some global sisterhood in that hora line, this wouldn't be happening...

But wait. What a dingbat I am, to think that our differences could drop away so easily. I am, and always will be, the rich American. But conversely, it also hurts that I'm not in a position to shower them with gifts, in return for their own generosity. Or that I could somehow finesse visas for them all to immigrate to the U.S., which the men will surely question me about if I stay long enough.

I thank them all profusely, grab the Blue Angel before someone else can snatch a ride on her, and pedal back to The Fortress, both blessed and discomfited. If only I could do more to help.

✳ ✳ ✳

When classes resume after Nowruz, the secretary at the front desk greets me with unusual amusement. "I saw you on TV, Miss. Both stations. Very nice. My whole family was very proud of you."

All the other Kurds at school have seen me too — Mohammed, the students, even the guy who drives our van to town. "*Kurdistan, min dulum khosh,*" they chant when I approach, waving an invisible flag. It's become my trademark jingle, winning me points wherever I go. Even in the village, people congratulate me, a mystery because I've never seen anybody with a TV that works.

❊ ❊ ❊

"Hevar say you very beautiful on television," Bezma informs me on Saturday evening after the holiday, for about the tenth time today. Dusk is falling and mosquitos are starting to pepper our ankles out on the porch. It's almost time for me to go back to my apartment and prepare for the week's classes. Every time I try to leave, though, Bezma comes up with another excuse.

"I think you just enjoy saying his name." This wins me a grin, but does not get translated to Ara, who is sweeping the steps hunched over a homemade broom that comes just short of her waist.

Bezma grabs my hand in reply. "Just wait a little longer."

A car door slams outside the gate, and her grip tenses. Ara keeps sweeping, a wonderfully soothing rhythm, oblivious to whatever is happening on the street. Her broom doesn't work very well, and she has to keep going over the spot she just swept, but she doesn't seem to mind. She reminds me of a monk raking gravel, with mindfulness being a path to — or substitute for — bliss.

Whaannnnnggg. The three of us freeze. An electric guitar out here? A mandolin? It hovers on a single note, buzzing like some gigantic insect, and then rises up, suspended, soaring, and falling in a cascade. Bezma jumps to her feet, throws her arms around herself, and hops with glee. Ara glowers, not understanding. Then singing floats over the wall. It's just one man's voice, strong and virile, confidently claiming the night. I can't make out the words, and don't understand this tortured kind of melody. But nobody — not a young woman, nor an older widow, nor a clueless foreigner — could mistake the intent of this serenade.

With each line of song, Ara becomes more agitated and Bezma more mesmerized. "Make him stop!" Crazed now, Ara pushes Bezma toward the gate, but the girl isn't budging.

Ara tosses on her abaya and flaps out to the street, shrieking. A few old men have already gathered; nothing this amusing has happened all day. Ara yanks Hevar inside by the elbow and clangs the gate shut behind him. "Quiet! Quiet!"

Hevar straightens himself like a conquering warrior, a rose peeking out of the folds of his cummerbund, and an oud cradled gently in one arm. Intricate arabesque carvings swirl around the sound hole of the instrument, and its amber-like varnish is cracked with age. Nodding a greeting to Bezma and me, he settles on the patio steps and resumes the song; his voice is lower now, husky and erotic. Ara and I have ceased to exist. He's spinning a gossamer mesh around Bezma, skillfully, deliberately, and she's a willing captive.

Ara picks up her broom again, and at first I think she's going to swat him off the steps. Instead, she squats alone over by the kitchen door, where the shadows hide her face. Although the darkness is almost complete now, I can make out her trembling. I crouch beside her, and rest a hand on her shoulder. Are you angry, or jealous, or fearful, or sad, my friend? Are you remembering what it felt like to be worshipped by a studly young man? Or are you recognizing how inevitable their togetherness seems now, as he seduces her with a song?

Even if I had known the words in Kurdish and had the guts to say them, I doubt that she would have given me a straight answer — or would have known the truth herself — because resistance to Hevar and his spell, we can both see now, is futile.

* * *

The next afternoon in class, we've opened up all the windows to let in the poignant kite-weather breeze, which only serves to torment us. The kids are tugged even worse than I am; their gazes keep drifting outside, helpless like little skiffs in a wind too strong for their sails. And we are condemned to reading about Alexander the Great, glossing over the typos and poorly translated segments in the text. For relief, our session later in the day will be mitigated by stimulating verb conjugations.

It's an affront to nature. No one will find out if we deviate just a smidgeon from the syllabus.

"So, kids, let's take a poll. Who thinks Alexander lived after Mohammed?"

About half raise their hands. Oh dear.

"Okay then, who thinks Moses came before Jesus?"

They're suspecting teacherly trickiness here, and only two risk voting.

Appalled at the gaps in their knowledge, I guide them on a period-long detour into a general timeline of history, from Moses to Gandhi, from the Ancient Egyptian Empire to the British Empire. We've got some semblance of a world map chalked onto the board, with gigantic arrows representing movements of armies and cultures marching around the world. I invite their questions, which we may or may not get to in future days, and promise chocolate bars for the best ones.

"Is it farther to drive to Sweden or Universal Studios?"

"Do they eat dolmas in China?"

"What happened to the dudes who built the pyramids?"

"Why didn't Mohammed convert the Americans?"

The bell surprises me; how did thirty minutes pass so effortlessly? I didn't have to give a single detention to keep order, either, although admittedly we got a bit rambunctious. But for once, my back doesn't ache with exhaustion. Instead, my cheeks feel zingy and bright.

As the kids file out, I notice a tiny sparrow alighted on the window sill, and go to wish him well and brush him back off into spring. A familiar, spooky voice startles me from behind. I spin, and there is Zaki in his Spy Who Came in from the Cold outfit, trench coat and dark glasses incongruous with the beautiful weather.

"Miss Turner, please explain the relevance of these drawings."

Rats. Caught. I laugh guiltily. "It looks pretty crazy, but that's my feeble attempt to draw Alexander's conquest of the entire known world."

"And these areas here?" Zaki demands, pointing toward what might have been porn drawn on the board.

"You mean the Americas. Yes, it's a fairly rough depiction. Art was never my strong suit. We were talking about why the New World never became exposed to Classical Greek thought and architecture. Because they were separated by oceans on either side…"

The rambling is not working. "I regret to note that this is your second infraction in a single week. I've written you up, and scheduled an interview with Madame."

Oh hell. What a waste of time.

✢ ✢ ✢

Madame, not rising from behind her desk this time, is surprisingly sympathetic. "I used to love that type of discussion too." She sighs, as if yearning for the horse-and-buggy days. "I can remember trying to draw out some little sweetheart who never spoke, getting her to join in a debate. But alas. That's not how we teach at the Academy. Same thing with the Socratic method..."

Her nostalgia encourages me to let down my guard a bit. "But what if the Academy's techniques aren't optimal for student outcomes?" Try some good pedagogical vocabulary on her...

"That remains to be seen. The experts in the Cairo office have done numerous studies that prove its efficacy." Ooooh -- more scholarly vocabulary right back at me. This is getting fun.

"I wish you could have been there yourself and seen it. The students were having a blast." I'm trying to remember to call them students, like she does, rather than kids, which we expat teachers do. "Everybody knows that engaged learners are the best learners. And nobody gets engaged following such a rigid curriculum, where you can't deviate a single iota. Where you can't go where the students' minds want to lead you." We've skated near these philosophical seismic rifts several times during our evening strolls. But then it had been a theoretical question, not one in defense of my behavior.

She glances behind my chair to make sure her door is shut. I wonder where we currently are on the continuum between friends and equals versus superior and subordinate. Come to think of it, maybe the whole idea of friendship with Madame has been delusional. "Remember that this is not a public institution, nor a religious school, like the places where you and I have taught in the past. It is a company. For profit. Tangible results are our product." Ah, that clarifies things. We're definitely superior/subordinate.

"Yes?" I wonder where this is going.

151

"And the Academy has established its reputation on uniformity. So that a child of a diplomat can transfer here from Buenos Aires, and be doing the exact same lesson here that he was there."

I've heard this once too many times.

"So we are essentially contributing to its brand when we follow orders. We are officers in a grand army of education. And like army officers, we are not hired -- or paid -- for our creativity."

I want to nod out of politeness, but can't get my neck to move.

"Everything in life is a trade-off. We make informed decisions, based on the knowledge available at the time." Now she's veering into a lecture. With each sentence, my black skirt gets balled up tighter in my fists. "That's why I emphasize the word loyalty with my teachers. If you are loyal to the Academy, you will definitely prosper."

"My" teachers? Do I belong to her in some nefarious way? "You mean choking out spontaneity? Snuffing out our souls?"

"I think that's being a bit theatrical, my dear. Let's not make a mountain out of a molehill. Keep the noise down in your classroom, stick to the textbooks, and everyone will be happy." She glances sideways with great meaning, like a co-conspirator. It makes me want to retch.

"Okay." I hate myself for saying it. But what choice is there? "I'll try to keep it quieter."

"That's a good girl."

Oh ick. There's that familiar old passive aggression kicking in again…

❈   ❈   ❈

I go on the Internet that afternoon and search for new class-taming techniques. The next day, I set up a cutthroat competition between my classes called the Silent Game. Near the end of each period, or earlier if we see Zaki at the peephole, I ding a reception-style bell and count the seconds out loud to see how long they can maintain absolute silence. One giggle, burp or fart brings the game to an end.

Their best score goes up on the board, and we compare it with my other classes. The winning class gets a pizza party. How I'll pull off a pizza party, I have no earthly idea, since food and drinks are prohibited in the classrooms. But that's a problem for sometime in the future. In the meantime, we've got a secret weapon against Zaki. Even such a tiny diversion from tedium is a gift I can give these beloved (if exhausting) children.

At first, none of my classes can sit quietly for even thirty seconds. After a week or so, we're getting up into the triple digits. Then four digits -- students squirming like they all needed to pee at once.

It isn't long before Pat and Jake's classes are asking for the Silent Game too. Pretty soon, we're all swapping survival tactics in the faculty room. Spelling bees. Word search games. Ghost stories about Academy witches who steal into classrooms and eat noisy children. Oh, we're a cagey bunch of guerillas, trying to outsmart the educational Stormtrooper brigade. The kids love it.

❈ ❈ ❈

"Treeza, I am sick." It's Friday again, and with spring here we don't need the kerosene heater in the main room. Instead, the window is open, and a heartening breeze flutters the faded yellow curtains.

"You look pretty good to me." Bezma has a rosy flush and a funny nervous energy, bustling around with the dishes after the midday meal. She waits until Ara leaves before sitting beside me on the carpet.

"Always I am hot." She plows through her school dictionary for the right word. "I have fever."

"The flu has been going around the school. Let me feel your forehead."

"No, not head. Here." She puts her hand on her stomach. "Also more low."

I laugh. "You're not sick. You're in love. Let me guess. You get hot down there whenever you think about Hevar. Right?"

"Please do not say name. Just say my love. My mother will hear."

"Okay. Your love. But you get this hotness when you think about him touching you, right?"

She nods. "I do not sleep in night. Very bad."

"But that's normal. Everybody feels like that when they're in love. I'm sure your mother did too, when she was waiting for her marriage. Didn't she talk to you about this stuff?"

"What this means, stuff?"

"You know. About what happens in bed after a man and woman get married."

"No. My mother say I never marry, do not have need for knowing. My two sisters dead. Also, very rude talk about this if not married. Forbidden in Islam."

"Well, it's not forbidden in America. And your mother can't understand a word we're saying. So, what do you want to know?" I can't stop grinning. My son Andy had never wanted to talk like this. This is a blast.

"Okay…" She's torn between shyness and curiosity. "What I must do? First time?"

Oh dear. This is going to be dicey, given our limited vocabulary. But I'll give it a shot.

"Well, hopefully he will touch you nicely and say sweet things to you, so that you start to get wet down there. You sometimes get wet now, when you think you have a fever, right?"

She nods with eyes lowered.

"Then when he is ready, when his penis —" Mistake. This is a word they haven't covered in the college English class. "— his thing down here — gets hard, he climbs on top of you and you open up your legs. Wide. Like so." My arms do a big splayed eagle.

She gasps. "No! This too much shame. With no pants?"

"Of course with no pants." Good heavens. "Then he puts his thing up inside you and starts pushing in and out."

"Oh, this terrible! Not possible. I have no space inside for anything. This very painful."

"Your body knows how to make room. And it's not painful if you're nice and wet. Except for the first time. For some women, the first time hurts. Oh, and you bleed a little bit the first time. Or rather, most women do. Some women who are virgins don't bleed, so you shouldn't get worried if you don't."

"Oh. I hear every woman bleed. Every woman hurt."

"No." Then I have a brainstorm. "If you use something to make sure you are wet, it feels much better. It kind of slides. You can use AstroGlide." I wonder if they even sell it here. "Or baby oil, if you can't get anything else."

"You give me some of this, if we have wedding?"

"Of course. Then you will probably really enjoy sex, once you get used to it. Most women do." If they have a considerate lover. Memories of a certain recent ex-spouse creep to the surface, but I squeeze them back; I don't want to go down that road right now. Come to think of it, something about Hevar's puffed-up posture makes me doubt his potential tenderness.

But then a chilling thought hits me. Before I can weigh the wisdom of asking, I blurt, "Wait. Bezma. Were you cut?"

She frowns at either my indelicacy or stupidity. "Of course. All womans cut." As if to say, "What a silly question."

"Not in the West." I wait for this shocking news to sink in. But there's no backing out now. "And it is the cut part that lets you enjoy sex."

She tips her head, incredulous. "I do not understand. Enjoy?"

How to explain this? "Sex can be really nice. Like tasting chocolate. Actually, it's much better than chocolate. It's like you are in heaven for a few minutes, like you are flying in outer space with your body just exploding with happiness. Except its a body happiness, not a heart happiness."

"Like when I think about my love..."

"Yes, but even more. It's what your husband will experience when he puts his thing inside you, and pushes, and then his seeds explode into you. Not really explode. It's like turning on the water in a hose for a minute. His seeds go way up high inside you, and if your egg is ready, you make a baby." Too bad my high school biology teacher isn't hearing this; he'd be in hysterics.

"I will get big happiness. I want this very much!"

Think fast, Theresa. What's the use of telling her about something she'll probably never know?

"You'll be really happy when he holds you, and touches your breasts. Some women even get the big happiness when their husband sucks on their breasts, and kind of bites on them a little bit." Heck, I read once that some women even have orgasms when washing their hands. Or sneezing. I hope it's true.

"I will be one of those." She has total confidence. "God cannot give something good to Infidel womans and not Muslim womans."

Truth or diplomacy? I take a deep breath. "I'm sure you're right, Bezma."

She relaxes and fiddles with her tea cup. "Everything different for Americans. Even bodies."

"Maybe you're right."

I'll find her an industrial-sized bottle of baby oil before the wedding, if it ever happens. Without a clitoris, she's going to need all the help she can get.

✻ ✻ ✻

I'm starting to pick up a little Kurdish. I can count to ten, and know the words for eat, full, delicious, tomatoes, cucumber, chicken, good night, sleep, school, bicycle, water, tea, yogurt, bread, sick, children, shut up, sit down, very beautiful, mother and husband. Oh, and marriage. At first, I had assumed "marriage" was a curse, because of the way Bezma and Ara threw it back and forth at one another.

I am also coming down with the flu -- along with about half of The Fortress, and Bezma herself, who's been throwing up. Plus it's drizzling. What a stupid idea, riding down to the village. But Bezma had insisted via text. "Vry mportnt come frydy." Via Seema, she also sent a note to class, which only added to the mysterious urgency.

When I reach their street, though, I regret it immediately. Bezma's yelling, and Ara's shrieked replies, are audible halfway down the block.

As I prop up the Blue Angel against the water tank, its regular spot now, Ara pulls herself together, straightens her head scarf, and *set tchows* me, like nothing is wrong. But Bezma is too angry to pretend. "We go to tailor," she commands. Before we can even have tea, she steers me out the gate and marches me off at full speed -- or rather, as fast as a young woman can trip through dirt alleys in patent-leather party shoes.

"My mother is goat. When Old Houda here, my mother say yes for my wedding. Then another day she say no. She very bad woman." We skirt a few stray sheep, and ignore two men

157

trying to push start a beat-up car. Her phone buzzes — Hevar, of course. As I struggle to keep up, she rants into the phone, then abruptly hangs up, smiling.

There's only one possible topic of conversation. "Have you gotten to see Hevar since he came singing?"

"Oh yes. He come almost every day. We have very much love."

"It's a long drive from the mountains. This guy's serious."

She blushes in reply, and speeds up our pace.

"I hope the grocery lady has stopped bad-mouthing you."

She gives a smug chortle. "Hevar told her *wiss ba*." She grins that I can understand phrases like "shut up" now. "Very soon my mother shut up also. Hevar is strong man. He say, 'Hevar want, Hevar get.'"

It's not the first time she's said something similar, and it gives me pause. "Based on personal experience, it's not always smart to marry someone who thinks that," I say, although she clearly thinks that it is.

Maia, the tailor, shouts a welcome when we rap on her gate, which screeches as we let ourselves in. We have barely embraced her when Bezma's phone buzzes again, and she disappears. While she's gone, I try on the different layers of the dress, feeling foolish with yard-long sleeve ends. Maia shows me how to knot them together in front, step through, and let them drape behind me. She scoots around me with pins in her mouth, adjusts the side seams, restitches them on her machine, and admires her handiwork. I try everything on again, and she is satisfied. Very beautiful!

She brings tea for the two of us while our wait for Bezma drags on. We have refills. We smile at one another a lot. I pay what she asks, about $15 for stitching the entire get-up, and she puts her hand over her heart in thanks. But with no common language, the afternoon stretches interminably. We both tire of the awkwardness. Finally, making a big deal of my sniffle and cough, and pantomiming that I must have picked up Bezma's stomach bug, she drags out heavy woolen blankets and tucks them around me on the floor mats.

Warm and comfy, but annoyed with Bezma for abandoning me for such a long time, I watch Maia stitch a hem by hand. I learned to hem on a stool beside my grandmother, on lazy afternoons exactly like this one. Watching Maia at her handiwork calms me. Tradition, tradition, the tempo of her needle seems to say; there is something solid and trustworthy about tradition that makes everything okay in the long run. If a lovely woman like Maia is content being a second wife to some old coot, then who am I to judge? If mothers and brothers have always prevented daughters from getting married and leaving home, then so be it. I sigh. Lying here is so good. A chicken clucks somewhere. A baby cries, cross, ready for a nap. Maia scoots over to her machine and cranks in a steady slow thump. Village life goes on. I am so blessed to be snuggled in here under a pile of blankets, reduced to a nameless set of ears, a silent spectator to it all...

It's almost dark when Bezma awakens me, beaming. She smells like cigarettes. Peeking inside my bag, she nods in approval at the dress, agrees briskly with Maia about it being gorgeous, and then tromps me back to Ara's.

"Why are we in such a hurry?"

She ignores me. Then I see for myself. There in Ara's yard is the white pickup. And there is Hevar himself, planted wide-legged on the porch with a parade-ground presence that takes command of the yard, and, in outward spirals of dominance, the house and the entire village. He stares down at Ara, crouched at her little chopping board on the concrete. It's a contest of wills. She drops her paring knife in a clatter, and squeezes her fists. Her eyes lance into his, stabbing him with hatred. No, no, no. She has lost so much in life. She will not lose this battle. He will not rob her of her one remaining treasure. She keeps hanging in there, matching his glare moment by moment. How much longer can she stand this?

"Mother. Please!" It's Bezma who breaks the impasse, beside me at the foot of the steps. Then she adds something very hush-hush, which Hevar and I aren't supposed to hear, and I couldn't understand anyway, being in rapid Kurdish. She ends with a plaintive "please?"

And that does it. Instinctively, Ara does what any mother would do -- turns at the sound of her daughter's anguish. And that breaks the game of chicken between Ara and Hevar. She purses her lips and hunches over, as if she's received a hard punch in the stomach. It's over. She is broken.

"Good," says Hevar to Bezma, his posture softening. He brushes off his hands on his pants, as if finished with an unpleasant task, and draws a set of prayer beads from his pocket. Two at a time, click click, click click; he's more rattled than I would have expected, and now looks a little vulnerable, even though he's won. So -- despite all that bravado, he hadn't been totally certain of the outcome after all. He reaches down and gives Ara a little touch on the shoulder, perhaps an attempt at reconciliation. I almost like him, just for a moment, for the generosity of it. Then he jumps down from the porch and tosses an arm around Bezma's waist. She's much too big to lift up, but he gives a convincing try. He's not laughing. Nor is he overjoyed. He's dead serious — and extremely pleased with himself.

Bezma, though, is delirious, spinning around, whooping at the top of her lungs, ignoring the mourning black heap of her mother. "Hevar, Hevar!" His name is too delicious, too full of virile energy and promise, to stop repeating it.

I know that look of hers -- the pride of being claimed, the glory of being fought over, the triumph of being a trophy. I really, really hope that it works out better for her than it did for me.

❊ ❊ ❊

Damned flu. Every joint and organ aches, like being beaten up on the inside. A million needles poke at my skin; my eyes can barely focus. It's just a fever, like everybody else has. Jennifer has been absent for two days now. Pat and Khalil are failing fast; Layla is just getting over it. I go next door to Layla's before bedtime and knock.

"Can I still have that flu medicine you were talking about?"

Layla hastily knots the sash of her kimono. She is curiously flat without a bra, and girlish-looking with bare legs and feet — an endearing side to her I'd never noticed before. "Sure. Wait here."

She shuts the door, leaving me out in the drafty corridor, and I hear voices inside, one low, raspy, and coughing. She returns with a bottle of Nyquil. "Here. Bring back what you don't need tomorrow, okay? Somebody else still needs it too."

I shuffle back to bed, miffed at the attempt at secrecy. How clueless — or narrow-minded — does she think I am? And why does she think I'd even care who she had in there?

❊ ❊ ❊

Even with a double dose of the school nurse's Panadol, I barely slog through until mid-morning break, and collapse into one of the faculty room sofas. "Okay, geniuses. Everybody tell me how I should have handled this one."

They pass around a Kleenex box. "Your beloved Jaber again?" Jake asks.

"Nope. Kaka Karwan this time, one of the big linebacker types. He had his hands down his pants, and before I could say anything he finished himself off and wiped it all over Helin's sleeve. Which, of course, caused her to scream and run around the room. Which, in turn, earned me an instructive visit from Zaki advising me to stop the commotion. And an 'invitation' to his office again."

I get a round of applause. "You win, Twinkle Toes," says Jake. "Best story of week, hands down. No pun intended." He gets a few feeble groans.

"But wait. I'm not done. So when I get to his office, Zaki asks me what it was all about, and I tell him, expecting that he'll discipline Karwan. And guess what? He says, 'Miss Turner, you realize why all the students call him Kaka, don't you?' And of course I don't. And it turns out that Kaka means something like mister or sir, and Karwan happens to be the son of some big honcho in the government, which means that he can pretty much do as he damned well pleases in this school and nobody's going to say boo. Including all-powerful Zaki."

Jake sighs. "I've got a Kaka in one of my classes too. So that's why …" He stops as a ghost-like Jennifer slumps into the faculty room.

"Whoa, girl," Pat says. "You should have stayed home another day. Whatever you've got, it's way worse than what we've…"

"I wasn't sick." She's sniffing, though, and her eyes are puffy.

"Let me guess. Mother's on your case again for not being pregnant yet," Pat says dryly. She and I are getting tired of hearing about "Mother" bullying Jennifer.

"Worse. Much worse." She stares at her lap." My sister's husband shot her over the weekend."

I gasp, and the breath stays stuck inside me. "That's awful. But you have such good gun laws in England."

"Not that sister. Shahaz's sister here in Kurdistan. Her husband checked the messages on her phone, and saw something he didn't like, and accused her of cheating on him, which of course was utterly absurd. But she got so scared she couldn't say anything. She's like that — sweet and quiet. So then her husband got mad, and took one of his guns, and shot her right in the back. In the kitchen. Next to the refrigerator." She's choking on the words now, gulping back tears. "I was really close to her. She was the nicest of them all."

"Wait a minute," says Jake. "I'm getting confused. Your sister-in-law's husband killed her over a couple of text messages?"

"Yes, but that's not the worst of it. Because then Shahaz and his brothers stabbed the husband, practically to death. And if he dies, then it's blood or money."

"What do you mean?"

"When there's a murder, the dead person's family gets to choose if they want blood — a life for a life — or money. If they choose blood, they'll come after Shahaz and kill him." Jennifer shivers with dread. "We hope they want money. I couldn't live without my Shahaz. But if it's money, it'll be a lot."

"Maybe the guy will pull through. Or maybe the police will arrest him for killing his wife." Good thinking, Pat.

"But it doesn't work like that. The police stay out of honor killings." Jennifer has clearly considered the angles.

"You mean a man can kill someone and get away with it if she's his wife?" Jake whistles in amazement.

She nods. "And you know what else?" Her voice cracks now as she sobs into her kerchief. "To bring in that much money, I'll have no choice but to teach at this wretched place for the rest of my life! Even after I get pregnant, *in sh'allah*."

"You'd better say a whole bunch of those Muslim prayers of yours," Jake says sagely. "Because staying here many more years would be a fate worse than death."

* * *

163

Early Friday morning a week later, the text buzz on my phone wakes me up. "Yu come tday. Hevar come 2." Bezma's texts are getting a little more readable. Still, did she mean "too" or "2:00"? Either way, I can't make it.

"Not possible. I am going to Suley with friends."

"Yes come. Imprtnt." She always says that. Everything is important.

"Not possible. Leaving now."

Suley is local slang for Sulemani, a smallish city in Kurdistan close to the border with both Iran and Arab Iraq. It's supposed to be the most liberal place in the country, whatever that means. And now that we have all recovered from the flu, more or less, Jake has found us a clunker car to rent. We're doing a road trip — with Rabinowitz driving. He's back in town, teaching at one of the fly-by-night English schools, and Jake ran into him in a bar.

"They let that lunatic loose?" Pat is outraged.

"He must have cut a deal," says Jake. "And now he wants to see Suley and the Red Jail."

"You'd think he'd have had enough of Iraqi prisons," Pat snaps as we stow snacks in the back seat.

"He says this one is the worst of the worst," Jake replies. "The ultimate tourist must-see. Plus there's supposed to be a world-famous martini bar downtown. I can't miss this photo op — a selfie of me in front of a genuine Iraqi martini bar..."

I've spent the night before trying to reconcile the idea of doing anything with Rabinowitz. On the plus side, we're both from the Pacific Northwest, a big togetherness thing when you're overseas. And I've got to admire his guts, staying in Iraq after a jail stint. But on the minus side, I'm primed to detest him for the way he abandoned my students.

The plus side wins. Yet when we pick him up at a seedy hotel downtown, he's even worse than expected — slovenly, fleshy and cocky. From the pallor of his skin, he probably hasn't eaten anything fresh for months. Claiming he's trying to blend in, he wears a local safari-style vest with pockets all over it, a black-checked Peshmerga scarf knotted around his neck, and the wool cap over dreadlocks Madame had complained about. He reeks of pot and unwashed hair. Jake doesn't seem to notice.

"Hey, bro. Lead us to the pits of hell. Let's make a party of it." Jake rips open a bag of Doritos and passes it around to kick off our adventure. Rabinowitz scoots in behind the wheel and empties half of the chips into his lap. Then he honks his way into the muddle of traffic, and starts pontificating as we head out of town, mostly to Jake. I get the feeling that Pat and I are irrelevant, invited mostly to share the expenses.

"Let me prepare you for the Red Jail experience," he begins. "Think Auschwitz. It's Saddam at his most ruthless. But then consider this." He raises a finger like some B-movie detective. "Who built Saddam's chemical weapons plants? An American company! I kid you not…"

As we career down the highway toward the south, he regales us with stories about Al Anfal, and how the U.S. was complicit through inaction. How we made obscene amounts of money arming Saddam as our ally during the Iran-Iraq war, and then turned a blind eye when he used our weapons — our tanks, our bombs, even our poison gas! — on minorities like the Kurds and Christians. How immoral the two U.S. Gulf Wars had been — oil, oil, oil. In the first war, we invaded to prop up a rapacious so-called royalty in Kuwait, and for what? Only to return a second time, leaving the entire region in a mess, still simmering even though our troops are almost gone.

I'm starting to sense that only three of the Americans in the car are personally guilty. Rabinowitz is absolved because of his attitude, his tone seems to say.

"But let's be fair." Pat leans between the front seats to protest. "It was the U.S. that finally set up a no-fly zone over

Kurdistan. That's the only reason many of the Kurds are alive today. And it was the Americans who got rid of Saddam."

"Only for their oil," Rabinowitz continues in a well-rehearsed spiel. "And greed, of course. Are we doing anything today when Sudan is doing something similar? Of course not, because Sudan doesn't have oil, or anything else we want. America is the greediest of the greedy, the slimiest in the swamp, when you scratch beneath the P.R. crap."

"So what would you suggest?" A bump jostles Pat forward, and she clings to the front seats for support. "I mean, it's so easy to blame. But it's another thing to find a better solution." Hurrah for Pat.

"Revolution. A return of the authentic Muslim civilization." He sounds too blithe to be serious.

"How old are you, Rabinowitz?" I venture. "All of twenty-four or something?" Okay, maybe pulling the age card isn't fair. But this guy seriously bugs me.

"Twenty-three," he answers huffily. "But I've studied world politics in great depth."

"Like at college in Oregon?" I immediately regret the cheap shot, but doubt that he'll notice it. Pat does though. She winks.

"AND in Pakistan before coming here."

"You lived there?" Despite my distaste, I'm dying of curiosity.

"Yeah, he camped up in the mountains with the Taliban or something. Or Al Qaida. Right, Binny? That's where you became a raghead?" Jake pokes him on the shoulder. Could he be tipsy this early in the morning?

"I learned Arabic, and the Quran, yes. But I wish you'd shut your trap about ragheads, Jake. It's effing offensive."

"Okay, rag-throat in your case, with that goofy bandana. Ha ha."

166

Rabinowitz lets it pass; he's got plenty more damning stories to tell us about our home country. He regales us with a lecture on the Japanese perfecting the first usage of biological warfare, killing millions in northern China. And then those same diseases and delivery methods — smallpox, meningitis, diphtheria, and even the plague — amazingly showed up in the 1950's -- used by the U.S. in North Korea. How had we gotten the germs? From the Japanese scientists, of course. The Japanese officers in charge of the biological weapons were never prosecuted for war crimes. Instead, they were hired -- hired! -- by Uncle Sam, and paid handsomely for their secrets. He's seen it all on an Al Jazeera documentary. And there is more...

Pat shoots me one of those looks. This is going to be a very long four-hour drive to Suley -- and then four hours back tomorrow. What good luck that she and I are both in the back seat, can morph into invisible older females and concentrate on our Sudokus.

* * *

Rabinowitz' Arabic is really pretty good, to my irritation -- or, more honestly, to my envy. How dare he have learned such a difficult language so quickly, when I taught for five long years in Saudi Arabia and can only remember the basics? Yet his skills sure come in handy at the roadblocks that crop up every twenty minutes or so. We'll be humming along through barren rocky wasteland, terrain that resembles the foothills of Nevada, following dun-colored ridges where no living creature could possibly exist, and run into a couple of beefy local soldiers with a pole swung down across the road. Rabinowitz (I refuse on principle to call him Binny) rolls down his window and starts shooting the breeze. The Peshmerga speak Kurdish and understand a smattering of Arabic, and Rabinowitz speaks the reverse. To my astonishment, it works. The soldiers pretend to read the English in our passports, study our local visas, nod solemnly, and motion us to pass. The roadblocks appear so frequently that Jake starts keeping our passports and visas stashed and rubber-banded together in the glove box.

Under steely skies, we drive mile after mile through undulating shades of brown; it's like a palette where the artist forgot to bring all his colors. Sandy brown cliffs, dusty brown plains studded with reddish brown boulders, dried grey-brown streambeds — yet there's an unmistakable drama to it. Steven Spielberg could film a great heroic scene here, with Mongol hordes or Old Testament throngs coursing down the hills' flanks, and only the rare house or village to PhotoShop out.

"We'll have lunch like Kurdish workmen," Rabinowitz announces when at long last we pull into the heart of Suley. It's mostly a low-lying jumble of run-down shops, with a three-story office structure here and there. He parks and uses his cultural homing device to find us an unmarked eatery.

"Are you sure it's okay?" Pat asks warily. "I don't see any women in there."

"No problem." He leads us to a metal table alongside guys fresh from a construction site, their coveralls stained with paint and oil, who very courteously ignore Pat and me. Behind us is an entire soccer team, sweaty and raucous in Barcelona and Manchester jerseys, banging the table in a post-game glow.

Without ordering, food appears -- a quarter of a roasted chicken each, white rice, tomato-bean soup, and fresh tomatoes. A turbaned fellow cruises the place with pizza-sized flatbreads draped over his arm, flipping down a few more when our stack gets low, and recycling them to another table when we're done. The whole thing costs $11 for the four of us, including bottomless glasses of tea.

"This was great!" My resistance to Rabinowitz is starting to melt, just the most infinitesimal bit.

168

He snickers. I can almost hear him saying, "I told you so."

✻ ✻ ✻

Sodden skies finally break into a chilly drip, and we hop puddles to the Red Jail, a poorly marked compound in the heart of the town. We'd driven past it twice without recognizing it. The high walls topped with razor wire and a flag resemble so many other Middle Eastern government buildings — until getting inside.

The Red Jail is not exactly a museum. It's more like a raw artifact, with everything left exactly how it stood when Saddam's regime fell. Bullet holes still pockmark the walls. Rows of tanks rust outside in clumps of weeds. None of us say anything. The awfulness of every square inch makes me want to gag. We don't need signs to explain how many Kurds were tortured to death here, or how many were shot in the quad. We recognize it in the marrow of our bones. It's that bad.

"Saddam built the Red Jail during Al Anfal as a holding tank for Kurds before transferring them to Abu Ghraib for execution," Rabinowitz explains in a hush. "Just being born a Kurd was enough to get you put here. Think about that. Your birth. The womb you ended up in. Something you had absolutely no control over."

We nod; we get it. But he continues. "You guys think before you get here that you understand how ghastly this was. You're liberals who have read books and seen movies about torture. But you can't really *know* it until you walk around a place like this. Am I right?"

Unfortunately, he is. Nothing could have prepared me for this misery. I shrink down into my raincoat in shame for the sheltered life I've lived, for all that I've taken for granted, and for the conceit that let me think I could fathom the depth of the agony that went on here.

We stumble through empty hallways and read gruesome explanations. One hundred prisoners crammed into a single cement cell with no running water. Only a rag to serve as a cloak against the cold -- the same rag that served as your bed and pillow and blanket at night. A cheap plastic bowl for your food and water, the kind used to feed a stray dog. A single light bulb. The children's cell held 80, and was the size of a small apartment bedroom. Eighty kids? What were kids doing in a prison anyway, separated from their mothers in such squalor? And kept here for months on end?

I expected crude graffiti, but instead see *Allah* written inside the cells. On one wall, an unknown prisoner had sketched the outline of a Kurdish mountain peak. My heart tugs like the artist's must have every time he saw it.

As the others proceed to the torture chamber with its meat racks, I stay behind at the women's cell and try to assimilate it. It's all too easy to imagine Ara here, shivering under one of these soiled rags. Or Old Houda, elbowing space so she could help birth a baby in this fetid place. Or me! What if it had been me here, straining to hear the feeble voice of my son behind bars in the next cell. A wretched desolation throttles me, and the imagined not-so-distant past melds with the dreary present in this empty, echoey dankness.

The misery suffocates; the heaviness clogs; my psyche becomes a grey block of concrete, like the floor of the prison itself, immobilized, as the months, the years of tears and blood soak down and in. I'm a drop in the ocean of human suffering, just a mere drop, helpless to fight against it, although I desperately want to. How does any one stay afloat in such a sea of despair? How does a person find the will to live for even one more hour when body and soul are saturated beyond endurance with fear?

I do not know. I honestly cannot figure out how human beings persist in the face of such evil -- inflicted systematically, unnecessarily, deliberately, by fellow humans. It goes beyond all logic, beyond what one would expect in the biology of a species. And yet, this cruelty keeps cropping up all over the world, throughout time. Not just Kurdistan, but Rwanda, Cambodia, Bataan, Germany -- practically everywhere. How can a person deal with the guilt of their entire species?

I try to take some photos that will capture the essence of it for my blog, realizing at the same time that no picture could do this place justice.

❊   ❊   ❊

Leaving the silence of the Red Jail, we stare at one another like wooden totem poles, grim and dark. "I hope you're a little more thankful for the freedoms of America now, Rabinowitz," Pat says pointedly as we start toward the car.

"Freedoms?" It's a verbal pounce, an instantaneous pole vault from gloom into rage. "Freedoms? Did I hear somebody mention Gitmo? Or Abu Ghraib?" His bitterness frightens me. "Oh yeah, virtuous Americans would never stoop to something so low as the Red Jail. Who do you think you're kidding? Don't get me started. You want to hear how we invented water boarding on freedom fighters in the Philippines a hundred years ago? Or how we trained the goon squads for our puppet Pinochet? How about the slave labor we orchestrated for United Fruit in Central America..."

"Stop it. Just stop." I want to strangle him. "I can't take this right now."

"Me either," says Pat. We storm away from them, across broken sidewalks, under tangled power lines criss-crossing over our heads, and wait for them beside the car. "I'm really regretting who holds the car keys right now," she says. "Too bad we can't leave the guys here overnight on their own and hitchhike home."

"Want to split a taxi?" This is way out of character. After my Wells Fargo debacle, I rarely even spring for a cab to The Fortress downtown.

"It's probably a hundred bucks, and I don't know where we'd even find a taxi or a bus to take us that far. But it would be worth it. Oh man, would it be worth it."

When the guys reach the car, however, Jake surprises us. "Hey, girlfriends. I was just telling Binny, it's okay by me if we skip the martini bar." It's a huge concession. He's been talking about that bar ever since our trip started taking shape.

"Same with going to Halabja tomorrow," I say quickly. "No more death. Please."

"Let's forget about staying overnight then and just go home." Jake adds in his best falsetto, "I think I feel a slight headache coming on."

Dusk is upon us. Rain is falling again. This is no time to be setting out onto treacherous unmarked roads, riddled with roadblocks and potholes and wandering flocks of sheep and goats. Still, sitting together in a tense, damp car in questionable mechanical condition is way better than staying around this town, which now feels as chemically polluted by both Sadaam and Rabinowitz as Halabja once had been.

We pile in. We pass around dried dates and Pringles and Coke from a minimart. I do my best to tune out Rabinowitz droning on about his conversion to Islam, the truest religion in the world, the religion of peace, the obvious answer to capitalism, imperialism, consumerism and racism. Then he waxes eloquent about his upcoming trip to Baghdad to get engaged, sight unseen, to a guaranteed virgin found for him by some brother in the jihad. It's the virgin part that he emphasizes the most. Oh lovely. Poor girl.

Jake's all ears. "What's it like, Binny, getting engaged to someone you've never met? Are you cutting off your dreadlocks before the wedding? Taking a bath? How old is she, anyway?"

"Sixteen." For some reason, it sounds like he's bragging.

"*Sixteen*? Oh my God. Binny, you're robbing the cradle. That's almost like one of our students. Even I wouldn't think..."

"Mohammed's favorite wife was nine years old when he married her." He's getting sulky.

"What kind of logic is that?" I can't help myself. I remember how innocent I was at nine, worried about getting VD -- or maybe even pregnant -- from a kiss or the water in a swimming pool.

The guys in front ignore me.

"Jeez Louise. Can she even read and write? No, seriously, Binny, think about this. What if she doesn't like sex? What if she cries for her mother? What if she has super-bad acne or a harelip?" And then Jake has a real stroke of brilliance. "Wait, I figured it out. She's gotta be as ugly and smelly as you are, right? Why else would any father in the world let some not-exactly-wealthy American convert like you take away his daughter?"

All he gets is an exasperated cough in reply. But Jake isn't done.

"Hey, you probably have to pay a dowry, right? Where's that gonna come from? Prying minds want to know."

Rabinowitz stares far off down the road. "As a matter of fact, that's a minor detail I'm still sorting out. Kurds don't usually do dowries. But this girl's a bona fide Arab. And Arab girls like this one don't come cheap."

"You probably couldn't get a Kurd though. Is that it?"

"I need a wife who will be as committed as I am to Islam and the Cause. Similarly, that's why this girl's father and brother have said yes — because I'm willing to prove myself for the Cause." The way he says "similarly" gives me the impression that he's practiced his defense. "So it's a dowry or the equivalent. I'm working hard on the equivalent."

Pat and I share a glance, close our eyes and lean against our respective cold dark windows, pretending not to hear. Did we really come from the same country as this immature retard? Neither of us speaks the whole way back.

※ ※ ※

"Treeza, you not here. You miss!"

I've survived another week of school, which helped me recover from Rabinowitz and the jail, and am visiting the village for another Friday lunch. I've barely gotten the Blue Angel inside the gate before Bezma starts hugging me and dragging me up to the porch. "I engage. Look! Look!"

Out comes the scarlet velvet box filled with the gold I'd seen before, but now even fuller. I ooh and aah over a matched set of twelve gold bangles, several heavy chains and ruby-studded dangle earrings.

She preens over a tiny gold ring with the letter "H" on her finger. "Hevar come and you gone. Family Hevar come too, many more this time. Old Houda talk my mother. Mother say yes, to all family Hevar. *Al ham du l'illah!*"

I embrace her. Who could resist such euphoria? I wonder if Rabinowitz' fiancee is this happy -- I hope so. Every woman deserves to be this radiant at least once in her life.

The details come bubbling out. The engagement party had happened then and there. Rather than a grand ceremony in a rented hall, they went to a little patch of meadow outside the village, and had a modest feast that Hevar's mother brought, spread out on sheets on the ground. They danced to music from Hevar's truck.

I'm devastated. It happened without me? How is it possible that I was suffering through Rabinowitz instead of being here for the second-most-triumphant day of Bezma's life?

"Wedding much more big," she assures me. "I get white dress, like America. And we get photographer. This is dream."

I kick off my shoes and look for Ara inside. Bezma follows, chattering away. "Hevar wonderful man. He say I am beautiful. He love my eyes. He say okay about burns on arms. He love me so much, he say yes for everything my mother want."

"So he'll let you finish college?"

"Yes, college. Also teach here, in village. We stay in house of my mother until family Hevar make house for us." She waves vaguely — there's plenty of vacant land on the outskirts of town to put up a house — and then laughs at herself when the motion causes her scarf to slip off.

Back in the gloom of the kitchen, Ara sits on the floor beside a propane-fired griddle making flatbread for the week. I've seen her serving these wafers before; she sprinkles them with water before a meal, to make them a little softer and less brittle. The greyish dough spits and crackles as she stretches it wider and wider across the dome, bigger than my bicycle wheel. She stacks them onto a round metal stand to dry, away from mice. Above her head, a battered wooden cradle hangs suspended from the ceiling, awaiting another grandchild. The propane tank, the rough wooden cradle, the hand-woven thatching, one above the next — the combination makes me cringe at the thought of fire.

"Can I help?"

She shakes her head without looking up. She may have agreed to the wedding, but nobody's going to force her to be pleasant about it.

"I'd like to learn."

No. She sniffs, twice.

"Ara, maybe it is good that Bezma will be a bride." At Bezma's insistence, *bo-ook*, bride, has been one of my early vocabulary words. I'm able to create a basic sentence now too.

"No. *Zor zor krappa*." Very, very bad. She wipes her face with the back of her hand.

"But Bezma no go. Bezma school here. Bezma children here, your house." I do my best to say it in Kurdish, wishing I knew even a few more phrases or tenses. I want to explain the value of an education, the power of a woman being able to earn a living and support herself and her children, just in case. With my feeble language skills, I can't even tell whether she gets my drift.

"*Krappa. Krappa. Krappa.*" The final word. With tongs, she lifts the flatbread, not even wincing at the heat. "Hevar *zor krappa*. Wedding *zor krappa*. Man *zor krappa*." She simplifies the sentences so I understand loud and clear.

This is one obstinate woman. I give up and sit there while she cooks. I watch the dust motes filter in between the burglar bars on the window; my pulse settles slowly, as I let go of taking sides. My breath finally becomes even. My mind wanders as her griddle pops.

"Ara, what if women have been sitting like us right here on this same spot, talking about similar things while they cook, for thousands of years? What if none of it changes? Children, marriages, all of it? What if everything just happens over and over again, in your country, in my country? And we women are just little pawns being pushed around the stage?" My Kurdish isn't half good enough to convey this, of course. But I give it a shot with basic words and a lot of grand gesturing.

She throws me a quizzical look; she's not quite ready to be cajoled out of her foul mood. Plus, what I said probably came out as nonsense.

"Well, thanks for letting me sit here with you anyway."

She may be illiterate, unrefined, and hard as nails when she makes up her mind. But in a way, I envy her her certitude. She's so grounded in place. So bitter, yet also accepting of her fate. So thoroughly sure of herself.

Six: Heating Up

AFTERNOONS ARE getting warm now, and it's harder to maintain order after the kids eat lunch. The Silent Game isn't working. Even putting masking tape on Jaber's mouth for a minute doesn't stop his chattering for long, or teach the other kids by example. On the right side of the chalkboard, the detention list stretches embarrassingly long. (What teacher worth her salt has to resort to detentions? Well, I am one of that sorry lot these days.) Things are at an all-time low when I lose my temper with little Seema, my one bridge between the village and The Fortress. In exasperation, I write her up along with the rest.

She hangs back after class, and waits while the more assertive kids try to wheedle me out of their detentions. "It wasn't me you saw unwrapping the candy. Really, Miss. It was Dilan." "It wasn't a gigantic poop sound you heard, Miss, it was a chair sliding on the floor." Right. And I was born before the Flood.

But Seema is different. She is usually too respectful to get a detention.

"Okay, Seema," I ask after the room had emptied. "So what's your excuse?"

"No excuse, Miss." Her posture conveys total despondency, or perhaps shame.

"Oh come on. Everybody else had one." Deep down, I want her to come up with some justification for having hit Helin during the spelling quiz. It would be a shame to ruin her perfect record.

"I deserved it, Miss. You were right to punish me."

In my long years of teaching and parenting, I've rarely heard anything like this. "Let's sit down." We drag two of the plastic student chairs close together, and I scoot them side by side, to feel less confrontational. "No, tell me what's going on."

"Nothing."

I wait. The air conditioner cycles, rattles, does its little asthmatic pshhh. The corridor gradually quiets. I wait even longer.

When finally she finds words, she directs them to the floor. "Miss, tell me what it was like when you had *khatana*. Nobody will tell me. I asked Helin, and she just laughed and said I'm filthy."

I freeze. Be careful. This could be tricky.

"Seema, women in my country don't get cut."

She sucks a short inhale and her eyes widen in disbelief. "YOU were never cut, Miss?"

"Of course not. And neither were my sisters, or my mother, or aunts, or grandmothers or girlfriends. Nobody that I know back home is cut, for that matter. Nobody -- in America, or Canada, or all of Europe. It is unheard of."

"Why not?" She's trying to tell whether I'm pulling her leg.

"Well, we don't think it's necessary. Or a good idea." Better not to mention that a lot of people don't even know such a practice exists.

"Oh. Well, my mother didn't have it done on me when I was small. She was waiting. I don't know why. But then she died, and I went to live with Grandmother. And now, being in the village, there's no choice…" She twists her feet around one

180

another and swings them back and forth while digesting an idea. "You aren't joking me, are you, Miss?"

"I wouldn't do that. Are they going to cut you? Is that what this is about?"

She tosses her head violently; I can't tell if she means 'no' or doesn't want to talk. She leaps up, grabs her bulging backpack, and bolts to the door.

"Should I talk to Old Houda about it?" I call after her. "Maybe she'd listen to me…"

As the door swings shut, she yells over her shoulder. "She'd never listen to someone who's unclean!" The sound of her running echoes down the empty hall. Similarly, her words echo in my mind long after I walk down the hall myself. Bezma must have kept my disgraceful clitoral condition a secret. But will Seema? And if she tells the rest of the village — or the other kids at The Fortress — will it matter?

❀ ❀ ❀

Once the other expats hear about our Red Jail adventure, they all want to go on a road trip. There are immediate problems. First, nobody wants the hassle of renting a car. Second, nobody has the guts to drive. Third, the Westerners can't speak Kurdish or Arabic to read road signs. Fourth, most cars hold five people at the most, and about 20 teachers want to go.

We road-trip veterans sit tight and wait for a plan to emerge. To our surprise, it's Khalil who organizes the next adventure. He and Layla invite Pat, Jake, Rabinowitz and me on a day outing to Shaqlawa.

"But that's six people," I protest. "Let's scratch Rabinowitz. He doesn't even work here any more."

"And he's a royal pain in the ass," Pat adds, to my relief.

"We want Binny to drive. We can all squeeze." Layla is at her most effervescent, with newly threaded eyebrows and lush false lashes. "All of the fruit trees up in Shaqlawa will be in bloom. We can grab food for a picnic and walk to the old monastery hidden up in a cave." Her breathy excitement is infectious. Pat and I lose.

Shaqlawa, a resort town, lies in the mountains. My students make it sound like paradise; whenever we talk about their favorite destinations, Shaqlawa is always up there with Disney World. I imagine something like the Swiss Alps, with grassy meadows, wild flowers and footpaths meandering to pristine waterfalls.

"Buy dried apricots there, Miss," they urge when I tell them about the expedition. "And figs. They make a special candy with nuts, too." My Christian students became ecstatic at the mention of Shaqlawa; it has been Christian since Roman times, and they speak with a pride of ownership.

Jake gets the dubious honor of sitting up front with Rabinowitz again. That means that Pat, Layla, Khalil and I have to cram into the back. The air conditioning doesn't work, and the car's shocks are shot. We start bouncing as soon as we hit the open road. Khalil, dapper in skinny jeans and a barely buttoned shirt, slips one hand around Layla's shoulder, and sneaks the other onto her fetching little knee. Pat notices right away.

"Whoa -- aren't you two the lovebirds." Wink wink.

The hand remains on the shoulder. Giggle giggle.

Jake glances back. "Well I'll be damned. Right under Madame's nose. How long has this been going on?"

Layla titters. In tight white jeans, a gauzy blouse, hair loose down her back and a frothy scarf looped around her neck, she could be a co-ed in California out on a first date. After a week of kids in uniforms, her saucy femininity is a balm to the soul.

"'And spring arose on the garden fair; like the spirit of love felt everywhere; and each flower and herb on earth's dark breast rose from the dreams of its wintry rest.'" Khalil's voice comes dreamily from over by the window.

"Is that some obscure Egyptian poet?" Jake asks.

"Nope. Shelley. I did a thesis on him once."

"You mean, like a master's thesis?" I had assumed he was fresh out of college.

"He's saving up to finish his doctorate," Layla explains, practically boasting. "At Cambridge. That's why he's here in Kurdistan."

"Well I'll be damned." Jake whistles. "You rock, kid."

"Layla, don't you have a son who went to Cambridge too?" Pat sneaks it in innocently, but I know where she's headed.

"No, London School of Economics. He's an investment banker."

"Oh, I see…"

"Jesus Christ!" A gargantuan semi truck barrels down straight toward us in our lane, passing another semi, blaring his horn nonstop. Rabinowitz swears, jams on the brakes, and swerves onto the shoulder. "Turks!" He honks over and over in frustration. "God damned Turks. They're everywhere. What do they think they're doing here, anyway?"

"How do you know it was a Turk?" Jake beats me to the question. Rabinowitz shifts violently and jolts us back onto the road. It takes him several miles of furious silence to reply.

"The bastard Turks slaughtered over two million Armenians in their own country. You all heard about that, right?"

Pat and I gave him an "mm-hmm." Khalil and Layla are off in their own private world.

"And you know how they did it? They got a bunch of Kurds to do the dirty work for them. Some of it, anyway. They paid the Kurds, gave them guns, and let them take over the Armenians' houses and farms when the dirty deed was done."

He's taking curves much more aggressively now, like a frustrated racecar driver.

"And then, get this. After the Kurds helped massacre the Armenians for them, the Turks went and made being Kurdish illegal. They outlawed having a Kurdish name. They stopped using Kurdish in schools. They went so far as to say that Kurds didn't even exist -- they were just 'mountain Turks.' AND they've been bombing Kurds for decades, claiming that the freedom fighters are terrorists."

"Oh Lord, Binny," says Jake." Don't make us listen to this stuff again."

"You asked, didn't you? How did I know it was a Turk? Well, obviously I knew because he was acting like a freaking idiot. That's how." Then, after several more tense miles, "You're aware that this very week, the Turks have been bombing so-called Kurdish terrorists on the *Iraqi* side of the mountains? That should be considered a violation of international law. And, need I add, that Uncle Sam supports our good friends the Turks? Hah. You can tell a man's character by the company he keeps. Who said that? Anyway, look at America's friends in the Middle East. Fascist Turkey. Nazi Israel."

Pat fires a look across at me. I can hear her asking whether we should be judged for keeping company with Rabinowitz.

"And corrupt Saudi Arabia?" Jake adds much too sweetly. "You forgot to mention them..."

"Leave Saudi Arabia out of this," Rabinowitz snaps. "They're the keepers of Holy Islam."

"Oh yeah. I forgot." Jake bats his eyelashes at the back-seat peanut gallery.

What a relief to finally pull into Shaqlawa after several hours and get out of the car. But where is the wonderland? The town is just another dusty collection of flat-topped shops with the ubiquitous chicken rotisseries, shwarma stands, poles with

Chinese-made acrylic sweaters dangling overhead, and cheap luggage piled for sale on the sidewalk. Careful observation, though, shows dried-fruit vendors on the two main streets, and a few ice cream shops for holiday-goers. The resort "chalets" are one-room cinder-block cabins thrown up alongside the river bank. A person would have to be desperate from the summer heat in Mosul or Baghdad to call this a paradise.

The surroundings, though, take my breath away. Shaqlawa lies sheltered beneath towering Mount Safeen, more like a long ridge than a peak, in neck-craning splendor. And blanketing the hillsides stretch endless acres of wildflowers — scarlet poppies, tiny yellow buttercuppy splotches, and lupine-like purples, much thicker and brighter than the plains surrounding The Fortress. Birds flutter over the meadows too; we've stepped into a travel poster for New Zealand.

"If you think this is something, you ought to see the Zagros Mountains between here and Iran," brags Rabinowitz. "They're 12,000 feet high, covered in snow, and you go through these huge ravines to get there, with waterfalls…"

"Let's hike," I interrupt. "Let's find that monastery." What I really mean is, let's get where we can feel fresh air on our cheeks instead of being wedged in this stuffy, contentious car.

"My shoes are hopeless," Layla whimpers. It's true; the prissy high heels that make her butt curve so gracefully will never make it on a dirt path, much less inside a dark cave. "Khalil and I will just stay here and wait for you. If it's okay with everybody else."

It's fine. Khalil isn't into monasteries that much anyway, he assures us. And we could use some space in the back seat. So we leave the Egyptian couple in town. We Americans spend the next three hours driving unmarked dirt roads, hurtling around the gullies and outcroppings of Mount Safeen, looking for some someplace that had supposedly been a Christian

185

pilgrimage site in 400 AD. Rabinowitz gets testier with each wrong turn.

We ramble alongside orchards heavy with blossoms, abuzz here and there with home-constructed apiaries. There are plenty of caves, and plenty of paths that look like they go to caves, but no signs telling us which is the right one. It's probably over 95 degrees, and with no trees as we get higher up on the slopes, there's no shade. Nobody suggests getting out to test any of the paths.

"You guys sure this place really exists?" Rabinowitz finally asks.

"Uh, not really," says Pat. "I read something about it a couple of months ago on the Internet." I groan. The guys curse.

By the time we make it back to Shaqlawa, it's too late to ask for directions. And we've stupidly forgotten to bring a lunch. We cruise up and down the two streets, now shuttered in the late afternoon, hot, thirsty and cranky, looking for Layla and Khalil.

"Maybe they gave up waiting and took a taxi back home," I suggest.

"Maybe they're at the No-Tell Motel," Rabinowitz says with a snide edge.

And indeed, there they are, emerging from a side street with several modest hotels, fresh and bright-eyed and grinning. They have obviously not been walking outside in the heat all this time.

"Oh, what a delightful town this is." Layla scrambles in after Khalil, hauling an oversized purse onto her lap, and glows in our direction. "We explored every little nook and cranny."

Rabinowitz revs the engine and jerks into first gear. "I'll bet you did. I mean, I'll bet Khalil did." From Jake, it would have been comic and prurient. From Rabinowitz, it slices like a knife.

"Cool it, Binny," says Jake. "Who are you to talk? You haven't exactly lived a life of virtue. Nor have any of us, I suspect."

"That was before I became a Muslim."

A little gasp comes from Layla's side of the seat. Khalil's thigh tenses next to mine. "Look, Rabinowitz old chap, there's no need to…"

"Don't 'old chap' me, you hypocrite," he snarls. "Are you Muslim or not? Tell me the truth."

"Of course I am." There's a slight tremor beneath Khalil's gentlemanly tone.

"And your little hottie girlfriend there. Is she Muslim too?"

It's a rhetorical question that needs no answer.

"And one more thing, Mr. Cambridge scholar. Wasn't your sweetheart *married* back home? And doesn't she have a *son* who's older than you are?" You'd think Perry Mason was storming back and forth in the front seat.

"Rabinowitz, this is none of your business." Thank you, Pat. "It's none of OUR business. You know that old saying? What goes on in Shaqlawa, stays in Shaqlawa." It's a feeble joke, but I give her an A for effort.

A long pause. "I've always had a soft spot in my heart for that particular saying, girlfriend," Jake says finally. "What happens in Bali, Bangkok, Budapest. You name it."

But Rabinowitz won't let up. "Listen up, everybody. I will quote. 'For those who keep from evil are Gardens with their Lord, beneath which rivers flow wherein they will abide, and pure companions, and contentment from Allah. Allah is Seer of all that His servants do.' That's not Shelley, buddy. That's from the Holy Quran."

"Duh, dude," says Jake. "As if any of us cares."

Pat leans over to whisper to me. "The new convert is always the worst bigot. Ever hear *that* old saying?"

It's awfully quiet over in Layla's corner, like she has vanished and turned into a rack holding up the enormous handbag. I reach across Khalil and pat her leg; we don't all agree with Rabinowitz, even if we won't argue with him. She keeps staring out her window, but Khalil puts his hand over mine in silent thanks.

It takes forever to reach The Fortress, given the white-knuckle atmosphere. And things don't sound so good in the apartment next door once we get back, either. The low murmuring and crying go on for hours, until one of them finally turns on the TV and I don't have to listen to it anymore.

In the faculty room the next week, though, we make our trip sound like a five-star event. Getting lost on the wild slopes of Mount Safeen becomes uproarious. There's no one to tone down the stories, though, because Layla and Khalil stop coming in except to get books.

Over our rum and Cokes at night on the patio, Pat and I pity the teachers at Rabinowitz's new school, wherever that is -- and speculate about why Jake brought him back in our lives in the first place.

"I can't get him out of my mind — the way he kept turning rabid on us," I say between sips. "I hate how he makes me off-kilter and defensive. What do you think makes him tick?"

"Who cares? Just another miserable expat gone nuts. You see it all the time." We gaze out at the weeds, now weaving knee-high through the chain link fence.

"No, I'm serious. You've known him longer than I have. You started teaching with him back in September. What do you think his game is?"

Pat jabs thoughtfully at her ice cubes. "Well, when he got here he was definitely strangeola. Weird, in a neo-hippy hate-America sort of way. Challenging everything Madame wanted us to do. We were worried for him, because he'd never managed a classroom before."

"I could have told you that after ten minutes with the kids he left me."

"Yeah, lucky you. Anyway, there was something different about his oddness, even at the start. Madame tried to get me to befriend him and tell her what was going on. She said she didn't like loose cannons on her staff."

I nod. I wouldn't have wanted to supervise him either. "So what's up with this Iraqi fiancee? You think that's why he bailed from the Academy? Because he couldn't find a girlfriend and got so horny that it made him desperate?"

"I can't figure it out myself. For a while I was pretty sure he and Jake were an item. They spent a lot of time together when we all got here, so naturally I assumed... But I must have been wrong. Unless Rabinowitz swings both ways."

This is an idea that needs to brew. "Jake's so fastidious. It's hard to imagine him being intimate with a slob like Rabinowitz."

"Rabinowitz always claimed that rolling deodorant all over his shirt and stomach worked better than taking a bath." She shakes her head in mock disbelief, and we have a good laugh at his expense. "But as for Jake? Beggars can't be choosers in a place like this." She does that wry eyebrow thing that cracks me up.

"You know, Pat, sometimes I can't believe that we're here. Two women, alone at our age, hanging out with characters like these -- people we never would have spent two seconds with back home. Isn't it a riot?"

"A riot indeed." She adds more rum to her glass.

"So let's say that, heaven forbid, Rabinowitz happened to be your son, or mine. What if we'd held him as a little baby, and changed his diapers, and taught him how to tie his shoes? How would we treat him now?"

"Bite your tongue, woman. I'd shoot myself."

"That's what I mean. We'd feel guilty about all that anger he's got. We'd hear him spouting this wacko fundamentalist Muslim stuff, and try to help him. Maybe even force him to take a bath so he could get a regular girlfriend."

She peers over the rims of her glasses. "I've got plenty of problems of my own."

"Okay, I'll put it another way. I don't want to understand him for his benefit. I want to do it for my own sake, so I don't carry around the weight of this resentment." But something else is swimming to the surface, dark and dangerous, a concern I've barely had the nerve to put into words, even in my own mind.

"Pat, what if he does something really stupid in the future? Like becoming a suicide bomber. I know, it sounds unlikely. Al Qaeda's been quiet in Iraq since the war supposedly ended. And Rabinowitz wouldn't get married if he was planning to be a martyr. But still, what if he did? Wouldn't we be guilty if we hadn't taken the time to figure him out? There's got to be a reason for him being such a brute."

Pat frowns. "I, for one, am not my brother's keeper. Rabinowitz has been at least partially unhinged for a long time. If you let his nonsense bother you, then it's your own fault when you feel bad."

"Yeah, you're probably right." But I can't totally agree, even when Jake tells me something similar later in the week. My worry won't go away. I continue to try to see some good in Rabinowitz, the good that his own mother would recognize, even when the universe fails to deliver handy insights.

※　※　※

It's April already, and Friday again. When I park my bicycle at Ara's, it's just her and Old Houda there. Although the muezzin's loudspeaker blasted about fifteen minutes ago as I

190

approached the village, the two women have decided that now is time for prayers. They each roll out a flimsy cloth on the carpet, cover in big scarves they produce from a nail on the wall, line up approximately in the direction of Mecca, and start murmuring and bowing. I offer to leave; no, they're happy if I just sit there and ignore them — down on their knees, foreheads to the floor, up again, standing, bowing, down on the floor again. Each woman seems in a world of her own, although they do everything in unison, voices low, talking privately with God. The proximity of holiness in their everyday life is so soothing; they take this ritual so thoroughly for granted. I promise myself to try harder to memorize the *Surah al Fatihah*. It would make them so happy.

As I watch them, the world becomes a little more sacred and balanced — something I desperately need. It's been a mess all week. Jennifer stopped showing up, even though we heard that her brother-in-law survived the stabbing. We've pitched in to babysit her classes, despite having no idea what to do with kindergarteners. And my own classes are more fractious, the kids less patient with the mandated grammar drills and spelling lists filled with tricky words like "harbinger." Emotionally, I'm spent.

When they're done with prayers, Ara goes to work on lunch, and Houda adjusts her snowy scarf, then tugs the air chiller into the doorway. The chiller resembles a bale of hay in a metal frame. A garden hose drips water onto the hay, and a fan forces air through it into the room. It looks weird, but it works; within minutes, the room is no longer a kiln.

I've been waiting all week to be alone with the old midwife. Gulp.

"Houda, would you tell me about cutting? I know it's none of my business. But..." But what? There's really no good excuse for prying.

I expect resistance or maybe embarrassment. Instead she fixes her deep green eyes on me, as if assessing my intentions, sighs patiently, and pulls a string of beads from inside her dress.

"*Khatana*? It is not something that I would expect you to understand. It's an old, old practice. No doubt it seems strange to an outsider."

"It must be so painful. So dangerous."

"True. Some girls die from the infection, if it's not done right. That's why I always use a fresh razor blade each time, and rub sifted ash in the wound for faster healing. Sometimes I have the girl sit in ice water, to dull the pain. Just as my mother and grandmother taught me." She sounds like an ER nurse explaining the latest antibiotics.

"How many times have you done it?"

"Oh, I couldn't even count. About the same number of times that I have birthed girl babies in the village." Again, that compassionate crinkling of the eyes. "There is some talk of the government forbidding the practice soon. But I doubt that many families will obey." She's not at all worried; everything is going to be okay.

"What if a girl doesn't want it? Like Seema." My heart is beating so loud that I'm sure she can hear it, and knows how badly I've wanted to ask her this.

"No girl ever wants it, my dear." She clicks the prayer beads with great dignity. "I am sure there are things in your country that children don't want, but parents do for their own good."

Dental work comes to mind. Inoculations. The hideous orthopedic shoes Andy supposedly needed. "But that's different. Those are scientifically proven."

"And what if some things are spiritually proven? Spiritual truths can be as important as scientific ones." She's turned this into a philosophy class.

"You mean the Quran says girls have to be cut?" I already know the answer for this one.

"No. I don't believe it is in the Quran. Still, things can be good ideas without being in the Book."

"Why is it a good idea?"

She is an inexhaustible well of patience. "The idea of cleanliness is very complicated. It goes beyond soap and physical hygiene. Lust can make a woman's heart dirty. It can cause her to go astray and do unwise things. If this happens, she might make bad decisions. Then God is unhappy." Then she chuckles. "Too bad men can't be cut too. We would have so much less rape. Less war."

"You've got a point there." But I'm not ready to give up. "I wish you would think about not cutting Seema. Times are changing fast. I hear that a lot of city girls are not cut. I'll bet they'll all find husbands."

Houda stretches her feet straight out in front of her. How on earth can she sit like that at her age?

"Treeza, I am thankful that you care so much for Seema. You have a good heart. But let me tell you a story. You probably do not know that I had another daughter besides Seema's mother, born late to me. Her name was Sana. She was a beautiful girl, like an angel. In my husband's heart, the sun rose and set for her. When the Anfal happened, she was just sixteen years old."

Uh oh. This isn't going to be good.

"When the Arab soldiers burned our village, Sana and I hid in a ditch. They found us after several hours. Sana was taken away in a truck with the other teenage girls and young wives. They were all screaming to be let out. They had never been far from the village. Sana had never been more than a few miles away from me. I cannot remember what I did after they drove away. I was crazy with grief."

My stomach cramps, imagining my own son disappearing like livestock in the back of a grimy truck.

"Did you ever hear from her again?" I'm afraid of the answer.

"I got a letter after several years. She had been sold to a family in Qatar, and was a slave there taking care of six children. Then I heard that she had been resold to a brothel in Dubai."

The blades of the chiller fan tick around and around, and time stops.

"Maybe she is still alive." What a stupid thing to say.

"I know in my mother's heart that she is dead. I had a dream that she jumped out of a very high window. That would have been like her."

I'm desperate for hope to exist. "Maybe there's some website where a person can look for missing people. I could... "

"No." She says it with great finality. "She is not missing. She is dead. I am certain. Just as I am certain that we will be together in paradise. Because no matter what happened to her at the hands of wicked men, I am confident that her heart was always pure. And that is what counts with God."

I'm trying to see how this all connects. "Because she was cut?"

"In part." I can't tell whether she is dismayed by my denseness, or pities me for spiritual retardation. "She was always innocent, always good. But being cut, I know that she was never tempted."

I am wondering how this can be sufficient consolation for such an enormous loss when she adds quietly, "And in that way, we are superior to the Arabs."

This isn't making sense. "What do you mean?"

She sighs, as if speaking with a child. "Arab mothers are unclean. They raise children like Saddam, like the Anfal soldiers. On the other hand, Kurdish mothers are pure. Their daughters may be kidnapped, raped or enslaved, but they treasure their honor, even unto death. So is it any wonder that we can never share a country with Arabs?"

Ara is there at the door. She puts down the heavy lunch tray to move the air chiller and bring in the food. Our time is up. Before we lose our privacy, Houda adds, "We have spoken today of only one Kurdish custom, out of hundreds. Customs are not always what they seem. They are like a beautiful carpet. One strand is connected with all the others. Or like the ingredients in a soup. You cannot remove the onions without changing the taste of the whole."

With that, she tucks her beads back inside her dress and helps Ara spread out the plastic on the floor, giving me a nod over her shoulder. Our time is up.

We have almost finished the meal when Houda turns to me and says, in Arabic so that Ara cannot understand, "I really don't like it, you know."

Ara's cooking?

"I hate doing it. And I never suggest it. Never. I wait until a mother or grandmother comes to me and begs. I know how long and hard she has weighed this decision, and I must respect it. After all, it's safer for me to do it than a stranger with less skill and care."

As I let this sink in, she twists her mouth and continues.

"The Quran tells us, 'The East and the West are God's. He guides whom He will to a straight path.' It was His will that I was born into this job, just as you were born into yours. So each of us does what she must do." She searches my face to make sure that I understand the quandary. "And then, when I have done what I must, I spend a lot of time praying. As you surely must do, when your teaching work is done each day."

It's an elegant explanation, but one I'll never be able to buy completely.

✳ ✳ ✳

As April grinds on, Madame requests my company less frequently on her strolls around the track; she must have sensed my reluctance, or not believed my lame excuses. So when an invitation does come, I feel pressure to join her. If only she would up the pace, though; it's painful to walk so slowly.

"Have you given more thought to staying on next year?" she asks after her normal pleasantries.

The answer is yes, but probably not the way she expects. I've been sending out resumes since my third week at The Fortress. "Well, the offer of a promotion is extremely attractive." Can she tell I'm lying through my teeth? "And I appreciate your faith in me. Plus, I love the Kurdish culture. But I'm not sure I can hold up, physically. Teaching here is really hard on my body." Not to mention my soul.

"When you're HOD, you won't be standing up all day." Heads of departments do paperwork in choked little offices, and have to work an extra half day on Saturdays -- not much of a trade-off for getting a chair.

"True. But I'm also finding it very difficult, ideologically."

"I understand," she says kindly. "I had many of the same objections at first. But then I realized that philosophy can be a luxury. One must evaluate cost versus benefit. So I hope you'll keep an open mind about staying."

I will myself to avoid judgment. She's entitled to her own life choices, as I am to mine.

"However, ideology is one thing, and ethics are another," she continues, surprising me. "Ethics are non-negotiable. Wouldn't you agree?"

"Of course. Except that ethics tend to be culturally determined. Something that's right in one culture might be wrong in another." I struggled with this particular point during my years in Saudi.

"Let's take the Ten Commandments, then. We find them in all three religions of the book -- Judaism, Christianity and Islam."

"Well, yes," I agree. "It's hard to argue against something like 'Thou shalt not kill'."

"Egg-sactly. Then you will understand my dilemma. I suspect adultery is occurring on our campus. When it's amongst Westerners, I don't say anything. But I fear it is amongst Moslems, which makes it much worse -- for me, at least. Because we are a Muslim institution."

"Hhmmm. That could put you in a difficult position." Stay vague, I tell myself. Stay out of trouble.

She stops walking, which means I have to stop too, and she stares up at me. "I need your help, Theresa. Without concrete evidence, I can do nothing."

"I'm not sure what you're talking about." My heart quickens.

"Oh, but I think you do. Layla and Khalil."

Damn; my cheeks are tingling with a flush. "But they're your friends more than mine. You said the three of you were a family..."

"*Were* family. Past tense. We have, most unfortunately, drifted apart of late."

She looks so small and forlorn, a stunted Egyptian woman on a barren hill in Kurdistan, unloved by even her ersatz expat family. She shrugs and starts walking again.

"I was hoping you would tell me something. And that you *will* tell me, when you see or hear something in the future. It's essential. For the moral integrity of the Academy."

Rat on my fellow teachers? She must be nuts.

"I don't have that much to do with Layla and Khalil," I waffle. "They came with us on a day trip to Shaqlawa a while back. But after that, they've kept scarce. I won't be able to be of much help."

"You live right next door to Layla. The walls are paper thin. I'm sure you hear things."

Of course I hear them at night — the giggles, the bed frame knocking, the gasps of pleasure. "She usually keeps the TV on," I try.

Her disappointment is palpable. "Layla ought to be ashamed of herself." Now hurt has transformed to rage. "She and I are friends with Khalil's mother. We promised to take care of him here. He's a virgin, you know. Or *was* a virgin before she seduced him. He'd be completely vulnerable to the advances of a beautiful temptress like Layla. It's scandalous."

I imagine my son Andy in a similar situation. My protective side would want to roar and claw the air at anyone compromising his innocence. My liberal side, on the other hand, isn't so sure. Initiation at the hands of a skilled lover, providing a safe outlet for all that pent-up libido — especially here in Iraq, where dating possibilities are zilch? It might not be such a bad thing. Better than whore houses, at least.

"If you don't have actual proof, maybe you could look the other way? Let it blow over?" I suggest hopefully. That's what I would have done, anyway.

"Impossible. Well, if you won't cooperate, I have other resources for getting to the bottom of this."

"You mean like hidden cameras?" At long last, an opportunity to find out whether the rumors are true.

"And other things." I sense a chortle.

Madame, you're jealous! The thought stuns me. You wish you had Layla's lithe little body, her flowing curls, that joie de vivre that comes with being in love, and a young guy panting after you -- instead of some old geezer back home who thrives on "distance" from you.

"I'm glad I'm not in your position." It's the best I can think of. She sighs bitterly in return.

We circle the court a few more times. Then she puts more bait on the hook. "There might be something even better than HOD for you next year. We'll have to see..."

What a shameless attempt to bribe me. Another academic year imprisoned with her in The Fortress? I shudder. No possible pay-out could make it worthwhile, much less endurable. I'm not *that* desperate, and hope I never will be.

❈ ❈ ❈

Bezma isn't interested in translating for Ara and me anymore, unless the topic happens to be Hevar or the wedding. "Hevar, Hevar, Hevar," I tease. "Can't we ever talk about something else?"

No, because he's been phoning every few minutes this afternoon. Twice during Ara's special pilaf lunch he rings, to Ara's great irritation. But the calls are important, Bezma tells us. Hevar's mother wants the wedding in just four weeks; preparations will have to get in gear immediately.

"What about your studies?" I haven't noticed textbooks lying around lately, nor any new vocabulary words cropping up.

With unusual energy Bezma flips her chin; it's taken forever for her to get over the flu. "No problem. I learn later. Now we plan house."

"I thought you were going to live here with Ara."

"Now Hevar want house with only me." That's understandable, given Ara's sour attitude. "Family Hevar build house here. My family fill house."

"So you have to buy things like a stove, fridge, pots and pans?" She nods. "How would Ara ever afford that?"

199

"This big problem, Treeza. Day after wedding, village peoples give gifts. Maybe cushions, pillows, blankets, pots, pans, dishes. Small things. But not big things. Not stove."

"You'll need a lot more than a stove. How will you manage the summer heat without a refrigerator? Or even an electric fan? How about a washing machine?"

"I wash using hands. Same like mother."

I'd guessed that was what they did, based on the clothesline by the water tank. Twisted black bloomers, black scarves, black-and-floral tunics are obviously wrung out by hand. It makes me sad every time I see it.

I have an idea. I'll ask the readers of my blog to contribute toward a stove, more essential than a washer. My meager post-Wells-Fargo savings will be a start, but not enough to pay for an entire appliance.

Hevar's family will also pay for the wedding itself, a good thing because Ara is in no mood to help. Instead, it's Old Houda who chatters away with us, indulging the bride-to-be in one of those rambly, we-have-all-the-time-in-the-world afternoon conversations.

"Okay to make my hair yellow like Treeza?"

"Certainly." Houda now seems authorized to make motherly decisions.

"Yellow hair nice with white dress and henna hands," Bezma says.

"My grandmother had red hands, but not from henna," Houda muses. "She wove carpets. And the red dye, *harmala*, gave her stains."

"Is that the same stuff they sell in the bazaar? To get rid of fleas?" I've seen it in a big powdery pyramid.

"Yes. Besides being a dye, it's an old medicine. But we shouldn't talk about that around a bride," Houda whispers. She needn't have worried; Bezma is busy texting again.

"Why not?"

She murmurs something about pregnancy, but uses an Arabic word I don't understand. "And it also gives dreams."

"What kind of dreams?"

"Djinns and houries. Magic carpets, flying carpets. Things younger people like." She smiles indulgently; she and I are much too old for such foolishness.

"How do you use it?" My hallucinogen-starved colleagues in the faculty room would die for information like this.

Houda shakes her head. "It's not a good thing for you to know. It's complicated and sometimes dangerous. I'll tell you some other time."

Just then we hear pounding on the gate, and here is Hevar, beaming at the surprise he's pulled off. He's been phoning all this time from the road, so Bezma wouldn't suspect he was on his way. And here he is in the flesh, giving Bezma a big smack of a kiss, whacking her affectionately on the butt, strutting around in his Peshmerga khakis. His cummerbund is especially flashy today, a floral scarf wrapped in complicated folds around his waist. He lets Bezma bring him inside and fuss over him; she insists that he take the cushion of honor farthest from the door, and goes to prepare tea.

Squirming, I dredge around in my mind for something polite to say. "Houda, please tell Hevar that I hope he will take good care of my little niece Bezma."

Houda must have accurately translated the "little" part, because he chuckles, and replies by placing his hand over his heart, saying something about Allah.

"Also please promise to be good to my sister Ara. She is a good woman."

Of course, he promises; it is nothing. He lights a cigarette, assuming that we won't mind. I take it as arrogance, but Houda doesn't seem to notice.

"And also let Bezma finish her education." I haven't asked it as a question, but it comes out that way when Houda puts it into Kurdish.

"Yes, Bezma will study. But only before babies. After babies, she will stay home."

Houda concurs with a nod; babies are top priorities.

"There are ways to make babies come later, so she could at least finish her degree," I suggest. Surely they know about the pill and condoms in places like this.

But now Houda refuses to translate. "This is women's talk," she whispers. "It's shameful to talk about it with a man. Bezma would be very angry if she heard."

So we make polite chit chat with Hevar about his family, his truck, his vague employment, his training with the Peshmerga. He had loved those years of his youth, shooting guns up in the mountains, sleeping under the stars, drilling with his comrades, singing and dancing around the fire at night. Ah, the good old days…

He likes telling me about his family, too. Since they had been refugees in Iran and then returned, the government owes them a repatriation house -- which they've never cashed in on. This is how they will buy land and build a new home for Hevar and Bezma. The family wants to build next door to their own property, high in the mountains. Bezma is still negotiating for a place here in the village. Surprise — I thought it was all settled, but agreements seem to be shifting all the time.

When I ask about his sisters, he frowns. The older one is fine. She stays home to care for his parents.

"He say sister fine, but this not true," Bezma adds in English to me, pouring out the tea. "Hevar older sister very unhappy. She has love for many years. Hevar, Mother, Father say no, not possible marry. Now she is 30, too old. Too dry."

I try not to smile at the thought of being dried up at such a young age. How many movie stars are still pretty juicy in their fifties or sixties?

"How about that gorgeous younger sister of his? The one who wore red?"

"Oh, you mean Soz? Hevar very angry with Soz. She also have love. But she promised from cradle to old man. Hevar say must marry old man, save family honor, no marriage with love-boy. Soz say yes. Hevar say no. Yes. No. Yes. No. Very bad."

"But that's so hypocritical. He's getting you, the girl *he* wanted."

She balks at translating, but I push. Hevar folds his arms in reply and stares insolently at me, not even bothering to answer. With that one look, my superior status as a foreigner vanishes; I am suddenly old, female and irrelevant. My shoulders hunch involuntarily. I'll bet Soz hates him even more than I do right now.

We listen dutifully as Hevar talks and smokes. Bezma laps up each word like a hungry kitten. He basks in her attention, ignoring Houda and me. Houda leaves and he barely notices.

He becomes quite the gentleman, however, when I make excuses to go, offering to drive me home. The Blue Angel fits neatly in the back of the pickup, and the three of us squish into the front cab -- Bezma inexplicably to the left of the steering wheel, giggling, Hevar driving in the middle, and me smashed up against the passenger door to avoid touching him.

"Don't we need Ara to come along, to chaperone?" It's got to be against Muslim law for them to be alone in the car after dropping me off, or at least highly scandalous.

"No, we engaged." Bezma flicks her wrist at such a trifling idea. "Everything okay." She snuggles against Hevar, who is doing his best to steer and shift with the same hand. When we reach the school's back gate, the guard doesn't even bring out his under-car mirror, for once. He gives Hevar a knowing half-salute and waves us through. They deposit me outside my apartment -- odd, because Bezma has been pestering me for weeks to look around inside -- and drive off happily towards Shaqlawa. It's the opposite direction from the village.

I'm not placing any bets on how long it will be before they arrive back at Ara's.

Seven: Dreams and Delirium

The next Saturday, Pat, Jake and I are on a mission. We've decided to do original research on Kurdistan, publish it in some international magazine or newspaper (*The New York Times* would be nice, we figure, or perhaps *Foreign Policy*), and use the coverage to further our careers. For Jake, that means getting into a decent grad school. For Pat and me, it means finding a better employer than The Fortress, as quickly as possible.

"Let's keep it fairly simple. We'll do a man-on-the-street thing, with three basic questions." I've supervised college students doing similar research. The more complicated the research, the worse the results.

"Okay. How about something really generic like attitudes toward gays? That'd be easy to sell." Thank goodness he's kidding.

"How about something that will not land us in jail, seeing as how we don't exactly have permission to do this?" says Pat, ever the pragmatist. "There's probably something in our contract against random research."

"So maybe not attitudes toward female genital mutilation either?" My turn to be just kidding. Jake throws a crumpled up homework sheet at me.

Fiddling around with ideas keeps us entertained for several days of lunch breaks. We range from political to economic to sociological. What do most Kurds think about Americans? About the share of oil revenue they get from the Baghdad government? The historical significance of the Anfal? How best to educate young Kurds for the future? Whether wealth is being distributed fairly? What to do about corruption?

In the end, we decide to ask just one question. "What is your dream in life?" Keeping it short will let us expand the number of surveyees. And it's a topic so generic that *Reader's Digest* might take it.

"But none of us speak Kurdish. How are we going to talk with ordinary people?" Pat asks.

"Oh yeah." We'd forgotten about that. I had assumed that we could do a mixture of Arabic and English, like I get away with in the village. But neither Pat nor Jake speak any Arabic.

Mrs. Zaki veers over from the tea kettle. "You could always ask one of the Kurds here to help."

Jake's face drops. I can almost hear him thinking, 'Well, I'll be damned. A heart beats inside there.'

"She's right," says Pat, filling in Jake's silence. "Theresa, you're pretty chummy with that Kurdish Government guy in the office. Mohammed? Want to ask him?"

"No!" It comes out much too hostile. They guffaw. "You guys can ask him yourself."

"Forget it," Jake says. "He doesn't have the hots for me." To my chagrin, the whole staff room finds this hilarious. Damn them. When we can't think of any alternative, however, we have no choice but for me to approach Mohammed, who eagerly accepts. He even offers to drive.

Mohammed picks us up the next weekend in a gleaming Volvo. In local garb, he's a totally different person; he seems more comfortable now that he's in khakis and locally made canvas shoes. We scramble in armed with Xeroxed survey sheets. To streamline the recording process, we've prepared check boxes to tick when we ask people about their dream: financial ("I want a million dollars"), educational ("I want my child to graduate from a good school or university"), geographic ("I want a visa to move to the U.S. or the U.K. or Australia"), social ("I want to find a good husband / wife for myself or my child"), and religious ("I want to see the spread of Islam"). Then we can write down details as our subjects get more specific.

We have also brought a small camera, hoping for portrait shots. "Like that Afghan girl on the cover of *Nat Geo*," Jake predicts. "Hauntingly gorgeous, coupled with a stellar quote. We'll be famous."

Our first stop is a muffler shop where Mohammed knows the owner. We tromp over power cords and pools of automotive grease, and accost the first hapless worker with our question. He looks up from the concrete floor and pauses to think.

"My dream is that all Kurdish people be united into one glorious country of our own." He returns to his ratcheting, dismissing us.

We move on to the guy in the muffler shop office, who interrupts a heated cellphone exchange. "Simple. I dream of an independent Kurdistan. Hey — are you from a newspaper or something?"

We pile back into the car. "Consistency of message in the automotive industry," Jake says. "Be sure to write that down."

Next is the European bakery we often go to for cakes and cookies. Pat reconnoiters. "Forget it. The workers are all Lebanese. We only want Kurdish respondents, right?" Right.

On to the next, an all-male tea shop. "Only Jake goes in with me," Mohammed says, retucking the corner of his red turban. "Western women will look funny."

They're gone an awfully long time. And it gets rowdy in the shop, with a lot of shouting. Pat and I roll down the car windows, but we can't understand a thing.

"What was that all about?" Pat asks when they finally return.

Jake slams the passenger door. "The first guy said his dream is to go live with his brother in Australia. Then everybody else started beating up on him, because he hadn't said an independent Kurdistan. Not physically beating up," he adds quickly. "Just words."

Oh whew.

"Can we count that as one for leaving the country?" Jake's got out the score sheets.

"No, because of how quickly he changed his mind." Mohammed is emphatic. He's really getting into this.

"Okay. Unanimity in the tea place." Jake sighs. "Crap, we'd better get somebody to say something different, or else it won't look like much of a scientific survey."

"Let's try some women." Brilliant, Pat. Mohammed lets us out by the vegetable stands at the central bazaar, and Jake stays in the car this time.

The women in the city, however, don't want to be bothered by pesky Westerners. They're bustling around with children in tow, toting heavy shopping bags, and negotiating tricky walkways in long skirts. They're not rude to us, just busy. So we end up at our favorite dried fruit stall; the crotchety old vendor recognizes us and is happy to oblige.

"I have had the same dream for fifty years now," he says, settling back onto his stool and basking in female attention. He launches into a story about his whole village hiding out in caves when he was a boy and surviving on roasted rodents. We know where this is going, even before he gets to the part about refugee camps in Iran.

By now, we've used up the morning; everything is closing for noon prayers. It's back to The Fortress with Mohammed at the wheel.

"I've got a great headline for our survey," says Jake. "Everyone in City of Half Million Gives Same Answer to Question."

"Don't get all huffy like that." I want to keep this upbeat. "It just means that we didn't hit a diverse enough population. We got answers from men in their twenties and above. But no millennials. Nobody with an education, or in a position of power. And no women."

"In other words, we didn't plan this very well. Or we were lazy." Thanks, Pat.

"No. In other words, we're not done yet," I say.

"Or, they see a whole pack of Westerners and only trust us with the answer they think we want to hear." Why didn't she think of something like this before we set out?

"That's not it at all," Mohammed says over his shoulder. "I could have told you what they would say, even before we set out this morning."

The three of us stare at him.

"If you ask people dying of thirst in the desert what they want out of life, you can't act surprised when they all say water. What did you expect?"

Jake leans over the seat and says balefully, "Yeah, girls. What did we expect?"

Mohammed isn't done. "However, as Massoud Barzani said once, we can't expect someone to present us our own country as a gift. We have a right to independence, and must demand it and make it happen. This saying is not just in our mouths. It runs through our veins. We take it that much for granted."

"We've been idiots." I mean it as an apology to Mohammed.

"Hell, we even forgot to take pictures," Pat says.

We slump into a group funk. This has not turned out the way we hoped.

"But what about you, Mohammed? I thought you wanted to leave Kurdistan." Oops. Too late I realize that this was probably a secret. He does not lash out or deny it, however.

"Of course I would like to live in other places. Temporarily. Isn't that why you three came here yourselves? But I still dream of a homeland for my people. Leaving is a personal desire, selfish. Greater Kurdistan is bigger than that — the ultimate dream. That's what you were asking in your survey, wasn't it?"

It gets very quiet in the car. Finally Pat says, "Thank you, Mohammed."

"Yeah, thanks," Jake adds, serious for once. "For putting up with us today."

"I thought it might help the cause," he says softly.

In the set of his shoulders and the carriage of his head is an unmistakable dignity. The word noble comes to mind. Astounding.

We decide to bag the article idea. We'll have to find some other way to get out of here.

❊ ❊ ❊

My first Iraqi sandstorm. It's like a gigantic hairdryer blasting grit at us from the Syrian Desert, all day and all night, thick as a blizzard. The air is so gritty that I wear a checkered turban scarf tied over my face in order to breathe. Even indoors.

Sand piles up in drifts inside the sliding glass doors of my apartment. I cover my head with the sheet to try to sleep.

Falling asleep is hard every night now, even without howling outside the door. Maybe I'm drinking too much tea. Maybe it's the stress of such big classes, the fear of Zaki's database, the BBC news reports about Turkey bombing less than a hundred miles from here, or Christian churches being blown up in Baghdad. Or it could be the unavoidable nap after school each day that's messing up my inner clock. But I blame it on the orange decor; if aqua colors on the walls help to

210

soothe patients and induce healing, then this awful orange everywhere must do just the opposite.

Suddenly, I sit upright and grab the sheets in terror. Someone is turning a key in my front door! Someone is opening the door, and stomping inside, rough and bold. I have no weapon except for my Bible beside the bed; it's hefty, so I grab it to my chest and peer out from behind the bedroom door.

It's a *mujahedin*, in a flak vest and checked gutra on his head, plunking down a sandy backpack on the floor.

No wait. It's Rabinowitz in his stupid thousand-pocket *khak* safari vest, tromping around like a crazy man and tracking in crud with each step.

"What in heaven's name? How …"

"Still got my key. Oh, for Christ's sake, Theresa. Don't be such a prude."

I bristle. "What do you want?" He doesn't deserve graciousness at this hour.

"I need a place to crash." He dumps his backpack on the sofa, as if he owns the place.

"No way. It's against the rules. How did you even get past the guards anyway?" How dare he?

"They all recognize me. Hey, don't get all pissy. This apartment was mine long before it was yours."

"Well, it's mine now."

"Just chill, would you? I won't jump your creaky old bones or anything. I'll stay on the couch, leave in the morning, and nobody will even know."

I do not like this person. I do not want him in my personal space. I do not trust him as far as I can spit, which is not very far.

Plus, he smells bad.

But above the scarf around his face, faded and stained, he's as forlorn as a stray dog on the side of the road. My motherly heart begins to soften.

"Go to Jake's."

"He wasn't home. I tried." The stray dog is wagging its tail.

"How about Pat?"

"I knocked but couldn't wake her up. And I didn't have her key. Hah."

So I'm the last resort. How flattering. I sigh. He's not looking so menacing now. "Okay. But just for tonight." I put on the teapot. I can at least be that hospitable. "You want a sandwich?"

"Sure." Then he adds, "Anything but pork."

"Right-o." What a conceited bastard.

He fumbles with the remote and switches on Al Jazeera News, turned low. "Okay, I've got to admit it. This place looks way better than when I had it. The woman's touch."

"Gee thanks." Would he even notice the sarcasm — or that I bothered to put his sandwich on a plate, instead of handing it to him on a paper towel? I've given him the cheese that needed using up, not the good haloumi. He won't care.

"Something happen with your job at your other school?"

"What a dump that place was. Total dirtbags." I wait while he chews. "They didn't pay us, so I got evicted."

"Oh. So what's next?" He can't be planning on a job at The Fortress. Madame would never take him back.

"Off to Baghdad. I'm just waiting for my visa to come through any day now."

"Oh yeah. Your wedding."

"Of course my wedding. Where's your laptop? I'll show you a picture of her."

Reluctantly, I open up Facebook and let him log on. He clicks on a black-shrouded face, with only the eyes showing. I burst out laughing.

212

"That's it? That's all you know about her?"

"It's enough. I'm set for life. *In sh'allah*. God willing."

"*In sh'allah*." I watch while he scrolls through their correspondence, impressed that he reads Arabic so well.

"Say, Rabinowitz, what got you started on this whole Muslim kick? If your family is Jewish, they couldn't approve."

He stretches out his feet on my coffee table. Correction — the school's coffee table — it's less irritating to think of it that way. "I studied imperialism and world religions in college. That was my major. And my family sent me on Birthright. You've heard of that, right?"

No, I haven't.

"Any young Jew can get a free trip to Israel to learn about their heritage. It's ten days, all expenses paid. Naturally, I took them up on it. But I went with my own agenda. Whenever we got any free time, I found Palestinians to talk to. Everybody else went to the bars, and I went to the slums. Hah!"

"Sort of counter-subversive?"

"Yeah. Exactly what the Birthright folks did not want. My Arabic wasn't very good at that point, but still, I heard an earful from the Palestinians."

"I'll bet." I wish I could have been eavesdropping in his backpack. A little ripple of resentment rises; the places men can go on a lark, that we women can't even consider.

"They're not all terrorists, like the Western media makes them out to be. Most of them are just normal people, wanting what any ordinary person does. A country to call their own. A future for their families. We should think of them as freedom fighters. Like the guys who did the Boston Tea Party."

It sounds like garden-variety undergrad revolutionism. "But what flipped the switch for you? What made you go live in Pakistan?"

"I almost went into the Peace Corps. But after Birthright, I was onto the Peace Corps' game, how they contribute to

America's imperialist expansion. How they prop up America's neocolonialist strategies all over the world. And therefore contribute to Zionism, which is just another name for fascism. The deeper I got into studying Islam, the more preposterous the Peace Corps seemed."

Indeed. "When did you convert?"

His face glints now, warming to his topic. "In Portland, before I left the U.S. There was a really cool *imam* there who explained things to me, and guided me to the best websites."

"They didn't mind your Jewish background?"

He laughs. "They thought it was great! They couldn't believe their luck, getting a Jew to see the light."

"They probably don't get too many like you." If I'd said this when teaching a college class, the other students would have howled. But Rabinowitz shoves out his chest.

"Damned right. I'm practically a hero."

"I'll bet your family isn't too thrilled about the marriage, though."

"They don't know. And I'm not telling them. Hey, can I have a beer?"

The best I have is rum and coke with no ice, which he finds acceptable. No appreciation, of course.

"No, the less people back Stateside know about what I'm doing, the better. For my work."

"What work is that?"

Oops; now he's frowning with a hint of suspicion. "No details. Sorry. It's decent of you to let me crash like this. But I've got to stay mum." He pretends to zip his lips.

"You mean you're a spy?" I can't help myself.

His look implies that I'm mentally challenged. "Hey, things are gonna heat up. Pretty quick now, too. And I'm gonna be right in the thick of it."

"What kind of things? It's been pretty quiet the whole time I've been here. Maybe trouble in other parts of the Middle

East, but not Kurdistan. Even the U.S. troops are practically gone."

"Things like the *Youm aδ Din*. Judgment Day. It's all written down in The Book."

"Oh, good grief. I thought you meant another 9/11 or something. Not the Apocalypse."

"You scoff now. But mark my words. Someday soon, you'll look back on this night when you gave refuge to a *jihaδi* in a sandstorm, and you'll be glad your good deed got recorded in the Book of Life."

"*Jihaδi*, my eye." No way could this kid survive without a cell phone and air conditioning.

"Believe me. There is no escape from the will of God."

"Couldn't you just find another teaching job and let that poor girl in Baghdad have a normal Arab life?"

A long pause. "There have been some unfair complaints about my teaching style. I probably couldn't get a decent reference."

Another long pause. "But it's not really about that," he continues. "I became a new person when I converted, and got a new name and everything. I only use Rabinowitz on official documents. You should really be calling me Waleed."

"No last name?"

"Only on a need-to-know basis. Sorry."

Lounging there with his sandwich and drink, he looks like one of the strays Andy used to bring home in high school, for a meal or to sleep on the couch when they quarreled with their parents. Under all of the camouflage gear, he's just a mixed-up American boy. Something in me softens.

"Rabinowitz." He bridles. "Waleed. If you were my son, I'd be staying up at night, worried sick about you. I'd want you to call me once in a while, to say you were okay."

"No you wouldn't. You wouldn't give a damn." His eyes squint like a boxer getting ready for a punch, more vulnerable than I would have anticipated. It prompts a tenderness in me that I hadn't dreamed possible toward him.

I try a more gentle tone. "How long since you're talked with your mom?"

No answer. Now he seems like a cornered animal, maybe a rabbit, something small and furry, threatened by an owl in the dark forest. "A month? Two months?" No answer. "A lot longer than that, then…"

I picture a haggard mother somewhere in soggy Oregon, hugging herself in a buttoned-up cardigan and plaid wool skirt, brooding. She's regretting harsh words she might have said over the years. Wanting to make amends. Then I have a brilliant idea.

"What time is it back on the West Coast? It's two in the morning here, so that's, what, three in the afternoon there? Let's get on Skype and see if she's home. It's easy. It's free…"

"No!" He's so loud that I worry that he'll wake up Layla (and no doubt Khalil) next door. "Absolutely not! Stop meddling, would you? Stop poking your nose. Jesus Christ."

He stomps into the bathroom, brings back my only big towel, kicks off his boots, and stretches out on the sofa. He pounds one of the sofa cushions in a vain attempt to make it soft, then doubles it up under his head anyway.

"When you wake up, I'll already be out of here," he proclaims from under the towel. "And forget anything I was stupid enough to tell you before I forgot what a Goody Two Shoes you are. Damn. Damn it to hell."

He turns to the wall so only his rear end and legs stick out from the towel. Ludicrous.

I shake my head and climb back into my own bed. Crazy kid. I guess he'll have to learn things the hard way — like practically everybody else.

The sand is still blowing strong outside. I get up and double-check that the bedroom door is locked before trying to go back to sleep.

❊ ❊ ❊

On my next visit, Ara is back at her red-hot metal dome in the kitchen, frying up bread for the week. She wipes away sweat with the back of her wrist, sees me and grins. "Treeza!" She calls to Bezma to bring me a chair from the porch. She knows I can't squat like the rest of them can.

Bezma fills me in on the latest. The wedding will be in early June. The hall is rented, food ordered, dress selected, music chosen. I wonder how all this happened so quickly. "Old Houda help," Bezma explains. "My mother not happy, do nothing. Family Hevar give me money instead."

I offer to contribute, but Bezma dismisses the idea. "No, big shame if you give money. You are guest. Most important guest."

She sure isn't acting like somebody about to be married in just a few weeks. "What else is wrong?"

"Nothing."

Her phone buzzes. I can hear Hevar yelling, even without the speakerphone on. He doesn't greet Bezma, but just starts in on the shouting; this must be part of an earlier argument. Bezma interrupts, gets cut off, shouts again, cringes when another barrage comes, and finally snaps the phone shut, hanging up on him.

"What was that all about?"

"Mother Hevar angry." She is crying. "Friend Hevar see me walking alone in city. Say to family, Bezma is bad woman. But I only walk to taxi after class. I do not speak to mans. I do nothing wrong."

"Of course you didn't!" What a preposterous idea.

"Mother Hevar say no wedding. No woman with black face come into family. She say I must give her gold." She twists the band with the "H" on it, as if it's a miniature life ring to a better future.

Hevar's voice, distorted over the phone, settles like ash in my stomach. I'm enraged that he won't stand up to his mother. Then I turn solid with dread, with deja vu, from having been controlled by a voice exactly like Hevar's for too many years. To hear it this early in a marriage — even before the ceremony — is sickening.

Very slowly, I ask, "Are you positive you want to spend your whole life with this man and his family?" It's not necessary to add, "with him having absolute power over you, forever?" She knows that better than I do.

"Not possible turn back now." She stares at the concrete floor.

"Of course it's possible. Just give back the jewelry and keep going to school. Somebody much better will come along..." I'm getting too insistent, weaving too much of my own disillusionment into this, but can't stop.

"Not possible now," she repeats, with a finality that silences me. "Cannot stop marriage. Some things happen, then future no change."

I want to get inside her brain and shake it up. I want to put new self-talk tapes into her head, so she'll be empowered and strong, and understand that she is not really stuck. She must be reading all this on my face, because she rests her fingertips on my arm, light and tender as a tiny bird.

"Treeza, you good person. But some things you not understand."

In other words, give it up.

"I know." I take her hand. "But neither do you. I'll bet this whole fuss blows over in a day or two."

She nods dolefully. Side by side, we sit like that for a while, watching Ara stretch and flip flatbread on her fiery griddle, one of us ready to rile up against fate and tradition, and the other cowed by identical forces, interpreting them in exactly an opposite manner.

❊ ❊ ❊

Fuzzy Wuzzy was a bear.
Fuzzy Wuzzy had no hair.
Fuzzy Wuzzy wasn't very fuzzy,
Was he?

I've written it on the board behind me before the kids come in for the last period of the week. In other words, hell period, when nobody's going to learn a blessed thing, and we're lucky if everyone just survives to the bell. With each passing week, hell period gets a little worse, and I've got to become more creative.

I pretend that there's nothing on the board except for the mandatory tactics and page numbers, and tell them to open to page 237. We're making progress reading about Alexander, who is now preparing for yet another gory battle.

"Miss, why did you write a poem on the board?"

It's Karwan. I stopped calling him Kaka once I learned what it meant.

"Oh, it's something that American children like to say. See if you can figure out why." I go back to reading aloud. But these kids have my number now. Then can intuit when I'm faking interest in something in order to divert them to something fun.

"Miss, I think it must be a joke." Whoa. Barav, Child of Martyrs at the back, contributing something? I want to clap for him.

"Yes, Barav, it is a joke. But you have to figure it out for yourself."

Barav's face furrows with concentration, and I realize how much I've come to adore these kids, even the ones who are slow or give me a hard time. They're such characters, each one of them. And who knows? Any — or all — of them could be key contributors to a more enlightened Kurdish nation some day. I try to spark as much as I can in their fertile minds while they're still eager to learn, and encourage them to think in different, even quirky, ways. Which is why we've been working on careful questioning to get information, with games like this one.

Finally Barav figures out how to get a clue. "Miss, please tell us what fuzzy means."

"Ah. A good question. It means hairy. Wooly."

I wait while the kids assimilate this. "Miss Miss!" Barav signals with his arm again. "I know the answer, Miss. It's funny because all bears have hair. It's impossible to have a bear that was bare." He doesn't realize that he's made a joke until everybody laughs; he's confused between embarrassment and pride, but decides on pride.

You poor sweet kid. "Uh, no. Nice try. Think harder."

I get through another sentence about Alexander.

Barav is determined to solve this before anybody else does. "Miss, nobody would name a bear Fuzzy Wuzzy. It's silly for a wild animal to have a name like that."

"True, Barav. But that's not the joke."

Jaber jumps out of his seat, hooting and hopping apelike in the aisle like he's going to wet his pants. "I get it, Miss! I get it. Wasn't very Fuzzy Wuzzy! Was he? Fuzzy Wuzzy was a bear…" And he repeats the whole thing quickly, over and over. "Get it, guys? Get it?"

Helin is the first to grin and whisper coyly to the girl to her left. Then Seema cracks up. In minutes, everyone is laughing.

And we've accomplished the real goal, which is to bring us together as a congenial group of humans, rather than a divided camp based on authority, counting down the minutes until the bell rings.

When the bell does finally ring, Karwan stays behind, a rarity; usually he's heading the pack of boys out the door with the swagger of an anointed leader. But now he is subdued, ashamed to be asking me anything. I get the idea that sons of Big Men are supposed to know everything at birth. "Miss, don't make fun of me. But I don't understand about the bear and the hair."

"Hhmm. And I don't understand why someone as clever as you won't keep his hands out of his pants."

He turns crimson. "I never…"

"Yes you did. But let's just assume that a real 'kaka' would be a gentleman and never do it again, okay? Fine. Now, if the bear didn't have any hair, he wasn't fuzzy, right? And 'was he' sounds just like…"

"Wuzzy! Wuzzy! I get it, Miss. Thank you, Miss!"

The gleam in his eye convinces me to make a Note to Self. Next week, we'll do "I scream, you scream, we all scream for ice cream" as a relief during hell period.

❀ ❀ ❀

"I owe you big time, Twinkle Toes." Jake waits until the Arab and Kurdish teachers leave the staff room before accosting me by the tea kettle. I can't tell whether he's elated or hung over.

"For what?"

"For the best, cheapest high this side of Istanbul."

I'm still not getting it.

"The rue! *Harmala*. You told us about it a while back, and I've been doing research. So this weekend, I bought a whole sack of it for about a dollar. Binny and I brewed up a batch of rue tea and … holy horse crap, Batman!"

"But that was just an old wives' tale."

"No way, Jose." He does a pretty realistic stoned imitation. "The barfing part isn't so much fun, believe me. For a while, we didn't think it would be worth it. But then the stuff kicked in, and it was very, very good." He kisses his fingertips. "Ooh la la. Almost as good as Maui Wowee."

"Quiet. What if it's illegal?"

"It isn't. Not even in the U.S. It's like weed before they made laws against it. Nobody knows about this stuff. I'm gonna make a fortune once I figure out how to export it."

"Jeez, Jake. Maybe it's dangerous."

"Only if you eat cheese while you're high. Or spend too much time in the sun. Oh, and it can cause you to abort. But hey -- I'm not pregnant." His eyebrows spring up and down, Groucho Marx style. Very funny.

"Did the guy in the bazaar tell you all this?"

"Oh ye of little faith. No, dearie, everything is right there in plain sight on the Internet. Go read it yourself. The guy in the bazaar thought I wanted to fumigate my apartment for lice, and tried to sell me an even bigger sack of it."

"Jake, you're just too much."

"And you, Twinkie, have just transmuted my sentence here. A million thank yous. I'm doing your bulletin boards for you from now until Doomsday." And he does his silly Parisian tart ta-ta farewell as he staggers off for class.

❀   ❀   ❀

It's really blistering now at noon, and any wildflowers alongside the road have long disappeared. As protection against the sun, I've worn a wide-brimmed traveler's rain hat and a long-sleeved shirt on the Blue Angel. I pedal fast to create my own breeze, eager to spring my surprise.

Bezma is elated when I get there. The wedding is back on, she chatters, and Hevar's sisters have sent gifts — delicate beaded chokers that they've strung for Bezma, Ara and me, with matching bracelets. "These my sisters now," she croons as she ties a choker around my neck. She's got a healthy glow back again. "See how they love me! And they love you too, Treeza!"

She's doused in a cheap rose oil perfume. I made the mistake of admiring it on a recent visit, and am now the proud owner of a whole bottle. My students like me wearing it; Jake and Pat say it's putrid.

"Now new idea for wedding. You remember Soz? Young sister Hevar?"

How could I forget such a vibrant beauty?

"Soz say we do one wedding — Hevar, me, Soz, her love."

"How exciting." My only concern is that Soz's glamour and pizazz will make Bezma look a little frumpy in comparison. "I've never heard of a double wedding in Kurdistan. Does Soz want to do it to save money?"

"No, so make wedding faster. Soz have so much love. Wait long time already. Soz wait more time Hevar and me. Now her love finally ask, bring gold."

"So it's settled then?"

"No. Big problem. Hevar no like Soz love. Always say no."

Good old Hevar. Trust him to mess things up. I nod in sympathy.

"Soz think, now when Hevar happy about his wedding, maybe he say yes for her wedding," she continues.

This doesn't sound like Hevar to me. But you never know. "She'd better hurry up convincing him. The wedding is coming right up, isn't it?" I've had a hard time getting a fixed date out of them, for some reason.

She giggles. "Soz say for me convince Hevar. Also say for you convince. Maybe this why she make beautiful jewelry."

Oh great. I'm not exactly a key influence in Hevar's world. Still, I let her tie the beaded bracelet onto my wrist, and wait for her to calm down before divulging my secret. "So, are you ready for some good news? Want to guess what it is?"

She has no end of ideas. I have decided to renew my contract and stay here next year. No. My son is getting married. No. The bank gave back all of my money in America. Alas, no. She gives up.

"My friends in America, and some of them at the school here, have given me money to buy you a wedding present. I have the money now. You and I are going into the city in a few days to pick out a stove."

"What?"

She makes me repeat it. "No, this impossible." Tears of disbelief well up. "Peoples, they not know Bezma, they give money for big present?"

I explain about my blog, but she doesn't get the idea of the Internet. She asks how much money, and I tell her. She runs to the kitchen to tell Ara, who comes out wiping her hands, shaking her head, incredulous. *"Ma sh'allah."* God is great. Neither of them can fathom it.

"Treeza, true, your friends do this?"

Yes, $10 here and $25 there. It was easier than I'd thought. "They've been reading about you for months now, and want you to have something nice for your new home."

"I tell Hevar." She searches for the cell phone, but Ara grabs it and stuffs it down the front of her dress. Lunch is ready, and Ara has made dolmas for me. We're not going to let them get cold.

The three of us ride a surge of gaiety. "So much money, we buy more than stove," Bezma says. I doubt this, but let her babble on about what appliances probably cost, which streets have the best vendors, how I will have to stand outside so we don't get rich foreigner prices, how we will have to hire a truck if the shop doesn't deliver, where she will store the stove at Ara's place until Hevar's parents build her new house. She has the air of a sweepstakes winner. Ara doesn't join in, but keeps sniffing back tears, shaking her head in wonderment.

And the dolmas have turned out especially well. Ara beams when I eat the second helping she spoons into my bowl. I love the onion and eggplant dolmas in particular, sweet and succulent. She's made an extra treat, too — a wild plant that she digs up in the fields in springtime. The name sounds like "kangareh". It tastes like fried artichoke hearts, dripping in grease but worth every calorie.

I ask how kangareh is prepared. Ara pantomimes walking for a very long time, up steep hills carrying a sharpened stick, digging around in stubborn dirt, carrying plants back in a sack, peeling, chopping, boiling, and frying. It turns silly. She's making fun of herself and all the work she goes to out there on the hillsides, and I start cracking up. I mimic her pantomime, and there we are, collecting invisible weeds for dinner and becoming giddy with the fun of it. I've never seen her like this.

Amazed at us, Bezma flips on a transistor radio, and now we're all three digging kangareh in time to some Kurdish guy wailing away to a bouzouki and drum. "Khsh khsh khsh," he repeats over and over as a refrain, and it's so hypnotic that we sing along. I shrug in time to the music, like the Kurdish dancers I spent Nowroz with, which makes Ara laugh even harder, and then Ara is shrugging too, and I grab her hand, pull her to her feet, link little fingers with her and we start dancing. I hand her my black scarf and she's twirling it like the dance leader at the head of a debka line. Skirting the plastic tablecloth on the floor, we kick back the cushions to make more space, hold up our hems, and prance even faster.

How can we get even more ridiculous? I stuff my Gore-Tex rain hat onto Ara's head; she catches a glimpse of herself in the little mirror as we spin past the door, and cackles. Too funny! Bezma rustles in my backpack, finds my camera and starts clicking. Here's a mother she hasn't seen in years. We stop for a quick pose, then go back to our insane dance. Let Bezma catch us if she can.

We're panting, sweating, delirious, and then the song stops and we fall onto the cushions. Every cell of my being is wide open, receptive; my body is millions of sea anemones waving in nutrients that re-make me whole. This mood is beyond priceless. We're drunk on the emotion of unexpected abundance, the taste of kangareh, the sound of "khsh khsh khsh," the springtime heat, and the great time we'll have buying something expensive together.

We lie back to catch our breath and I stare up at the roof; what looks like corn husks are woven into intricate thatch patterns, tied together with thick twine, laced across bamboo-type poles. Ara, beside me, takes my hand and squeezes. "It's beautiful," I say, meaning everything — the thatch, the lunch she worked so hard to make, the dancing, the laughing, and especially her, this dazzling soul who somehow burst through ordinary existence to laugh into the camera under a silly hat.

"Yes. Beautiful," she replies. And we just lie like that, letting the world return to normal, but also wishing it never would.

"Now give me phone," Bezma is saying somewhere back in real life. Ara fishes it out of her dress, and we can hear Bezma outside telling Hevar about the stove. There are a lot of "Amreeka"s, and some "Soz"es too. I wonder if the stove will make him change his mind about a double wedding. How could any husband-to-be resist such happiness in his fiancee's voice?

❊ ❊ ❊

I'm out of oatmeal, and that means a mid-week trip into town on the faculty bus. I'm the only passenger until Khalil jumps on just as the doors close. He takes the seat next to me, and leans his head close. The cuffed white shirt makes his bony shoulders look like coat hangers, and his attempt at a moustache isn't filling in too well yet.

"Okay if we talk?"

"Sure." I smell garlic and cilantro, probably from one of Layla's aromatic stews. "What's going on?"

"Too much." He hasn't planned this; the bus must have been a last-minute decision. "I think I have made a mistake."

"Oh, you mean about Layla?" Let's just cut to the chase.

"Yes, about Layla." His voice drips with melancholy. "I may have let everything go too far, too fast."

He's taking this way too seriously. "Oh, I don't think a little romp in the hay ever hurt anybody. But maybe that's the American in me. I'm sure it's different if you're Muslim."

"It's not that so much. I grew up in the U.K. It's not all that uncommon to, uh, well, sow a few wild oats. For a man, anyway."

"You don't say."

"I was hoping you could give me an older woman's perspective. Layla is close to you and Pat in age, although nobody would ever guess it."

I decide to overlook the prick to my vanity. "Mmm hmm." Where is this going?

"I don't exactly know how to put this." His throat clearing sounds fake, to stall for time. "You see, she has not yet gone through the change."

The change? Oh yes, that. She must be a bit younger than I'd thought. "And you have trouble abstaining for four or five days a month?"

"No…" He drags it out, waiting for me to catch his drift.

"You can't mean that you've gotten her pregnant."

"Not yet." He twists a stretchy watchband around his graceful wrist. This boy should have been a pianist, or maybe a ballet dancer. "But that's what she wants. For us to start a family together back in England."

I'm sorely tempted to laugh, but something about the little moustache stops me. "And let me guess. You had something else in mind?"

"I'm bloody terrified." He'd be using stronger language if I was more his contemporary.

"Understandably."

We let a few miles rumble by, past a salute at a police checkpoint.

"Of course, I am incredibly grateful to her."

"For all the good meals, right?"

He doesn't hear the irony. "For everything. But does that have to translate into a lifetime commitment?"

I'm disappointed in Layla. She's pressuring this kid into marriage? It seems so out of character. "I wouldn't think so. But then, I'm not Layla. I'm not an Arab."

"But you passed through the stage she's in. You're divorced -- probably for excellent reasons, just like hers -- and live alone and travel all over the world, and you don't need a man in order to exist. So why should she?"

"Is that what she's saying? That she needs you? Sounds like manipulation to me."

He draws himself up straighter, as if to remind me that a gentleman need not worry about being manipulated.

I let a few more blocks of auto repair shops and minimarts rumble by.

"Khalil, you're young and handsome and smart. You have your whole life ahead of you. Don't get stuck in something you don't really want."

"That's what Madame says."

Uh oh. "You told Madame all this?"

"I needed a sounding board. And she's a friend of my parents. Like a second mother."

Oh dear. "I don't consider Madame to be the most disinterested party here." Wait. Maybe he'll think I'm implying that he should have come to me first. My face is getting hot.

"True, but she understands Layla." Oops. Now he's defensive. "She said she might be able to transfer me to a different Academy school. There's an opening in Abu Dhabi." He brightens.

"So you wouldn't have to break up with Layla, or say no to marriage? You'd let the transfer do the dirty deed for you."

He nods, miserable again. "I realize it would be cowardly."

"But an easy way out. Right?"

"Right. And Abu Dhabi is supposed to be a nicer place to live."

I have my doubts about that. I let the dusk enfold us in silence and stare out the window. We're almost at the new shopping center, but will have to do several tricky U-turns in traffic to reach the parking lot. There's not much time left to resolve this.

"Layla's a grown woman. She can handle the end of a romance. Don't worry about her."

He shakes his head. "She really wants another son. This is probably her only chance."

Good lord. "You're like a son to her, for heaven's sake."

Nothing is sinking in. "It's not that I don't love her." The double negative is less than convincing. "I feel so guilty. I've taken advantage of her good heart and gorgeous body, and now won't give her what she wants in return."

We've reached the mall, and the bus door opens. I give his arm a little squeeze. "Trust your instincts, Khalil. There's part of you that knows exactly what you want to do. What you want to do is what you should do. Follow that impulse."

He leaves me at the mall's security check, where they will go through my purse and shopping bags to make sure that I'm not bringing in any concealed weapons. And I wonder at the improbability of this conversation, a young Arab man pouring his heart out to me in the outskirts of an Iraqi city. Despite the strained topic of conversation, it's great to be alive.

Eight: Leaps (Of Faith and Otherwise)

IT'S NOW early June, and I'm still doing promenades sometimes with Madame. She is already walking by the time I meet her at the track, striding at about double her normal speed, panting on her stubby little legs. "Bad, bad bad." She mutters to the pavement itself. Does she even notice me?

"What's bad?" Perhaps she found out about my village visits and friendship with Seema. Perhaps she's sending me home.

"Theresa, we are friends, correct? Not just work acquaintances. Real friends?"

I would never rank this woman among my friends. "Of course."

"I am facing a professional dilemma. No, not about you, don't be silly. About Rabinowitz. He emailed the president of the Academy in Cairo, reporting Layla and Khalil. So now I officially know about the affair. I have no choice but to fire her and send her home."

"What a rat!" And I let him sleep on my couch? I abetted a traitor to the expat teacher ranks?

"No, don't blame Rabinowitz. He was doing his duty as a Muslim, keeping the faith pure."

"Rubbish. He's jealous that Khalil is getting some action and he isn't."

She sighs. "I wish he had come directly to me, instead of to the president. I was handling things in my own way. Now it looks like I don't know what's going on in my own school."

Yes, it had been a particularly insidious maneuver.

"I've already spoken with Layla, and told her to start packing. Maybe you could have a word with her? The two of you have been close."

"Not exactly close. But we've lived next door." Hearing muffled noises through the wall hasn't exactly made me her confidante.

"I don't know what she'll do after this," Madame says. "She needs the money. Her family didn't approve of her divorce, and they won't support her. Needless to say, I can't give her a good reference letter now." Another sigh. "For years, we have been sisters. And now this."

"What about Khalil? Doesn't he bear a certain amount of responsibility? You can't blame the whole situation entirely on Layla."

She ignores the question, lost in a cloud of worries. If I've learned anything over the past many months, it's that Madame can't be budged, and doesn't have many listening skills.

I stifle my outrage, agree to comfort Layla, and we cut the walk short. On the way to the apartments, though, I fume, and not just about Khalil. Layla has been a sister, but Madame can't bend the rules enough to write a measly letter? I'm already drafting one for Layla in my head, which Jake can put on forged letterhead, with a forged version of Madame's signature. Oh, I'll wax eloquent on Madame's behalf, citing delighted parents, high-performing students, an award in the offing; what a pity we're losing her. It's the least Jake and I can do.

But what will I say to Layla in person? She should have known better? No, that sounds righteous. She'll find better husband material at a different school? No, that sounds like pablum. I salute you for going after life with such gusto? Possibly, because that's more like the truth. But maybe I won't have to say anything. Maybe she'll just cry in my arms. Or yell.

When I reach Layla's apartment, the door is propped open with a waste basket. Clothes are strewn everywhere, lacy little negligees and thong undies, a peach-colored bra mixed in with the sweaters and skirts she wears to teach. An enormous suitcase the size of dance-hall speakers lies splayed face down on the bed. Why such haste? She won't have to leave for a day or two, maybe a week. There aren't that many flights out of the country. She still has time to buy souvenirs, and for us to have a party for her...

And then I hear a scream over by the classroom block. It's one long wail of anguish echoing against masses of concrete, and then silence. Horrible, ghastly silence.

My stomach knows in an instant. An internal Richter scale jags off the charts, the world convulsing and caving in around me, and I'm paralyzed, like the neighbors must have been when shrieks or shots came over the walls at the Red Jail. I take the stairs two at a time to the classroom quad.

But of course it's too late. There's too much blood splattered everywhere. She must have leaped from the rooftop — not just stepped off meekly, but jumped with a vengeance for extra momentum. I can't see Layla's sweet, lovely face, or what's happened to it, mashed into the concrete, but wouldn't want to. She is much too still.

Madame is right behind me. "Layla!" It's a mad woman's howl, at odds with the rigidity of her back. She kneels next to the crumpled pile, mindless of all the blood, and pokes at her friend's back with an arm stiff as a stick.

"She's still breathing. Get an ambulance!"

How does one call for an ambulance here? Is it 9-1-1, or something else? Rescue seems only a feverish delusion anyway. But you never know.

"You foolish, foolish woman." Madame mutters in Arabic.
I can't tell whether she means Layla or herself.

*   *   *

En masse, we stare as the shuttle's tail lights wend their way
down the hill to the main road— every teacher, administrator,
secretary, and even the Bangladeshi janitors, mustered in haste
by the scream. We've been standing around helpless until a
vehicle can be found for Layla. The Arab and Kurdish women
fall into one another's arms, weeping with great shuddering
abandon. We expats grasp at our elbows awkwardly, avoiding
one another's eyes, shifting from one foot to another. Madame
has abandoned us, disappearing into the admin building with a
mixture of hurry, confusion and self-importance.

"I can't believe it," says Jake finally. "WTF. Sure, things
suck here big time. But *that* bad?"

"It was your buddy Rabinowitz," I blurt. "Why couldn't he
just keep his big fat mouth shut and mind his own business?"

"About what?" Jake still hasn't gotten it. He squints as Pat
silently mouths "the affair", then buries his face in his hands.
For once, the melodrama seems appropriate.

"Listen." Pat's voice trembles. "You bring that self-
righteous bastard anywhere near here again, and I promise, I
will personally report him to the embassy for being Al Qaeda.
You got that? And I don't even care whether he's really Al
Qaeda, or Taliban, or whatever. Theresa and I will swear on a
stack of Bibles that he's planning a suicide attack or something.
Right, Theresa?"

"I'm ready to call them right now." Yet I barely hear
anything, even my own words coming out on autopilot,
because I'm too numb; nothing registers above the bass
pounding of my pulse, reverberating like ongoing sonic booms
throughout my body.

234

Hunched over in grief, Mrs. Zaki breaks out of the Arab / Kurd huddle, staggers toward our expat group, and drags Pat and me to her bosom. She's heaving with sobs, great gut-wrenching moans; and now we are weeping along with her, unabashedly, for she has unleashed something primal that can't be borne alone. Jake too — now we all clasp one another tight, Arabs, Kurds, poor wretched Khalil, Teflon-coated Roboteacher, Mohammed, the secretaries, commando Zaki himself, everybody, smelted into a sodden lump of agony.

A clanking makes us look up. The Bangladeshis materialize behind us with mops and pails. They don't start cleaning the mess right away, though. Instead, they mumble what sound like prayers around the blood, reluctant to so much as touch it with their mops. When the praying winds down, one of them tosses out his pail onto the blood, diluting it to a softer pink that pools out, leaving a brighter stain in the middle. They shake their heads. This is going to be one ghastly task.

The rest of us stand there in the quad, wordless, sniffling, watching the janitors swoosh and swirl soiled water around. There's nothing to say. Nothing to do. When there's nothing left to look at, we drift back to our apartments in silence. Aside from proceeding with lesson plans tomorrow, we have no idea what any of us are supposed to do next.

❀   ❀   ❀

Mercifully, the next morning begins with a fire drill, eating a good forty minutes out of the day. The students are just settling back into their seats for homeroom when Zaki's voice comes crackling over the loudspeaker.

"Your attention please. All students must proceed immediately to the school bus loading zone. Calmly and in orderly fashion, board your buses and go home for the rest of the day. If your parents normally drive you to and from school, wait for them inside the gate. They have been notified to come get you. We will resume classes again tomorrow. I repeat. Proceed in a calm and orderly fashion to the school gates. That will be all."

What is this, war? Has the President been assassinated? Petrified, I wait for an explanation. My kids, in the meantime, are jubilant, stuffing books into backpacks and crowding the door. "Bomb threat again, Miss. Isn't it wonderful?" They're acting like they've all won free passes to an amusement park.

Did Jake pull the fire alarm, or phone in a bomb threat? Or did Madame or Zaki take pity on us, knowing what emotional wrecks we'd be today? Where is Madame anyway? I'd expected her to brief us about Layla's condition before class in the faculty room, and not leave us shrugging at each other in concern.

Madame is still missing the next day too. Khalil hangs like a specter around the faculty room, saying nothing, drinking endless cups of rancid coffee; none of us dare ask him if there's any news about Layla. Zaki has probably been told something by the headquarters people, but the thought of him delivering grim news to us grates like nails on a chalkboard. So I'm nominated to go ask Mohammed, who may have the inside story from the Kurdish Government.

Mohammed's office is now heavy with self-importance. Massoud Barzani, father of the nation, gazes protectively from a massive golden frame on the wall. A new metal filing cabinet bulges open, folders zig and zag in careless stacks, and there's even a red Afghan carpet under the desk. Mohammed must be coming up in the world.

"A very sad situation," he murmurs. "But not as bad as it might have been, *al ham du l'allah*. Miss Layla is safe in a hospital in Istanbul, getting very good treatment. She has many fractures, including her pretty face, such a pity. Her condition is no longer critical, and she will recover *in sh'allah*. But the Academy will certainly not bring her back, not after this."

That's it? I wait, to shame him into telling me more.

"The school has insurance. You teachers needn't worry about her."

"Insurance? You think we're worried about money?"

He clears his throat politely. "Okay, she is covered for the broken bones. But not for reconstructive surgery. That will be her family's responsibility."

I stare in disbelief. "What about the ethics of the situation? Doesn't the government investigate this sort of thing? To make sure she wasn't being coerced about something? To see whether her, uh, accident could have been prevented. Or doesn't happen again, with somebody else?"

Mohammed's face ages about two decades in the blink of an eye. "Miss Theresa, look around you. Remember what country you are in. Remember what has happened here in just the past ten, twenty years. My heart goes out to Miss Layla and the rest of you. Really it does. But..." He turns both palms up and shrugs. "What can anybody do?"

"I don't know," I say helplessly. And I don't. But the sanctimonious Westerner in me wants to make a fuss anyway, organize a march with big placards protesting intolerance and meanness in general, and make sure Rabinowitz gets deported to someplace like Guantanamo. Or better yet, locked back up in the Baghdad jail, the miserable hypocrite.

Mohammed shows me to the door with exaggerated courtesy, and I thank him with equal courtesy, sensing a new level of fellowship. "My advice?" he says gently, touching my elbow. "Get on with your work. Carry on, for the sake of the children. It helps during times like these. The children feel these things even more deeply than you do. And they are counting on you a great deal to help them succeed in the final exams, you know."

It's a good reminder, however trite. I assure him that we teachers will not let our charges down, and head back to my colleagues to tell them the sorry news.

❖ ❖ ❖

It's yellow-hot now outside in the daytime, the hillside grasses desiccated to a ragged brown mat. Nothing in the village stirs this afternoon except for us, unloading a brand-new four-burner gas range with oven and a smallish refrigerator from a hired Datsun pickup. Bezma bosses three men straining beneath first one enormous carton, and then the other, staggering through Ara's gate and up to her porch. Bezma shoos away the children gathered around us; I'm busy snapping pictures for my blog. We did it! While I sweated outside on the sidewalk for an eternity, Bezma and Ara wrangled such a great discount at the appliance shop that we could afford both a stove and fridge. And now she is storing them here on Ara's porch until the Big Day arrives.

Hevar already knows. The whole way back to the village from the city, Bezma yacked on her phone with him until she ran out of battery. As soon as the delivery guys leave, Hevar pulls up in his truck, adjusts the gun tucked into his waist, and admires the cardboard boxes. He turns solemn with gratitude.

"Treeza, Bezma big woman in my village with stove gift," he tells me, with Bezma interpreting. His hair is lacquered into a dashing pouf, giving him a distinctive 1950's look; I wonder how he keeps the creases starched so nicely in this heat. "Nobody see anything like this, never. Now Bezma very special."

Embarrassed, I shrug to make light of it. "Famous far away in your village, but not here?" I'm joking, but also surprised that none of her friends, or her sister-in-law, have heard the commotion and come to check it out.

"Here they know, but jealous," Bezma says, as if any dummy would have known this. "They jealous you buy only for me, not them. They ashamed to say this, so stay away."

"But we only had enough money for you. And besides, you're the one getting married…"

"No matter. Do not think about this."

"I'm just one measly teacher. I can only do so much." I hadn't expected such defensiveness.

"Never mind. I am very, very happy. Hevar very happy. My mother very happy." She dusts her hands together. Finished.

"And wedding very soon!" says Hevar.

"Sooner is better," she adds.

I rarely have a chance like this to speak with Hevar. "Say, whatever happened to the idea of a double wedding? With your sister Soz?"

At the sound of her name, Hevar looks daggers at Bezma. She hastens to explain.

"Not happen. Not possible."

Now I'm curious. "Why not?" I want to hear it from him. They bicker back and forth in Kurdish as they decide what to tell me.

"Hevar must protect family name. He will find Soz good husband. But later. She must let Hevar make decision."

This seems patently unfair. "But Bezma got to pick you. Why can't your sister pick *her* husband?"

He struggles to keep his temper; one look at the appliance boxes restores a bit of his patience. Bezma jumps in to speak for him.

"Hevar is bad brother if say yes for wedding. Family lose face. And more things, I cannot say now. So we talk something else." She placates him with a peck on the cheek, and it seems to work.

239

"Okay." Even better, we should *do* something else. As every teacher knows, when a situation gets uncomfortable, switch to a different activity.

Today I have brought my male *khak* outfit, stitched for me as a souvenir by a tailor in the city. The baggy pants, with a crotch that reaches practically to my knees, cinch up easily with a drawstring, and the jacket has simple buttons. But I don't know how to tie the sash or turban. I ask Hevar to teach me.

Great idea; both he and Bezma are delighted at the diversion. I fish the outfit from my backpack, put on the pants and jacket over my clothes, and wait for him to demonstrate.

The belt is a silky polyester scarf at least six yards long. He explains that different tribal groups tie it in their own way, and I should really learn his village's technique, the most elegant, rather than doing it sloppy like people from Zakho or Sulemani. This requires an assistant. He spins me while Bezma stands back with the ends taut, until I'm wound like a spool with fabric criss-crossing in front. He tucks in the ends, and ta-da. A blonde Peshmerga wearing Nikes in their midst. Then he unwinds me by pulling on the ends. I'm all dizzy now. "Do it yourself," he instructs me, and of course I mess it all up so that it slips to the ground in a big messy coil. We're in hysterics. Too bad Ara has gone off to the grocery and is missing all this.

Then there's the turban. Hevar settles my crocheted skullcap on his own head, folds the cloth I've bought, and deftly whips it around. He praises that I have bought red, meaning the right tribal affiliation. Then he takes the whole contraption off and sets it on me. After admiring his craftsmanship in a hand mirror Bezma brings, I stow it in my backpack as is, like an antiquity, knowing that I'd never be able to rewrap it properly on my own.

He stares at me meaningfully, at the gate, at me. What am I missing? Then I get it — here's a rare chance for them to be alone. I wheel out the Blue Angel, still in the Peshmerga pants and top, and head back to The Fortress, despite their half-hearted protest.

As I reach the edge of town, I hear a familiar "Miss!" There is Seema, sitting alone under a tree, just beyond the last house. She chews on the end of a dried weed, watching as absolutely nothing happens on the road. She can't help puzzling at the get-up. "Miss. You look like a man."

"I'm a cross-dresser." But she doesn't understand; nobody cross-dresses in Kurdistan. "Seema, what are you doing outside in this heat?"

"It's quiet out here." She helps me rest the bicycle against the tree trunk, and brushes off a place for me to sit. She waits for me to mop my face. Riding even a few blocks in this heat has given me a headache.

"Miss," she starts tentatively, "do you think I'm getting better in school?"

I try to concentrate on talking. The stones are sharp under me, and I have to tilt over to one side to get comfortable. "Funny you should ask that. I was just talking with the other teachers a few days ago, to see whether you've improved as much in their classes as you have in mine. They all said that you had." Well, two did anyway. The ones who couldn't place her don't count.

She's pleased.

"And the girls have been nicer to you too, haven't they?"

"When you're around, Miss. Not the rest of the time."

Oh damn. So much for my lecture on the Golden Rule. We stare at the heat rippling off the asphalt for a while.

"Miss, you will be my teacher next year won't you?"

Not unless the dozens of resumes I've been emailing all get rejected, and no school from Bolivia to Mongolia wants to hire me. But I want to prolong this lazy camaraderie, and not

241

disappoint her yet. "If I'm here next year, I'll see if you can be in my class."

It's enough to satisfy her. She clearly hasn't considered the vagaries of the international job market.

A few sheep meander down the hill, a lame mongrel limping behind them. A kindergartener in a faded Real Madrid soccer jersey follows, whistles at the dog, and tosses a rock at the sheep when he sees us. Seema, the dog and the sheep all pay him no mind. It's too hot to care.

"Miss, if you're not staying here for sure, then maybe you'll go back to America. Right?" This girl isn't missing a beat.

"It's possible," I admit. Anything is possible right now, even Timbuktu.

"Then I have something very important to ask you."

I've grown accustomed to requests from people all the time, even total strangers. Will I get President Obama's autograph for them? Will I send them a flat screen TV? Someone even asked me once to get them on a game show, so they could win a million dollars.

After a long wait while she gathers her courage, she whispers, "Will you take me with you to America?"

Oh dear. "I can't do that. You belong here in the village, with Old Houda."

I'm ashamed of such a patronizing answer, insulting her intelligence. Yet how to explain the visas, the red tape, the costs, the needs of paying for Andy's college, my nearing a grandmotherly age, my saving for eventual retirement — much less my unwillingness to shoulder such an enormous responsibility?

"Grandmother would let me go. She trusts you."

We both know it's impossible, don't we? No; the way she's grabbing my sleeve and wringing it reminds me of trying to ask my own mother for things I desperately wanted; how I would practice a question for weeks, waiting for just the right moment until she seemed in a receptive mood, and then chicken out or ask for something lesser — out of fear of hearing "no".

"I would be very good, Miss. I would do everything you told me. I would clean the house for you after school, and iron your clothes. I'm learning to be a good cook." She is pleading now, pulling out all the stops.

I see Seema's future twisting like a poorly marked country road. If she's extremely lucky, stays motivated, gets exceptional grades, and has someone to guide her through the minefields of adolescence, she might make it to a local college some day. She might get a technical degree, or learn computer programming, or become a dental assistant, or qualify to be a teacher, and eventually support herself. On the other hand, a bomb could explode some day when she's in the wrong place at the wrong time. She might get married off young — or, heaven forbid, kidnapped or sold if someone like Saddam comes into power again or overruns this part of Iraq. Part of me therefore has to take her request as seriously as she intends it. And yet...

"The school does not permit things like this. I am not supposed to even be friends with students outside of class. They would never let me adopt you. I am very sorry."

But that's only a piece of the truth. Because, despite all of the affection I have for her, and despite my understanding of her need, and despite what an unnamable former spouse scorned as my bleeding liberal heart, and despite the sincerity of my desire to help make the world a better place, when push comes to shove I am not ready to put this adorable little girl's future ahead of my own.

She flings herself into my lap. "Nobody would cut me in America, Miss."

It's her last bit of ammunition, the final bullet she's been holding in reserve. I gasp, like she's socked me in the stomach.

"Please, Miss. Please!"

I hold her in my arms, and wish that things were different. I wish I was wealthier, younger, in a more stable situation, and that the Western world had never double-crossed the Kurds. I wish I could whisk Seema off, spread out fresh sheets for her in my spare bedroom, send her to school, and give her just a few of the advantages my own son had. But I can't. That's the hard, cold truth of it.

Suddenly, collecting money for a stove and fridge now seems like such a hopeless drop in the bucket. There's a whole world of Seemas out there, orphans, amputees, child brides, refugees, children starving to death. I am too small to make anything better.

"I'm sorry, Seema. I'm sorry from the bottom of my heart." It sounds so lame. Words. I have nothing else to offer her.

I struggle to my feet and remount the Blue Angel. Can she tell I'm crying? I pedal with great weariness uphill, turning back to wave to her before disappearing behind the rise. I pedal through wavy heat mirages, through a razor-wire fence, past a security check manned by machine-gun-toting guards, and back to a stack of ungraded exercise books. The raggedy homework pages mock me. Sure, I can teach some English grammar. But that's about as far as I'm getting in being the change I want to see, and the realization is too much to bear.

❊ ❊ ❊

"I realize this comes at a bad time," says Madame as Jake, Pat and I take seats in her office.

No kidding. It's only been a week since Layla's leap, and the air in the faculty room feels polluted. A ghost echo of her scream seems ever-present in the quad. Khalil left the Academy yesterday with touching chivalry to take care of Layla while she convalesces in Istanbul. He gave Jake one of his Alfani dress shirts, which Jake is wearing now, and Pat and me his email address with a promise to stay in touch; we gave him a little album of photos from the Shaqlawa trip, which may not have been the most thoughtful gift, we concluded afterward. We'll miss his ingenuousness in the faculty room, but the real losers have been Khalil and Layla's students, left adrift until next school year. Madame and Zaki try to pop into the classrooms at random times to maintain order, a patently futile endeavor, and the resulting pandemonium leaches out in quantum resonance throughout the school.

In addition to this sorrowful chaos, we're ramping up for final exams, and it's as serious as training for a desert Iron Man race. Acne flares across anxious preteen foreheads. Once-friendly jabs across the aisles have become pointed and tense. Both students and teachers walk a treacherous emotional tight rope together: exam tension on the one hand, and the proximity of summer liberation on the other. For the kids, the deadly threat of summer school for those who fail makes it all the more tenuous.

The pressure for our students to do well, and outshine other Academy sister schools around the world, gives us little time for anything but hard-core teaching. No more spelling bees, word searches or silent games. Which is why Pat, Jake and I are surprised to be summoned to Madame's office for this meeting. Other teachers have similar appointments, in groups by subject and grade, wasting our precious free periods. We suspect the worst.

A stern furrowed look from Madame warns us not to mention Layla, and we obey, enduring a drivel of pep talk. Exams have been received from headquarters in Cairo. The reputation of our school and its faculty are at stake. This is our opportunity to prove our professionalism. By the way, we shouldn't forget that our year-end bonuses are tied to our students' results. Madame steals a look at her watch. Her phone rings. "I see. Right away." With not-very-convincing nonchalance, she prods a small sheaf of papers toward us, stands, and excuses herself. "Please stay in my office. I'm not sure when I'll be able to return." And hurries out.

Jake starts fuming. "So, we're supposed to just sit here waiting for her the whole effing period?" Then he follows Pat's eyes to the papers, and whistles. "Holy crap. I do not believe this. Don't tell me this is some sort of weird coincidence. Final English exam for sixth, seventh and eighth graders. Hmmm."

I check the tiny window in Madame's door, but no one is there. "Maybe this is a test of morality. She's trying to see if we'll peek at the tests while she's gone. She's comparing us infidel teachers with the virtuous Muslims. What if she's got secret cameras in here after all?"

"I don't think so." Pat scans the corners of the room and ceiling anyway. "No, I think the phone call was a set up, and she's hoping we'll read the questions. Maybe even copy them down."

"She wouldn't do that." But now he's not sounding so sure.

"How else will her school look smarter than everyone else's?" Pat pulls the papers closer and leafs through them. "How else will she get a plaque for Principal of the Decade, especially after what happened with Layla? She's probably up shit creek."

I'm getting a bad taste in my mouth, like when we kids used to put tin foil on our teeth as fake braces. The window in Madame's door is still empty. She's been gone much too long. "It seems nutty. But I think Pat's right."

"Okay, Twink. We'll trust your judgment. We'd better hurry." I wish Jake would stop calling me that. I'm not feeling very twinkly at the moment.

We divide the exams into thirds, and rush to write as much as we can onto the blank sheets conveniently provided at the bottom of the sheaf. By the time the bell rings and our "appointment" is over, Madame still has not returned, and we head back across the quad to our respective classrooms. The test questions are devilishly hard, more appropriate for college students than middle schoolers. Who the heck cares what a hoplite phalanx is? I have a hard time remembering what the past perfect continuous tense is myself. My poor kids. I will have to teach to the exam nonstop to get even half of them to pass.

"This is not education," I grumble for about the hundredth time as we trudge across the quad to the classrooms.

"What ever made you think it was?" Pat asks.

"And it's not right, either," I continue. "Our kids will learn about half as much if we just focus on what's on the test."

"'Ours is not to wonder why. Ours is but to do or die.' Funny how often that comes in handy," Jake says, squaring his shoulders.

"Pat, tell me we're not going to use these copies," I plead. My palms are starting to sweat.

"When in Rome…" she replies. "Besides, who knows the back story here? Madame had to have some reason for giving us these, a reason she couldn't share with mere underlings like us."

"Yeah, Old Baldy's no fool." It's the first not-totally-obnoxious thing I've ever heard him say about her.

"Look, she's bringing everybody into her office, so there's got to be some grand scheme here. I say we go with the flow, since none of us will be here next year anyway. Okay?" She stops at the foot of the stairwell and waits until she gets a grudging nod from both of us before doing her segue. "Say, speaking of next year. Keep this to yourselves, but I've got an offer in Saudi. It pays more than twice what we get here."

"Hot damn." Jake sniggers. "Schools pay the absolute minimum they have to, to get warm bodies in classrooms. So let's do the math. Twice the pay means twice the misery you've got to endure. Not worth it, even for a whore like me."

"It can't be that bad," says Pat, turning to me hopefully.

"Oh, but it is," I reply. "Maybe not the school itself. But absolutely everything else."

"You'll look adorable in an abaya." Jake flutters his eyelashes. "Hey, if it wasn't for the no-alcohol thing, I'd consider Saudi myself. You could get away with murder under one of those black abayas."

"I'll really have to wear one?" Pat asks.

"Yep," I reply. "And forget about walking around outside by yourself, too."

Pat sighs. "I could handle that, I think. My biggest problem has been getting a recommendation from the Academy. Anybody figure out how to do it, without Madame knowing that we're trying to leave?"

"Kiss that bonus goodbye once she finds out." Jake blows her a smooch. "But no worries about the letter. Twinkie and I've got it all worked out now. Practice makes perfect. Right, Twink?"

Our recommendation, which Madame supposedly wrote over the weekend for Khalil to bring to Layla, looked pretty dubious on paper. But after we photocopied it a couple of times and scanned it to a PDF, giving it that "authentic artifact" effect, it wasn't half bad. We figured that other places would give it the benefit of the doubt, coming as it did from a war zone. When word gets out, everybody in the staff room will want one.

❖ ❖ ❖

Getting on the computer is always something to look forward to back in the apartment when classes are over. Every "like" or comment on my blog is an upper. So is anything from Andy, or even a marketing email from an insurance company, proving that I still exist in the Real World. Today there's something from a mysterious "fgmlaw," which I click on out of curiosity. Bad idea. It takes me three readings to understand all the legalese.

"Pat!" I bang on her door, find her napping on her orange sofa, and thrust the laptop into her hands. "Take a look at this. This time I'm getting sued!"

Reluctantly, she tips down her glasses from on top of her head and squints at the screen. "Let's see." She gets the gist faster than I did, and does a low groan. "Holy shit. You're screwed, baby."

Fester, Gerber and Moscowitz regret to inform me that certain business liabilities have not been paid by my beloved former spouse and have been accruing interest, fees and fines, causing the liabilities to more than double in the past several years. As co-signer to a loan…

The muscles in my face have started to quiver. "What kind of slimebag lawyer would try to strong arm a penniless expat teacher like this? Don't they know Wells Fargo already took everything I had? It's an outrage!"

"Of course they know," she says. I hate it when she gets calm and practical like this in an emergency. "That's why they bought the debt for pennies on the dollar. They also know you've probably got some assets somewhere. Or somebody in your family does. Hey, want a cup of tea?"

"Sure." Good thing she gives me a saucer, because my shaking jostles tea all over the place. And good idea she has, spiking it with rum. It tastes great.

"What are my options?" I ask when my heart slows down a little.

"Let's see." She clicks up the air conditioner so it blasts directly down onto us. "Pay it. Or fight, spend a fortune on lawyers, and then pay it on top of the lawyer's fees. In other words, pay it."

"No way." It's almost my entire year's salary. "I'll sue The Financial Genius. Or pay the Mafia to squeeze it out of him. He got a nice car and an RV out of this, the little snake."

"Hah!" she explodes, spluttering her tea. "Professional leaches cover their tracks. I'll bet you dollars to donuts he registered everything in somebody else's name so it can't be traced, and on paper he looks even more strapped than you actually are."

My toes curl. I'm too embarrassed to admit that, in fact, he did this to his previous ex-wife. But naturally it never occurred to me that he'd do it to *me*. I can't even look at Pat now; I'm sure that she's got ESP, and has already guessed how stupid I've been.

"One more option," she continues. "You pay up with Fester and Company, and they conveniently neglect to record it, and then a second sleazeball buys the debt at even fewer pennies on the dollar, and sues you again, and you pay it a second time, only with a lot more interest, fees and fines."

All the orange in the apartment is starting to swirl around me. I shut my eyes and try to breathe. Pat takes the empty cup from my hand and the clattering stops. I can hear her heading back to the kitchen.

"So your best bet is to go home and hire a lawyer to resolve it all." The rum bottle glugs behind me. "Of course, then you end up paying lawyers AND the debt. But at least it'll be behind you once and for all."

"But that will cost a fortune!" The cup is back in my hand, nicely refilled. I open my eyes, but still slop it onto my lap. I'm drowning in self-pity. "But hey — how do you know all this stuff?"

"Hah!" This burst, sounding something like "I may be more street-smart than you but I still pity you," has become her trademark now. "I was married to the second sleazeball."

She's kidding. No, she's not. "Oh man, Pat. This is unbelievable."

She leans back with her hands behind her head. "Yeah, tell me about it, kiddo."

❈ ❈ ❈

The next evening, Pat and I take the back seats on the shopping bus where nobody can hear us talk.

"You look like a wreck," she says once we start bouncing down the hill.

"I haven't heard from Andy in a while…"

She gives me one of those knowing looks. "That's not it, is it? You're still fretting about that lawyer business."

How did she guess? "I just want to disappear off the face of the earth, and never pay another penny of that jerk's debts. It's so unfair."

"Who told you life was fair?"

"And what's worse, to pay a lawyer I'll have no choice but to keep teaching here next year."

"Heaven forbid." She's serious. "HOD doesn't pay that much more than what you're making now. You'd be better off in Saudi with me."

"What — you didn't believe me about what it's like there?" Part of me is miffed that she hasn't obeyed my advice, even though it's irrational. Even though I hadn't obeyed my family's advice about the Financial Genius, long before the divorce, for instance.

"I emailed the contract off last night after you left. Hey, don't look so disappointed. It can't be any worse than you becoming a blonde Zaki. Enforcing the Academy's Nazi policies all next year."

My jaw clenches so hard it hurts. "I'll do it as penance. For trusting that loser with my credit."

She squeezes my arm. "Don't be so hard on yourself, sweetie. You were just being a good wife, like we boomer girls were brought up to be. Stand by your man. And other such rot."

"Like Madame? Stand by your school. I wonder if she gets a retention bonus, for teachers she can convince to stay." I shiver with the realization that this could very well be true.

Pat laughs wickedly. "Oh I get it. You mean you believed all along that she liked you and was trying to do you a favor? That's a good one. Talk about gullible."

I glare out the window. "I resent that word, gullible."

"Now you're pouting like a goddamn victim. Cut it out."

"If I'm gullible, I can't be a victim." I seriously object to that righteous tone she's got now, patronizing me for being a fool. "It makes me responsible for not knowing better, even when the other person is clearly taking advantage of me. And if you don't know something, how can you be expected to know it? See what I mean? It's just not fair."

Pat draws in a breath, getting ready to speak. Before she can, though, I continue, "Don't say it again. Please?"

"Say what?" There's a long pause, and then she darts a sneaky look at me sideways. "Whoa — I finally got you to smile."

And she's right, sort of. But it's mostly a smile of thanks for her friendship.

"If it's any consolation," she adds right before we pull up at the shopping center, "I should be the last person to call the kettle black. You ran away from a bad situation and ended up being sentenced to six months in Iraq. Plus maybe one more school year, the way things are going. Big effing whoop. Whereas yours truly tried the same thing, and got sentenced to twenty-four cursed months in a hell hole called Ouagadougou. And got paid in Peace Corps cowrie shells."

She snickers so loud that the teachers all the way up in the front of the bus turn around to stare.

* * *

Everything I've heard about Kurdish weddings sounds grandiose — three days of celebrations, live bouzouki bands, banquets in elegant halls, and scads of 21-karat gold. But as Bezma's wedding day approaches, the house is oddly subdued. I offer to help with preparations, but am told to just arrive at the crack of dawn on the day itself, in my black Kurdish glad rags, to give the bride moral support.

Moral support means a hasty breakfast of *mast ow*, watered-down yogurt, homemade cracker bread and a few almonds, then traipsing in a caravan of festooned cars and pickups to a beauty shop in the city. Half of the village must be here, including Maia the tailor, the grumpy grocery lady, and even the old men who used to scowl at me in the street, plus a host of women from Family Hevar. It's a sea of sequins, spangled vests, and gold — belts and headgear and necklaces and bracelets — everyone's finest.

"TV! *Kurdistan, min dulum khosh*." Boys and young men mob me the minute I emerge outside the beauty shop. One mimics a cameraman; another shapes his fingers like a screen. For a place with so few television sets, and the fact that I've never seen one turned on in the village, my fame is remarkable. "Both stations," they tell me. "Very beautiful."

I pose like a Hollywood star on a red carpet, to make a joke out of it, and follow the women into the salon.

We admire Bezma as she is crammed into an old-school corset. Old Houda cinches up laces through reinforced eyelets at the back. I marvel that Bezma has gotten so much heavier so quickly; perhaps the pot belly was always there, but didn't show under the baggy house dresses, or she's been eating too

253

many pre-wedding sweets. Why didn't she rent a bigger gown? A tune pops into my head, and I stifle a smile; "June is busting out all over." It's Bezma's boobs that are busting out, most impressively, from the decolletage. The cleavage is downright breathtaking.

While her newly lightened hair is being styled, sprayed, re-styled, resprayed, and layer upon layer of pasty make-up applied, the women ululate in high-pitched trills. It hurts my ears and makes me tired. And the cultural incongruity of seeing Bezma dolled up, like some prom queen from Iowa, makes me sad. By the time they lower the veil over the gobs of mascara and eyeliner, it's a wonder she can even see; they have to help her stand in the stilettos, and half-carry her to the waiting car. All the perfume makes my head swim.

"Miss, it's very exciting, don't you think?" Seema has slipped beside me at the back of the crowd.

I agree, of course. But something's not quite right. It feels, in fact, a lot like my wedding to the Financial Genius, where my family was present but far from celebratory. They could see something that I could not.

Or maybe it's Soz spoiling the mood. She's literally raining on the parade despite the dazzling red outfit, dark rivulets of mascara streaking down her cheeks back by the salon bathroom.

"Are you okay?" I ask her.

She doesn't want to talk, but I insist. She shakes her head. Yes. No. It doesn't matter, because we can't speak the same language anyway. I dig out Kleenexes from my purse and dab at her face. "It'll be all right. Your turn will come, I'm sure of it." I search for reassuring words in my limited vocabulary. "You're so lovely, Soz. You'll find a husband. After the wedding is over and Hevar is married Bezma, he'll change his mind…"

Her arms tense at the mention of Hevar's name; her eyes narrow to slits, and she disappears somewhere inside her mind. I retreat too. I have no idea how to console someone in a rage this deep.

We pile into waiting cars and honk all the way to a hillside halfway between the village and The Fortress. It's a hillock I pass on every bike trip, just beyond the smoldering trash heap. What? I thought they were renting one of the halls in the city. No, this is definitely the place, because Ara and Houda have spread out sheets and blankets, and are dishing out bowls of food from big pots, like at the funeral. They make piles of little breads shaped like footballs in the middle of each sheet, and hand out individual plastic cups of water sealed with foil. They're working fast, glancing at the sky; the clouds are getting darker, and a peevish wind is picking up.

Seema takes charge of me, fills my paper plate with vegetables and dolmas, and peels a tangerine for me with serious self-importance. I'm thankful for her chatter, explaining in English who is who, what will happen next, when the music will start for the dancing, and where I should join the dance line. It helps me feel less out of place. Bezma made a big deal insisting that I leave my hair uncovered, pulled up in a local *toqa* clip with outrageous fake feathers sprouting out the back; but nobody else shows their hair. Even in my conservative black Kurdish tunic, vest and pantaloons, cross-legged on one of the women's blankets, I am painfully conspicuous.

"Won't there be a ceremony?" I ask. "An *imam*, a trip to the mosque?"

"The *imam* has already blessed them, Miss," she explains. "That part was very quick. The good part is now, with the eating and dancing."

"It's kind of the same in America." I laugh. "Guests usually care more about the reception afterwards than the church part." Still, I wished I'd been able to see the official act, and witness the melding that must have happened between the two families. Even more than watching Bezma and Hevar's expressions, I would have liked to see the two mothers as the imam blessed the union — because the mothers are avoiding one another now at the picnic, sitting on separate blankets. But perhaps families always sit separately. What do I know?

Soz, on the other hand, crouches alone away from the party, her face hidden behind her scarf. I motion for her to join us and have some food, and get only a violent head shake in reply.

"Miss Turner." I spin around; nobody calls me that in the village. The face beneath the elaborately coiled turban doesn't register at first; unexpected, it's in the wrong setting. "Mohammed!"

He squats beside me, without getting too close to the blanket, but still near enough that I can smell a recent cigarette. "So, you turn down my invitation to one Kurdish wedding, and then we meet at a different one. Should I be offended?"

He doesn't appear offended in the least; in fact, the thrust of his shoulders says he's proud to know me outside of the wedding, to be able to hunker down casually like this.

"How did you get here? Hold on. Maybe that was rude. I didn't mean it that way."

"I understand." He smiles, and I'm glad to have a friend here. "Perhaps I should be asking you the same thing? But to answer, these people are like family to me. The bride's father was a driver for my uncle, many years ago. We stay in touch. And let me guess. You are the famous Miss Stove and Refrigerator?"

"Nothing escapes you." I'm not sure whether to be flattered or irritated. What else does he know about me? What if he's told Madame about me spending so much time here?

"I have another appointment and can't stay for the dancing," he explains. "Otherwise I would offer you a ride home. Now excuse me. I will leave you in the hands of charming Seema."

"Yes, Kaka," Seema says, glowing that he knows her name.

"Why does Bezma look so sad?" I ask her when he's left. Even when posing for the photographer, she wears a doleful pout.

"Oh, the bride is supposed to. It would be shameful if she seemed happy. She might attract the Evil Eye."

The wind is whipping the edges of the sheets and blankets now, so Ara and Houda hurry to gather the dishes and food scraps and weigh down the corners of the cloths with stones. Somebody produces an old boom box. A teenage boy tries first one cassette, then another, until he locates the dance tune he wants.

"Come on," Seema says. "This is a great one. You can learn it really easily." We scramble to our feet and join in the line at the back, along with older women and children. They're doing more intricate steps than at the Nowruz picnic, which is problematic on such a rocky field. I search for Soz, hoping she'll dance on my right to show me the steps; she's nowhere to be found. Ara and Houda refuse to join, even though a lot of other black-shrouded women have lined up.

Seema has me in tow, though. "Watch Bezma's feet," she instructs. "Women don't dance as wild as the men. Bezma is one of the best." However, the women's feet barely peek out from under their long hems. I do my best to follow along, two quick steps to the right, a dip forward and back, a lot of shoulder shrugging up and down. The steps don't seem to matter too much if one just keeps progressing in time to the right.

"Okay now watch Hevar!" He's leading the line with Bezma on his left, twirling a scarf, whistling excited whoops, prancing like a stallion. Bezma can't hide her joy any longer. She matches him step for step, even in her high heels, veil flipped back over her head so she can gaze up adoringly into his face, shimmying her shoulders like a belly dancer, making all her cleavage jiggle, dangerously close to spilling out.

I catch her eyes, and pretend we have telepathy. "Yes! Yes, my dear Bezma, you made it! You got what you wanted. Emblazon each moment of this afternoon in your mind, so you'll remember this zenith of your life forever." And although the sun is totally clouded over, I imagine a beam of blessings shining down from the sky, straight through the sparkly white bodice to her essence.

Magnificent — that's the only word for Hevar now, king of the dance line, slapping his knees, then his heels as he leaps, squats like a Cossack, stealing the stage while the music ratchets up a notch. I can see us in a Discovery Channel film on this windswept hillside; the camera captures Hevar and Bezma at just the right angle, stretched tight with lust and yearning and boldness. The pistol handle poking out of Hevar's sash makes him even more exotic and macho. How proud he is of her, and she of him; how proud they all are of their Kurdishness, belting out this song that they all know the words to, even the youngest children singing their hearts out.

With each song the frenzy mounts, becoming so fierce that we're just jumping up and down in place like on pogo sticks. We're a bunch of dervishes, crazed with fresh air and hypnotic music, plastered with sweat, stamping our feet into earth that has drunk so much Kurdish blood over the millennia. 'Our music, our land, our people,' their feet insist. 'The brown of our men's outfits that blends in with the hills; the rainbow colors of our women like the flowers we love so much.' Despite the lack of alcohol, I'm tipsy and undignified, but who cares. All I need now is a chance to slip Bezma the AstroGlide, which I finally found in the new mall downtown and have hidden in my purse.

So intent are we that nobody notices the smell at first. Now and then a dancer will sniff and look puzzled; the smoky breeze seems to be coming from downwind, not from the direction of the trash heaps. With each dance it becomes a bit more noticeable, a strange meaty smell, like grilled kabobs mixed with singed wool. As one especially long number finishes, a mother sends a boy over the rise to check. He races back, berserk, hopping in horrified excitement, waving his arms. "Hevar! Hevar!"

The dancing halts. We drop little fingers, even though the music is still chugging away and a few men are still singing; baffled, we stare at one another up and down the line. Hevar races to the top of the hillock, pauses, and bellows at the top of his lungs. The entire wedding party now runs to reach him, men and children getting there first, then women stumbling after, holding their skirts up above their knees, many with babies clutched tight. From the rise, we can see Hevar chasing to a barren depression where smoke rises within a cluster of plastic gas cans. A blackened body lies singed in flames, the mouth tied tight with a gauzy red scarf. The matching vest, tunic and bloomers are mostly burned away already. Underneath is merely the humiliation of naked charring flesh — the remains of a gorgeous young body — which Hevar hastens to tamp frantically, and then cover, with his Peshmerga jacket.

"Soz!" Over and over, Hevar shrieks his sister's name, ripping off his turban, his mother now throwing herself onto the embers, his father dragging her off, all the guests yelling, everyone tight around the body, batting away the smoke and coughing but glued in anguish to the spot of the pyre itself.

Then a single gunshot thunders through the babel. My ribs rattle at the sound; I've never been this close to a shot before, and had no idea how the air itself quivers afterwards, how time stops in shock and wonder.

Hevar stands there with legs spread wide, eyes ablaze and crazed, gun pointed to the sky.

I can almost hear him daring God to fire back.

As if Hevar had fired into the wedding crowd itself, the guests scatter. Two men I don't recognize roll Soz in one of the heavy picnic blankets, tight as plastic wrap around a sandwich, hoist her sack-like by both ends, and rest her tenderly in the bed of a pickup. Cars and trucks start gunning off in billows of dust. In the chaos, I can't even tell how Bezma leaves, or by whom she is whisked away.

❀ ❀ ❀

We women — Ara, Houda and I, plus Seema — are left alone, gazing in bewilderment at the empty fields around us. My knees wobble. Ara and Seema blink blindly, like people emerging from a darkened theater. Even Old Houda wears a baffled frown. But not for long.

"Come," says Houda gently. "We have work to do."

We glance at one another, questioning, and she gestures at the picnic litter surrounding us. "Ara and I will put the trash into a sheet. Treeza, you and Seema go down to the road and see if you can get us a taxi to come up here."

I tilt my head, glad for an order to fulfill, but still too stunned to move.

"Come dear," she repeats. "You must learn to accept. Everything —even this — is God's will. You will see."

I doubt that. At the same time, I'm grateful to her for taking charge, for putting her arms around Ara, then guiding her through the motions of cleaning up.

Dark has almost fallen by the time we convince a taxi to drive off-road to our picnic site and take us back to the village with all of our gear. Ara serves rounds of tea until we receive

Bezma's text, confirming what we already knew, that Soz has died. We sit, numb.

Everything was so perfect. Bezma's joy was so complete. And now this. I can't process it.

"Houda, it's just not right! It's — it's stupid."

Rather than being offended, Houda nods. "Yes, dear. Beautiful Soz thought she had no other choices. However, it is best that we not mourn too much. Perhaps God in His mercy was protecting her from something much worse."

"Worse? What could be worse?"

She sighs. "You never know. Sometimes it is better not to ask, and merely trust God and His plan."

As if to underscore our inner ambience, the power flickers and goes out. Passively, we sit in the gloom, without the will to search for candles and matches. Fingering the beads from her bosom, Houda prays aloud. Ara, Seema and I rock in time, murmuring *"Allah, Allah."*

But Allah doesn't send reassurance. He feels much too distant to help.

"What will happen now?" I ask when the prayers have died down to mumbles, and Houda is gathering up her skirt to leave.

"Seema and I must go home. But you stay, please. We shouldn't leave Ara alone."

At the mention of her name, Ara raises her face, and her haggard, desolate look frightens me. There's some rapid Kurdish back and forth, and Ara grabs my hand, pleading. "Of course," I say. "I'll stay."

❊   ❊   ❊

The room is even darker when Houda and Seema have left. I rustle around in the cupboard for the soft comfort of my house dress, and feel a little better once I've changed. Candles are in the cupboard too; the trigger lighter always lives on the window sill, so it's easy to find, and we drip wax to stick a couple of candles upright onto saucers. The glow helps.

We could be having our own private wake, the way Ara and I sit here on the floor, she moaning and rocking again, me twisting hair around my finger, then clasping and unclasping my hands, wishing for something to do. How do people while away the time when there's no TV or radio for distraction, no chores to be done, barely enough light to see what's going on but still too early to sleep, and too few shared words to really talk? I'm not used to this.

"Pain," Ara says, holding her waist. Her rocking is more pronounced now; she leans far forward with each bend.

"Yes. Soz dead. Bezma gone. We are very sad." I put my hand over my heart.

She shakes her head at my misunderstanding. "Sad *and* pain."

"Where? Head? Legs? Stomach?" I could go to the grocery to get the local equivalent of aspirin or antacid...

She rubs near her kidneys and sighs. Nothing that over-the-counter pills could help, then. Come sit beside me, she gestures. No, not so far away. Closer, so our knees are right beside one another. Like conspirators. Partners in grief.

An idea brightens in me, but also sounds scary. Is massage taboo? In Saudi, women were polluted by the touch of an infidel like me. But maybe not here. I have nothing to lose.

"Lie down on your front," I suggest, in English but she gets the idea. "Here. On the cushions. Put your face this way."

I'm a confirmed massage addict, but have no idea how a professional goes about giving one. However, maybe it's the laying on of hands that heal, rather than the skill — the magic of just being human together.

Ara is so "other", though. The black she wears from head to toe gives the air of armor, walling her off from normal interaction. I need some kind of bridge across the black, an "open sesame" to make her touchable. So I murmur *"bism Allah, al rahman, al raheem,"* one of the few Muslim prayer snippets I know. In the name of God the merciful and compassionate; it's what Houda says when starting anything, even putting a key in a lock. If I touch Ara in the name of God, it can't be taken badly. I hope.

As my fingers alight on her shoulders, she does a quick flinch, even through all the layers of clothing, like I've zapped her with static electricity. Then, as I start kneading, a deep groan filters up, first from her chest, then from her belly, and finally from what I imagine to be the cavern of her womb.

"Let go, Ara." She doesn't understand the English, but what the heck. "Just let it all go. Release the muscles, the tension. Forgive. Forgive. Everything's going to be okay." I start humming, any old thing that comes to mind. Nursery songs. Hymns. Reggae. The tunes help me get into it, if nothing else.

Under my hands, her body is like a burlap bag filled with unshelled nuts, clumped and miserable. Long minutes pass before my fingertips stop meeting active resistance. Then deeper breaths, more regular ones. And trembling. She stops me so she can wipe her eyes with the corner of her headscarf, then motions me to keep going.

The humming went okay, so I get braver and start chanting out loud. "Let go." Over and over. In time with the chant, my fingertips press hard and firm. I imagine goodness flowing through my hands, piercing the tattered layers of black. We're so alone now; the chickens cackling next door are so far away, on another planet maybe, the chattering in the street like a distant memory. Palms on knotted shoulders, then down the ridge of her spine, then on both sides of the lower back. I am learning the territory of Ara, venturing into an interior of sorts.

This tired body of hers is saggy and elderly at 47. This belly like a deflated basketball, loose and coarse, used up and colorless. Lifeless. Four children in rapid succession came from this exhausted old womb, plus probably a few miscarriages along the way. That means a whole lot of sex there for a while. Then he left her for a younger woman. And she raised the children alone and poor and bitter.

I scoot down to reach her knotted calves, rubbing gently at first and then deeper, and on to the gnarled feet, all split and crusty in my hands. That's when it hits me. Aside from a peck on the cheek, or a hug on the shoulder, or the embrace of a child, it's probably been a decade or two since anyone has touched or rubbed Ara's body with affection. She hasn't been one of those women in magazine commercials, either, caressing her own skin with lotion. This is a body long forgotten, making a slow lonely march to the grave.

Decades? Now sorrow ebbs in a backwash, from her body up through my arms to my core. A rope around my chest squeezes. This sadness is too big for just the two of us. I want my father here, with that sage knowingness and authority he had, which could take the terror out of anything.

It passes. I calm down. The energy starts going back the right way. Only now something has shifted; gone is any pride in being a healer. What a silly arrogance. Ara and I are two parts of a single whole, her breath and mine going in and out in unison and back out into the dark village. A circle, with neither part stronger or wiser or more "evolved" than the other. Just two women in a cramped little concrete-block room, with a dog barking somewhere nearby, on worn mats on the floor, and me with my knees going numb and back cramping and stomach rumbling. Doing that thing that women have done for time immemorial. Simply being.

When the fullness of the moment wanes, we unfold blankets from the stack in the corner, scooch two of the mats closer together, blow out the candles, and fall asleep holding hands.

* * *

When classes start on Sunday, I do my best to focus on the young faces before me, and hold tight to the affection that's grown between us. I owe them my very best during these last few weeks we have together. But instead, I keep smelling smoke in my hair, despite having washed it twice. I keep imagining soot from the pyre, human ash, clinging to the insides of my lungs. Why didn't I think to look for Soz earlier? How did she have the courage to gag herself so tightly, and stay silent long enough to burn so badly? Didn't anybody notice how thoroughly engulfed by rage she must have been, to do this on Hevar's wedding day? Or rather, on what she had hoped would also be *her* wedding day?

One look at Seema in the front row brings it all back in a torrent. I've got to shake myself out of this. I search for a gimmick in my mental bag of teacher's tricks. Hokie Pokie? No, irrelevant. Heads Up Seven Up? No, nothing useful there. With a flash of inspiration, I grab the chalk and write.

I before E
Except after C
Or when sounded as "eh"
As in "neighbor" or "weigh".

"It's another joke, Miss?"

"Fuzzy Wuzzy was a bear?" They jump at the slightest opportunity to twist their tongues around it.

"No, it's a way you can remember how to spell better." I explain how the poem works, and we experiment with different words. Brilliant Jaber's face lights up when he gets it. He's been amazingly cooperative since the proselytizing episode, despite the rejection. And he's become a bit full of himself for rising to the top of the class, too.

"Look, guys!" He takes the chalk from me and writes 'Piece'. Then 'Relief.' 'Chief.' "See? But now when we have a C word…" He writes 'Receive.'

One by one, their faces light up; it's that moment of comprehension that teachers live for.

"See if you can think of more words," I urge.

"Deceive."

"Perceive."

"But it's 'relieve' because there's no c,'" Jaber says. "Look, guys. It works."

We chant the poem a few more times. A few of the slower ones, like Barav, look resentful of those who have already caught on. Karwan, to my dismay, is messing around with his pencil case in the back. He hasn't paid attention for weeks.

Then Seema's hand shoots up. I can't believe it. She hasn't volunteered anything in class all year. And after the trauma of the weekend, I'm amazed that she even came to school today. But here she is now, with one finger stuck in the paperback dictionary they all have to lug around in their backpacks. "Miss, it doesn't always work."

"No?" I draw the question out, so she'll have to be totally certain of herself. In fact, I've been waiting to see if anyone would catch this.

Her smile resembles a little minx. She's nervous about proving me wrong, yet is so triumphant she can't help herself. "What about 'weird'? I looked it up, Miss. It's not I before E. It's not after C. It doesn't say eh. And it's E before I. You can look right here in the dictionary…"

Yes! I want to cheer. "Wow, Seema. You found an exception — the only one I personally know of. Weird is weird. Makes sense, doesn't it?"

I give her a high five and write her name on the board with a big star beside it. What I really want to do is lift her up and hug her, right in front of everybody, and say to all of them, "Look at how far little Seema has come! Be like her. Think outside the boxes. Be curious, test the limits, become independent learners, and maybe even start a Kurdish cultural renaissance some day ..."

But of course, I can't. It would just humiliate her. So we go back to reading aloud about Alexander's battle at Massaga, where he slaughtered every last inhabitant, and reduced the entire city to rubble. Charming stuff for preteens. We're accustomed to it by now, however; like a desert platoon we have bonded through endurance.

At long last, the minute hand reaches twelve. Seema stays behind when the other kids charge out.

"I was so proud of you today!" I gush once we're alone. "You've become so courageous in class."

"Thank you, Miss." An awkward silence descends while she tries to find the right words. "Thank you for staying in the village overnight too, Miss. I felt safer with you being at Ara's. Grandmother said so too."

"It was nothing. It helped me feel a little better myself." Not enough, though. My insides are still freeze-dried, waiting to thaw into some semblance of normalcy.

"Miss? About Soz. You mustn't take it too hard, Miss. Things like this happen. Not all the time, but not rarely, either."

"As if that makes it any better!" It's sweet of her to try to console me, though.

Shyly, she looks down, and her braids cover her face. "It's just the way things are here, Miss. So maybe ... So I was wondering ..."

I wait. We don't have much time until next period. "Yes?"

"So, Miss, maybe now you will change your mind and take me with you to America? Not only because of the cutting. Because of everything else, too."

"Oh, little Seema. I wish. Truly, I wish…"

She hears the "no" between the lines. Hope drains, leaving her shrunken. She grabs her backpack and slumps out the door in defeat.

✻ ✻ ✻

"Headquarters is pressing me for your answer." Madame has called me to her office later that week. "Once the end-of-year results are in, I can point out to Cairo that you're clearly a master teacher. So we won't need confirmation from them to name you HOD."

I'm wracked with guilt about Seema. I'm worried about Bezma and Ara. Plus I haven't replied yet to Fester, Gerber and Moscowitz. Perhaps this explains my vanishing patience with Madame and her political gamesmanship. "Actually, I'm looking at something where I'd make a lot more money than here." It's a bit of a stretch, since Pat hasn't gotten me the Saudi offer yet. But I don't care any more. "I had another financial issue arise back home…"

"So I heard."

I snort in disgust. How much of my personal business has she learned about — and how?

"Now don't get defensive — it's my job to know what's going on with everybody here. Just hear me out. The students love you. From early results, I can already see that you've rescued 6/7 Accelerated, so none will have to repeat the year, as we feared. You are an important asset to the Academy, worthy of special consideration." Now she lowers her voice. "And I can sweeten the deal, so to speak."

268

"Better than what they pay in Saudi? I find that hard to believe."

"Not as a salary. But I can give you an advance on this year's bonus and next year's earnings, immediately upon signing. You could go home for the summer, wrap up whatever issues might be going on there, and return here to start the next school year."

"That's a lot of money."

She clears her throat. "The advance would have to come out of my own pocket. That's how much I trust your loyalty. Strictly unofficial, of course."

"I'm stunned." More like speechless. "Do you have any idea how much I need?"

She nods, and pushes a document across the wide expanse of desk. "Sign right now, and you will have your advance by the end of the semester. Either cash, or wired to the bank account of your choice."

My mouth is suddenly parched. My shoulders start to ache at the thought of another entire year at The Fortress. The ache is less, however, than my fear of more Wells Fargo-type surprises, ongoing creditor letters, and the terror of living under their shadow until my dotage.

"I don't have a pen…" It buys me less than a second to think.

"Here." It's a gold Cross pen embossed with the Academy's crest.

She smiles with obvious relief when I'm done. "Keep it. You're part of the Academy management family now. And, Theresa? Congratulations. We both know you've made the right decision."

We do? My stomach does an unsettled lurch that reminds me of signing a marriage certificate about ten years earlier.

Nine: Desperation

PREPPING THE kids for exams has been even worse than normal teaching. We've been under pressure to make every single minute count, and cram extra useless factoids into malleable minds. The kids suffer too; if they fail, they're stuck sweating here in summer school. Given the stress, even Zaki has lightened up on us.

And it's white hot; even walking from the apartments to the classroom quad is a torment. I can't wait to turn on the a/c in my bedroom — it cools down faster than the living room — and crash on the sofa. I throw down the book bag and open the door to the bedroom, wondering where I left the a/c remote. It's not on the night stand, where it should be. Maybe over on the other side of the bed?

I gasp. A rough wooden crate hulks beside the bed where the Blue Angel ought to be. It's nailed shut and striped with black duct tape. Resting on top is a page torn from an exercise book. "Twinkie, be a doll and don't touch. J."

Of course, I have to try to lift it. It's way too heavy to budge. I lock the apartment, storm down to Jake's, and pound with a clenched fist on the door. He's expecting me. And so is Rabinowitz in a grimy tank top, lazing on the couch with a beer.

"Count to ten, Twink. It's not as bad as it looks."

I'm too rattled to count past two. "The nerve! How dare you? What's in it?"

Rabinowitz burps. "Information on a need-to-know basis only. Don't ask."

"It looks scary. And illegal. Take it back!"

"We don't have space." Jake gestures around the room with a vague air of apology. I notice suitcases strewn amongst empty beer cans. "Binny's been couch surfing with me. The stuff wouldn't be safe here, if anybody searched."

"Stuff?" What a stupid euphemism. "Is it guns? Grenades?"

"Think of it as a dowry." Rabinowitz is slurring his words; I despise the way he tries to make things mysterious.

"See, if Binny does this favor for his father-in-law, he gets out of paying for the bride," Jake explains. "You and I are saving him about a hundred grand. Small price for a friend in need."

"Friend!" I stamp my foot and instantly feel childish. "Friend? I absolutely loathe you, Rabinowitz. You'd endanger Jake and me with contraband —"

"Sshh. They might have our rooms bugged. You never know."

"If they did, Rabinowitz couldn't have been here the past couple of days." I nod at the chip bags and beer cans, about a week's worth of trash.

"We have nowhere else to put it," Rabinowitz says matter-of-factly. "Tag, you're it."

"Plus, we heard you signed on for next year. Old Baldy will do anything to protect her star returning teacher. Or HOD, or whatever you're going to be." Jake says this with an oddly self-justifying air, as if he realizes how stupid he sounds. Or maybe he's buzzed. Maybe that's how Rabinowitz got him to cooperate.

"That has nothing to do with it. I demand that you get it out." To my mortification, it comes out as a sputter.

"No can do. It's only for a couple of days. I think. Allah's got everything all figured out in His book." Rabinowitz eyes me with a little "gotcha" when he says "Allah", knowing it will infuriate me. "So we're all safe. Just chill."

"I can't *chill* next to a box of things that kill people, you moron."

But I also am not strong enough to drag the horrid thing anywhere. So I stomp back to my apartment. Tossing and turning all night, I fantasize in endless loops about tying Rabinowitz to one of those bee hives we saw in Shaqlawa. Naked, and smeared with jam, so the bees will torture him to death. It takes two melatonins, double a normal dose, to fall asleep.

❊ ❊ ❊

"Com now pliz mothr hous. NOW." The text from Bezma comes while I'm proctoring in the cavernous exam hall, walking up and down rows of overwrought students for ninety minutes without a break. Once I read the message, the kids could have cheated as blatantly as they wanted. However, I can't leave The Fortress until late afternoon. The ride to the village swishes past in a blur of worry.

"What happened?" Bezma won't even look at me until she bolts the gate shut and leads me to the porch. Her face reminds me of Mary at the foot of the cross in a Renaissance painting, haggard with weeping. Ara and Old Houda wait on the plastic chairs. For once, Houda has switched out her snowy white scarf for black, which makes her look at least twenty years older. We greet each other with half-hearted *ser tchows*. Covering up an eye feels appropriate right now, although they haven't told me why.

"Bezma, what are you doing here?" I ask. "You told me that brides had to spend a whole month with their in-laws, before they could see their parents again."

Bezma chokes. She motions for Houda to tell me.

"Yesterday Hevar shot the boy that Soz loved. Hevar's mother has sent Bezma home."

"Wait. One thing at a time. He shot Soz's boyfriend? But that's insane. It won't bring her back. She's already dead."

Houda exhales with a soughing sound. "Hevar is sometimes crazy with anger. His family is known for that. It's one of the reasons that Ara was not in favor of the marriage. After Soz died, day after day Hevar became more angry. Last night he drove to the boy's house and shot him."

That gun he liked to keep tucked into his sash. That fury so close beneath the surface. I can see him striding into a little concrete-block house like this one, finding a young man in *khak* reclining on cushions against the wall, pulling the trigger, blasting blood and guts all over the walls, carpet, tea tray… "So Hevar must be with the police."

Houda shakes her head. "There will be no police. The boy's family decided on blood, not money. Hevar has had to disappear. If the boy's family can find him, they will kill him."

Where could a man hide in such a small country, where everybody knows everybody else — and their business?

Bezma's ashen face tells me that there's more. "Then what will happen to Bezma?" I ask. "Why is she here, rather than with her new family? It wasn't her fault about Soz."

Houda searches for words that will be both delicate and easy for me to follow. "Hevar's mother says that Bezma is a bad girl, and spoils their reputation. The mother is being very cruel. She says Bezma gives them a black face."

Bezma hurls herself onto the cushions. "Mother Hevar take back gold," she wails. "Too good for me, she say." She bawls so

274

loud that all the neighbors must know catastrophe has struck. "She keep stove and fridge. Make Family Hevar look better."

This isn't making sense. "But that isn't right. How could they say you are bad? How did you make his mother angry?"

Bezma can't manage to answer for several breaths, and then she speaks so softly I can barely hear. "Treeza, no blood."

Huh?

"No blood on sheets in morning. Mother Hevar look. Show to everybody. Big shame to me. Everybody in Hevar village know. Impossible show face now." She dashes to the outhouse and drags the iron door shut behind her; sobs reverberate from the windowless cave.

I frown at Houda, who nods. It's true. "That's positively medieval," I say. "Everybody knows that virgins don't always bleed the first time."

The word "virgin" wasn't a good choice. Houda coughs.

"Treeza, maybe you did not know. Hevar's family is claiming they did not know. They are using it as an excuse for sending her back."

"Know what?"

The minute the words are out of my mouth, I sense my own lack of street smarts. My gut has been figuring it out in the background, while my mind wasn't listening. Ara had been trying to tell me for weeks now, without words, to avoid the shame. She'd been urging me to share her motherly grief. The realization is an awful, world-changing thud. Despite the almost-summer heat, I'm suddenly so cold that I can't move. "When is she due?"

"In five, six months, *in sh'allah*."

"But how? It's only been…" I let the information trickle down into my heart. I juggle memories, trying to make them fit, trying to figure out when Bezma and Hevar might managed to be alone together, how intimacy could even be possible in a place like this. Could it have been over three months already since that day at the tailor's? Or had they snuck away even before that? Slowly, the reality gels into place, all the details that I've been oblivious to. With reality comes mortification. Bezma must have been in hysterics with my pathetic little talk about Hevar's "thing down there." My face stings with embarrassment all the way to my ear lobes.

"It has to be Hevar's," I say lamely.

"Certainly," Houda replies. "But his mother says they cannot be sure. Either way, Bezma's life would be terrible in that household now. It is better that she is here, safe with us. It will work out. God never gives us more than we can bear. That's what The Prophet told us, may peace be upon him."

"But Bezma's life will be hell here too, won't it? Who will support her and her child? Ara barely has enough to live on as it is. This is unbelievable!"

One look from Old Houda tells me to stop babbling nonsense.

"Houda, listen. Everything is Hevar's fault. Soz's death. The murder of the boyfriend. And now a baby. Right? He has to take responsibility. He will have to send Bezma money. When something like this happens in America…"

I stop mid-idea. In America, men have to support their children? Who am I kidding? Andy's father never sent me a dime in child support. But at least I was educated, and was able to work. Unlike poor Bezma.

Houda shakes her head. "Hevar was within his rights to forbid Soz to get married. Most likely he was within his rights for shooting the young man, too. As for Bezma, even if a woman is raped, she can be blamed. It's all about honor. And I doubt that Bezma was raped."

Me too. But I care too much about her to admit it out loud.

"What can we do?" I'm ready to call the BBC, make a report to the police, or scream at some village elder.

"Nothing."

I can't believe how calm she is. "What do you mean, nothing? We can't stand by and let this happen."

She sighs. "That's all that anybody can do. It is written in God's Book. Bezma played her part, and Hevar played his. Shameful things happen sometimes, even when a girl is cut. Now do you understand why it's a good custom? Think how often this would happen if the girls were not clean. Anyway, it is finished."

"How about giving her rue? *Harmala*?" My mouth tastes filthy even suggesting it.

Even this cannot ruffle old Houda. "Too late," she says. She's obviously considered it, though. "It would no longer be safe. If only she had come to me when she first found out. But then, who would have ever thought things would turn out this way?"

Much as I love Houda, I'm ready to shake her. "Doesn't this make you angry?"

She sighs. "There's no sense in being angry with God, or doubting His plan. As we Kurds say, not all clouds bring rain."

My Arabic isn't nuanced enough to ask whether she means that rain is a blessing or a misfortune.

"But it's true that I am sad," she goes on. "Very sad. For all of them. I hope you'll help me pray for them all — Ara, Bezma, and Hevar. God hears the prayers of both Muslims and Christians."

Pray? My fists wouldn't unball enough for something as passive as that.

⁂ ⁂ ⁂

All that evening, my apartment mocks me. Each time I look around, the walls taunt me. "See you next year, you loser." The hills outside the windows jeer too. "Look what your happy little village experience turned into." The bedroom is the worst of all, where Rabinowitz's hateful crate sneers wordlessly. There's only one obvious answer for surviving my last week or two here, and that's a rue vision quest.

It starts out inauspiciously. The rue leaves smell like fusty mushrooms or termite dust, and the tea I brew with them leaves a rotten taste on my tongue. Even worse, it induces an explosive vomit, more bitter coming up than going down. But Jake assured me that the escape will be worth it.

The Internet didn't really specify how strong to brew the tea, or what to expect once it starts to take effect. Also, the article had to have been written by a man, because it didn't mention cramping — almost as bad as the beginning stages of childbirth once the retching stops.

But that agony is behind me. I set out on foot for my cosmic experience after the campus has settled down for the evening. A full moon, more brilliant than I've ever noticed before, silvers the tops of the hillsides; it's easy to follow the dirt road up past the smoldering dump, avoiding the deepest ruts. I spread a sheet out over the rocks, align toward the south and settle in for a good, long wait. Who knows how long this could take?

While waiting for the rue to do its thing, whatever that is, I've prepared a lengthy meditation. I call out to the ancient gods (or preferably goddesses) of Mesopotamia to come visit me with visions and bless me with insights. I ask them to let me in on timeless secrets of the universe (I'm a little hazy about what these might be), all the while suspecting how laughable this must look to any enlightened beings hanging around the neighborhood. I don't care any more, though. Nothing harmless like this could be as upsetting as what's been happening in real life.

Although the day has been a scorcher, the ground beneath me is now cold as a grave, and a piercing wind tugs at my jacket. Somehow, this makes it even more romantic.

My mind won't stay focused on the meditation, though. My hands hurt, and I look down to discover my fingernails scoring sharp little moons into my palms. I've been obsessing about another year at The Fortress again, trying to scheme my way out of it. And I've been back in Ara's little sitting room, suffocating under the image of Bezma stuck there with the shame of a fatherless infant. And I've been sniggering with glee, imagining The Financial Genius stamp his feet and howl with rage as a sheriff tows away his R.V. to pay back Fester, Gerber and Moscowitz.

Come to think of it, my mind is getting a bit fuzzy for a meditation. Ideas just aren't sticking.

What was it that Gilgamesh and Enkidu did around here anyway? Why were Abraham and Sarah wandering around these parts? Why would anybody have wanted to live in such a barren, forbidding place as this? Too bad I hadn't paid more attention back in World Civ.

I think Gilgamesh was searching for immortality. Abraham wanted a homeland for his lineage. Those were pretty tall orders. Sarah, on the other hand, just wanted a son. I've already got one of those. So what do I want? I'm not sure any more. Financial security? Might as well forget that one for a while. Adventure? Got that one in spades. To make a difference in the world? Hah. I can't even figure out what that might mean in a place like this.

I'll wait for a message. I'll empty out my mind and see who or what comes drifting in, besides the usual suspects.

It gets colder. I swat at mosquitos whining around my ears, but can't see the ones already stinging my wrists and neck. Damn. This is so not worth the effort...

A wispy cloud softens the moonlight, and a swarm of bat-like creatures zip past my face, fast and flappy; wakes from their wings brush over me, along with the smell of malevolence. I duck and cover; what if they fly into my eyes? Surely their touch is poisonous and will scar me forever. Wait. What if they're not vicious after all? What if they're the messengers I've been waiting for? But by the time I've found the courage to sit up again, the bat-thingies are gone. Amazingly, I have not perished. I command my heart to cool down out of warp speed. It doesn't cooperate.

The moon is totally clouded over now; eyes are useless. I strain my ears, and discover that it's not my ears but the very cells of my body that can hear now; they're like little radio receivers that detect signals from far, far away. No wait. The signals are coming from right here; they're like invisible barcodes resonating from the soil and dust, and the molecules inside my forearms can read them. They're saying two words. See if I can concentrate harder and decrypt them. I want these words to be something universally profound. I'm all set to receive Light and Love. Or maybe Peace and Oneness. Something New Agey, that will transform me effortlessly into a yogi or prophet, giving me a new inner compass that makes decisions effortless for the rest of my life. I strain, awaiting Great Revelation.

But as I tune in to make out the words, they're not at all what I've anticipated.

They're Shock and Awe.

What the heck? I dismiss them and ask for something different, but there they are, twin sisters, Shock and Awe, reverberating like the tolling inside a massive cathedral bell. My frail mind is the bell, about ready to split; my body is the clanger, in trauma from the violence of impact, with skin aquiver in gooseflesh.

What have my people done?

How did we plant these words, grotesque with implication, into the mountainsides along with all of the bombs we dropped?

This isn't fair. I protested against the Iraq wars when the Bushes marched off America's young men, both times. I wrote to the newspapers and the presidents, and tried to make sense of the chaotic, biased news reports, and sent donations to refugee funds, and basically did anything that a normal citizen can be expected to do to stop the deranged actions of her government. So don't try to lay Shock and Awe on *me*, of all people.

Now the bat-thingies return, but they don't flap on by. This time they form a pulsating cloud of black, even darker than the night surrounding them, and I ache to scream. But my throat has frozen, like in a nightmare. Go, go, go, I command them in my mind. Instead, they coagulate into a figure in a long black trench coat. Furious eyebrows join above aviator glasses, and there is hideous Zaki the Academy zealot, glaring at me, then smiling at me, then inviting me into an embrace. Disgusting wretch.

Now he is morphing into a guy in a Western suit and a Kurdish turban, Mohammed the too-friendly government liaison guy, standing above me with palms out like Jesus after the resurrection. "Come to me," he entreats. "Once you see the big picture, everything will be okay."

But I can't tell whether to believe him or not, because part of my mind knows that he probably isn't real, and I don't know anything about this rue stuff, haven't ever gotten high before in my entire life, and my mind is the only thing I've had to guide me, the only thing that people like my father ever put any faith in, but for a long time now my mind hasn't been so trustworthy either, if you consider getting married to someone I'd only known for five months and despite Andy, presciently, not being able to stand him, and then me signing on with The Fortress without even Googling to read former teachers' comments, for instance, which would have given me some pretty horrific details...

About the only thing that has been a true friend lately has been the Blue Angel, and my eyes well up now thinking of Rabinowitz touching her — the nerve — to make room for his despicable crate. And Andy. Why isn't Andy out here on this hillside with me, helping me with the purity of adolescent wisdom, asking me some perfect question again that mystically fits all the kaleidoscopic pieces of my confusion into a single glorious comprehensible image?

Then it's over. As quickly as it began, the bonging vanishes, and I'm left sitting there on my sheet with a gazillion mosquito bites, a leaden stomach and a queasiness lodged in my bowels. My womb is now filled with a lustrous, possibly radioactive substance, only it's not distressing. It's more like a glowing weight or magnet, and oddly reassuring; I've become a holographic, luminous version of a blow-up clown that pops back up each time it's punched.

I allow my womb to expand and become my whole being. It's so languorous that I lie back on the sheet and stare contentedly into the void. I am pregnant with something nameless, incandescent, a golden metallic rose color, and that something is grateful when I lie flat on the earth and submit.

We hum together, the earth and I.

We are creative. Something has quickened between us, a nascence that carries me like a formidable ocean wave, rising, swelling, then hovering at the crest, and I am on a longboard poised to angle into the ultimate curl, suspended just before the barrel, where thoughts, muscles, breaths, drops of ocean and particles of sunlight all glisten together in perfect azure alignment.

I surf it. I dissolve into it. It absorbs me. I spin out this instant of grace, moment by glorious moment, searching for a word that will capture its essence — shut up, insatiable mind, don't wreck this for me — so I can re-enter again when it subsides. But the only word that materializes is Witness. I know who I am, and it is Witness. Witness am I. Right Now. Witness as a single pinprick of awareness, surrounded by a glistening sea of wonder yearning to be observed. Witness stripped of name, personality, nationality, gender, age, profession, role, or history. No purpose, even, except to pay attention. And to marvel at it all.

When time returns, I discover that I am safe. And for the first time in my entire life, I am enough. It's okay to relax. I am part of something, although I have absolutely no idea what it is. Or what it means. But it doesn't matter.

Something is Good.

❀   ❀   ❀

A hairy stink wakes me, then a tinkling, and all around me are hooves, beards, udders and stumpy tails all matty with dung. They'll stamp my face! I bolt upright, and there is my shepherd friend pushing his way through the flock.

"Good evening," he says, as if we're meeting in a drawing room. Then he frowns in a protective manner. I shouldn't be out here.

I shrug. My head is very thick now, and so are the clouds over the moon. I've forgotten which direction home lies, but my tongue is coated in fur.

"Bicycle?" he motions.

No, I've come on foot.

"Okay, come." He reaches a hand to help me to my feet, and shakes his head in amusement when I stagger. He hoists me onto the back of his little donkey, and my cheek ends up resting against a scratchy mane. He taps me awake again when we reach the back gate of The Fortress. Heaven only knows how I make it into bed.

When my mind ungrogs a bit, I decide to leave this particular escapade out of the blog.

❅ ❅ ❅

The whole post-rue day has passed in a mellow fuzz; I've mostly just sat and stared out the patio window at the chain-link fence and the hills beyond. Pat brings me soup, along with her vodka-cayenne-lemon-honey flu remedy, which only intensifies the blur. I observe cloudy snippets of concern hovering around my apartment, but they don't settle, nor do they threaten me very much. The crate. The school contract. The village. Seema getting cut. Money for the lawyers. Bezma being a single mom.

In the background, the Witness is watching a movie of my life. The climax is upon us, and we in the movie theater hear the music brimming up, heightening the tension. Meanwhile, we're basking in the fun of the show. What terrific drama. What brilliant acting. What incredible special effects. Is there any of that popcorn left?

When dark falls, I pull the curtains but keep staring toward the hills. There's something out there that I'm related to, a power that I can't name. Because of the power, stuff happens. Things come and go across the ancient landscape. And the Witness merely watches...

Tapping on the patio door startles me from reverie, soft but insistent. I ignore it; it's probably that bastard Rabinowitz. But when I pull aside the curtains, it's a crowd of Kurds on the patio. I rush them inside before anybody can report me. Bezma. Ara. Old Houda. And Hevar, with a ratty duffel bag slung over his shoulder.

"What in heaven's name?"

They're never been inside my apartment before, or probably any foreigner's home. They take in the flat-screen

TV, microwave, sofa and gleaming kitchen in amazement, but don't waste any time in getting to the point.

"Treeza, please, you keep Hevar." Bezma acts like a woman kidnapped from an insane asylum, her voice tight and crazed.

"Hide Hevar here in my apartment?" His name smacks of rancid cheese. "Are you out of your mind?"

Bezma and Hevar exchange frantic looks. They must have taken it for granted that I would let him stay.

"If not stay here, he dead," says Bezma matter-of-factly. "Here nobody look."

All the Kurdish words I've learned evaporate into thin air, replaced by my shock at their audacity. Only English remains. "Absolutely not! He's been a total ass this whole time. He doesn't deserve anybody protecting him. Let that poor dead boy's family kill him, for all I care."

Nobody translates; they don't need to. The "no" is pretty clear. But nobody moves, either. The Kurds pose like statues around my coffee table, as if silently restrategizing. Each time Bezma does a panicky glance at the door, the urgency ramps up.

"Look, his anger problem is not my responsibility." This comes out as too Western, like something from a college communications class, but my mouth can't stop itself. "Besides, they could take me to prison for this." I have no idea who "they" might be, not that it matters. Bezma translates, so briefly that I wonder about her accuracy.

"Yes. That is very possible." Nodding, Houda stays calm. "We are putting you in considerable danger. We know that." She doesn't apologize for it, either. She's stating the obvious, but with that magnetic glow of hers, even in the midst of trouble.

Think fast, Theresa.

"Okay, I would do anything to help Bezma and Ara. Anything. But not Hevar." I can't even rest my eyes on the creep. Have him here, alone with me in this tiny apartment? With his zero-fuse temper? For who knows how long?

"Treeza, help me, help Hevar, same thing," says Bezma, knitting her fingers over her tummy. "You family. Hevar family. Hevar father my baby. "

I turn to Houda. She tips her head in agreement. That's how they see it all right.

I do not want to be deported or imprisoned for abetting some violent, impetuous person I despise. I do not want this man anywhere near me, especially in my one sanctuary within this country. I have to hold out, emotionally and mentally, until final exam results are released tomorrow. Then I have to manage for several more days, until I can step on a plane for summer vacation and blissfully return to my nice safe home in a sane, logical country where I understand the rules. How would I sleep even a single night, much less enjoy the little time I have left here, with Hevar in the apartment?

"Give me a minute to think." And clear out the remaining rue fog.

I step outside onto the patio, and there is the Blue Angel, propped up against the railing where Rabinowitz stuck her to make room for the crate. She's all dusty now, dinged up from the shepherd, the Nowruz boy, and most recently the kids in the village once I stopped being so protective. Dents distort the poor old basket, which hangs on for dear life with wire. Such a simple vehicle, so inexpensive, really, yet she sure has liberated me. Just being beside her helps me breathe. What should I do with her when I leave for the summer? Oh yeah — leaving. I'm getting out of here in a few days. Well, since I'm leaving anyway, would anybody really deport me for hiding Hevar for a while? Oh wait. I signed Madame's contract. I've got to return in August. If I get deported, I can't come back, and then the advance she promised me goes out the window. But then, if I'm returning to The Fortress, I'll be seeing Bezma and Ara and Houda all next year. Part of the family, like they said. Spending every weekend with them. I can't let them down. Damn this rue and the mishmash brain it's left me with.

And as I think the word "rue", the poise of the surfer / witness / kaleidoscope pieces returns, just for a second or two. I can sense my pores expanding, the molecules of my organs too, uncrimping, unfurling like tiny green shoots in a time-lapse nature video, morphing into ports for a knowingness to come shooting my way, connecting with something, clicking, engaging, sopping up, digesting, tranquil and certain when I was expecting desperation...

It's not much, but enough to toss me a lifeline to a larger self, and with it the smell of the Pacific Northwest — my father, my son, the way Puget Sound sparkles on a crystalline summer day, the virtue I've always assumed for choosing a teacher's life, and a solid surety that reason and order can reign, even in a world seemingly gone mad.

I slip back the glass slider, gulp, and address the waiting Kurds. "I will let Hevar stay here on one condition."

They wait in confusion for Bezma to translate; they'd expected a simple "yes" or "no".

"Of course," Bezma replies immediately; after all, what could I possible want of any consequence? "You say, we do."

The risk of alienating these proud people is so great. Intuition warns me how perilous a few wrong sentences could be. I suck a breath deep down into my belly, and commit to taking the wave ...

"No more *khatana*. Not Seema. Not Shirin. Not Bezma's baby, if it's a girl. Nobody. No more blood on Houda's hands. Finished."

Before Bezma translates, she squints up at me. In body language, she silently asks, "Are you sure? Couldn't you just keep this uncomplicated and say 'yes' instead?"

My hands stay planted on my hips, doing my predator teacher pose that brooks no opposition, so the class realizes there's no chance of compromise or changing my mind. I hold the pose, willing my eyes not to blink. Can they tell that my hands are actually trembling? Do they realize to what degree I'm bluffing?

Bezma sighs, and translates with obvious ambivalence. They go rigid in surprise; nobody moves or speaks or so much as rustles. I can't tell whether the silence means disbelief, relief or hostility.

Then Hevar roars at me, a long invective of Kurdish. Bezma blushes and wrings the end of her scarf around her hand. "I am sorry, Treeza. Hevar say *wiss ba* about *khatana*. Shut up, but not so rude. He say *khatana* and staying with you, not same. He say you not think he is big man. He say your heart not big."

My heart, whatever its size, is thumping so hard that the guards can probably hear it down at the gate. "Tough." I bite my lips together, hard, partly to say "take it or leave it," and partly so I won't snivel, or, worse, cave in to his overpowering maleness.

Each churn of the air conditioner ratchets up the tension. I'm all alone on one side of the coffee table, with the Kurds clustered on the other, all of us scowling at the impasse. This damnable pride of theirs, this unwillingness to lose face, no matter what the cost. At the same time, I can imagine Hevar swearing vile epithets at me for being an interfering foreigner, someone who comes here for a brief interlude and thinks she knows best, dictating against customs passed down for thousands of years...

A touch shakes me out of reverie. Ara has shifted over to my side and taken my hand in hers, course and scratchy. She gives me a quick squeeze, pulls herself up to full height, and motions for Bezma to translate.

"I say yes with Treeza. *Khatana* not good, not happy. I cry when Bezma, other girls get *khatana*." A pause. There's surely a "but" coming. "But *khatana* is work of Houda. *Khatana* give Houda money. She widow. She need money. We must be kind to Houda."

"Oh." I'm stunned. I hadn't thought of the revenue part of this. I turn, questioning, to Houda, who has moved apart from us, perched on a bar stool by the kitchen, and taken out her prayer beads.

Houda ponders the beads for what seems like an eternity, ignoring Hevar's impatient huffing. Finally she says to me in Arabic, "This is not a question of money. It is about God's will. We Kurds like to say that for every misfortune, there is always something worse that can happen. I just am not certain what is the misfortune, and what is the worse."

I can't help her on that one.

"There is only one answer," she continues. "I must pray. Do you have a towel I could borrow for a prayer rug?" She hoists herself off the stool and hobbles toward the bedroom with my only clean towel, the same one Rabinowitz once slept under.

Oh Lord. Can a person pray next to a case of armaments? I guess so, because she stays in there long enough for me to make and serve two very awkward rounds of tea for Hevar, Ara and Bezma. They marvel at my ability to accomplish this simple act of food preparation, and remark among themselves at the ceramic mugs that came with the apartment, so clunky compared with the dainty shot-glass-size cups they're used to. There's barely enough sugar for the way they like their tea, a deficiency they overlook when I bring out the last of my Cadbury bars.

In defiance of my cringe, Hevar lights up a cigarette; he accepts a saucer as an ash tray, ignoring the rest of us. Curse him for this mess.

When at last Houda returns, her eyes are pools of jade-colored serenity; a sweetness softens the room.

"Here is what the Holy Quran teaches," she announces with great solemnness, first in Arabic for me and then in Kurdish for the others. "'Tell the believing women to reduce some of their vision and guard their private parts and not expose their adornment except that which necessarily appears.' It's from *Surah An Noor*."

Hevar blurts something that sounds like "What the hell is that supposed to mean?" albeit with a deference I hadn't noticed earlier.

Houda explains with remarkable patience. "'Guard their private parts,' it says. This is usually quoted to support wearing *hijab*. But I suppose that 'guard' could mean protect, or not cutting. I cannot think of any other verse that might apply to guide us. God is Great." The implication is, "The oracle has spoken."

But the oracle has not been exactly clear, at least for me. In fact, to my chagrin, I find my tongue poking out one cheek like a kindergartener. I glance around at the others to see if they're as baffled as I am. They are.

"You'll stop then?" I whisper, not daring to believe it.

Houda nods; it's as if a halo appears to consecrate her decision. I hold her tight in a hug while Kurdish curses resound from a male voice behind us.

"Maybe you are angry with me?" I murmur in her ear. "Maybe I spoke out of place."

She shakes her head. "Everything is God's will. *Al ham du lillah*." Praise be to God.

"*Al ham ðu lillah,*" I agree.

No matter what happens, she will praise Him.

The snap in tension is too much for Ara to bear. She falls into my arms, sobbing, blessing me, grabbing Houda's abaya and pulling her tight too, babbling. Meanwhile Bezma and Hevar huddle in a corner, talking fast, making plans; his anger has dissipated by practical necessity.

So it's settled, and everyone but Hevar (and me) traipses back out the patio door into the night. Once they're gone, Hevar decides he can look at me again. He slips off his *khak* vest, shakes it out as if it might have bugs, and gives me a serious nod of thanks. That's it. He sits cross-legged on the sofa in a big slab of entitlement, lights another cigarette, plugs earbuds into his smartphone, and zones out, presumably to music. I no longer exist.

I heave my stack of ungraded exams into the bedroom, shut the door, and try to concentrate on the complicated marking scheme. Rabinowitz's container on my left, with heaven knows what in it. His Majesty, Ticking Time Bomb Hevar out in the living room, for heaven knows how long. No way am I going to offer to cook him dinner; let him smoke himself to death out there.

Before getting into bed, I prop a chair against the locked bedroom door, but even that doesn't seem secure enough. But then, really, is "secure" an appropriate word for anywhere in the Middle East these days?

This is not exactly how I'd planned to spend my final days in Kurdistan.

Ten: A Crown for Every Achievement

FINALS ARE over. The kids got all weepy after the last one, and so did I; a true Day of Atonement for the trials we put each other through. They want to friend me on Facebook, forbidden by Madame during the school term, but probably okay during the summer. To their delight, I give them my best *ser tchow* as farewell.

Although we haven't received any specifics, we've been told that exam scores are in from headquarters. This means we can go home in a couple of days. Headquarters is processing our airline tickets, and all the expats are giving away extra clothes so their suitcases will shut. About half are requesting stop-overs in Europe; the promised bonuses will stretch far at backpacker hostels, and the faculty room is abuzz with place names like Ibiza, Mykonos and Carrapateira. So when Jake, Pat and I are summoned together to Zaki's office, our spirits are high, expecting the best.

"I'll bet HQ told Zaki to hand us our cash bonuses in person," says Jake on our way across the quad. "Mine'll cover two glorious months in Thailand."

"Maybe they're giving us a special Expat Perseverance Award for sticking it out to the bitter end," says Pat.

Oh, we're so full of ourselves. Amazing what a pending departure date does for you.

We're still horsing around when we reach that officious sign on his door. "Mr. Nazir Zaki, B.Science (Honors)," Jake mimics in a stage whisper, not quite softly enough. "How fatuous, bragging about a measly bachelors degree. And Representative of the President, International Academies Worldwide. Such a big frog in such a tiny pond. Har, har."

For my part, I can't help but smile at how Zaki appeared to me in the rue dream, or whatever it was, and how harmless he turned out to be compared with all the scary bat thingies. No longer can he be the threat he'd seemed earlier in the year.

The spymaster voice behind the aviator glasses welcomes us with typical formality. "Miss Pat. Miss Theresa. Mr. Jake. Take seats. Please. Your classes did exceptionally well in the final exams. Congratulations."

Something's fishy. I glance at Pat and Jake; they sense it too. The jolly mood evaporates.

"You achieved miraculous results," he continues. The 'miraculous' has a snap to it, like the click of a mouse trap.

"However," Zaki continues, "there's a problem. You see, your students scored in the upper three percent of all Academy classes worldwide. Even Miss Theresa's accelerated students, who started so far behind. Consequently, headquarters would like to know how this amazing feat occurred."

We squirm, unable to look at one another. I grip for dear life to the bottom of my chair. We can't blame it on Madame; she didn't explicitly tell us to cheat, after all.

"You don't have to confess," Zaki says when the torment has gone on long enough. "I know what happened in the principal's office. We have the tapes."

What? He was spying on Madame all this time?

Zaki raps his fingers on the desk, the nails doing an impatient tattoo. He's waiting for something. Probably an apology.

Pat makes an attempt at appeasement, just a notch above groveling. "Sir, we've never done anything like this before in our lives." Remarkable, that she can find it in her to call him "sir".

The "sir" evokes a lift in his forehead, which gives me the courage to pipe up. "We'll take the blame, Mr. Zaki. I hope the students won't suffer because of our mistake. It wasn't their fault. Really it wasn't."

He deliberately rolls up the trench coat sleeves, as if preparing to bite into a juicy shwarma sandwich, revealing the hairiest forearms I've ever seen. As he leans toward us on his elbows, his tone lowers, hushed and conspiratorial. "No doubt you were under some pressure, since it wasn't only the three of you." Cough cough. "The Academy understands that. So we have decided that you will not be terminated immediately, as regulations would have otherwise stipulated. You will remain here to wrap up the paperwork for your students before summer vacation, as planned. That way they can advance to the next grade. However, this is an ethics violation. The Academy obviously cannot offer any of you a contract for next year. And naturally you will not be receiving bonuses."

Suddenly stiff in disbelief, Pat, Jake and I dart hasty glances to one another. Their cheeks are as white as fresh sheets of printer paper, and mine must be too. "Holy crap," says Jake. I silently thank him for the euphemism.

"Isn't there something … I mean, we've worked so hard all year, handling these enormous classes for you, doing the tick marks like you wanted, grading boatloads of final exams for the Academy, which wasn't technically even in our contracts…" I trail off, because one look at Zaki's mouth tells me this line of logic is pointless. But we wait anyway, hoping against hope.

"Just out of curiosity, what about Madame?" says Jake, at last breaking the silence. "Since this happened on her watch, so to speak."

"Oh, she's already packing." Zaki runs his fingers through his hair and almost chuckles. I wonder how much friction there had been between him and Madame all along — which she never divulged during all of our strolls together. Maybe she had been chafing against his methods as much as we were, but believed all of that loyalty nonsense she kept spouting.

"To go where?" asks Pat with a confused frown, as if anywhere outside of Kurdistan would be like banishment. "This school was her whole life. She devoted everything to it. She'd probably planned to retire from here."

"In fact she asked for a ticket to London." Zaki replies while studying the wall clock. He's such a busy, important fellow. "She leaves tonight."

"Doesn't the Academy owe her some leniency or a second chance in return for her service these past years? For the way she helped build the school up from nothing?" I can't believe that I'm sticking up for the woman, given how critical I've been for months. But now that she's in the doghouse like the rest of us, I'm discovering remarkable new springs of compassion.

Zaki leans back in his chair and unrolls the cuffs, dismissing us. "As they say at Academy headquarters, no one is irreplaceable. Not even expats." He stays seated while brushing us toward the door.

My ribs ache from the callousness — and the ultimate truthfulness — of the dig. We slither out, humiliated equally by our guilt and for having gotten caught. And also by the grudging realization that Zaki and the Academy, whatever their crimes against modern pedagogy, actually proved to have some integrity after all.

❖ ❖ ❖

Our woeful threesome slinks straight to Pat's apartment, where she pours more rum than usual into the Cokes. "I sure didn't see that one coming. Did you guys?"

"Nope. And all this time we thought Zaki was some nobody prick. Jesus Christ. We're screwed. Here's to the pity party." Jake downs his drink in two hasty gulps and holds out his plastic cup for a refill.

"It's probably less about cheating, and more about an excuse to withhold our bonuses," Pat says. My jaw drops. Why hadn't I thought of that?

"That bonus was a whole summer of vacation," she continues, sighing. "So much for Turkey and Greece. Hello to my daughter's basement — and then beautiful Saudi in August. Fun fun fun."

"Want to hear what I've got lined up?" Jake takes a long slurp. "Don't get too jealous now. Binny's future father-in-law has a graphic design house in Dubai. Guess who's the new creative director? No more little brats for me. If it pans out, that is." He's doing his best not to be smug, but it's not exactly working.

"I'm worse off than both of you. No job next year. No bonus. Nothing to hire lawyers with back home. No savings to live on during the summer. Not even a daughter's basement. I might as well just go jump off a classroom building or something."

Jake jerks forward. "You're kidding, right Twink?" He's truly concerned.

"Yeah, of course I'm kidding." The thought of Layla still makes me tighten up, though. I regret kicking the conversation in that direction.

"I could try again to see if they still need somebody else in Saudi." She's trying to be nice.

"Thanks, Pat." Returning to Saudi Arabia is about as appealing as being nailed in a narrow pine box. Even worse is the thought of returning home penniless, to mooch off of relatives until I find a job somewhere. And nobody will be hiring this late in the year. I'm toast. "Come to think of it, I guess there's no choice, is there?"

She shakes her head, and there's not an ounce of gloat in her. "None that I can think of."

I turn to Jake. "Any ideas for me?"

He starts to say something but I interrupt. "That do not involve Rabinowitz, that is?"

He hesitates. I can almost see the wheels turning in his head, deciding whether to confide in us. "Well, just between friends, I've been thinking about starting an import business. There's this herb that's dirt cheap here, and it could be a hot commodity back home. We could bring it in as an insecticide, like for fumigation, or for tie dye or something, and then spread the word about multiple other uses. If you get my drift."

Pat doesn't miss a beat. "Tell me I'm not really hearing this."

But he's not done. "I'm short on marketing talent, though. Binny's cool for finding me money, says he owes me. But he's probably on some terrorist list by now. I've got to keep him in the background. I need a partner to give me credibility — somebody who doesn't look suspicious to the authorities either East or West. Like maybe somebody with twinkly toes?"

I set down my plastic cup very carefully. "Have you gone stark raving mad?" I turn to Pat for moral support, and she's nodding emphatically. "You know how dangerous something like that could be?"

He shrugs, like he must have when the waves disappointed him at Malibu. "I'll bet we could pull it off, with the right connections and some seed capital." Jake's forehead lifts hopefully; he has no idea how funny he sounds uttering phrases like "seed capital."

"Well, thanks but no thanks. Although I appreciate the thought." They both know this is a lie, but it doesn't matter. "So, damn. A girl's got to do what she's got to do. Right, team?"

Pat nods and gives my shoulder a squeeze. Jake blows me a kiss, and with a sad wink, pantomimes pulling an abaya over his head.

I promise to get Pat my resume as soon as we've finished the Coke.

❊ ❊ ❊

I unlock the door to my apartment and do a double-take. How could I have forgotten? Hevar sprawls on my sofa, smoking, with the a/c cranked up full blast. He waves a welcome, then goes back to watching his TV soap opera, which reverberates even into the bedroom.

This is too much; nowhere to hide, to lick my wounds from the Zaki episode. Nowhere to concentrate on revising a resume. I've got to get out of here. I lace up my Nikes, grab my phone, lock him back in the apartment, and head out on foot toward the hills.

This proves to be a dumb idea. It's way too hot to be out here. I'm dizzy and headachy by the time I pass the dogs at the back gate. Scrambling off the road to the shade of Seema's tree, I lean back against the rough trunk. I'm not sure whether it's sweat or tears dripping off my face; probably a mixture of both.

Who could I call for advice? My mind scans through possibilities, anybody who might understand my predicament. The Financial Genius? I could phone him long-distance collect and yell at him for the mess he left me in. My sister, or my son Andy, or my best friend back home? They'd just worry.

I close my eyes and feel the tree trunk poking through my blouse. It hurts a little, but I don't shift. I pretend I'm able to listen to the silent sap running beneath the trunk.

To my astonishment, without invitation the Witness emerges from the bark and seeps its way into my blood stream. The Witness is immense and throbs pulse-like in a very pleasant way, boosting my awareness up an octave or two. The Witness looks at me from the inside out and embraces this solitary woman on a hillside. The Witness has a dreamy two-fold essence — simultaneously an innocent infant in a cradle, and also a loving mother adoring the infant as she rocks with her foot. The rocker. The rocked. The resonance between the two, which both are aware of, although it cannot be seen.

All is well. Everything is exactly as it should be. In truth, I have no idea what this means. But I know that it is true.

❊ ❊ ❊

When I let myself back in the apartment, Hevar is still watching TV with the a/c blowing. I shiver after the heat outside. The air is blue-black like a welt, thick with recycled smoke. It steals my last ounce of courtesy, but not my composure. My neck suddenly feels elongated and elegant, like a prima ballerina.

"Hey, get up. I've got a job for you."

He tilts his head in puzzlement; he's never heard me speak in this tone before, the one I use with the boys at the back of the class.

"Come with me."

He hesitates when I gesture toward the bedroom; his shoulders protest that it's a moral affront to so much as suggest that he'd step inside a woman's chamber. Then the shoulders relax, and he shrugs with a mocking smile. Ah, he thinks he's getting lucky, and I'm one of those Western hussies after all. I can't resist his studliness. He's assuming I'm unbuttoning my blouse behind him as he strides toward the bed, because he turns confidently, expectantly, with his hands on his hips like a fresh young buck claiming his due.

"See that box?"

In erotic haste he hadn't noticed the crate. Now he's more puzzled than before.

"Well, we're going to push it. Out the patio door. All the way down to the other end of the parking lot. And we're going to leave it right outside a particular idiot's apartment. Got it?"

He's not following any of this. He could be a mule, for all I care. I make him do the heavy work, while I give directions. He's sweating like a pig, soaking right through all of the spiffy starched creases on his khaki; so am I by the time we've reached Jake's patio, knocked on his door, waited for him to see what we've delivered, and started walking away.

Let's call a spade a spade. It's passive aggression. Hevar knows it; he has that glare of a person who is all too conscious of being used. Jake knows it; he's doing that female "you can't do this to me" whiny thing, wringing his hands, pleading for us to take it back. Rabinowitz knows it when he comes out onto the patio, dreadlocks wooly around his shoulders, dressed only in a skimpy towel tucked around his waist. So does Pat, who's out on her patio now seeing what all the ruckus is about. And so do Roboteacher, Mrs. Zaki, every last one of them out to catch the latest installment in the ongoing teledrama we call the Academy.

"You'll pay for this, Theresa Turner!" Rabinowitz screams. "You'll see what happens when you mess with holy *jihad*."

Hevar stops in his tracks. Like the sheriff in an old-school Western, he turns slowly to Rabinowitz, twists his face as if in the presence of road kill, and draws the pistol out of his sash. He points it straight at Rabinowitz's nose and clicks the safety. Rabinowitz quivers; the towel is coming dangerously close to unwrapping. A trickle seeps down between Rabinowitz's bare legs, out from under the towel, and forms a puddle around his feet.

Hevar waves his pistol at the puddle. He bursts into disdainful, mean laughter, and slowly lifts his arm high, outstretched as if raising a triumphant banner. A single shot rings out, straight up into the clear Kurdish sky.

One shot. It rings through the concrete of the school, echoing around through the teachers' apartments, the basketball court, the classroom quad, the admin offices, the parking lots. Two guards race from their post, machine guns clutched at the ready. They screech to an abrupt halt when they see that it's Hevar. They follow his gaze to Rabinowitz, frantically clutching his towel back into place while still standing in the puddle, then to wide-eyed Jake beside him, and they double over laughing. Thumbs up, Hevar. Bravo for you, buddy. High fives all around. Disgrace to the whiteys, liberators though they might be.

Hevar stuffs the pistol back into his sash, and sucks in his cheeks at me in wordless closure. With the dignity of a chaperone at Buckingham Palace, he takes my elbow and escorts me back to my apartment, past the Blue Angel locked to the patio grill, and inside to the safety of our little shared haven of orangeness. Once inside, we collapse on the couch in hysterics.

❋ ❋ ❋

Hevar and I pass a peaceful, respectful evening together dining on microwaved leftovers. We polish off the last of my dried figs and cookies while acting out the afternoon victory over and over. We're war buddies now. Nevertheless, I prop the chair against my bedroom door again when we turn in, just in case.

In the middle of the night, the rumble of his snoring wakes me up. Although my rational mind knows he can't control it, there's something about the noise that rings in my mind like a boast. "I'm such a Big Man, I can make any old kind of noise I feel like and you, woman, just have to deal with it." I chew on the acrid cud of this idea for a long time, as the glory of our crate triumph over Rabinowitz fades, and in its place steals a horrific new danger…

Rabinowitz has probably already reported me for harboring Hevar here — the perfect revenge. He probably called up his radical cohorts and figured out how to get maximum political leverage out of the intel. And I never thought to ask Hevar how long he was planning on staying with me. So here we both are, sitting ducks until the police or Al Qaeda or the Taliban or whoever knocks on the door to arrest Hevar for murder, and me for complicity. Why oh why did I ever have to be Miss Smarty Pants and do something so rash?

With each snore, the reality of my situation gets worse, the way that wee-hour ruminations tend to do. By the morning, however, there's the tiniest pinprick of a solution. As soon as the school opens for business, I head over to the admin building.

Mohammed is there sipping his first cup of tea, his dress shirt an even higher quality suit than the last one I saw him in. "*As salaam aleikum, ya Mohammed. Choni?*"

He grins; my accent is no doubt atrocious, but at least I've made an effort. "*Bashi*, Miss Turner. What a pleasant surprise. How can I help you?"

"Mohammed, I'm in way over my head." I have vowed not to cry in front of him, but it's not going to be easy, even with avuncular Massoud Barzani beaming benevolence down onto me from his big gilt frame.

"Yes?" He is remarkably composed, maybe buoyed by the inevitability of me crawling to him at last.

"I've gotten into a really messy dilemma." Talk about an understatement. "Actually several dilemmas. One with my job, and one maybe with the law or the government. What's worse, I have no idea who to trust."

Mohammed puts his hand over his heart and inclines closer, with the manner of a caring attorney. "Speak truth to power. Some famous Westerner said that."

Spare me the platitudes; I'm hanging on by a thin thread. "But who is power? Zaki? The police? Come on, Mohammed. Help me get a grip here."

He leans back behind the now-cluttered desk and fiddles with a cell phone.

"Do you love the Kurdish people? If yes, you will know the answer." He waits about three heartbeats for me to get it.

I have no choice but to trust him. But it's so humiliating to explain this predicament. Where to start?

"Look," he continues. "Do you realize whose nephew Karwan is?"

"Not really. Somebody important, anyway…"

"His uncle is one of the true *kakas* in the country. They've got to look good everywhere, even in a foreign-run school. At the beginning of the year, Karwan was behind more than one whole grade, and his family was furious. Now he is back on track for his age group. The family no longer looks stupid, and they're grateful."

My ears heat up. Karwan is probably "back on track" only because of his test results, which, under the circumstances, hardly qualify as education. But in the big scheme of things, how much does it matter? I'm accustomed to a loftier idea of learning, and a society that at least gives lip service to meritocracy. Here, saving face for a politico's family probably counts for as much as mastering a verb tense.

"I was just doing my job. I tried to teach all of the kids as best I could." Which, not counting all those weeks we were cramming for exams, is true.

But he's not done. "Also, you made public comments on television praising the Kurdish people. You spoke a little Kurdish. You held a flag. People in the right places noticed."

Ah, that was just a lucky fluke, because I happened to be out on my bicycle in the right place, at the right time, on the country's biggest holiday, with a flag a child had just stuck in my hand. Any fool would have done the same.

Now he props his chin on his elbows and stares deep into my eyes. He's not hitting on me, however. He has the manner of a cousin or male mentor, trying, albeit clumsily, to convince me of sincerity. "Whatever you have to tell me, I guarantee in the name of Allah that you will be protected."

"Anything?" This could so easily be a trap. I trusted a husband with my finances, and look where it got me. I trusted the American banking system, and got screwed. I trusted Madame, too, and did what she wanted, even when my gut told me not to. Look where that landed me.

He nods. "Unless you have killed someone. Which I very much doubt."

I try to swallow but my mouth is too dry. "Okay. How should I put this? Is it possible that you can find a safe place for somebody who made a very big mistake in anger? Who may need to hide for a while?"

His whole countenance brightens in surprise, and he barks a tough little laugh. "Ah, Miss Turner, you never cease to astonish me. Even this you got involved in? No wonder you said 'over your head.'"

He's accusing me of meddling. He's going to give me a lecture, well-deserved, for being part of something I don't understand and have no business tampering with. In terror, I realize that I've abetted a criminal. Two criminals, counting

305

Rabinowitz and his crate. Mohammed probably has his police cronies at the ready, and with one push of a button can have me hauled out of here onto the next plane home. That's the best case scenario. The worst case is having me hauled off in handcuffs.

But no, I've misunderstood again, because he tilts farther forward with unexpected tenderness. He works his mouth, as if worrying a piece of meat from his teeth, before licking his lips with decision. "He shall be safe with us. We do not forget our martyrs, nor their children. Do not worry. We've actually been wondering where to find him, once we heard about the problems. We had no idea that you would know. Very clever of him, to think of you. Very good."

An unexpected blip of self-congratulation ripples through me, and then a much bigger blip of admiration for my family's cunning. "My" family. Yes. I notice that my feet have been wrapped like jungle vines around the chair, and disengage them into a more ladylike cross at the knee.

"In your apartment, perhaps?" he asks. When I nod, Mohammed picks up a new-model iPhone and taps the screen. He rattles off about three sentences in Kurdish and clicks off the phone. "He will be collected shortly. Set your heart at rest. The guards will be notified to watch for unauthorized guests. You can stop worrying."

A sigh rises from the pit of my stomach, and with it the Witness taps gently for just an instant at the back of my mind.

Now Mohammed shifts gears. We're apparently done with the serious stuff, forgiven, and the clean slate lets us start a new conversation. "So, what will you do next, if I might ask? Someone like you probably has a host of job offers awaiting."

"My contract is not being renewed," I reply, ignoring the flattery. "You probably already knew that. Pat's trying to get me a job in Saudi with her, but that's a last resort. Plus I have a small legal problem back home. Over the summer break I'll have to borrow money from my mother to take care of it. Then I'll have to save up all next year to pay her back." One year in Saudi hell, to make up for a single poor decision.

"I think you can do better."

Obviously he has no idea how hard I've been trying to leave ever since the first Zaki put-down back in January. Or how seriously finances restrict my choices. I can't accept just any job now. Any new position has to let me do some significant saving. "Maybe so. But in two days I'll be on a plane back to the U.S., with a lot less money than I came here with. Sorry. I don't want to burden you. There's nothing you can do."

"Hmmm. That remains to be seen." He pushes a small lumpy bag across the desk.

"This is from the government for your work here — nothing to do with the Academy. We'll just say that it's for things like 'I before E, except after C'. A gift for extraordinary services rendered to the state."

I'm shocked. "I can't accept anything like this. It's forbidden in my contract."

He stifles a chuckle, not very successfully. "This is not from a student's family. It's not a bribe. It's more like an official gift, which you would be unwise to refuse."

I peek inside to find a leather box; it springs open to reveal a Rolex oyster watch, like the expat wives in Saudi used to pine for. It looks real. I would never wear something so ostentatious. But I'll bet somebody can tell me where to sell it. I'll bet it will buy me a whole lot of attorney time.

"Now, to continue. Someone high up in the government is dissatisfied with the Academy. Many children have been vocal about their unhappiness. They hate coming here. Perhaps you have noticed this as well."

His irony finally makes my mouth twitch. "Oh yeah, just about every single day. But I haven't been in a position to do anything about it."

"Yes. The Minister feels the same. We are a young country, still forming our infrastructure. At the outset we needed to import a school like the Academy for the elites. Now we are ready to build several of our own. The Minister has ideas."

"The Minister?"

"He went to college in the United States, and has his heart set on an American-style curriculum. Your name came up. Well, to be more specific, a poem you taught came up. Something about a bear? The Minister wants to meet a teacher with a sense of humor, as he puts it. Who cares about making learning fun."

He checks his watch. I can't help but notice that it's not a Rolex. "A car will arrive to pick you up at three this afternoon. I believe you are free?"

This is surreal. "Hold on. You think the government might offer me some sort of a job?"

He's not hiding his amusement now. "I think that the contract may already be drafted. Actually, it's possible that you might even be working with a few educators you already know. As the old Kurdish proverb says, learn from new books but old teachers." Was that a wink he did? If it was, I'm too astonished to react.

"But I can't tell you anything further. The Minister will fill you in himself."

I glance down at my dorky teacher's outfit. "I'd better change into my suit. And maybe cover my hair?"

He nods. "Good thinking. Not necessary, but culturally sensitive. He'll appreciate that. You could skip the *toqa*, though."

Oh, he's enjoying this. *Toqa* my eye. "So maybe I can stay here in Kurdistan after all." Probably not close enough to ride a bike to the village. But still, here when Bezma's baby comes.

"*In sh'allah.*" He holds the pause, like an orchestra conductor dragging out the coda on a final encore. "Gives me more time to convince you to be my wife."

But by now I know that he's just kidding, especially after the crack about old teachers. Which is why I can be flippant now over my shoulder as I bounce out. "You never know, Mohammed. That's what I'm learning about this place. *Kurdistan, min dulum khosh.*"

❄ ❄ ❄

We're killing off the last of the rum in Pat's naked apartment, her suitcases already weighed on her handy travel scale and clicked closed. Unlike mine; I still haven't given away enough stuff to get the zippers shut.

"So, Saudi's a no-go for Theresa," she says, sniffing in disappointment. "For now, at least. Assuming that this whole Kurdish thing comes through. Personally, I've got my doubts. Things have a way of happening really fast, and also fizzling really fast, in this part of the world."

"You can say that again," says Jake. I hadn't wanted to share our rum with him, still sore about his complicity with the crate. But Pat reminds me that really, I'd won, and Jake's got plenty of problems of his own in the Rabinowitz department.

"I feel awful letting you go to Saudi alone," I say. "But not awful enough to go along with you."

She knocks back her drink without looking at me; we've been over this a couple of times before.

"If this Kurdish gig actually happens and you end up living in the city, be sure to keep us in mind." Jake stirs his ice with a finger. "Who knows? Pat and I both might need a place to go in a few months. If, say, she doesn't bring enough Prozac to make it in Riyadh. And if Binny's bride changes her mind once she sees what a douche bag she's getting. Then kabam, Daddy doesn't need the world's most hugely talented designer, and guess who's up shit creek." His lusty "har har" doesn't quite cut it; nerves must be kicking in.

Pat turns to him with a reassuring air. "The darned thing is that you just never know what to believe when you're an expat. For instance, take Theresa here. You really think that midwife friend of hers is going to hang up her razor blades once Theresa's gone?" She does that trick where one eyebrow drifts upward and the other stays in place.

Goosebumps prickle my arms. In my euphoria, bragging so confidently to them about my feminist triumph, I'd never even considered this possibility. Now it's as if somebody caught me in a doping scheme I hadn't even known about, and stole my Olympic gold medal for humanitarianism.

"Pat. You're my friend…" I can barely make my mouth move to get the words out. How could she puncture my balloon like this?

"What does friendship have to do with the price of beans? We're talking real life here."

But when she sees how much the feat, or perhaps fantasy, about stopping the cutting has meant to me, she scoots closer on the couch and puts a chubby arm around my shoulder. "Come on," she murmurs in her best motherly tone. "You did what you could. Who knows what will stick? Isn't that all we can do as teachers — cast our bread out on the waters and hope for the best?"

"She's right, Twink." Jake pours me another shot. "If I've been a role model for some little gender-confused rag— uh, adorable patriotic Kurd —and helped him or her come out of the closet about two decades from now, well then it's all been worth it. I guess."

"Not to mention the Rolex," says Pat.

I freeze. How did she find out?

Then Pat rolls up a sleeve. Jake does the same; they grin at each other, and at me.

"Huh? Where did you guys get those? They're Polexes, right? From the guy down in the bazaar…"

"Nope. Parting gifts from grateful families. For countless hours of faithful tutoring, and a couple of lazy little brats passing eighth grade against all odds."

"You guys were tutoring all this time? And I never knew about it?"

"Ah, our clueless little Twinkle Toes, spending all her time in a poverty-stricken no-name village. How did you think we were keeping ourselves out of trouble these many months? Cutting out stencil letters for our bulletin boards?" Now he's cracking up, slapping his knee at my naivete.

"Pat. You never let on. And you knew how badly I needed money."

"And there you were," she says, continuing Jake's theme, "walking around that blessed track with Old Baldy night after night, confiding heaven only knows what in her."

"You — you didn't trust me!" I stammer.

"We couldn't." He says it so matter-of-factly. "Anyway, we set up tutoring gigs during Parents Night in September, long before you got here."

"We? You mean all the other expats?"

"Almost. Well, except Binny. No family wanted to hire him." His "har har" sounds a lot funnier this time around.

"But hey. It's not so bad. You got out of Leechland back home." Pat's voice is genuinely consoling now, maybe to make up for keeping me in the dark. "And you got to do all that fun anthropologizing."

She's right. I shouldn't begrudge them a secret or two. Besides, although I can't put this into words that would make

311

sense, I know that I have leveled up in the video game of life, as Andy would put it. And that's worth more than a Rolex. My son would be proud.

"Let's not forget about your cosmic tripping out there in the hinterlands, either," Jake adds. "You wouldn't have done that in a million years if you'd stayed back on your little island with the pine trees."

I still haven't told him that much about what happened, and don't plan to either, not with that eager leer that he's wearing.

Pat starts to say something, as if she's got one more plug of reality for me she's been keeping up her sleeve. With a piteous look, she shakes her head and purses her lips.

"Go on. Tell me, whatever it is. I can take it." What I really mean is that our friendship can take it. I can envision us side by side in rocking chairs on the porch of some old folk's home one day.

"Ooohh kaaaaay." Her reluctance tugs at my heart, even before knowing what's on her mind, and I brace myself against the back of the chair.

"You may have some ill-defined job lined up here for next year, which I seriously doubt, by the way," she begins. "So you're not exactly home free, financially. But have you thought about your young friend in the village? What's going to happen to her, pregnant and disgraced, living as a single mom in her mother's hovel forever? All three of them, when the baby comes, eking it out on a widow's measly pension? Without an education, in a place where women can't get jobs anyway? Hey, being minus a clitoris is practically nothing, in comparison. That's what really tears me up."

My effervescence dissolves into a hunk of sticky asphalt. Think fast, Theresa. "Maybe I could —"

But Pat doesn't miss a beat. "No, don't tell me you're going to support them for the rest of their lives, either. That would be just plain stupid, given your own situation. Oh crap — that *was* what you were thinking, wasn't it? Okay, come on, get real, girl. Swear to me that you're not going to make any wild promises to these people. Much as you love them. Much as you want to do something good. Much as you were hoping to be Mother Teresa the Second. Nod your head yes. Listen to reason."

Jake fondles his chin like a sage old psychotherapist. "She's right, girlfriend. Stay cool. You can't save the whole world all by yourself."

Why not?

"Doggone it, Pat." Does she really have to bring me down like this? "I kind of hate you right now too, Jake."

United, they both give me a familiar teacherly look. It's that steady gaze that reminds a student that yes, they know the correct answer, while maybe even mouthing the first syllable as a prompt. "Come on, come on, you can do it."

Silently my friends urge me on, certain that this time I'll get it right.

Epilogue

HIGH ON a hill overlooking the plains of Iraqi Kurdistan, around a school track beside a razor-wire fence, a blondish woman runs alongside a wobbling bicycle. Clamping the seat, she balances a waif-like girl who shrieks with both fear and excitement. The woman lets go, just for an instant, and the bike and rider totter precariously — until she catches them and yanks them back upright. Dusk is gathering; lights wink on in the city far in the distance. The woman keeps jogging, winded despite her exhilaration, cheered on from the bleachers by two women in black headscarves and one in white. Now she holds the seat with only her thumb and two fingertips.

Soon Seema will be riding on her own.

Any minute now, it will happen.

Author's Afterword

The Kurdish Bike is based loosely on my experiences teaching in northern Iraq in 2010. It started as a memoir, describing true events but set in a fictional school. The characters quickly took on lives of their own, however, morphing and demanding changes in the plot, narrative and circumstances. Thus the book in its entirety should be considered a novel.

The few years leading up to and following 2010 were something of a golden era in the Kurdish Autonomous Region of Iraq. A boom in oil production and high oil prices brought quick riches and sparked rapid development. A new airport, high-end malls, international hotels, Western-style gated suburbs, and even a water park sprang up; in a mere six months, entire neighborhoods became unrecognizable.

Then two disasters struck. One was the rise of ISIS with their take-over of lands throughout Syria and Iraq, and their threat to Kurdish sovereignty, a dire situation unresolved as this goes to press. The second was a fall in oil prices, which left the region financially compromised. The government stopped paying salaries and pensions. This has left the most vulnerable Iraqi Kurds, namely widows and orphans, at tremendous risk.

On a more positive note, the Kurdish government outlawed female genital mutilation (*khatana*) in 2011, and undertook publicity campaigns to raise awareness about its dangers. In the first four years of the campaign, the practice reportedly decreased from 95 percent of women in many areas (including the village described in the novel) to about 60 percent.

In real life, the character on whom Hevar was drawn went into hiding after the "honor" killing. He notified his wife that she should consider herself to be "abandoned", meaning that she remained married to him (and thus could not remarry), but would receive no money or other support from him or his parents. He fled to another country, remarried there, and already has a new child. The woman on whom Bezma's character was based now lives with her infant daughter at her mother's house. Until government payments ceased, they survived on her mother's widow's pension. Now they subsist on government food rations and whatever other family members can spare them.

As for me, I returned home, spent the summer with a person much like Andy, and became a professor at a very interesting college overseas. But that's another story...

About the Author

Alesa Lightbourne has been an English professor and teacher in six countries, lived on a sailboat, dined with Bedouins, and written for Fortune 50 companies. She lives close to Monterey Bay in California, where she loves to boogie board and ride a bicycle. Read more at www.kurdishbike.com.

If you have enjoyed this book, please review it on Amazon.com and/or Goodreads.com.

Glossary

Abaya — Black outer garment that drapes from head or shoulders to the floor (Arabic); also called *burqa* in some countries

Ayatul kursi — The most famous verse in the Quran

Al Alfal — The systematic destruction of Kurdish and other ethnic minority communities by Iraq's Baathist regime between 1986 and 1989, including massacre, torture, gassing and enslavement, literally "the spoils of war" (Arabic)

Al ham du l'illah — Praise be to Allah (Arabic)

Bashi — Good (Kurdish)

B'kher hati — Welcome (Kurdish)

Choni — How's it going? (Kurdish)

Dolmas — Vegetables stuffed with a rice and meat filling, the Kurdish national dish

FGM — Female genital mutilation, also called female circumcision, where external genitalia are cut or otherwise injured

Hijab — Islamic practice of women covering their hair and bodies, typically in an abaya (above)

Imam — Muslim cleric (Arabic)

In sh'allah — God willing (Arabic)

Kaka — Mister or sir, an address of respect (Kurdish)

Khatana — Female genital mutilation (FGM), involving removing all or part of clitoris (Kurdish and Arabic)

Khak — Traditional khaki outfit worn by men consisting of long-sleeved shirt and very baggy pants secured by decorative cummerbund (Kurdish)

Madrassa — School (Arabic)

Min dulum khosh — My heart is glad (Kurdish)

Mohammad rasul Allah — Mohammed is the Prophet of God (Arabic)

Mujaheddin — Holy soldiers (Arabic)

Peshmerga — Nationalist soldiers or freedom fighters, literally "those who face death" (Kurdish)

Ser tchow — Literally "On my eyes," an endearment or intensifier said by women while covering right eye with right hand (Kurdish)

Surah Al Fatihah — First chapter of the Quran, and the first Surah recited in each cycle of Muslim prayer (Arabic)

Toqa — Decorated hair clip used to form a bun or pony tail (Kurdish)